"Aren't you sugar and spice and everything nice!"

"You are confusing me with my sisters." Esther grew warm beneath his intense scrutiny.

Gabe tugged gently on her *kapp* ribbon. "I think not. They may be sweet, but I haven't seen a sign of spice among them."

"Sweet is usually enough for most young men."

He didn't take his eyes off her face. "Not me. I like spicy."

She knew she was blushing. "We should go to the house before the storm gets worse."

He took a step back. "You're right."

The rain was coming down in sheets. Esther's *kapp* and her hem were soaked by the time they reached cover.

She laughed as she ran up the steps and shook out her dress. Gabe pulled a handkerchief from his pocket and began to mop her face. "I didn't help much."

She saw his eyes darken. She couldn't look away from him. She didn't want to.

Why hadn't she realized it before now?

She was halfway to falling in love with this wonderful man.

After thirty-five years as a nurse, **Patricia Davids** hung up her stethoscope to become a full-time writer. She enjoys spending her free time visiting her grandchildren, doing some long-overdue yard work and traveling to research her story locations. She resides in Wichita, Kansas. Pat always enjoys hearing from her readers. You can visit her online at patriciadavids.com.

Growing up on a farm, **Jocelyn McClay** enjoyed livestock and pursued a degree in agriculture. She met her husband while weight lifting in a small town—he "spotted" her. After thirty years in business management, they moved to an acreage in southeastern Missouri to be closer to family when their eldest of three daughters made them grandparents. When not writing, she keeps busy hiking, bike riding, gardening, knitting and substitute teaching.

USA TODAY Bestselling Author

PATRICIA DAVIDS

Someone to Trust

&

JOCELYN McCLAY

Her Forbidden Amish Love

LOVE INSPIRED

INSPIRATIONAL ROMANCE

LOVE INSPIRED®

INSPIRATIONAL ROMANCE

ISBN-13: 978-1-335-41889-0

Someone to Trust and Her Forbidden Amish Love

Copyright © 2021 by Harlequin Books S.A.

Someone to Trust
First published in 2021. This edition published in 2021.
Copyright © 2021 by Patricia MacDonald

Her Forbidden Amish Love
First published in 2021. This edition published in 2021.
Copyright © 2021 by Jocelyn Ord

This edition published by arrangement with Harlequin Books S.A.

For questions and comments about the quality of this book, please contact us at CustomerService@Harlequin.com.

Harlequin Enterprises ULC
22 Adelaide St. West, 40th Floor
Toronto, Ontario M5H 4E3, Canada
www.LoveInspired.com

Printed in U.S.A.

Recycling programs for this product may not exist in your area.

CONTENTS

SOMEONE TO TRUST

Patricia Davids

This book is lovingly dedicated to nurses,
respiratory therapists, doctors and
all medical personnel working tirelessly to
save lives. May God give you strength and wisdom.
May He guide your hands and hearts
as you bring comfort to all His people.

Trust in the Lord with all thine heart; and lean not unto thine own understanding. In all thy ways acknowledge him, and he shall direct thy paths.
—*Proverbs* 3:5–6

Chapter One

"I'm happy to tell you that your mother's cousin Waneta is coming for a visit."

Gabe Fisher looked up from the glowing metal wheel rim he was heating in the forge as something in his father's voice caught his attention. Ezekiel Fisher, or Zeke as everyone called him, wasn't overly fond of Waneta, so why was he trying so hard to sound cheerful?

Gabe glanced around the workshop. None of his three brothers seemed to have noticed anything unusual.

Seth continued setting up the lathe to drill out a wheel hub. "That will be nice for *Mamm*. She has been missing her friends back home. I know she and Waneta are close."

Seth was Gabe's younger brother by fifteen minutes. They might look identical, but Seth was the most tenderhearted of the brothers. He was twenty minutes older than no-nonsense Asher, the last Fisher triplet, who was readying wooden spokes to be inserted into the finished wheel hub. Asher bore only a passing resemblance to his two older brothers. Where Gabe and Seth were both blond with blue eyes, Asher was dark-haired with their mother's brown eyes. All three men shared the same tall, muscular frame as their father.

"Is she bringing her new husband to meet the rest of us?" Moses asked, greasing the axle of the buggy they were repairing. At twenty he was the baby brother by four years and the one that looked the most like their mother, with his soft brown curls and engaging grin. He was the only one who hadn't yet joined their Amish church. He was still enjoying his *rumspringa*, the "running around" years most Amish youths were allowed before making their decision to be baptized.

"This isn't the best time for a visit," Asher said, expressing exactly what Gabe had been thinking.

"Apparently your mother and Waneta have been planning this for ages, but she only told me last night. She wanted it to be a surprise for you boys."

Asher's brow furrowed. "Why?"

"You know Waneta. She likes to surprise folks. They should be here later today."

Gabe continued turning the rim in the fire. Both his parents had gone to the wedding, but he and his brothers had been busy keeping the new business running. A business that didn't look like it would support the entire family through another winter. If things didn't improve by the end of the summer, the family would have some hard choices to make.

"They? Her new husband is coming with her, then?" Seth said.

Gabe glanced at his father and saw him draw a deep breath. "He isn't, but his children are."

Seth finally seemed to notice their father's unease and stopped working. "How many children?"

"Five."

"The house will be lively with that many *kinder* underfoot," Moses said. "How old are they?"

"The youngest is ten. The others are closer to your ages," *Daed* said, keeping his eyes averted.

Seth, Asher and Gabe exchanged knowing looks. They shared a close connection that didn't always require words.

Asher's lips thinned as he pinned his gaze on his father. "Would they happen to be *maydels* close to our age?"

Their father didn't answer.

"Daed?" the triplets said together. Moses stopped what he was doing and gave them a puzzled look.

Their father cleared his throat. "I believe your mother said they are between twenty and twenty-five. Modest, dutiful daughters, as Waneta described them."

"Courting age," Moses said with a grin.

"Marriageable age." Seth shook his head. "I don't have any interest in courting until we are sure our business will survive."

Gabe crossed his arms over his chest. "Has *Mamm* taken to importing possible brides for us now?"

There was a lack of unmarried Amish women in their new community in northern Maine, but that didn't bother Gabe. Like Seth, his focus was on improving the family's buggy-making and wheel-repair business while expanding the harness-making and leather goods shop he ran next door.

"Tell *Mamm* we can find our own wives," Asher said.

"When we are ready," Seth added.

Daed scowled at all the brothers. "That kind of talk is exactly why your mother was worried about sharing this news. She wants you boys to be polite to Waneta's new stepdaughters and nothing more. Show them a nice time while they are here. No one is talking about marriage."

"Marriage is the point of this trip, girls. Do not make me tell your father he wasted his money paying for it. We should be there within the hour."

Esther Burkholder kept her eyes glued to her brother Jonah's hands as the ten-year-old rapidly signed their stepmother's conversation. Seated with Jonah in the back of the van their father had hired to drive them to Maine, Esther couldn't lip-read what Waneta was saying or what her sisters were answering because all she could see was the back of their white Amish *kapps*. Waneta didn't know sign language and showed little interest in learning. Julia, Pamela and Nancy could sign, but they often preferred to talk among themselves, leaving Esther out of the discussion.

Unlike her Deaf friends, who found it isolating to be left out of conversations with hearing family members, Esther normally didn't mind. Even before she lost her hearing, she had preferred to spend time alone. She enjoyed her silent world. All she had to do was close her eyes and nothing intruded on her solitude unless someone touched her. Today was different. She needed to know what Waneta had planned so she could avoid getting caught in the web her stepmother was weaving. Did the poor Fisher brothers know what was about to descend on them?

"I've known these boys since they were babies. The three oldest sons are triplets. They are twenty-four, so a good age to be looking for a wife. Seth is the tender-hearted one who loves children. Pamela, I think you and he could make a match. You have a very caring nature. Asher is the practical one. Julia, I think he might be best suited for you. Your no-nonsense attitude should appeal to him. Nancy, you and Moses, the youngest son, are the same age and not yet baptized. I think the two of you will find you have a lot in common."

"How are we going to tell them apart if they all look alike?"

Jonah rolled his eyes and signed, "Pamela has a good point for once."

"What did Waneta answer?" Esther signed, wishing Jonah would keep his thoughts out of the conversation.

"She said only Gabriel and Seth look alike. Gabriel has a small scar in his right eyebrow. Seth looks like him but no scar. She says Asher and the younger brother are both dark."

He leaned forward over the seat to speak to his stepmother, frustrating Esther. She tugged on his suspender strap. "What are you saying?"

Because she hadn't completely lost her hearing until the age of ten, she spoke almost normally, although she had been told that ability might gradually leave her.

She worked hard at practicing her speech so that she wouldn't lose what she had.

Jonah turned back to her. "I asked which brother Waneta thought would make a good match for you."

Waneta turned in her seat and gave Esther a knowing, sympathetic smile. "I believe the oldest son, Gabriel, would suit you. Sadly, he was jilted when he was twenty and of course was heartbroken. According to my cousin Talitha, he has been put off by the idea of marriage ever since, so I don't hold out much hope for a match. Now I don't want the rest of you to take an interest in only one son. Keep open minds."

Esther knew what Waneta was really saying. None of her cousin's sons would be interested in a deaf woman for a wife. After a moment of self-pity, Esther sat up straight. She wasn't shopping for a husband and certainly not a hearing one. She had a wonderful job working in their community's school for children with disabilities. She and her three close friends who were also Deaf taught twenty hearing-impaired and deaf children in special classes along with assisting the other teachers when needed. She dearly missed her friends and the children already. This trip needed to end quickly.

Jonah touched her shoulder to gain her attention before signing again. "Waneta talks too much. My hands are getting tired. Can I stop?"

Esther smiled and nodded. It had been a long two-day trip from Millersburg, Ohio, and he was growing bored. "Watch out the window. I have read there are many moose and bears in this part of Maine. Perhaps you'll catch a glimpse of one of them," she said.

He eagerly turned his attention outside, leaving Esther alone with her thoughts. This trip was such a waste of time. She sighed and opened the quilted satchel on the floor by her feet. The sketchbook or the sewing projects she'd brought along to occupy her time? She was making new *kapps* for her sisters. Because she enjoyed sewing, she made the clothes for everyone in the family, including her father. She withdrew her sewing kit as fond memories of learning to sew with her mother filled her mind.

She glanced once more at the back of Waneta's head. The woman wasn't a replacement for her mother, but she was good for Esther's father. He smiled more and seemed to enjoy life with her. Because of her father, Esther had tried hard to please Waneta, but she'd failed more often than not. Waneta was impatient with Esther's lack of ability to understand her. So Esther simply stayed out of her way.

Had it been up to her, she wouldn't be on this trip at all. Her father had insisted Esther come along. He told the family he wanted them to see some new country and meet Waneta's favorite cousin and her family. Privately he told Esther he hoped that the trip would bring her and her stepmother closer. He knew there was friction between them. Because she loved her father, Esther had agreed, but two days in a van had certainly not strengthened the bond between her and Waneta.

At least she had gotten to see the ocean that morning. It had been a stunning sight she would never forget. The highway they had traveled along skirted the beautiful rugged Maine coast from Portsmouth to Brunswick before turning inland. The views of the sparkling waves stretching to the horizon took her breath away. She could never reproduce such beauty with her limited talent for drawing, but she couldn't wait to tell her friends back home about it. She would write as soon as she had the chance.

They had been traveling for almost an hour when Esther felt a change in the vibration of the van and looked up from her sewing. Bessie, their van driver, was pulling off to the side of the road. Jonah began to sign. "I think something is wrong with the engine. Bessie says we should get out and stretch our legs while she takes a look. We are only about a mile from the Fisher farm."

Esther was happy to leave the confines of the van for even a little bit. Outside the afternoon air was fresh with a cool breeze that fluttered the ribbons of her *kapp*. She admired the farmland interspersed with wooded areas that lined either side of a broad valley. She could see a river sparkling in the distance, and closer to the road, a small pond reflected perfectly the clear summer sky and the trees that surrounded it.

Her sister Nancy came to her side. "It's pretty country," she signed.

Esther nodded. "It is. Has Bessie discovered what is wrong?"

"It's nothing she can fix."

Esther glanced up the road. "If it's less than a mile, we can walk."

"Waneta has already sent Jonah ahead to tell the Fishers where we are and what has happened. They will send a buggy or wagon to fetch us and our things."

A car zipped past on the highway, startling Esther. Cars always frightened her if she didn't see them coming first. She looked both ways. There wasn't any other traffic in sight, but she stepped farther back from the roadway. She faced her sister. "Are you as eager to find a husband as Waneta is to find one for you?"

Nancy shrugged. "I'm not eager to find a spouse— I just turned twenty—but I'm open to the possibility. Julia and Pamela are more hopeful than I am that the trip will be the answer for them, or maybe they are feeling a tad desperate. Julia will be twenty-six soon, and some folks have started calling her an old maid since she rejected Ogden Martin's proposal in such a public way. Of course she was right to do so. He wasn't a good man.

"Pamela is only a year behind Julia in age. Very few men in our area have shown an interest in us, and Father has discouraged those fellows. He would rather we marry outside our community." Nancy blushed and stopped signing.

"Because our incidence of inherited deafness is so high," Esther finished for her. She was aware of her father's feelings, but it still hurt to be reminded that he saw her deafness as an affliction to be avoided rather than embraced. Thankfully his views were not shared by all, but they were shared by the one person who had mattered the most to Esther—Barnabas King, the young man she had fallen in love with and had hoped to marry. Until he'd made his true feelings about her deafness known last Christmas.

She pushed that unhappy memory to the back of her mind. If she ever thought of marrying, she wasn't going to seek a spouse in the hearing world. Only a man who was Deaf could understand the struggles and rewards of existing in a silent world. God would provide such a man for her if that was His plan. If not, she had her job and the children she loved.

Nancy smiled sadly and signed, "All of us want to find someone to love who loves us in return. I won't settle for less, no matter what Father and Waneta have in mind."

"She can be persuasive," Esther said, looking to where her stepmother was talking to Julia and Pamela.

"I know the two of you don't get along, but she isn't a bad sort."

"She's so different from our mother. I know it's wrong to resent her. I'll work on being a better daughter."

"She's calling me. I'm glad to be out of the van, aren't you?" Nancy walked away without waiting for Esther's answer. It wasn't an unusual occurrence.

Esther's gaze was drawn to the pretty picture of the little pond across the way. She couldn't believe her eyes when a moose with enormous antlers stepped out of the forest and waded into the water. She thought he was going to drink, but he plunged his entire head beneath the surface and came up with a mouthful of pond weeds that he munched on contentedly.

Oh, she wished Jonah was here to see this. A real live moose a mere hundred yards away. She had to get a closer look.

Gabe had hitched up the wagon as soon as the boy called Jonah arrived at the farm and explained his family's ride had broken down about a mile away. Now they were both on their way to the van. "Are you excited about spending a few weeks in Maine?" Gabe asked.

"I would rather spend the summer at home playing ball with my friends, but *Daed* said I needed to come along to look after my sisters."

"Do your sisters take a lot of looking after?" Maybe he could learn something useful about his mother's imported bridal prospects.

"Esther needs my help sometimes, but the others don't. They're all going to be too busy trying to find husbands to need me." The kid rolled his eyes.

Gabe grinned. Jonah was exactly the person he needed to pump for information. "All of your sisters are looking for husbands?"

"My stepmother claims she is a *goot* matchmaker and will have them engaged before the end of this trip. She even said we aren't going home until at least two of the girls are promised. I think the whole thing is silly."

"I couldn't agree with you more."

"I'd like to get back to my friends before the ball season is over. I'm the pitcher on our team. Are you looking for a wife?" the boy asked hopefully.

"*Nee*, I'm content being a single fellow."

"So am I. Girls are nothing but trouble. Just ask me. With four sisters, I know what I'm talking about," Jonah said with long-suffering conviction.

Gabe tried hard not to laugh. "How does your stepmother hope to get all your sisters engaged so quickly?"

"I don't know her whole plan. I got tired of listening, but each one is going to concentrate on one brother."

"Who plans to set her sights on me?"

"I don't remember. I was getting pretty tired by then."

A white van with the hood up came into view along with a group of Amish women standing beside it. Gabe pulled the horse and wagon to a stop beside them. Which one was going to concentrate her attention on him? He wished Jonah knew the answer. That way he'd know which sister to avoid. His mother's cousin Waneta came rushing toward him with a cheerful smile.

"Gabriel, it's *goot* to see you again."

He got down from the wagon, determined not to give any of the women undue encouragement. "Nice to see you, too, Waneta. If your stepdaughters will get in the wagon, I'll collect your things."

"Our driver, Bessie, will help. Let me introduce you to my family."

"There will be time for that when everyone is settled at the house," he said and walked to the back of the van where Bessie, a gray-haired *Englisch* woman, was pulling out the luggage. He heard the rumble of a truck approaching and then a horn blaring. He glanced in that direction and saw a woman walking into the roadway. Her gaze was fixed on something in the distance. Didn't she hear the truck? She looked at the ground. The trucker would never be able to stop in time. Gabe dropped the suitcases and dashed toward her.

The truck's brakes squealed. Over the noise Gabe heard screaming behind him. He yelled at her to get off the road. She didn't move a step. He closed his eyes and launched himself toward the woman, knowing they were both going to die.

He hit her and locked his arms around her as they landed on the hard pavement. His momentum sent them rolling to the grassy verge on the opposite side of the road. The wind from the truck tore his hat off. When the vehicle flew past, he kept his eyes closed for several seconds until he realized he was alive.

Thanks be for Your mercy, Lord.

He opened his eyes and gazed at the woman beneath him. She stared at him with wide, frightened, amber-colored eyes. She pressed her hands against his chest. "You saved my life."

"Are you hurt?" His arm was starting to sting where he had landed on it.

"I don't know. My head hurts." Her words were slightly slurred.

The rush of adrenaline drained away, leaving Gabe weak and shaken. "Don't move until you're sure. What were you thinking? Didn't you hear the truck? We could've both been killed."

She was staring at his mouth. "I saw a moose. I've never seen one before. I wanted a closer look. Something scared it away. Please let me up."

He rolled off and sat beside her. "It was almost the last thing you saw."

Her family surrounded them and helped her to her feet. They were chattering and motioning with their hands as they hugged her and checked her for injures. It dawned on Gabe that they were using sign language. At least that's what he thought it was. Was the woman deaf? Was that why she hadn't heard the trucker's horn or his shouts?

The big rig's driver had managed to stop the truck a hundred yards down the road. He came running up to Gabe. "Are you okay? Is she all right? I couldn't stop in time. She just walked out in front of me. Man, what you did was the bravest thing I've ever seen."

"Or the most foolish."

"I've always heard there's very little difference between the two." The man patted his chest. "That took ten years off my life. If you had been a second slower—"

Visibly upset, the man sat down in the grass beside Gabe. "Are you folks Amish? I've heard some of you have moved here."

"We are."

"After today, I might trade my truck in for a horse and buggy."

"You won't haul near as much lumber that way."

The man chuckled. "You're right. Maybe I'll just slow down and keep an eye out for folks like you."

"We would appreciate that."

Jonah, pale and shaken, left his sister and came to sit beside Gabe. "You saved Esther's life. *Danki*, but it should have been me. I'm the one *Daed* sent to look after her. I reckon I didn't do such a *goot* job."

Gabe draped his arm over the boy's shoulders. "You brought me here. Looks like that was *Gott's* plan for both of us."

"I just remembered something."

"What?" Gabe asked.

The child looked up with his eyes full of wonder. "Esther is the one *Mamm* picked for you."

Chapter Two

Esther couldn't stop shaking. She was afraid her knees wouldn't hold her up much longer. Her shoulders, her hip and the back of her head were starting to hurt. Tomorrow she would likely be black and blue all over, but she was alive. God be praised. She leaned heavily on Nancy's arm.

Julia immediately took charge and signed as she spoke so everyone would know what she wanted. "Let's get Esther to the wagon."

Julia turned to Gabriel. "Are you able to drive the team? If not I will."

"I can drive." Gabriel got up with a grimace as Jonah helped him to his feet. The truck driver added a steadying hand to his back. Gabriel nodded his thanks.

"You're hurt," Esther said, pointing to his arm. His shirt was torn from his elbow to his shoulder. There was blood dripping from his fingers. She swallowed hard against the pain of knowing her disability had almost cost him his life as well as her own. How could she have been so foolish?

He tried to look at the injury, but the blood was soaking his shirtsleeve. "It's nothing."

Esther was able to read his lips, but Jonah signed for her, as well.

"It's more than nothing. Let me see." Julia made a quick examination. "That's a nasty gash. You might need stitches." She turned to Bessie but didn't sign, so Esther had no idea what she was saying. Bessie hurried to the van and came back a few moments later with a first-aid kit.

Esther was grateful for her older sister's competence. Once Julia had a dressing on Gabriel's wound, she ushered everyone into the wagon, where Bessie had loaded their luggage. Esther sat facing Gabe as he leaned against the side boards of the wagon bed. He cradled his injured arm across his chest. Jonah got in beside him and handed him his hat.

"Danki."

Esther carefully studied his face.

He was a good-looking man with blond hair and sky blue eyes. He had strong features, a square chin and a nicely shaped mouth. She thought he must smile often, for he had tiny laugh lines bracketing his lips. "I'm sorry you got hurt saving me. I was careless."

"I hope you're more careful in the future. I might not be handy." He glanced at her brother. "I don't know sign language. Can you tell her that for me?"

"Esther can speech-read pretty well."

"I thought she read lips."

"Some call it speech-reading, but calling it lip-reading is fine. I guess that's the most common term. It's more about interpreting expressions and face muscles' movements. You have to look directly at her when you talk. She can get the gist of what you're saying, if not every word. I'll sign for you."

"*Danki.*"

He looked ill at ease. Esther was used to having hearing people feel uncomfortable around her, but she didn't want this man to feel that way. She owed him too much. How could she repay such bravery?

"You are Gabriel, am I right?" She smiled to put him at ease.

"Folks call me Gabe."

"We haven't actually met. I am Esther." She gestured to the front of the wagon, where her stepmother sat beside her sister on the bench seat. "You already know Waneta. Julia is driving. She is my oldest sister. This is Pamela and Nancy." She indicated the women sitting on their suitcases behind the wagon seat.

"I'm happy to make everyone's acquaintance." He nodded to her sisters, but his eyes held wariness, not happiness, as his gaze slid over them. Something wasn't right.

She looked at Jonah and signed, "What did you tell him about us?"

"I don't know what you mean," he signed back without speaking.

Having a conversation in sign without explaining what was being said to Gabe might be considered rude, but Esther didn't care. "Jonah, the truth."

"I might have mentioned Waneta's plan to find everyone husbands."

Esther pressed her lips together tightly. "Why would you do that?"

"It just slipped out," he signed with an apologetic grimace.

"Tell me you didn't mention that I was looking for a husband."

Jonah looked away and then back at her. "I did say Waneta had picked him out for you."

"Jonah, how could you?" Esther closed her eyes and leaned her head back to pretend she was alone in the world. No sights, no sounds, no humiliating suspicious looks from the man who had just saved her life. Somehow she would have to make it clear to him—when her stepmother and her sisters weren't listening in—that she wasn't husband hunting.

Someone tapped her foot. She opened her eyes to see Gabe frowning at her. "Are you okay?"

"I'm fine." She forced herself to smile. Humiliated, bruised from head to toe and stuck in Maine. She was about as far from fine as she could get. A headache began pounding away fiercely at what few wits she had left.

Gabe wanted to know what she and her brother had been saying to each other. Whatever it was, it made her blush. Her cheeks were as red as the barn he had helped paint in the spring. He suspected the conversation had something to do with him. Otherwise, why wouldn't she share it? Jonah looked guilty and contrite. None of the sisters spoke.

Waneta, on the other hand, hadn't stopped talking about his prompt action, his quick thinking and his disregard for his own safety since she had climbed to the wagon seat. Her voice had become almost a whine, like the sound of the band saw running in the buggy shop.

Julia drove the wagon into the farmyard. His family came out of the house to greet them.

His father took hold of the horse's bridle as he looked at Gabe and frowned. "What has happened?"

"It was the most frightening thing, Cousin." Waneta got down and threw her arms around Gabe's mother then launched into her dramatic version of the story as Gabe's brothers helped him and the women out of the wagon. Gabe's mother's face grew pale as she listened.

"I'm okay, *Mamm*." Gabe touched her shoulder. "It's just a scrape."

"He needs stitches," Julia said, getting down. "Is there a physician nearby?"

"There is a new clinic in Fort Craig. I'll hitch up the buggy." Asher jogged toward the corral to get their buggy horse, Topper.

"I don't need a doctor," Gabe declared. He'd lost enough working time already.

Moses helped Esther down from the wagon. The color left her face, and she crumpled. She would have hit the ground if Moses hadn't swept her up in his arms. "I think this one might."

Moses carefully lowered Esther to the ground. His mother and her sisters gathered around. Gabe was relieved when her eyes fluttered open. She frowned. "What happened?"

"You fainted," her sister Nancy told her.

She raised her hand to her brow. "My head hurts."

"We're going to take you and Gabe to a doctor," Julia said and signed.

"I'm sorry I'm being so much trouble." She closed her eyes again. Gabe knew how hard he had struck her when he tackled her. He had tried to protect her when they hit the ground, but she could easily have serious injuries.

Seth quickly unhitched their workhorse from the wagon and took him to the barn. Asher had Topper hitched to the buggy in a matter of minutes and drove him up to the house. Gabe's mother got in and had Moses lift Esther in beside her. Gabe climbed in and sat across from the two women. His mother looked out the door. "There is room for you, Cousin Waneta."

Waneta took a step backward. "Nancy should go with her. I haven't learned enough sign language to be of any help."

Gabe's father climbed in and took the driving lines. He looked at his sons. "Help our guests get settled. We will be back as quick as we can. Topper, step trot." The horse took off down the lane.

Gabe hadn't had a chance to tell his brothers what he knew about Waneta's matchmaking plans. He would as soon as he returned. If his brothers wanted to find wives, that was up to them to decide, but they should be warned they were now the targets of their mother's matchmaking cousin and her brood.

The trip to the clinic in Fort Craig took almost an hour. Esther was seen immediately. Gabriel ended up waiting thirty minutes before the physician was able to get to him. When the young man in a white lab coat entered the room, Gabe's father, who had been waiting with him, sat up straight. "How is the woman who came in with us?"

"She gave her permission for me to share her condition with your family because she knew you were worried so I can tell you she has a concussion. I told your wife and her sister that someone should be with her around the clock for the next twenty-four hours and to wake her at regular intervals to make sure her symptoms aren't getting worse. She could lapse into a coma if there is bleeding in her brain. In that case she will need immediate surgery. After that I want her to rest for at least another day."

The doctor read through the notes the nurse who had admitted Gabe had written. He looked at Gabe. "I want you to lie down on the table."

"I hit her pretty hard," Gabe admitted as he complied.

"She told me. She's thankful it was you and not the truck." He put his stethoscope in his ears and listened to Gabe's heart and lungs and pressed several places on his belly. "Does that hurt? Do you have pain anywhere else?"

Gabe shook his head. "I have a few aches and bruises. Nothing more than that."

The doctor seemed satisfied. "Okay. Let's take a look at this arm." He unwound the bandages. "Ouch. Oh, this is going to need stitches. I'll get the nurse in here to help me."

When he left, Gabe's father paced to the door and back. "He sounds concerned about Esther."

"So am I," Gabe admitted.

"Waneta should have come with her."

"You heard her say she doesn't sign well enough."

"She'd known the family for more than a year before she married Carl. You'd think she would have made a point of learning to talk to the child even before the wedding."

"Maybe it is a hard thing to learn, and Esther is hardly a child."

Daed shook his head. "Even if it is difficult, that's not a good excuse. Your mother has had concerns about their relationship. Just things she has gathered from Waneta's letters. She claims the girl is stubborn and resents her trying to take her mother's place."

"She's a grown woman. Does that seem likely?"

"Who can say? I think there is more to the story."

The doctor and the nurse returned, ending their conversation, but it gave Gabe something to think about. If Esther was unhappy with her new stepmother, maybe she was eager to find a husband and get out of the house. He could sympathize with her, but he wasn't going to give her a hand with that. He'd already done enough by saving her life.

It didn't take long to get ten stitches in his arm. Hearing that he wasn't to use his arm for several days was disappointing.

"We can spare you from the repair shop," his father said as he helped Gabe slip into his shirt after the doctor and nurse left the room. "Work in your harness shop can wait a few days, too."

"The Potato Blossom Festival is only three weeks away. I've already paid for a booth at the event to sell my leather goods. As of now I don't have enough pieces ready to make it worth my while."

"Your plans to expand your harness business with other leather goods is ambitious, but don't think the fate of the family rests in your hands. We will get by. *Gott* provides. We have enough repairs lined up to take care of our needs."

"*Daed*, you know as well as I do that we won't be able to make the loan payment on our land in August unless we can bring in additional income. Seth and Asher are talking about moving to the city and taking jobs there."

His father sighed heavily. "That would break your mother's heart. I brought us here to get away from the influences of so many *Englisch* moving into our part of Pennsylvania. To have my sons find work in a factory is not what I wanted. I thought more Amish from our area would follow us here. I thought we would be the only buggy builders in this part of Maine and that we would have more work than we could handle. It pains me to say I was wrong. Two of the new families left last winter because the weather was so harsh. The New Covenant Amish community is too small to support us. If we had stayed in Pennsylvania, at least the boys could have found work in the factories with other Amish men and women. Here they will be alone among outsiders."

Gabe laid his hand on his father's shoulder. "If I can

sell enough of my leather goods to the *Englisch* tourists, and if we have a decent potato harvest, we will make the loan payment and have another year together. More Amish will come. This is a fine place you brought us to, *Daed*."

The thousands of tourists who attended the Potato Blossom Festival each year were Gabe's best chance of earning the money the family needed. He was sure his quality wallets, belts, ax and knife sheaths, among other things, would appeal to the festivalgoers. If he could finish more items in time.

Out in the waiting room, he saw his mother sitting with Esther and Nancy. The sisters were conversing in sign language with a nurse. Gabe had seen people using sign language before, but he hadn't known any of them personally until now. It looked complicated.

Esther caught sight of him and smiled. "How are you?"

He patted his arm gingerly. "Almost as good as new. What about you?" He gestured to her head. Her hair was down and loosely braided, but she had her kapp on.

"I still have a headache, but I don't feel faint anymore." She touched her prayer covering. "I had to take my hair down for the X-ray. The doctor thought the padding my hair provided may have saved me from a worse injury. This is Nurse Heather. She knows sign language."

"I see that."

Heather touched Esther's arm to gain her attention then handed her several pieces of paper. "These are instructions for you and your family," she said as she signed. "Things to watch for. Do you have any questions for me?"

Nancy and Esther looked at each other and shook their heads. "We will take good care of her," Nancy said. "I'm so glad you know ASL. It makes things much easier for my sister."

"What is ASL?" his mother asked.

Heather smiled at her. "American Sign Language. My husband and I had to learn it when we realized our son had been born deaf. Because of that we foster two twin girls who are also deaf, and we hope to adopt them. What we once saw as a tragedy was instead a blessing in disguise for us and for our girls."

"Were they also born deaf?" Gabe's mother asked.

"Their hearing loss is due to untreated ear infections when they were five. Their mother was a single woman with a drug problem. Sadly the girls suffered from neglect and abuse at her hands. However, they are happy and healthy now. It was amazing how quickly they learned to sign. We are investigating bone-anchored hearing devices for them."

"What is that?" his mother asked.

"A small metal post is surgically implanted in the bone behind the ear. When the bone is healed, a hearing device simply snaps onto it. Sounds, which are only vibrations, are transmitted to the inner ear through the bone. It won't help people with nerve deafness like my son, but my grandfather has age-acquired hearing loss in both ears, and eventually his hearing aids no longer helped. He retreated from his friends and became depressed. He had the surgery, and it has made a world of difference for him. He enjoys being around people again. The girls will wear temporary devices held against the bony place behind their ears with soft headbands for several months before having any surgery. We want to see if it is the right choice for them. I have some literature on the procedure if you would like."

"Thank you, but it isn't something I am interested in," Esther said.

"Are you sure?" Nancy asked.

"Very sure." Esther looked away.

Gabe and his mother exchanged puzzled glances. Why wouldn't Esther want to learn about something that could let her hear? He wished he knew more about deafness. Maybe she knew she couldn't be helped.

The nurse turned to Gabe. "You need to come back in a week to have those sutures removed. I've made an appointment for you." She handed him a small card.

"Danki." He took it from her.

"Okay, you are free to go."

He opened the door. His mother rose to her feet and took Esther by the arm to shepherd her outside. Nancy hung back and turned to the nurse. "I'd like some information on the device you spoke about."

"Of course." Heather went behind her counter and handed Nancy a brochure. "There is a phone number you can call."

"Thank you." Nancy slipped the paper in her purse and hurried outside.

On the return trip, Esther sat with her eyes closed and her head leaned against Nancy's shoulder. Neither sister said a word.

When the buggy stopped, Esther sat up. Her furrowed brow told Gabe she was in pain. He got out and gripped her arm to steady her as she got down. She leaned heavily on him.

His mother had noticed her discomfort, too. "Nancy, why don't you take Esther upstairs and let her lie down? She looks worn out. Your room is at the end of the hall."

"All right." Nancy signed something to Esther, who merely nodded, and they both went in the house.

While his father put the buggy and horse away, Gabe followed his mother inside. He found Asher and Seth in the living room playing a board game with the two oldest Burkholder sisters and Jonah. The women were smiling and laughing. Waneta sat in the corner with a smug look on her face. She rose to her feet when Gabe's mother entered the room.

"How is your dear brave son, Cousin Talitha?"

Was it odd that she didn't ask about her stepdaughter first?

"He will be fine. Esther needs to be watched closely for the next two days. I had Nancy take her up to their room."

Waneta pulled a long face. "That girl is always making more work for her family. Her carelessness is the reason your son was hurt, and I'm so very sorry."

Gabe scowled at Waneta's unkind comment about Esther but held his tongue.

"All is forgiven," his mother said. "We will speak no more about it. By God's grace, both our children were spared."

Gabe looked at his brothers. "Have you finished the

wheel for Jedidiah Zook? *Daed* told him it would be ready today."

"We were just about to go out and finish it," Seth said. The men murmured their apologies to the women and got up.

"What did the doctor say about you?" Asher asked as they stepped outside.

"He put in ten stitches and said not to use the arm for several days. I get the stitches out in a week."

As soon as they were out of earshot of the house, Gabe stopped walking. His brothers turned to face him. "I want you to know that matchmaking is the only reason Waneta has brought her stepdaughters along on this visit. Be aware that they are all husband hunting."

A frown appeared on Asher's face. "They seem like nice women, but I'm not on the lookout for a wife."

Seth shrugged. "I wouldn't mind getting to know them better. Just because Waneta and *Mamm* have hatched a matchmaking plot between them doesn't mean it's a bad idea. Waneta has known us since we were babies. If she thinks her stepdaughters would suit us, we should keep an open mind."

Gabe scowled at him. "You have changed your tune since this morning. I've got better things to do than to start courting someone who lives in another state. If our business doesn't improve, we could all be taking jobs in the city."

"We put our faith in *Gott*. He will provide," Seth said quietly.

Gabe felt his brother's gentle rebuke. "The Lord sends the rain and the sun to make our garden grow, but we must still hoe the weeds." It would take faith and effort to keep the family together. The brothers had never been apart for more than a few days. Gabe would do everything in his power to see that didn't happen.

Asher crossed his arms over his chest. "We won't neglect our work because we have visitors, Gabe."

"I know. I'm sorry if I sound cranky. Pay me no mind. What did our cousin and her stepdaughters have to say?"

"*Goot* things about you." Moses grinned.

Asher chuckled. "I thought Waneta was never going to stop praising your brave deed. You must be more careful, *brudder*. That could have been the end of the Fisher triplets, and twins are just so common."

"I did what any of you would have done, and you know it. Come on, I'll give you a hand with the wheel. I've got one good one left."

They chuckled at his little joke and went into the workshop at the side of the barn. Gabe glanced over his shoulder at the second-story room where he knew Esther had gone. He caught sight of her standing by the window.

He wanted her to be okay. He wanted to see her smile. It appeared that things weren't good between Esther and her new stepmother. Family was second only to God in Amish life. Gabe never had to worry that his wouldn't stand by him.

Esther raised her hand in a brief wave before turning away. It was a shame she was trapped in a silent world. Why hadn't she taken the information about a device that could let her hear? And why had her sister taken it after Esther left the clinic?

Chapter Three

Esther woke early the next morning. There wasn't a place on her body that didn't hurt, but at least her headache was manageable. The moment she moved, she remembered everything that had happened yesterday. The vibration under her feet that had confused her, then the glimpse she'd had of the truck from the corner of her eye when she knew it was too late to run. The impact against her that wasn't hard steel but rather muscle and bone. When she had opened her eyes and found herself looking up at Gabe's face, she could hardly believe she wasn't dead. She had been given a second chance at life by an amazingly brave man.

How was Gabe this morning? Was he as sore as she was? She thought again of his sky blue eyes and his pretty mouth. Maybe it wasn't right to call a man's mouth pretty, but she spent a lot of time looking at that part of people's faces, and she knew a pretty one when she saw it.

She sat up and stretched her stiff muscles. Her brush with death had given her a new appreciation for life.

She might be sore, but she wasn't going to waste this precious new day lying in bed. If she didn't get up, all she would think about was Gabe—his strength, his kindness and his smile. It was all that had occupied her mind yesterday whenever she woke. It was probably only natural given the way they had met, but he was occupying far too much of her thoughts. The thing to do was to get moving and work out the kinks from her body and her mind.

She glanced around the room and saw her sisters were all still in their cots. Two of them had their pillows over their heads, so she guessed that Waneta had been snoring. It was a complaint they had shared about her on this trip and one thing Esther was glad hadn't disturbed her rest.

She dressed quickly and went to the window. There was a faint pale pink light across the eastern sky. The sun would be up in an hour. What to do until then? Going back to sleep was out of the question, but a solitary walk in the predawn light held an allure. She would take her sketchbook in case she happened upon some unfamiliar flowers. She slipped the pad and her colored pencils into a quilted pouch and slung it over her shoulder, wincing at the movement but undeterred.

Downstairs she saw Talitha starting coffee in the kitchen. The family would be up soon if they weren't already outside doing chores. She didn't want to bother her hostess, so she slipped out the front door.

The morning air was cool and crisp. It might be summer in Maine, but the air felt like early fall at home in central Ohio. She drew a deep breath. The smells of pine and wood smoke came to her on a gentle breeze. A walk on this beautiful morning that the Lord had made after resting in bed was exactly what she needed. But to where?

She looked down the lane toward the highway. Would the moose return to his feeding spot? She'd had so little time to admire the massive creature yesterday. She would take a chance and see if her curiosity was rewarded.

Walking down to the highway, she followed along the verge of the road until she came to the place where the van had broken down. There was a puddle of oil in the grass, but the van was gone. Bessie must have had it towed away.

Esther hoped the repair wasn't costly. Bessie made extra money driving the Amish in their community. She had agreed to this trip because she was meeting some friends in Bar Harbor for a two-week vacation. She had promised to check with Waneta before she returned to Ohio in case the family was ready to go back with her. Waneta thought they would be staying a month or more and had said she would make other arrangements. Esther prayed two weeks was all she would have to spend away from her Deaf friends and the job she loved. Maybe by then she could convince Waneta to let her return with Bessie.

After looking carefully in both directions, she stepped out onto the highway. The moment her feet touched the pavement, she shuddered. How long would it be before she could walk down the road again without worrying about being struck by a vehicle? Or tackled by a large man?

Poor Gabe. She would have to find a way to repay his daring action. And she would have to find the right time to tell him she was not husband hunting.

She checked both directions three times as she hurried across the road to the edge of the pond. She sat down, drew her knees up and wrapped her arms around them as she waited for the sun to come up.

Gabriel raised his arm to hang up his hat and stopped halfway at the pull of his stitches and sore muscles. He had gone out to help with the morning chores, but his brothers and his father had made him go back into the house. Switching his hat to his other hand, he hung it up and turned around. The kitchen was full of women chatting and laughing. His mother looked happy amid the company. He searched the room but didn't see Esther. He didn't blame her for sleeping in. It had been a wildly dramatic day yesterday.

He went into the living room until breakfast was ready. He found Jonah reading one of his favorite books.

"That's a good adventure story." He gestured toward the novel.

"It is," Jonah said and signed something.

"Do you always do that?"

Jonah looked up. "Do what?"

"Sign although your sister isn't in the room?"

"Did I? Habit, I reckon. I want to make sure that Esther knows what's going on, especially when she isn't with her Deaf friends. And that's Deaf with a capital *D*. They are an amazing group of people. To them deafness isn't a disability. Sometimes my sisters forget that

Esther is around and they don't sign. She so quiet, so it's easy to do."

"She speaks very well. Was she able to hear at one time?"

Jonah closed his book, keeping one finger in between the pages. "*Daed* told me she became completely deaf when she was ten, but she started to lose her hearing when she was eight. We have two deaf cousins, but my folks didn't think much about it until Esther became hard of hearing. The doctors told them it was an inherited type of deafness that doesn't show up until the child is older, but she was born with it. They learned more of their children might become deaf."

"Does that mean you could lose your hearing?"

"It's possible. Since I'm already ten, *Daed* thinks it has skipped me as it did the rest of the girls."

"Maybe it's not my business, but I noticed that Esther and Waneta don't seem as close as your other sisters."

"Esther likes to be alone. I mean, she helps at the school near us for special-needs children. She loves doing that, but when she's in a group of hearing people, she just retreats into a corner or against the wall. It's hard to look at everyone's face at once to try to guess what they're saying."

"What do you mean, guess? I thought she could lip-read?"

"With people she knows well, she can get most of what they are saying, but strangers are harder. Only about half the words we use can be understood by someone who lip-reads. The person has to be looking right at Esther and speaking slowly. Waneta has a habit of putting her fingers on her lips and tapping them and speaking very quickly. Waneta thinks Esther misunderstands her on purpose."

Gabriel heard his father and brothers come in. Nancy stepped into the room. "Jonah, tell Esther breakfast is ready."

"Okay. Is she upstairs?"

"*Nee*, she was already gone when I got up. I thought she must be with you."

He shook his head. "I haven't seen her this morning."

"She has to be around somewhere. Look in the garden. You know how she likes flowers." Nancy turned on her heels and went back to the kitchen.

Gabe had read through the information the nurse had given Esther's family. One of the complications they were to look for was confusion. Had she become confused and wandered off before anyone was up? People in their right senses could easily become lost in these woods if they were unfamiliar with the area. He got to his feet. "I'll help you look for her."

Outside he opened his mouth to call her name and closed it again. That wouldn't help. She couldn't hear him.

"You take the garden. I'll check in the barn. She likes animals," Jonah said.

Gabe didn't find her in his mother's flower garden. There was no sign that she'd been there. The dew was heavy and undisturbed on the grass walkway. She would have left footprints if she had walked along it. He returned to the front of the house and scanned the farmyard. Where would she go? She couldn't hear him calling. She hadn't heard the blare of the semi's horn yesterday. Surely she wouldn't go back to the highway. Then he remembered something she had said. She had wanted to see the moose.

Jonah said she loved animals. Enough to try to see a moose again? It seemed unlikely, but he didn't have anywhere else to start. He called for Jonah and heard the boy answer, "I haven't found her."

"I'm going down to the highway. You keep looking around here."

"Okay."

Gabriel walked quickly down the lane and followed the edge of the highway until he came within sight of the pond. She was there. Sitting in the grass with a sketch pad on her lap while a huge moose grazed on water plants a hundred yards from her. He let out a breath of relief.

He crossed the highway, sat down beside her and touched her shoulder. She turned to him with a huge grin on her face. "Do you see him? Isn't he beautiful?"

Impressive, yes, but not as beautiful as her face in the morning sun. Her amazing amber eyes sparkled with delight, like honey in a clear glass jar, only warmer. Momentarily at a loss for words, he looked down and cleared his throat. "Breakfast is ready."

He felt her hand under his chin as she lifted his face and turned it toward her. "I can't see what you are saying unless you are looking at me."

"I said breakfast is ready if you're hungry."

She turned back to the moose. "*Nee*, I could sit here all day watching this fellow. He's so big. He can keep his head underwater for the longest time. I wanted to get closer, but I wasn't sure it was safe." She looked at him again. "I wouldn't want to force you to save my life again."

Gabe smiled, rose and pulled her to her feet. He wanted to make sure she could see his lips. "A cow with a calf can be dangerous. As can the males during the mating season, but this time of year they are mostly interested in food. You are safe enough at this distance."

"Say that again, and slower, please."

"You're safe as long as he's eating. Speaking of food, I'm hungry. Now that I have found you, I'm not going back without you. Your family was worried."

She shook her head. "*Nee*, they were not. They're used to my odd behaviors. They know I'll turn up eventually."

"Okay, then, I was worried."

"Why?"

"You hit your head hard enough to get a concussion. The papers the doctor sent said confusion was one of the signs we should look for." Her gaze drifted back to the moose.

Gabriel cupped her cheek and turned her face toward him, remembering he had to speak slowly and distinctly. "I was worried you might have become confused and gotten lost."

He realized how close he was to her. His hand still cupped her delicate cheek. If he bent closer, he could kiss her softly smiling lips.

Why would he even think such a thing? He released her abruptly. "We need to go back before my rumbling stomach scares the poor moose into thinking I want his waterlilies."

"I am a little hungry, now that you mention it."

He rubbed his hands on his pant legs to erase the feel of her soft, warm skin against his palm. She caught his arm before he turned away. "I have something to tell you."

"Okay, I'm listening."

"My stepmother believes she is a wondrous *goot* matchmaker. I know Jonah mentioned that she had picked you as a potential spouse for me. I'm grateful for what you did. You've been very kind and I'm sure you would make a fine husband. For someone. Just not for me. I can't—I won't begin a romantic relationship with a hearing man. It's too hard. For me and for him. I hope you understand. I owe you a great deal, my life in fact, but all I can repay you with is honesty."

Gabe was taken aback by her candor. "I appreciate that."

"I'm so glad to clear this up. My sisters hope to wed one day soon, so if you'd like to take one of them out while we are here, that would be more than acceptable."

He managed a wry smile. "I am not looking for a wife."

She tipped her head to the side. "Why not?"

He thought about explaining his business plans but remembered her brother saying she might only understand half of what he was trying to tell her. He would need Jonah or one of her sisters to help. "I'll show you after breakfast," he said slowly, hoping she understood.

Esther walked beside Gabriel with a much lighter heart. Even her headache was nearly gone. Now that he knew she wasn't angling to become his wife, perhaps they could enjoy a friendship while she was staying with his family. She liked him and wanted to get to know him better. She cast a covert glance his way. Was it only because he had saved her, or was there something else that attracted her to him? She wasn't sure.

And if she did find him attractive, there was nothing wrong with that. She could admire a fine horse without having to own it or a cute puppy without taking it home. She could enjoy the company of a handsome man without thinking of him in a romantic fashion. She realized how liberating it was to have finally admitted the truth to someone. She didn't want a hearing husband.

At breakfast she met the rest of the family. Zeke Fisher was a burly man in his early fifties with streaks of silver in his blond hair and beard. Seth bore a striking resemblance to Gabe, but she could have told them apart without the tiny scar in Gabe's eyebrow. Seth's face was softer, less angular than Gabe's, but he had the same sky blue eyes. If he was uncomfortable with her deafness, it didn't show. He made an effort to converse with her through her sisters. Asher and Moses, on the other hand, reacted the way most people did when they met her. They kept their eyes averted except for covert glances and they avoided speaking to her. They weren't trying to be unkind. They were simply uncomfortable. She understood but wished she could slip away to the moose pond again. He hadn't minded her presence at his breakfast. Animals were much more accepting than people.

She was buttering her toast when Nancy touched her

arm to get her attention. Everyone was looking at her. She laid the knife aside. "What?"

Nancy spoke and signed, "Several friends of the Fishers are hosting a picnic for us in a few days at the school. Waneta doesn't want you to feel you need to go."

Holding back a grin with difficulty, Esther rubbed her brow. She was being given a chance to say no. She should take it. "I will have to wait and see."

"I'll stay with you if you don't feel up to going." Nancy said.

"*Nee*, I don't want to spoil anyone else's fun. I'll be fine here alone."

Nancy shook her head. "You won't be alone. Gabe isn't going."

Esther looked at him. "Why not?"

"I have my leatherwork to catch up on," he said, staring straight at her.

She tipped her head slightly and watched his mouth. "What kind of work?"

"Leather goods. I will show you my shop when you are feeling up to it."

She didn't need Nancy to sign—she understood him. It was unusual to find someone she could speech-read so readily.

"I would like that. I feel well enough at the moment. My headache is bearable." She smiled at him and finished buttering her toast.

After breakfast Gabe led her and Jonah to his workshop beside the barn. He opened the door with a flourish. "This is where I make harnesses and other leather goods."

The smell of leather and oils delighted her. She gazed

about in awe. There were harnesses and straps of every kind for working horses, but it was the small items that caught her attention. Wallets, key chains, dog collars of every size with matching leashes. There were sheaths for knives and hatchets as well as tool belts. There were even small boots. She picked one up, thinking it was the wrong shape for a child's moccasin. She held one out to him. "What are these?"

She looked to Jonah as he signed Gabe's answer. "Dog boots. In the winter there are a lot of dogsled races here and in neighboring areas of Canada. The dogs wear boots to protect their feet from the ice and snow while they are running."

"I never knew that."

She touched some of the belts and ran her fingers along the perfectly aligned stitches. "You have a steady hand."

She caught sight of a familiar apparatus and stepped over to it. She turned to grin at him. "This appears to be the moose-size version of my humble sewing machine."

He patted the top of it. "It's old and has seen better days, but it is hand operated and can stitch through three thicknesses of leather."

"And this?" She pointed to a set of rollers that resembled the wringer on her washing machine only with different size grooves in it.

"It's a creasing machine. Let me show you how it works. I'll make a strap." He picked up a tool. "This is a draw knife. I use it to cut strips of leather from the tanned hide. Once I have a strip the length I want, I feed it into the creaser. It comes out perfectly trimmed with creases that give me a stitch line as a pattern pressed into the leather. Then I take it to the sewing machine."

He demonstrated how to position the piece, set the pressure foot and then reached to pull down a lever with a ball on the end. He stopped with a grimace, unable to raise his injured right arm high enough. He motioned for Jonah to operate the lever and set the first stitch. With Jonah's help he stitched about four inches and stopped. "That's how it's done."

"May I try it?" Esther asked, intrigued by the machine.

"Sure." He showed her how to set the stitch length and how to make a turn, then he stepped back. She quickly found the rhythm and was able to complete the strap.

He snipped the threads and examined her work. "*Goot*. Very straight. Nice and even."

She grinned at his praise. "I told you I like to sew. This is very interesting. How do you sell these things? I didn't see any signs advertising them. Do you have a shop in town or someone who sells them for you?" She looked to Jonah to sign Gabe's answer.

"These are the inventory I'm taking to the Potato Blossom Festival in three weeks. I paid for a booth there, and I plan to sell them during the festival."

She raised one eyebrow. "You can't run a business on a single festival."

He tipped his head toward her and grinned, deepening the laugh lines bracketing his mouth. "You are absolutely right. I will need a storefront in time. There isn't enough room in this building right now, but it will be easy enough to add onto it."

She enjoyed his enthusiasm. She could see he liked his work. He had an artist's gift, something she hadn't expected. "Have you thought about selling on the internet? I ask because I have a friend who makes reed baskets. She sells them online. She hired a manager, an *Englisch* woman, to handle the orders and the computer side of her business."

He sobered. "It's an idea I mean to explore in the future. For now, I plan to hand sell my items."

"If your church district allows it, you should look into it sooner rather than later."

He shrugged and turned away. She tapped on Jonah's shoulder to relay Gabe's words to her. Jonah scowled. "I know. He said a man needs to make a living to feed his family and help in the community, but he doesn't need to make a lot of money. If he has a business that makes a profit, he doesn't need to go bigger."

He was right. There was a lot to like about Gabe Fisher. He believed in living the values taught by their church. God first, family second, community third. He would make a fine husband for a woman who could hear. She checked the pang of self-pity that hit her and turned her attention to the enormous sewing machine. When she had her emotions under control, she smiled at him and gestured around the room. "How much more inventory do you want to take with you to the festival?"

"About twice as much. My problem has been finding the time. Spring and summer are busy times for buggy and wheel repair with all the farmwork underway. I can't slack on the work that is paying our bills while I daydream about earning more." He flexed his injured arm gingerly. "This is not going to let me catch up."

Suddenly she saw a way to repay some of his kindness. It was so simple and something she liked to do, anyway. "Maybe I could help."

Both his eyebrows shot up. "You? How?"

"I'm known as a good seamstress. I could do your stitching while you did the tooling on the pieces. Some of the items in here don't need tooling. The dog leashes are just simple stitching. So are the belts. Even some of the gun holsters and knife sheaths don't require much tooling."

She held up a small holster. "Take this piece. I could add a concho threaded with leather fringe for decoration and sew the two pieces together in no time. I wouldn't mind helping."

She saw his indecision and put the holster down. "You gave me my life back yesterday. I feel this might repay you in some small way. Please allow me to help."

He rubbed his hand across his chin as he considered her offer. He didn't look convinced. She held her breath, wanting him to say yes. Only because she wanted to stay busy until she could return home. Not because the thought of spending time in Gabe's company was appealing. Even if it was.

Chapter Four

Gabe considered Esther's offer to help. He looked around his workroom. It was filled with his cutting table, stacks of tanned hides, rollers, presses, machines to stitch and mold leather. There was barely room for him to move around as it was without adding another person underfoot. Two, since she would need Jonah to convey what he said.

Anyway, how much help could she be if she wasn't familiar with the equipment or even sewing leather? Completing one strap wasn't enough to make her an expert. He didn't want to hurt her feelings, but he would be better off if she stayed with her sisters. She would be better off, too.

He shook his head. "I understand you want to repay me in some way. It isn't necessary. It's kind of you to offer, but you are here to enjoy a visit, not to work."

Disappointment flashed in her eyes and then something that looked like defiance.

Her chin went up a notch. "You think I can't do it?"

He sought to smooth over the moment. "I'm sure you could if someone taught you."

"You can teach me."

He glanced around again. "I wouldn't know where to start. There's a lot more to harness making and leatherwork than simple sewing. It isn't like making a dress."

She crossed her arms. "Have you made many dresses?"

He shifted uncomfortably from one foot to the other. "*Nee*, I haven't."

"Then you don't know if the skill required is similar or not. I'm not offering to make a complete harness. I have no idea how to operate your equipment. I'm offering to stitch and perhaps embellish some of your smaller items."

He stared at her intently. What was behind this offer? "Why?"

She held out her hands and gestured around the room. "This would keep me from becoming bored while I'm here. I like to sew."

Or was it her way of trying to ingratiate herself to him? She might say she didn't want a hearing husband, but she hadn't come all the way to Maine to view the wildlife. He didn't like the feeling that he and his brothers were on Waneta's shopping list. It made him suspicious.

The outside door opened, and Waneta stepped in. "There you are, Jonah. I need your help with something. Come along."

"But I'm signing for Gabe," the boy said.

Waneta sent Gabe a knowing smile. "I'm sure he

can make himself understood. Esther reads lips better than she lets on. Don't make me wait." Waneta held the door open. Jonah sighed heavily but went out with her.

When the door closed, Gabe looked at Esther. She was still staring at the door. He hesitated, then touched her arm. She glanced at him. "Do you?" he asked.

"Do I what?"

"Speech-read better than you let on?"

"Is that what she said?" Anger flashed in her eyes before she schooled her features into the appearance of calmness. She did it so easily he wondered how often she was forced to practice the move. He admired her self-control.

She kept her gaze fastened to his. "I didn't know she had come in. I wasn't looking toward her until I noticed Jonah staring behind me. All I caught was 'Don't make me wait.' I have no idea what she said before that."

"That has to be frustrating, only catching part of a conversation because you happen to look away or don't see someone behind you."

She tipped her head slightly as she regarded him. "It is. Few people make that connection unless they are used to being around a deaf person who lip-reads."

"I don't know any deaf people personally. It just seems logical."

Her eyes sparkled as a slight smile curved her lips. "You would think so, but not everyone is as observant as you are."

He wanted to ask her why she hadn't taken the information about the hearing device yesterday but thought better of it. It wasn't any of his business. He needed to get to work, not stand here wasting time visiting with Esther, no matter how interesting she was turning out to be.

"About my offer?" she prompted.

"I appreciate it, but I think not." He hoped he wasn't going to wound her, but she deserved his honesty. "I don't have the time to teach you what you would need to know."

Her expressive face went blank. "I should go back to the house." She hurried to the door.

He had hurt her feelings. "Esther, wait. I'm sorry."

She left the shop without looking back. Of course she didn't turn around. She couldn't hear him.

He stood staring at the door for several seconds. He could chase after her and apologize, but maybe this was for the best.

He picked up a length of leather and fed it into his shiver to cut down the thickness of the piece. When he was done, he added it to the pile of belts on the table waiting to be stitched. Working the shiver to decrease the thickness of the leather didn't pull his stitches the way trying to operate the sewing machine did. He would cut out as many pieces as he could and do the sewing when his arm was better in a day or two. He hoped.

A little past noon, the door opened. His father looked in. "Gideon Beachy's feed wagon has a busted axle and broken rear wheel. It will take all of us to get it repaired before he has to feed his dairy cows again this evening. Seth has gone into Fort Craig to see about some scrap iron for sale."

Gabe laid aside the leather stip. "I thought I'd get some work in here done today, but reckon I thought wrong."

"I'm sorry, *sohn*. I can't neglect a paying job or our neighbor. I need you."

"Of course." Gabe laid the last strip of leather on the pile, grabbed his hat and followed his father. As he climbed on the wagon with his brothers, he caught sight of Esther in the garden with her brother. He should have taken her up on her offer. She could have stitched a belt or two for him while he was gone. He nodded to her. She pointedly looked away. It didn't appear that she would be willing to help him in the future. He resigned himself to another lost day of work.

"Where are Zeke and his sons going?" Esther asked Jonah, who was helping her weed Talitha's garden.

He shook his head, not bothering to sign. Esther stared at Gabe's empty workshop. He didn't think she had the skill required to stitch a few simple straight lines. That was basically all the belts and dog leashes required. Unless he wanted to produce fancier pieces. She was quite capable of stitching a zigzag if that were the case.

She resumed hoeing the weeds with renewed vigor. Being deaf didn't make her incapable of learning. Unfortunately some people assumed that it did. She would love to prove him wrong.

She stopped hoeing. She shouldn't be this annoyed. Why was she?

Because she'd had a few glimpses of empathy from Gabe Fisher. She thought he was different.

Jonah tapped the handle of the hoe she was leaning on and signed, "Maybe Pamela knows."

Esther looked toward the house and saw Pamela walking toward her with a bowl in her hands. She stopped at the first row of green beans, squatted down and began searching among the leaves for pods that were big enough to pluck.

"Where did the Fisher men go?" Esther asked.

Pamela looked up. "To help a neighbor with a broken wagon."

Esther glanced at the workshop again. "Will they be gone long?" She looked at her sister to see the answer.

"I heard Zeke say they wouldn't be back for several hours."

Several hours. How much stitching could she get done before Gabe returned? Enough to prove that she was capable of doing more? Would he be angry if she invaded his workspace without him? Was it worth risking his ire just to show him he was wrong about her usefulness?

Maybe it was.

She resumed hoeing. As soon as she finished this task, she was going to take another look around Gabe's workshop. If there happened to be something that she could sew for him, she would. If there wasn't anything cut, she wouldn't risk ruining one of his pieces of leather. She'd just leave, close the door and pretend she had never gone back. She began to hoe more quickly.

Fifteen minutes later she put her gardening tool back

in the shed and hurried around the side of the house before Waneta noticed she was done with her chore. If Waneta saw Esther wasn't busy, she always found something for her to do. At the door to Gabe's shop, Esther glanced around to make sure no one was looking for her and then she slipped inside.

The wonderful smells of leather and tanning oil made her smile. Perhaps she couldn't hear the sounds of the world, but there was nothing wrong with her nose. She took delight in the different fragrances of life and the way the scent of something could bring a treasured memory into sharp focus. Only now she needed to concentrate on finding what work, if any, she could do for Gabe.

There were tanned hides stacked in one corner of the room waiting to be cut into usable shapes. Some of the leather was thick and black. Other pieces were thinner, more supple and dyed different shades of brown. There was little she could do with the uncut pieces. She turned her attention to the other side of the room and saw a stack of leather cut into strips of varying lengths but all exactly the same width. Unless she was badly mistaken, these were for belts. She grabbed the top three and carried them to Gabe's sewing machine.

There were several spools of colored thread to choose from, but she decided to go with the creamy color that was already on the machine that Gabe had set up earlier. She looked back over her shoulder at the closed door.

She could put back the strips and leave. He would never know she had been inside without his knowledge. A quick retreat was tempting. She focused on the machine again. Proving him wrong was even more of a temptation.

After she stitched five of the belts with the creamy thread, her eyes were drawn to the spool of red thread. It would look pretty against the black leather. It took her a few minutes to figure out how to rethread the machine. When she was done, she set the needle for the first stitch and stared at the belt. What if she made a series of Xs instead of doing a straight stitch? How would that look? She pictured it in her mind's eye. It certainly wouldn't be plain. Would customers like it?

The more important question was, what would Gabe think of such a design? If she went ahead and he didn't like it, the leather would be ruined.

She took a deep breath and began to sew. With each pull of the lever, she adjusted the angle of the strap and soon had a row of Xs almost done when light spilled in, brightening the room. She knew the outside door had been opened.

She turned around slowly. Gabe was standing in the doorway with a frightening scowl on his face and one hand clamped over his injured arm. She kept her chin up with difficulty as she focused on his mouth. She didn't want to miss what he had to say.

He stood there for a long moment before he stepped into the room. His eyes moved from her to the stack of leather belts on the table beside the sewing machine. He didn't say anything. He walked over and picked up one of the belts. He turned so he could examine it in the brighter light.

Still without speaking he spread the others out, looking carefully at each one. Then he noticed the piece still on the machine. One eyebrow shot up and he looked directly at her. "Interesting."

While it wasn't praise, it certainly wasn't condemnation. "I thought so."

His gaze roved over the room. She sat up straighter. "I didn't touch any of your equipment other than the sewing machine."

He nodded and then walked to the piles of leather. He withdrew one from a smaller stack and walked to the cutting table. He continued to hold his injured arm tight against his chest. She thought he said something but couldn't tell for sure. He sent her a questioning look over his shoulder.

She crossed her arms. "What?"

"Sorry. I asked if you wanted to learn how to cut patterns. I'll show you what templates I have. You can finish that piece later."

"You aren't angry with me?"

He cocked his head to the side. "Why should I be angry?"

"You were when you opened the door and saw me in here."

"*Nee*, it was not an angry expression you saw. It was only discomfort."

"Your arm is paining you?"

"Some. How is your head?"

She unfolded her arms and settled her hands on her hips. "Do you want the truth?"

"Certainly."

"Throbbing, but not as bad as yesterday. Now tell me again, how is your arm?"

He cradled it with his good hand and grinned. "Stinging and aching something fierce. I think I may have torn a stitch."

She looked at him, aghast. "Did you just say you might have torn your stitches?"

He sobered. "That's what I said. Am I hard to understand?"

"I get most of what you are saying. I can guess at the rest. I'm just shocked that you came in here to work. March up to the house and let me take a look at your arm. You will need a new bandage, anyway. It has bled through onto your shirtsleeve." She pointed to the door. "Now. Go. Did you understand that?"

"I got it." He walked to the door and held it open for her.

Her shoulder brushed against him as she walked past. She sucked in a quick breath as the contact sent her pulse racing. Why did he have such a strange effect on her?

She smelled like a garden in the sunshine. It wasn't something Gabe had expected to encounter in his workshop. Perhaps she used a shampoo with a floral scent that lingered, or maybe it was simply her.

She was a breath of fresh air. More direct than any woman he knew except his mother. He liked her. But she wouldn't be here long, and she wasn't interested in a walking out with a fellow like him. He'd never thought having good hearing would be a drawback in a relationship, but it was in her case. Not that he had the time or the inclination to court a woman this summer. He didn't. He had work to do.

At the house his father was seated at the kitchen table with a cup of coffee in his hand as he waited for supper. Esther pointed to a chair. "Sit. Roll up your sleeve."

Esther gently unwound the bandage. His mother and Waneta came in from his mother's quilting room. "What has happened?" his mother asked.

"I tore a stitch loose. It's nothing. Esther is taking care of it."

Waneta called for Julia, who came in from the other room. "See to Gabe's arm. Julia has taken first-aid training and helps our local volunteer fire department," she explained as she drew Esther aside.

"Esther was doing fine," he said, watching her retreat to the living room.

His mother scowled in disapproval at his father. "You told me the doctor said he wasn't to use his arm for a week."

"I told the boy not to lift with that arm, didn't I, Gabe?"

"You did, but it couldn't be helped. We got the wagon fixed. That's what counts." Gabe hissed as Julia cleaned the rest of the stitches with peroxide.

"You will have to watch for any signs of infection," she said, stepping back. "I'll change the dressing again tomorrow."

"*Danki.* Am I free to go?"

Julia nodded. Waneta beamed at her, then looked

at Gabe. "Julia is calm and capable in an emergency. Wonderful traits for a wife to have, don't you think?"

"I reckon so." He stood, rolled down his sleeve and went into the living room. Esther was seated by the window staring outside. Her hands were clenched into fists on her lap. Jonah stood nearby with a scowl on his face.

Gabe crossed the room to stand beside Esther. She looked up at him. He nodded toward the front door. "We have work to do."

Her eyes widened in surprise. She grinned and jumped to her feet. "I'm ready if you are."

"Then come on. Jonah, I may need your help." Gabe led the way through the kitchen and out the door.

Jonah hurried to keep up with him. "Gladly, but can we go look for a moose later? I've been hoping to see one."

"Did your sister tell you about the one we saw this morning?"

"*Nee*, she did not." Jonah touched Esther's arm and signed quickly.

Esther signed back, ruffled his hair and went into the workshop.

"What did she say?" Gabe asked.

"She said if I get up early I might be able to see him tomorrow. Do you think he'll return?"

"They tend to feed in one area for several days. It's possible."

Inside the workroom, Gabe went to his cutting table and pulled out several of the templates he had made for cutting out holsters, knife sheaths and wallets. Jonah was able to convey his instructions to Esther as Gabe had to keep his eyes on what he was cutting so he didn't ruin a piece of leather. Esther watched and asked pointed questions about the properties of the leather he chose for each item. She had a quick mind, and she didn't waste time with chitchat.

When Gabe had enough items cut out to keep her busy stitching for the rest of the day, he sent Jonah back to the house and turned his attention to making the pony-size harness that Willis Gingrich, the local Amish blacksmith, had ordered. He was cutting the driving lines an hour later when he noticed the sewing machine had stopped. He looked over to see Esther rubbing her temples with both hands.

She glanced his way. "I'm done."

He shouldn't have put her to work so soon. "That's fine. Go to the house and rest. I will finish them tomorrow."

"I mean I'm done with what you gave me. Do you trust me to cut out more?"

He made his way to her side. The neatly stitched items were stacked together on a table beside her chair. He picked up several of the wallets, knowing they took the most work, and examined them closely. The stitching was flawless. He shook his head in disbelief.

Worry filled her eyes. "Is something wrong? Did I make a mistake?"

"*Nee*, your work is every bit as good as I could have done, and you did it in a quarter of the time it would have taken me. To think I wondered how much help you could possibly be."

Her eyes narrowed. "Because I'm deaf?"

"Because you said you hadn't used a machine like mine or worked in leather before." He held out the wallet. "Tell me the truth. Do you do this at home?"

She laughed. "I do not, but it's easier than making a dress or a shirt. I can do more if you will cut some for me."

"Not now. I want you to go rest. Your headache is worse."

"How do you know that?"

"I can see it in your eyes."

She rubbed her temples. "I said you were observant. Very well, I will go lie down for a bit."

He watched her leave and then looked at the work they had gotten done in one morning. With Esther's help, he could finish more than enough pieces in the next three weeks to sell at the upcoming festival. His hopes rose for the first time in ages. His plan just might work.

Chapter Five

Esther only meant to lie down for half an hour or so, but when she woke, she realized she had been asleep for over four hours. It was too late to go back to Gabe's shop. She sat up and discovered her headache was almost gone.

Nancy was sitting on a chair nearby. "Feeling better?" she signed.

Esther grinned. "Much better."

"Gabe was concerned when you didn't come down for supper."

"I promised to help him in his workshop. He must think I deserted him."

Nancy shook her head and signed, "He said you were not to do any more work for him today."

"Oh." Esther was surprised at the sharpness of her disappointment. Had he decided he could get along better without her?

"He said rest and tomorrow will be soon enough to get started again."

Relief made Esther smile. "That's *wunderbar*. I'm happy to help him. I owe him so much."

"He seems like a nice fellow. Waneta certainly thinks so."

"I do, too. What about you? Have any of the brothers caught your eye?"

"After a day? I hardly think so. You sound like Waneta. She asked us all that very question this morning. Why is she so set on having us marry?"

Esther had wondered the same thing. "Perhaps she wants our father all to herself."

"She won't have that until Jonah marries, and he is only ten. Are you ready to go downstairs?"

"I am. I'm starving."

"I'm sure Talitha can find you something. A soup bone to gnaw on or a crust of bread."

Esther gave her sister a playful shove. "I'm sure our hostess has more than that laid by for her guests."

"You wouldn't be so sure if you saw how much food her sons eat. Moses must still be growing. He ate more than any of them."

"Then someone should point out that you are the best cook among us, little sister," Esther said, holding back a grin.

Nancy stuck out her tongue and signed, "I expect Waneta will get around to mentioning it soon enough. We are working on a quilt in Talitha's sewing room. Will you join us?"

"I think not. It's difficult to quilt and gossip if you must stop and sign everything for me. You go and join the fun. I think I'll have a bite to eat and go back to sleep. I can't believe how tired I am."

"You are trying to do too much too fast."

"Maybe you're right."

The sisters walked downstairs together. Esther discovered that Talitha had left a plate of roast beef, carrots and potatoes warming in the oven for her. She enjoyed her solitary meal and then went back to bed.

The following morning she came down to breakfast to find everyone had already finished. She stepped outside and paused on the steps, wondering what she should do, when she caught sight of Gabe coming out of his workshop just as his brother Seth came out of the barn. Gabe must have called out to his brother, because Seth stopped, nodded and then continued his way. Gabe walked toward her. He held a pair of bridles in his hand.

He paused in front of her with his eyes focused on her face. "Are you feeling better?"

"Much. I'm ready to do more sewing for you."

He shook his head. "Not right now. How about a walk in the fresh air?"

She sighed. "I know you have work that needs doing. You don't have to babysit me."

He grinned and held up the bridles. "Didn't you hear me tell Seth just now that I'm walking over to the Arnett farm to deliver these?"

His grin vanished. He flushed a deep red. "You couldn't have heard that. I'm sorry. That was an inconsiderate thing to say."

"Don't be sorry, Gabe. You haven't offended me. I am as I am."

Esther could see he was still uncomfortable. He shifted from one foot to the other. "Mrs. Arnett is our neighbor. Her place isn't far. It's a pleasant walk through the woods. Would you care to join me?"

She didn't want him to worry that something he said or did would upset her. "I would like that. *Danki.* You realize you will have to walk backward most of the way so that I can see what you're saying to me."

She tried not to smile, but she couldn't help it. The look of puzzled confusion on his face was priceless. She burst out laughing.

It quickly dawned on Gabe that Esther was teasing him. Was she joking about her condition to put him at ease? It was a generous move. "Laughing at the man who saved your life isn't the nicest way to repay him."

"What would be a better way?"

"If you could forgive his fumbling words."

"You are forgiven, as long as you promise not to treat me differently from my sisters or your other friends."

"I'll try my best. This way." He nodded toward the barn.

"Let me get something first."

She rushed back inside and soon returned with a blue quilted bag slung over her shoulder. "I'm ready."

"The path through the woods is just beyond the barn. If I have anything important to say while we are walking, I'll make sure I get your attention first."

"That sounds like a sound plan. If you hear of a better one, you should give me a shout." She arched her brow. "Get it?"

He rolled his eyes. "I get it. I'm free to use words that refer to hearing. You won't be offended."

"Excellent. I like the sound of that." Her wide grin made him smile, too.

"Enough. I'm going. Tag along if you like." He started toward the path. She quickly fell into step beside him. Less than a hundred yards beyond the barn, they entered a grove of pine trees. The path skirted around moss-covered boulders thrust up through the earth and skeletons of old fallen pine trees. The dappled sunlight was broken in places by openings in the canopy that allowed the brightness to reach the forest floor. Those spaces were filled with shrubs, plants and young trees eager to take advantage of the light.

The air was filled with birdsongs and the sighing of the wind in the branches overhead. Gabe kept alert for the sounds or glimpses of animals. There were black bears in the area as well as moose. It wouldn't do to surprise either one of them.

They skirted the edge of a shallow pond when suddenly Esther stopped. "Oh, how pretty."

Gabe turned to see her crouched beside a cluster of small blue flowers. She looked up at him. "What are these called?"

"I don't know." He pointed overhead. "But that is a Harris's sparrow. A rare bird in these parts."

She stood and moved closer to him. "Did you say a rare bird? Where?"

"Near the top of that spruce." She looked where he was pointing.

"He's kind of streaky brown and black. He has a

black bib, a black face and a small black crown." Gabe stopped talking when he realized she wasn't looking at him. She couldn't hear the bird's call or his description.

"Is it that black-and-brown bird with a little black hat on his head?" She turned to look at Gabe.

He nodded. "That's the one."

"He's pretty, but I like flowers better. Are you a bird-watcher?"

"I am. I keep a record of the rare ones that I see."

She knelt beside the flowers again. "I keep pressed petals in an album. I like to sketch them in their native setting, too. I wish I knew the name of this one."

He touched her arm to get her attention. "Take a sprig. Mrs. Arnett might know. She's a Maine native."

"I hate to disturb the plant until I know it's a common species. I'd like to make a quick sketch instead if you don't mind."

He had work waiting but he couldn't deny her this simple joy. "Go ahead."

"Danki." She opened her satchel and pulled out a pad along with some colored pencils.

He moved a few feet away and took a seat on a fallen log to watch her. She bent close to the flowers, looking at them from several angles before she settled on the ground, opened her book and started drawing.

She seemed at home in the woods. The patterns of sunlight filtering down on her made her blend into the surroundings, for her dress was nearly the same shade of blue as the flowers at her feet. She chewed the tip of her pencil as she regarded her subject before bending over the paper once more.

He heard a rustling in the leaves behind him and scanned the woods for the source of the sound. A gray squirrel scampered up a nearby tree and chittered loudly from a dead branch.

"What are you looking at?" Esther asked.

"That squirrel. He's upset with us." He glanced at her and realized she was still waiting for his answer. How long would it take him to learn he had to be looking at her before he spoke? It wasn't as easy as it sounded.

"A squirrel is scolding us. Are you finished?"

"I am."

"May I see it?" He held out his hand.

She hesitated then handed over her sketch pad. She had captured the size, color and even the texture of the plant. "The Lord has given you quite a talent."

She took the picture away from him. "I think flowers are easy to draw."

"Not for me they aren't. I tend to avoid floral designs on my tooled leatherwork for that reason."

"Perhaps I can give you some pointers when I get back to work."

"I look forward to it," he said and realized he meant it. She was an intriguing woman. He found he wanted to know her better.

They started along the path again, but it wasn't long before she stopped to examine another cluster of blooms. "What are these?"

"I haven't a clue."

"Oh." She walked on but soon stopped beside a group of miniature daisylike blossoms. "These are lovely. Do you know what they're called?"

"Weeds."

She shot him a sour look. "Weeds or not, they're pretty."

"At this rate we won't get to the Arnett farm before dark."

"Okay, I'll stop looking at the flowers."

"Weeds."

Her eyes flashed with annoyance. "I refuse to call something with such delicate petals and this sweet scent a weed."

She walked off ahead of him, so she didn't see his grin. She might pretend to be annoyed with him, but he could tell she wasn't. He was discovering that Esther Burkholder was a very interesting woman even if Waneta had brought her here on a husband-hunting mission.

The thought drew him up short. He wasn't in the market for a wife. He had to keep his focus on improving the family's precarious financial situation.

Esther was sorry when the woods opened suddenly into a field until she realized she was walking out amid acres of blossoming potato plants. The air was filled with their delicate fragrance as the white flowers atop the bright green foliage trembled in the breeze. Gabe came up beside her and gestured around them. "Not weeds," he said when he was sure she was looking at him.

She rolled her eyes. "Are you trying to be funny?"

"I am. Did it work?"

She chuckled. "I'm mildly amused."

"I'm usually much funnier."

"I can hardly wait to see a sample. Is that where we're going?" She pointed toward a farmstead a few hundred yards away.

"Yup."

Together they walked toward the farm. An *Englisch* woman wearing jeans and a red plaid shirt came out of the barn carrying a bucket. She caught sight of them and waved.

Gabe waved back. The woman put her bucket down and came to greet them. "Hello, Gabe. I see you have my bridles. Who is this with you?"

Gabe looked at Esther. "Esther, this is Lilly Arnett. She farms here by herself. Lilly, this is Esther Burkholder. She and her family are visiting from Ohio. Esther is Deaf but can speech-read or read lips, as they sometimes say. You must be looking at her when you speak. She is also a wildflower lover. Perhaps you can identify one she sketched."

Lilly held out her hand. "I'm pleased to meet you. I'd be happy to look at your drawing."

Esther pulled her sketchbook from her bag and opened it before handing it to Lilly. "I think it must be a violet of some sort."

"It's a New England violet. They are rare. Where did you find it?"

"Alongside a small pond just off the path that leads here."

Lilly smiled. "They do like moist ground. I may go gather some seeds and plant a few in my wildflower garden. You must come and see it. It's my pride and joy."

Esther happily followed Lilly to an area at the side of her house, where a stepping-stone path led down to a small stream. A profusion of flowers graced the gentle slope in a multitude of colors and sizes, from small bleeding hearts clustered beside the path to tall nodding white yarrow, blue spires of lupine and everything in between. A stone bench stood beneath the spreading branches of an oak tree that overlooked the area. Esther's fingers itched to get out her pencils and paper.

She grinned at Lilly. "It's beautiful."

"Thank you. I feel close to God when I come down here to just sit and admire His handiwork."

"I know what you mean." Esther, too, felt close to God when she was in her flower garden at home.

Gabe handed Lilly the bridles. "I hope these are what you wanted."

"Let's see." She led the way to a corral where two horses stood. She opened the gate and slipped a bridle on one of them. Both she and Gabe checked the fit, and Lilly seemed satisfied. The two of them spoke briefly, but Esther couldn't see what they were saying. When Gabe returned to her side, she waved goodbye to Lilly and waited for him to speak.

"I invited Lilly to the picnic. I hope you don't mind. I thought you might enjoy visiting with someone who shares your hobby. She'd like to see more of your sketches."

It was kind of him to invite someone she knew and would have something in common with. Large groups weren't comfortable for her unless she was with people who could sign. Her sisters often performed that service, but with Waneta insisting they focus on finding mates, Esther wasn't sure they would have time for her.

"I'll be happy to show Lilly my drawings at the gathering. Have you decided to go to the picnic?"

"If we get enough work done this afternoon and tomorrow, I might."

Esther smiled, amazed at how happy it made her to know he could be coming. "*Goot*. Then I'll sew up a storm."

Gabe was busy in his workshop early the following morning when Esther came in. He had a dozen leather knife sheaths tooled with a basket-weave pattern ready to be assembled. "I didn't expect you until after breakfast."

"I wanted to get an early start to make up for our lost time yesterday morning," she said, moving to take a seat.

"We made up for most of that in the afternoon. I'm nearly caught up."

It didn't take long for him to show her what he wanted done. After that they worked in silence with only the sound of his mallet tapping designs into leather pieces and the steady thumping of the sewing machine. He glanced over several times to make sure she wasn't having trouble. Once she looked up and caught his eye. She frowned slightly. "Did you say something?"

He shook his head, and she went back to work. After an hour he heard his mother calling him. Gabe put his tools aside and touched Esther's shoulder. When she looked up, he nodded toward the door. "Breakfast is ready."

"I'll be in as soon as I finish this piece." She went back to pulling the lever on the stitcher.

He pulled her chair back. She frowned at him. "What are you doing?"

"Finish after we eat. Our families will be waiting on us."

A mutinous expression crossed her face but quickly disappeared. "Very well."

He followed her out the door and across the farmyard to the house. Inside, his brothers and Jonah were lined up on one side of the table while her sisters and Waneta were seated across from them. His father sat at the head of the table. His mother filled all the cups with coffee, returned the pot to the stove and took her place at the foot of the table. Everyone bowed their heads for a silent blessing.

There was very little conversation until everyone was finished eating. Jonah, seated opposite Esther, signed for her when needed.

Gabe's father cleared his throat. "We have a broken spring on the bishop's buggy to repair today. Seth, you and Asher can manage that. I want to get a few more spare buggy wheels built so we have a ready supply when one is needed. Moses, do you have anything going on?"

"*Nee*, I'm free to help you."

"*Goot*. Waneta, what are you and the girls going to do today?"

"We are almost finished with Talitha's quilt. After

that we'll bake a few things for the picnic tomorrow. Nancy works in a bakery in our town. She's very skilled, as I'm sure you will agree when you sample her creations tomorrow."

Nancy signed something for Esther, who smothered a laugh. Waneta scowled at them.

"Esther will be helping me today," Gabe said quickly.

His mother took a sip of her coffee and put her cup down. "I hope you aren't taking advantage of her kindness in offering to sew for you?"

"He isn't," Esther said. "I enjoy it. I'm hoping he will show me how to tool some of the pieces, too." She picked up her plate and began to clear the table. Her sisters quickly joined her. Gabe waited outside for Esther to join him. When she came out, he smiled at her. "Would you really like to learn to tool leather?"

"I would."

"Once we finish the pieces I already have cut, I'll show you the basic tools I use. Does that sound okay to you?"

She smiled broadly, proving she recalled their conversation yesterday. "You are a quick learner."

"I try."

They entered the workshop and spent the rest of the morning concentrating on their own tasks as the finished pieces piled up. He looked at the growing stack. With Esther's help over the next two weeks, he would have plenty of items to sell.

It was almost noon when the outside door opened. Waneta came in, followed by Pamela.

"I see Esther is still taking up all your time, Gabriel," Waneta said. "You don't have to continue to indulge her."

"I'm not humoring her," he said with a pointed look at Waneta. "She is a skilled worker."

Waneta ignored his rebuke. "Why don't you show Pamela some of your work? She is interested in leatherworking, too. Pamela, tell Esther Talitha would like her to work on the quilt with us for a while and then I have some errands I need her to run." She turned around and left.

Gabe watched the exchange take place in sign language. Esther wasn't pleased. She shot an angry look toward the door but got up and allowed Pamela to sit down. Esther glanced at Gabe. "I'm sorry, but I have to go."

"That's okay. Pamela can help me."

Pamela looked the sewing machine up and down. "I'm not too sure about that."

He spent the next hour teaching Pamela the basics of stitching leather while his own work went by the wayside. She had dozens of questions, which he answered patiently, but she didn't possess the skills Esther had. He was glad when they had to go in for lunch.

Waneta and Nancy served up the meal. He didn't see his mother or Esther. He turned to his father. "Where is *Mamm*?"

"She went into Fort Craig to pick up some material for a new dress."

"And Esther?" Gabe looked at Waneta.

"I sent her along to keep your mother company and

to buy some things I need. I'm sure Pamela can help you again this afternoon."

"I'm not really much help," Pamela admitted. "My talents lie more with quilting."

"I see," Waneta said with a tight smile. "Nancy, perhaps you would like to give Gabe a hand."

"I guess I could," Nancy said.

She clearly wasn't eager to do so, and Gabe wasn't eager to waste more time teaching a reluctant pupil. "I have harness cutting work to do this afternoon. I don't need help with that." He concentrated on the meat loaf and mashed potatoes on his plate, but his appetite was gone. It looked like he'd miss the picnic tomorrow after all.

Was Waneta suddenly intent on keeping Esther away from him? If so, why?

Chapter Six

When Esther returned from town with Gabe's mother, she found Pamela and Nancy in the kitchen rolling out pie dough. Talitha was putting away the horse and buggy.

Esther laid the packages her stepmother wanted on the table. "Waneta, I have your things. Pamela, I thought you were helping Gabe."

Pamela put aside her rolling pin and looked at Esther. "He said he needed to work alone on cutting a harness." She glanced at Waneta, who was slicing apples and signed, "I don't think I was much help, anyway. I'm sorry she made you leave."

"That's okay. It wasn't your fault," Esther signed. She cleared her throat. "Gabe was going to show me how to decorate leather with stamping and tooling. I think I'll go see if he has time now."

Waneta turned around. "You shouldn't monopolize his time, Esther. You've made no secret of the fact that you won't consider marrying someone who isn't deaf.

Give your sisters a chance to get to know Gabriel. One of them may suit him. How will they find out if he is constantly with you?"

"It won't be me," Pamela signed then transferred the pie dough into a pan and crimped the edges.

Waneta scowled at her then looked at Esther. "I've decided you may return to Ohio with Bessie. I walked to the phone booth today and called her. She said she'd be happy to have your company on the return trip."

It was what Esther had wanted, so why wasn't she happier about the prospect? Because Gabe needed her help and she liked helping him. "Did *Daed* agree to this? He wanted me to come."

"And we both know why. I'll write and tell him tomorrow. I'm sure he won't object when I explain."

"When is Bessie coming back?"

"In ten days. Take over on these apples, Esther." Waneta left the kitchen with her packages. Esther hadn't agreed to go, but she knew she had little chance of changing Waneta's mind when it was made up.

Esther grabbed the paring knife and began peeling the bright red fruit. Maybe it would be best if she did leave. She hadn't been trying to prevent her sisters from getting to know Gabe. She only wanted to repay him for his kindness. She was a little amazed that she enjoyed fashioning leather pieces as much as she did. In fact she had a few ideas for new items for him to sell.

She had seen several leather purses for sale in Fort Craig and realized Gabe didn't have any among the items he'd made. He had men's wallets and men's belts but nothing specifically for women customers. She was eager to suggest he add some and see what he thought of the idea. She even had several sketches to show him.

Now she wouldn't get to see how well his booth did at the festival. She would be going home before then.

She drew a deep breath. She had ten days left. She would show Gabe her drawings and see if he liked the idea, and then she'd find a way to help him make them. If she worked hard enough, she might manage to stitch all the items he would need for the festival.

An Amish man from a neighboring community arrived after supper to inquire about a new buggy for his son who was getting married. Zeke and his sons spent the evening going over plans, helping the man choose interior fabric and seat covers and then settling on the price in the living room. Esther didn't get a chance to speak to Gabe alone.

After supper the women set to baking cakes, cookies and pies that would be taken to the picnic along with a large ham, fried chicken, potato salad and fresh vegetables from the garden. As Esther was helping clean up the kitchen afterward, Talitha touched her arm.

"Are you feeling well enough to go with us tomorrow? The gathering is at noon."

Esther grinned and nodded. "I'm looking forward to it. Gabe introduced me to Lilly Arnett. It seems we share a love of wildflowers. She is coming, so I will know someone besides your family. I still have a slight headache, but I barely notice it most of the time."

Talitha turned toward the living room. Esther looked that way and saw Gabe standing in the doorway. He nodded toward her, but there was an odd wariness in his eyes.

"I'm glad you're feeling good enough to go. Lilly is looking forward to seeing your flower sketches. I wish I could go," he said and looked at his feet.

Esther frowned. He wasn't coming? "I thought you were going to join us? You said you could afford to take the day off."

"I've fallen further behind in my work. I need to do some catching up."

"That's a shame." Her anticipation faded away. She hadn't been eager to go until Gabe said he was going.

"He needs a day away from that shop," Talitha said to Esther. "He takes on too much." She walked past him and left the room.

"I'm sorry you're behind in your work." Esther sucked in a quick breath when she noticed a stain on his shirt. "Gabe, there's blood on your sleeve again."

"I overused my arm trying to stitch. It's nothing."

"I thought Pamela was helping you."

He shook his head ruefully. "She doesn't have your skill at leatherwork." He took a step closer. "Did I upset you? Is that why you didn't come back this afternoon?"

"*Nee*, my stepmother had errands for me to run in town. They took longer than I thought they would."

"I hoped it wasn't something I said or did."

She gazed at him quizzically. "Why would you think that?"

"Jonah said only about half our words can be understood by a person reading lips. Sometimes I forget to look at you when I speak, or I look away when I'm talking. I was worried that you didn't understand how much I appreciate your help."

Esther decided he needed to know the truth. "My stepmother doesn't want me taking up all your time."

"You're not. How can she think that?"

Esther swallowed hard. "She wants you to have a chance to get to know my sisters better."

Comprehension dawned on him. "Because they are hoping to find a husband here and you are not?"

She nodded. It sounded so cold when he put it that way.

His brow furrowed as he shook his head in disgust and threw his hands up. "I don't have the—courting someone." She missed part of what he said when he looked down.

"My work must come first. This family has—on— my success. Your sisters will—with brothers—fellows they'll meet at the picnic tomorrow. Single women—in New Covenant. They'll—sought after, I'm sure."

Esther stood quietly waiting for him to finish.

The scowl left his face. He took another step closer. "I'm sorry to rant at you. Did you understand all that I said?"

"I think so. You don't want to court anyone. My sisters can look elsewhere."

A wry grin tipped up the corner of his mouth. "That's about it."

"I can understand you fairly well. You're one of the rare people I find easy to read. For the most part you speak slowly and distinctly, and you have an expressive face, but if you look down or away from me, I miss things. Reconsider and come to the picnic. It will do you good and give your arm a chance to heal."

He stepped back. "I wish I could. I'll see you in the morning. *Guten nacht*, Esther."

"Good night, Gabe."

He turned and walked away.

Esther leaned on the table with both arms. She didn't want to go to the picnic if he wasn't coming. He needed to come. Even his mother thought so. Esther pushed away from the table and walked toward the stairs. How could she convince him to change his mind?

Gabe rose before first light, grabbed a cold biscuit from the bread box and washed it down with a glass of milk. If he got started early and worked through the morning, he might be able to spare an hour to attend the picnic. He wanted Esther to meet his friends. He wanted to see her enjoying herself.

Opening the front door, he paused when he noticed a light coming from the window of his workshop. He distinctly remembered turning off the overhead propane lamp when he left the building yesterday. Who had business out there at this hour?

He hurried across the farmyard and opened the door. An Amish woman sat at his stitching machine. He knew it was Esther without seeing her face. He walked up behind her. She raised her head. "Good morning, Gabe." She turned around with a smile.

"How did you know I was here?"

"I felt the vibration of someone walking across the floor. I assumed it was you."

"What are you doing?"

"I'm stitching the pieces I didn't get done yesterday."

"How long have you been out here?"

"About two hours. I have at least another hour of work to do. Hadn't you better get busy? We don't want to be late to the picnic today."

"I said I wasn't going."

"And I'm helping you catch up on your work so you can. You mother said you need a day off. I agree with her, and you should do as your mother bids."

"I don't stand a chance of getting my own way if you've teamed up with *Mamm*."

She frowned. "Say that again but slower."

He repeated himself, and she chuckled. "Very smart of you to recognize that. I'm almost done with what I have here. What's next?"

"Dog collars and leashes. I cut. You stitch."

She grinned. "Easy straight lines. What color thread are you wanting?"

"What do you think?"

"Mostly red, but I would do a few in blue and a few in pink."

"Pink? For a dog collar?"

"*Englisch* women like their dogs to wear fancy things. I saw pink collars with rhinestones on several little dogs in town yesterday."

"I don't have any rhinestones."

"You do have brass and chrome dots in round and diamond shapes. You even have little brass bells. I checked. Plain items are all good and well for your Amish customers, but the *Englisch* like fancy."

He rubbed his jaw as he considered her suggestion. She could be right. Only a handful of the festivalgoers would be Amish, but over half of the rest would be women. "What else might an *Englisch* woman want to buy from us?"

"Not ax and hatchet covers."

"There are plenty of lumberjacks in this part of Maine, and they like to protect their tools."

"Women lumberjacks?"

"Some."

She arched one eyebrow and gave him a skeptical look.

"Okay, not many."

"Women like bags and purses, pretty belts, soft leather baby boots, perhaps."

It was his turn to be dubious. "Plain bags and plain purses?"

He saw her take a deep breath. "Some plain, but some with fancy designs in the leather. Flowers, leaves, feathers, vines, and the inside of the purses would need to be lined with fabric. I've made several sketches." She slowly handed over her drawing pad.

The shapes of the bags themselves were simple enough, but her elaborate designs would take hours to complete on each piece. "Fabric? Flowers? I thought your plan was to help me so I had less work to do, not more."

"You're right. I'm sorry." She reached for her sketches.

He held them away from her and carried them over to his workbench to study them. If he simplified the scrollwork and reduced it so it was only on the flap or even down to a border, it could be done in a lot less time.

He turned around to face her. She had her hands clasped tightly in her lap. "You would have to do the artwork. I have no skill at drawing. We'd have to reduce the size and area of the decorations, but I think you are onto something."

Her smile lit up her entire face. "You do?"

Her joyful expression was more than payment enough for any added work. "Let's finish what we have cut. Tomorrow I'll teach you the basics of tooling leather and we'll see if we can produce a sturdy leather purse that someone will gladly part with their money to own."

"Gabe, please. Speak a little slower."

He swallowed a tinge of annoyance. It wasn't her fault. He would have to learn she couldn't always follow his long, rambling conversations. "Tomorrow I'll teach you to tool. Hopefully someone will want to buy your purses."

"They will. I'm sure of it."

He pointed to the stitcher. "Get on with your work so you can enjoy an afternoon at the picnic."

Her smile vanished as she crossed her arms and raised her chin. "I'm not going unless you go."

"You've just given me more projects to get done, and besides, Lilly is expecting to see you."

"Then she will be disappointed, and it will be your fault. I think if you promise to speak to all my sisters today and to visit with each of them in the evenings, I believe Waneta will be satisfied and continue to let me help you. Provided you make her understand ours is only a working relationship."

That's all it was.

Only could it be more? He liked her. A lot. Spending an hour or so with each of her sisters in the evening would be a waste of time, he already knew that. But if it meant spending the majority of the day with Esther working beside him, it would be worth it.

"Well?" she asked.

"It's a deal."

"Did I hear you right? You'll do it? And you'll come to the picnic?"

"You heard correctly."

"I thought so." Her smile returned.

He grew serious. "There is one problem."

"Oh?"

"I don't want one or more of your sisters to get their hopes up. They could misinterpret my attention."

She frowned. "I hadn't thought of that. You're right. That would never do."

He could get to know the sisters, but he wouldn't raise anyone's hopes. Not even Waneta's. Somehow he had to make his cousin understand that he needed Esther's help.

She turned around and sat at the sewing machine. "I'll get as much work done as I can before my stepmother starts finding other tasks for me."

Since Esther wasn't looking at him, Gabe knew she was finished with their conversation. He knew a moment of envy. She could shut herself off from anyone and any problem simply by not looking. It had to be a small consolation for all that she was missing in the world. He followed her lead and set to work.

Several hours later the door opened and Waneta stepped in. She frowned at Esther, who hadn't seen her yet. Gabe moved quickly to speak with his mother's cousin. "Good morning, Waneta. How are you and your family this morning?"

"We were wondering where Esther had gotten off to. I see she is troubling you again."

"Never think that. She has been a wonderful help. It was nice getting to work with Pamela yesterday, but Esther needs little direction and she is amazingly skilled at leatherwork. She is making my job easier."

He paused, not certain his parents would approve of what he had to say, but he did need Esther's help. "I'm sure my mother has shared her concerns about the family's financial situation. I know how close the two of you are."

Waneta drew back. "She hasn't mentioned anything to me."

"Then perhaps I shouldn't. I don't want to spoil your visit."

"How would our visit be spoiled?"

"I confess Jonah told me you and *Mamm* had hoped to spark a romance or two between the families."

"Did he? I must speak to the boy about that."

"Don't. None of my brothers are opposed to the idea of finding the right woman, but now may not be the right time."

"How so?"

"Please don't mention this to *Daed* or *Mamm*."

"I can't promise that until I hear what you have to say."

He hoped he was doing the right thing. "Business hasn't been good since we moved here. If things don't improve before the fall, my brothers will have to leave to find work in the city or even return to Pennsylvania. I don't believe they will consider taking wives this year with such an uncertain future."

"Your mother never mentioned this in her letters."

"I'm not surprised. *Daed* did not want to worry her and only shared this news with her recently. As you can imagine, she is concerned about her sons moving away. She has been looking forward to your visit for ages. Having you here is a blessing for her. She has missed you and her friends back home. The thing is, I think I may have a solution to our troubles."

"How so?"

He gestured behind him, where Esther was still sewing. "If I can sell enough of my leather goods, expand this part of the family business, my brothers can remain here working with *Daed* and look to the future with more confidence. Amish families will move here. We'll be the only buggy makers for two hundred miles. We just have to hold on until that happens."

"I see."

"I hope you do. I've rented a booth at our upcoming festival to sell my goods to the *Englisch* tourists who attend. I need a well-stocked inventory of items for people to buy and to place orders for more." He gripped his sore arm. "I'm not going to achieve that without help."

"Can't your brothers work with you?"

"They do when I'm making harnesses. For the

smaller items, I need someone who knows how to sew and sew well. None of them have mastered the skill. I can't tell you how grateful I am that Esther offered to help. Without her I don't know what I would do. She's a fine worker. I only wish I could pay her for her labor."

"I'm sure that isn't necessary. We are family after all."

"Still, it doesn't feel right. I'll keep track of her hours and reimburse her when I'm able. With her help I may even have time to get to know your charming family instead of working out here until late at night. I know you must miss Esther's company. If you need her, I will manage somehow."

Waneta raised her fingers to her lips and tapped them. "Now that I understand better, and you're sure she isn't a bother, I'll allow her to continue assisting you. She is handy with a needle."

"You are a dear, Cousin Waneta. I'm glad you and your family are here. It will take *Mamm's* mind off her worries, and perhaps in a few weeks and with the Lord's blessing we'll put an end to her concerns and she can focus on her real goals."

"Which are?"

"Getting grandchildren. She constantly reminds her sons that she isn't getting any younger. And neither are my brothers and I."

"She *should* remind you. Grandchildren will be a great comfort to her in her old age. Esther may continue to help for as long as you want."

Gabe patted his cousin's hand. "*Danki.* I knew you'd understand."

"Your mother sent me to tell you breakfast is ready."

"I'll let Esther know."

"Her deafness makes her such a bother."

Until that second he had been thinking he'd misjudged Waneta. He let go of her hand, struggling to keep his disgust from showing. "It doesn't bother me," he said in a flat tone.

"Your attitude is a credit to your parents and your upbringing."

"All Amish consider children with disabilities a special gift from *Gott* to be treasured by the entire community," he reminded her, since she wasn't practicing her faith where Esther was concerned.

"That is true, but when such a child refuses to be healed, she can only be considered willful and ungrateful."

He glanced at Esther and then back at Waneta. "What do you mean? Are you saying Esther's deafness can be cured?"

Chapter Seven

Gabe waited for Waneta to answer his question. She simply shrugged and walked away, leaving Gabe confused. He looked to where Esther was working. If her hearing could be restored, why wouldn't she do it?

Should he ask her? If Waneta spoke the truth, there had to be a good reason why Esther chose to remain as she was. Perhaps her family couldn't afford the cost, or she didn't wish to burden them with the expense. He had no idea what it would even entail. He recalled her turning down the nurse's offer of information about a hearing aid. He also remembered that Nancy had taken a copy of the brochure from the clinic. Maybe Nancy could explain Waneta's remark.

He walked to Esther's side and touched her shoulder. She looked up at him with a smile. "Is breakfast ready?"

He nodded. She got up from her chair. "*Goot*, I'm starving. We made a lot of progress, didn't we?"

"We did."

"Enough for you to feel comfortable going to the picnic?"

He smiled at her. "As long as we can keep up this pace tomorrow and the next day and the day after that."

"If my stepmother agrees that I may continue working with you."

"She has already agreed. You are free to help me for as long as needed."

"She said that? When?"

"I spoke to her a few minutes ago. She came to tell us breakfast was ready. I explained the situation, and she readily agreed with me." He rubbed his hand over his sore arm. Would Esther be embarrassed or annoyed that they had discussed her behind her back?

Her eyes narrowed suspiciously as she stared at him. "What else did Waneta say?"

Maybe now wasn't the time to reveal Waneta's accusation. There was already too much animosity between Esther and her stepmother. He didn't want to add to it. "Not much. I thought you were hungry?"

Esther relaxed. "I am. Your *mamm* makes the best biscuits. I hope she shares the recipe with Nancy."

"I'm sure she will." He led the way outside. His concerns about Waneta's comment could wait for another time.

After a quick breakfast, Gabe and Esther returned to the shop and managed to get in a few more hours of work before his mother came to the door. "We're ready to go. Are you coming?"

"Esther has convinced me to join you."

"Then Esther has my thanks. But hurry. We don't

want to be late when people are coming especially to meet my cousin and her family. We need to stop at the Jefferson farm first. Who knows how long that will take."

He glanced to where Esther was seated with her back to the door. He would have to rearrange the sewing machine and stitcher so that she could have a view of anyone who walked in. That way she wouldn't be excluded from conversations. "I'll tell her that you're ready."

He went back to Esther and tapped her on the top of the head. She tilted her head back and looked at him. "Are they ready?"

"Come along. It was your idea for me to waste an entire afternoon."

She turned around to face him. "I didn't get any of that. It seems I can't speech-read upside down."

He chuckled. "I said time to go." He nodded toward the door.

She sighed heavily. "I guess we should get it over with."

"My thoughts exactly. Do you have your sketchbook?"

She lifted a quilted bag from the floor beside her chair. "Right here."

"Okay." He held out his hand to help her up.

Esther gave Gabe her hand and allowed him to pull her to her feet. The grip of his strong calloused fingers made her heart stumble as her breath quickened. She looked into his bright blue eyes and saw them widen in surprise. They stared at each other for what seemed like an eternity. Did he feel it? This strange connection that seemed to arc between them.

She looked down and pulled her hand away. Such a simple gesture shouldn't affect her and yet it did. She moved past him quickly, determined to gather her wits and pretend nothing had happened. Because nothing had. It was only her imagination. Or maybe a lack of sleep plus her head injury had affected her senses.

She couldn't be attracted to Gabe. They were working partners for the little time she had left in Maine. Nor could she forget that she owed him her life. She wouldn't repay him with unwelcome attention. He wasn't interested in dating any more than she was. They were friends and coworkers. That was all.

Outside she saw both families were seated on hay bales in the back of a large wagon. Two massive black draft horses were hitched to it. Their harnesses gleamed as shiny black as their coats. Chrome tacks and buckles decorated their breast bands and the bridles. Chrome bells jingled as they tossed their heads.

Esther stopped to look up at Gabe. He shrugged. "I know their harnesses are much too fancy for an Amish family. It's called a parade style. We have promised to show a prospective client what the harnesses look like when in use. He has asked my father to stop by his farm today."

"I hope your bishop won't object to such a display at the picnic," her sister Julia said as she helped Esther climb in.

Jonah who was seated on a large wooden box behind the driver's bench seat began to sign. "The bishop won't." **He patted the box he was sitting on.** "We have their regular harnesses with us. If the customer likes the look of the fancy ones he may buy them on the spot. The bishop is the one who gave the man Zeke's name."

"They're beautiful."

"According to Gabe this harness style has a three-strap breeching with a scalloped spider. It also has decorated traces and hip drops. The spots are steel and standard size. Gabe could decorate them with diamonds shapes or even stars if the fellow wants that. He put a lot of work into these."

She smiled at her brother and signed, "You like Gabe, don't you?"

"He's a fine fellow. He never tells me I ask too many questions. His brothers are nice, too."

Esther sat back and watched her sisters converse with Gabe's brothers who were seated across from them. She tried to gauge the amount of interest between the couples. Moses and Nancy seemed the most at ease with each other. They were frequently laughing about something. Since Nancy wasn't signing, Esther had no idea what they were saying. She didn't have a full view of her mouth.

Julia was seated across from Asher. To Esther's eye they showed little interest in each other. Pamela, on the other hand was showing a great deal of interest in Seth. It was hard to miss. She gazed at him with the eyes of a lovesick puppy. Esther couldn't tell if he was interested in return or not. While he occasionally glanced at Pamela for the most part he kept his eyes riveted to the tips of his boots. Waneta sat up front with Talitha and Zeke but she glanced back frequently.

Gabe leaned forward and gained Julia's attention. Esther couldn't see his face. She looked at Jonah. "What is he saying?" she signed.

"He asked if she was enjoying her visit so far. Please don't make me sign through the entire picnic."

Esther flushed. "I'm sorry. Enjoy the ride and keep an eye out for any moose."

The farm where they stopped was two miles past Lilly Arnett's place. The man who came out of the barn to look over the harness was a short stout fellow with curly black hair. Glancing around, Esther saw eight matching black draft horses inside the corral and several brightly painted antique carriages and wagons parked in a long low shed. Gabe and his father got down to speak to the man. Together they walked around Zeke's horses as the man closely inspected the harnesses.

When Gabe returned to his seat Esther could tell he was disappointed. "He didn't want to purchase them?"

"He wants to think it over. Something tells me we won't hear from him again."

"The harnesses are beautiful."

Gave managed a rueful smile. "*Danki*. I spent many hours making them. Our price is reasonable. I don't know what more he wants. He just purchased a new team of eight horses and was talking about getting parade harnesses for an eight-horse hitch. It would have been a substantial sale for us. Maybe the difference between keeping my brother's home and seeing them leave."

"Someone else will buy them if he doesn't."

"I don't think they are what our Amish neighbors are looking for. It's rare to find a local *Englisch* customer for my harness work. Hank Jefferson and his horses travel to many events around New England. He also gives sleigh rides to the tourists in winter. He would've provided a good way to showcase my work far beyond New Covenant."

"Perhaps he'll change his mind and buy them after all."

"Let's pray that's true."

After changing out the harnesses and stowing the fancy ones in the box behind the wagon seat, the family headed toward the schoolhouse in New Covenant. When they arrived there were already a dozen buggies and carts lined up in front of the building. Food was being laid out by several women on long tables. There were colorful quilts spread under the shade of nearby trees. Adults clustered together in groups while the children played on the school ground equipment.

Esther and her sisters piled out of the wagon and stood off to the side while the Fisher brothers and Jonah unloaded several blue-and-white coolers and carried them to the tables. Talitha and Waneta gestured to the girls to follow them.

Esther kept her chin up and a smile on her face. This would be the hard part. With so many new people to meet and all of them talking she would never know where to look. The result was that people often felt ignored by her if she didn't respond to them. It was easier to remove herself from the group and pretend she wanted to be by herself. If she took her sketchbook and went to sit under a tree who would care?

She saw Gabe smiling at her and knew he would. She suffered through the introductions to a dozen women from the New Covenant church district, including the bishop's wife. Nancy and Julia took turns signing for her. They casually explained that she was deaf but could read lips if people spoke slowly and looked directly at her. The women all started out speaking that way but as more families arrived the conversations became livelier and less directed at her. One by one her sisters moved away as they met other people. Soon there wasn't anyone to sign for her. She lost the gist of the conversation going on around her. Awkwardness kept her looking at her feet more and more.

She glanced up and saw Lilly Arnett getting out of a small blue pickup. She happily left the group she was with and hurried toward her. Lilly smiled, waved and waited until Esther stopped in front of her. "I'm glad you decided to come," Esther said.

"I didn't want to miss a chance to meet your family and introduce you to some of my friends."

A tall teenage boy came jogging over to them. Lilly took Esther by the arm and turned her to face the boy. "This is Harley Gingrich. He works for me when he isn't in school."

Harley nodded to Esther and pointed at the picnic basket Lilly was carrying. "I'll take this to the table."

Lilly handed it over, and Harley walked away. "Harley's brother is Willis. He is our local blacksmith. He recently married the new Amish schoolteacher. Her name is Eva. They are raising Willis's siblings. Harley, Otto and little Maddie, who will be in the second grade when school starts again. Maddie had a most interesting imaginary friend named Bubble who got up to all kinds of mischief. I'm told Bubble moved away to Texas. I think we all miss her."

"Which one is Maddie?" Esther asked using it as an excuse to look for Gabe. He stood with a group of clean-shaven men that Esther knew were bachelors. Only married Amish men wore beards.

Lilly tapped Esther's arm and pointed toward the swings where one little blonde Amish girl was pushing another. "Maddie is on the swing. That is Annabeth Beachy pushing her. Annabeth lives with her mother, Becca, and her grandfather Gideon on a dairy farm not far from here."

Esther was impressed. "You know a lot of the Amish folks in this area."

"I met most of them under unusual circumstances last fall when Maddie followed Bubble into the woods and got lost. Everyone came together to search for her and many of us have remained friends ever since."

"It's amazing how the Lord can use a difficult or frightening time to bring about good things."

"It is. Isn't that how you met Gabe?"

Esther felt a blush warm her cheeks. "It was very frightening."

"Then something good will surely come of it. Did you bring your sketchbook?" Lilly asked.

"I did." Esther opened her bag and pulled out her drawing pad. Lilly took it from her and began to slowly turn the pages. Finally she looked at Esther. "These are wonderful."

"Danki."

"Would you sell some of them to me? I'd love to frame them and hang them on the wall of my breakfast nook."

"You can have them. You don't need to pay me. Choose the ones you want."

"May I keep this and look through it again later."

"Of course."

"Thank you. I see Gemma Crump and Jesse. I need to speak to Jesse about getting a larger garden shed. Excuse me."

Lilly walked away and Esther found herself alone. She moved to the shade of a maple tree and watched the people gathering together near the tables. There were a few *Englisch* but most of the picnic goers were Amish. The women clustered together in small groups. Several of them held babies. The younger children were chasing each other in a game of tag. Several teenagers began setting up a volleyball net. The married men stood near the tables visiting and laughing. She could see people's mouths moving but she couldn't tell what they were saying. Everyone was talking to someone. Everyone but her. A heavy ache centered itself in her chest. It hurt to be ignored, to be overlooked by the people she that had secretly hoped would accept her. She blinked back tears.

Suddenly she was glad she was going home in nine days. She missed her Deaf friends. They understood what it was like to be on the outside looking in. But when they were together it didn't matter. There was joy in signing freely. Among her friends she didn't have to stare at someone's mouth to understand what they were saying.

From the corner of her eye she caught sight of Gabe. He motioned her over. She rose and walked across the grassy lawn to where he stood with a group of young men near his own age. He smiled at her. "These are the fellows I'd like you to meet. I've told them about your hearing. Shall I get Jonah to sign for you?"

It was kind of him to offer. Had he noticed that her sisters had abandoned her? "I think I can manage."

She nodded to each of the men as Gabe introduced them. The one to Gabe's left was Danny Coblentz. "Happy to meet you, Esther. Gabe tells us you have been a great help to him. I'm the new schoolteacher. I've taken my sister's place after she married, but she continues to help me find my way with the children."

Gabe turned to his right. "This is Tully Lange. He's a newcomer, not yet Amish but working toward joining us."

Esther had never met an *Englisch* person who wanted to join the Amish faith. Tully tipped his hat and started speaking but Esther couldn't quite understand him. She got "cowboy" and "dairy" but couldn't make sense of what he was saying.

"I'm sorry. I'm afraid I didn't catch that." She looked at Gabe.

"Tully is a cowboy from Oklahoma. He works with Gideon and Becca Beachy on their dairy farm."

"Does he have an accent?"

Gabe chuckled as he looked at his friend and then back to her. "He has a terrible Western drawl."

"That would explain it." She smiled at Tully. "It may take me longer to learn to understand you because of that. I'm used to our Amish way of speaking."

The third man was Jedidiah Zook. He was a tall lean fellow with a somber expression. He looked toward where her sisters were standing with Waneta.

"Have you met my sisters?" Esther asked.

"Not yet," he said but he looked hopeful.

"Let me introduce you." She pasted a smile on her face and walked toward her stepmother. "Waneta, this is Jedidiah Zook. He is a friend of Gabe's. These are my sisters Julia, Pamela and Nancy."

Waneta's eyebrow rose a fraction. "My stepdaughters and I are happy to make your acquaintance. Are you also a farmer?"

"I have a nice place along the river between here and Fort Craig."

"You must tell us about it," Waneta said with a genuine smile.

Esther turned on her heels and went in search of Lilly. She found her seated on a blanket beside the school leaning back against the building and balancing a paper plate loaded with food on her lap. Esther sat down across from her.

"The Amish ladies in this community sure know how to cook. I never miss a chance to eat with them." Lilly laid her plate aside. "I'll choose a few sketches so you can have your book back."

"You can do that after your lunch. We have all afternoon."

"True." Lilly picked up her plate again. "Your sisters seem to be gathering admirers."

Esther looked over her shoulder. Danny had joined Jedidiah along with another man Esther hadn't met. "Who is the younger fellow with them?"

"That's Ivan Martin. He recently started a small engine repair business."

"He looks young to have his own business already. Most fellows in their late teens are still working with their fathers."

"Ivan is an orphan. He lives with his sisters Jenny and Bethany. Bethany is married to Michael Shetler. He owns a clock and watch repair shop. I see Gabe coming this way."

He sat down next to Lilly so that he was facing Esther. His plate was piled high with ham, corn on the cob, potato salad, green beans and two slices of pecan pie. "Aren't you eating, Esther?"

"Did you leave anything for me?"

He laughed. "There might be some church spread and bread left."

"That sounds *goot*." Esther was fond of the peanut butter and marshmallow cream mixture that was popular among the Amish.

"Gabe, I saw a bird near the river yesterday that I've never seen before. I looked it up on my computer and I think it might be a swallow-tailed kite. Is that possible?"

"Not likely but I guess it is possible. There have been a few sightings in the state. Was it flying when you saw it? Did it have a white head and body with black-tipped pointed wings and a deep forked black tail?"

"That is exactly what it looked like."

Gabe's eyes lit up with excitement. "Where did you see it?"

"You know where the bog lies west of my cornfield?"

"Sure."

"He was flying over the water and then landed in a dead pine."

"I wonder if he is still in the area. Could you show me? When you're done eating and visiting, I mean. Not right this minute."

Lilly grinned. "I'll eat fast."

He looked at Esther with a huge smile on his face. "Would you like to go birding with me this afternoon instead of hanging out here?"

Chapter Eight

Gabe watched a bright smile transform Esther's face. It gladdened his heart to know his simple suggestion made her happy. He wanted to keep her smiling. To see her delight every day she was near him.

"May I bring my sketch pad?" she asked.

"Of course."

"Then I should dearly love to accompany you on another walk in the woods."

"You had best go get something to eat first." He pointed toward the tables. She rose and hurried away.

"Esther is a charming young woman," Lilly said.

Gabe continued to watch Esther as she made her selections from the bounty remaining on the serving tables. "She is. I've never known anyone quite like her."

"You've never known anyone who is deaf?" Lilly asked.

He looked at her. "It isn't Esther's deafness that makes her unique. At least not to me." With a jolt he realized he was beginning to like Esther much more

than he should. Why did he find her so attractive? He
barely knew her.

"Still, it takes a special person to overlook what
many would see as a drawback to a relationship where
free communication is impossible."

He sighed and looked down at his plate. "It can be
difficult. Sometimes I wonder how much of what I say
she truly understands and how much she guesses at."

"Have you considered learning sign language?"

He glanced at Lilly again. "Wouldn't that take a long
time?"

"I imagine it would take years to become proficient.
Learning a few simple words might not be difficult. I
can do some research on the subject if you'd like?"

He saw Esther talking to Jonah. The boy rapidly
signed and then took off toward the ballfield where a
game was getting underway. Gabe took a bite of ham.
He could ask Esther to teach him or he could surprise
her by having Jonah show him signs for a few words.
He liked the idea of surprising her. "I think her brother
might help me with that. Don't say anything to Esther.
I might not be able to master a single word."

Lilly chuckled. "I think you'll do much better than
that, but I won't tell her."

"Danki."

Esther returned and sat down across from him.
"Jonah is going to let Waneta know where I've gone so
she won't worry. Not that she would."

Gabe let the comment pass. He had no idea how to
heal their relationship without knowing the cause of their
discord. Maybe one day Esther would confide in him.

It didn't take them long to finish their lunches. Gabe told his father where he was going. His brothers were visiting with friends, except for Moses who was enjoying a game of volleyball while Nancy looked on.

Gabe and Esther got in the pickup with Lilly. "Could you stop by our farm so I can get my binoculars?" he asked.

"Sure. Esther do you need anything?"

Esther didn't answer. She was searching inside her bag. He touched her arm. She looked up with a smile. "What?"

"Lilly wants to know if you need anything from the house."

Esther turned to Lilly. "I need my colored pencils. I thought I had some but apparently I left most of them in my room. Do you mind stopping at the Fisher farm?"

"I don't mind at all," she said making sure Esther was looking at her when she spoke this time.

It didn't take long to reach his farm. Lilly drove faster than Gabe liked, but he didn't say anything to her. He simply wasn't used to speed so he didn't know if hers was excessive. He and Esther quickly gathered what they needed and were soon back in Lilly's truck. She drove to her place and turned into one of her potato fields. Skirting the edge she continued along the bumpy track to a second field, this one planted in corn.

She stopped the truck and pointed. "Follow the edge of this field until you come to a split rail fence. Just beyond it is where the bog starts. Be careful—the ground is mushy. In places you can easily sink up to your knees so stick to the grassy areas. You can spot the dead pine I spoke of from the fence. You know to be careful of the wildlife. The moose have been frequenting this area."

"I'll watch for them." He got out and waited for Esther. She quickly joined him, still grinning. Lilly turned the truck around and drove away.

Esther looked at him. "How does one go about watching for birds?"

"You find a place to get comfortable then watch and listen for their calls."

She chuckled. "I can watch. You'll have to listen."

He smiled. "Come along but watch your step. Stay to the grassy places or you might sink up to your neck in the mud."

"Not how I would want this day to end."

She scrambled over the fence without his assistance. He followed, scanning the area for any sign of moose and saw none. He spotted the dead tree Lilly had mentioned. It was on a small rise of land that jutted out into the bog. It looked like a good place to settle. He should be able to see quite a distance from the base of the tree. He pointed in that direction and Esther nodded. Together they made their way carefully toward the elevated ground. They reached it after about fifteen minutes of circumventing puddles and leaping from one patch of heavy grass to another.

At the base of the tree he noticed a clump of bushes that would provide them with suitable cover. "I think this will do."

"What are we looking for exactly?"

"Birds."

She rolled her eyes at him. "I gathered that much. Any special type of bird?"

"A swallow-tailed kite, but who knows what other interesting species we might discover while we wait to see if he returns to this spot."

"What would tempt him to come back?"

"They feed mostly on flying insects. I understand they like dragonflies and there are plenty of those around. They'll even snatch lizards and snakes out of the trees."

She looked up at the dead branches overhead. "There are snakes in these trees? Why would you want to sit under one?"

He waited until her gaze returned to his. "There aren't any snakes in this tree."

"How can you be so sure?"

"Because I'm familiar with these woods." He hoped he was right. After clearing away some dried pine needles, he sat cross-legged on the ground. He scanned the sky and then raised his binoculars to his eyes.

"Do you see something?"

He lowered his glasses. "Clouds. Aren't you going to sketch flowers?"

"I was until the thought of a snake falling on my head was mentioned."

He chuckled. "I never thought of you as someone who would be scared of snakes."

"They give me the creeps." She scanned the ground around them and looked over the tree again. "Now you know what frightens me. What scares you?"

"Seeing a woman step in front of a speeding truck. That took a few years off my life."

"I am sorry about that. And thank you again for your quick thinking and quick action. What else?"

"Spiders, mice, the usual."

"I don't believe you." She continued to stare at him waiting for his answer.

"I reckon I'm most afraid of failure."

"How so?"

"I'm concerned that my business venture will fail and make things worse for my family instead of better."

"That I can believe. You seem to be a driven person. So what makes you that way?"

"Failures in the past."

"Like what? Business failures?"

He wasn't sure he wanted to dredge up his past mistakes, but Esther was staring at him with such an open and honest expression. Somehow he knew she would understand. "I was engaged to be married once."

"Waneta mentioned it in passing."

"I'm not surprised. She had a lot to say about it back then. The girl was the daughter of her close friend."

"I can imagine she had strong opinions on the subject. What went wrong or do you mind my asking?"

He shook his head. "It was years ago. I fell head over heels for a woman named Gwen, but she secretly wanted someone else. Most Amish couples date quietly and their engagement isn't announced publicly until the banns are read in church. After I proposed and she said yes, Gwen told a lot of people including the fellow she hoped to make jealous. It worked. A month before the banns were to be read she told me it was over between us. She was going to marry the man she truly loved. They were wed on the date she and I had chosen for our ceremony. Did you understand all that?"

It didn't hurt to talk about it as much as he thought it would. Maybe because Esther was such a good listener in spite of being unable to hear.

She nodded. "I got most of it. I understand it must have been a painful time, but why do you consider it your failure?"

"Because I couldn't win her love, nor could I see that she didn't love me. Now I realize it was the best thing for both of us." He had forgiven Gwen long ago but now he could let go of the hurt.

"I was in love once, too," Esther said quietly. "So I understand a little of what you went through."

Gabe saw the pain in her eyes and reached over to cover her hand with his. "Do you want to talk about it?"

Unexpected tears filled Esther's eyes at his compassion. She looked down at his hand where it rested on hers. He was a good man. "There isn't much to tell. Barnabas King didn't want a deaf wife."

He had seen her as broken, not as a whole person who was simply different. He wanted her to be fixed before he would consider marrying her. This was the life God had chosen for her. She wasn't broken. She wasn't!

Gabe lifted her chin with his fingers so she had to look at him. "Barnabas King sounds like a fool."

She managed a wry smile. "Perhaps I'll think of him that way from now on."

"If I were you, I wouldn't give him a second thought. I know that's easier said than done. But try. You will make some man a fine wife one day."

It would have to be a deaf fellow because no hearing man could understand the way she truly was. She smiled at Gabe's attempt to comfort her. "You aren't getting much bird-watching done."

"And you haven't drawn a single flower." He sat back and raised the binoculars to his eyes.

Esther got out her sketch pad, but it wasn't flowers that interested her. She wanted to draw Gabe. She started with the part of him she liked the best, his mouth. It took her several tries to get it right. It wasn't perfect but she thought she had captured the feeling of his laughter waiting to break free.

What did his voice sound like? She could imagine it a little from the voices she remembered from before she lost her hearing. She recalled her father and her grandfather's voice and the bishop who had preached on Sundays. Gabe's would be different. Softer maybe? Or did he have a gruff growling voice to match his large frame? It was something she would never know.

She rubbed the scar behind her left ear where a cochlear implant had been surgically placed when she was fifteen. Five years after she lost her hearing. It hadn't been the cure her parents prayed for. Even with therapy and multiple visits to the doctor, the device didn't allow her to hear normally. While she could hear voices and sounds, they were distorted and hard to make sense of no matter how hard she tried. She heard everything through a ringing noise that she finally couldn't cope with. She stopped wearing the external processor after a year and refused to put it back on. She couldn't remove the parts inside her head, but it didn't cause her discomfort. Her father never understood why she wanted to remain deaf. Neither had Barnabas.

She had met him when he came to help repair the special-needs school roof along with a number of young volunteers following a damaging hailstorm. She had been flattered by his interest and had started using her CI again because she wanted to please him. It had been as awful as her first attempts. She only turned it on when they were together. She thought once he learned sign language she would be able to leave it off for good.

He had listed all the reasons why he was a good catch for someone with her problem as if that somehow made up for the fact that he saw her as defective. He couldn't believe it when she turned down his proposal. He had appealed to her father and her new stepmother to pressure Esther into changing her mind. It had driven a wedge between her and Waneta that hadn't yet healed.

Being deaf wasn't always easy, but when she was with other Deaf people it didn't matter. She had a happy and productive life. If she had someone to share her life with, someone who accepted her the way she was, she would be the happiest woman in the world. Her gaze was drawn to Gabe. Someone like him.

Which was a foolish thought. She looked down at her drawing. Gabe was turning out to be a good friend. Something she hadn't expected to find on this trip or ever with a hearing man. She chewed on the end of her pencil for a moment and then drew him smiling with a sparkle in his eyes and tiny crow's feet at their corners. She added the scar to his eyebrow and wondered how he had gotten it.

Gabe lowered his binoculars. She quickly closed her sketch pad. "No sign of the bird you were hoping to see?" she asked.

He shook his head and turned to her. "I saw many species, but not the swallow-tailed kite. I didn't really expect him to remain in this area. Northern Maine is far outside the kite's normal range. Have you found something interesting to draw?"

"Not really."

"Are you wanting to start back?"

"I'm in no hurry. There is enough of a breeze to keep the bugs down and the bog is pretty in its own way." She spied a dark shape moving through a stand of bushes toward them. "Is that my friend the moose again?"

He lifted his glasses briefly and quickly lowered them. He stood up and offered his hand. "We should go."

"Why?"

"Because that is a black bear coming this way."

"What?" She surged to her feet and gripped his arm dropping her sketchbook in the process. "Should we climb a tree or something?"

"It wouldn't do any good. Black bears are excellent climbers. The best thing is to walk, not run, away from them. Bears are more frightened of people than we are of them."

"I doubt that." Her heart hammered in her throat.

Gabe started walking back the way they had come

still gripping her hand. She hurried to keep up with him, glancing over her shoulder frequently expecting to see the bear charging toward them. How fast could a bear run?

Gabe glanced at her, squeezed her hand reassuringly but kept walking. If he said anything she couldn't tell. It wasn't until they reached the fence that he stopped and faced her. "He isn't following. I think we're fine."

"Praise the Lord for His mercy."

"Amen."

"That was the first bear I've ever seen. Please don't tell Jonah about this. He'll be out here trying to find him or her in a heartbeat."

"Okay. It will be our secret." He smiled at her, and she realized he was still holding her hand.

His touch was comforting. She managed a smile. "You always seem to be pulling me out of danger. It must be getting old."

"We weren't truly in danger."

"This time." She eased loose from his grip and slipped her hands in the pockets of her apron. "I'm ready to get back to the house."

"Agreed."

She climbed over the fence without his help and together they walked along the edge of the cornfield. When they reached the potato field, he turned into the woods. She thought it was the same path they had been on before but couldn't be sure. Other paths and game trails intersected it. The sun was still high in the sky, pouring in light. The lack of shadows made things look different. When they reached a small pond with the delicate violet growing along the shore she knew where she was. "May I rest a moment?"

He nodded. She sat on a fallen log and tucked a few tentacles of loose hair back under her *kapp*. "I can see how easy it would be to become lost." She smiled at him. "I'm glad you know the way so well."

Gabe sat down beside her. He might know his way around the woods, but he was at a loss for how to handle his growing attraction to Esther. The time he had spent with her had not been boring. "You'll have a lot to tell your friends back home when you write."

"That's the truth."

He wondered what she really thought of his adopted state. He loved it and wanted her to feel the same. "Have your experiences given you a distaste for Maine?"

"Not at all. I like it here."

"I'm glad. It's a wonderful place to live even when the snow gets five feet deep. You will always be welcome in our home," he said softly.

Would she consider returning to New Covenant someday or even staying on when her stepmother left? She would make a welcome addition to the community. And then he could see more of her.

He gazed into her eyes for a long moment. Did she sense how much he was starting to care about her? Should he tell her? Or was it too soon? They barely knew each other and yet it felt as if he had known her for ages. She put him at ease. He was comfortable with her. Something he couldn't say about any other woman.

Maybe after the festival was over he could explore

his feelings more closely and gage her interest in return. When he knew if his endeavor had helped the family or not.

Lilly's suggestion that he learn sign language was a good one. He'd ask Jonah to teach him as soon as they returned home.

Esther looked away first and got to her feet. "I'm ready to go."

He wanted to take her hand again, but she walked on ahead without waiting for him. Maybe she didn't share his growing feelings. Maybe he was reading more into their relationship because he wanted to believe it. The same way he had with Gwen. He did not want to play the fool again.

Chapter Nine

The following morning Esther hurried down to breakfast with lighthearted steps. She would be spending the day working with Gabe, and she didn't have to worry that her stepmother would be upset. Gabe had seen to that. She was grateful to him for yet another rescue.

She concentrated on her plate of scrambled eggs and sausage in order to keep her eyes off him. It was difficult. Just seeing him smile did funny things to her. She didn't want anyone else to notice how much she liked him. It was her secret.

Julia nudged her with an elbow and started to sign. "Have you finished our new *kapps*? The day after tomorrow is the church service, and I want to look my best."

"For which brother?" **Esther signed.**

"I didn't say I wanted to impress a Fisher."

"So it is someone you met yesterday."

"Are the *kapps* done or not?"

"I will finish them this morning." **It meant she would**

be late getting out to the workshop, but she had promised to make all of her sisters new head coverings. Since she began working for Gabe, she had put that chore aside.

She looked over and met his gaze. "I will be out to help you directly."

"Is something wrong?" he asked.

"I have some work of my own to finish, that's all."

"Any time you can spare for me is appreciated." He rose with the rest of the men and filed out of the house with them.

Esther helped to clear the table and then raced upstairs to put the ribbons on the *kapps* she had made. It took her nearly an hour. In her haste she made one ribbon longer on the right side of Julia's *kapp*. She had to pick out her stitches and do it over. Satisfied at last, she laid one *kapp* on the end of each cot where her sisters slept. Then she hurried downstairs and out the door. When she reached the workshop, she saw Gabe had turned the sewing table around.

"Do you like it?" He was smiling as if he had done something special.

"It's fine. What was wrong with the way it was facing?"

"You had your back to the door. This way you can see when someone comes in. I can't always be here. I thought this would make it easier for you to see if a customer or someone comes in."

"This is very thoughtful, Gabe. I get better light from the window, too. *Danki*."

"I'm glad you like it. If there's anything else you want rearranged in here, just let me know."

"This is your shop. You had it set up the way you like. I'm not going to be here long enough for you to rearrange the equipment on my account."

Some of the happiness left his eyes. "I can always move it back after you're gone."

"Shall we get to work?" she asked.

"Right. I have cut out four of the purses you sketched. Let's see if you can stamp and tool as well as you draw."

Esther pressed a hand to her forehead. "My sketchbook! I left it out at the bog."

"It should be fine. It hasn't rained, and there's none in the forecast. I will fetch it for you tomorrow. I was planning to look for the kite one more time, anyway. You're welcome to join me if you aren't afraid of meeting another bear."

"Or having a snake fall on my head?"

"You'd rather not go. I understand." His disappointment was plain.

She took a quick step toward him. "I didn't say that."

"So you will come?" He looked so hopeful that she didn't have the heart to refuse him—nor did she want to.

"I will be better prepared this time. I'll take my umbrella."

He threw back his head and laughed. She wished she could hear what that sounded like. There were so many things she wanted to discover about him.

The day went by quickly. Esther discovered stamping leather required a strong wrist and accuracy. She couldn't count the number of times she accidentally thumped her thumb and forefinger with a mallet while trying to hit the head of the small tool she held positioned just so on a strip of leather. Gabe made it look easy.

Gabe tried to make everything easy for her. He always made sure he was looking at her when he spoke. He left his own work frequently to check on how she was doing. He made sure she took breaks when she could have spent hours at her machine without stopping. He was almost the perfect boss. She would miss him dearly when she went home.

The following day she left the tooling to Gabe and began stitching the assortment of items he had ready for her. She was pleased with the way her first purse turned out. All it needed was to have a cloth lining added with several pockets to hold keys or cell phones. She would have to ask Lilly what size pockets would be needed, since Esther wasn't sure how big a cell phone was. She had seen them in use and her sister Nancy even had one for a while, but Nancy had given up using it because she intended to be baptized into the faith and cell phones were not allowed by their church district.

Esther held the purse up for Gabe to see. "What do you think?"

He took it from her and examined it inside and out. "Nice work."

"But will it sell?"

"Perhaps we should ask a few of our *Englisch* neighbors what they think?"

"That's a good idea. We can ask Lilly."

He gestured toward the cutting table. "I've finished here for today. How about you?"

It was early afternoon. She could have kept working. Instead she stretched her tired shoulders. "I'm ready for some fresh air and a little exercise."

He walked to the door and held it open for her. "Let's go over to the bog. I'll get my binoculars. Why don't you wait here?"

She couldn't keep a happy grin off her face as she watched him cross to the house. A walk in the woods with Gabe promised to be the highlight of her day. More wildflowers and his company. What could be better? She saw Jonah coming her way.

He tipped his head to the side. "What are you smiling about?" he signed.

She wiped the grin off her face. "Nothing. Gabe and I are going to do some bird-watching. If anyone wants us, we'll be at the Arnett farm."

"Since when do you like bird-watching?"

"Gabe looks for birds. I look for flowers to collect and draw."

"I still haven't seen a moose. Are you sure he was at the pond by the highway?"

She nodded. "I saw him there twice. Be careful when you are out walking. There are bears about."

His eyes brightened. "Really?"

She scowled at him. "Do you know what to do if you see a bear coming your way?"

"Run?"

"Wrong answer," she said. "Ask Gabe. He will tell you the best way to avoid them."

"I will." Jonah turned and jogged to the house.

Esther smiled as she watched him. Having Jonah to talk with was almost as good as being with her friends. She waited impatiently for Gabe to return.

Gabe had his binoculars and his book on bird identification in his hand when Jonah came rushing into the kitchen.

"Esther says I'm supposed to ask you what to do if I see a bear."

"I thought she wasn't going to tell you that we saw one."

"You did? Where? Esther never said she actually laid eyes on a live one."

"It was a long way from here, and I wasn't supposed to tell you because she's afraid you'll go looking for it."

"I promise I won't."

Gabe nodded and told the boy what he needed to know if he encountered a black bear. He started to leave but stopped and turned to the boy. "Jonah, is it difficult to learn sign language?"

"Not really."

"How could I go about learning to sign? Could you teach me?"

"Sure. If you tell me where you saw the black bear."

Gabe crossed his arms over his chest. "Nope. So thanks, anyway."

"I was just kidding. I'll be happy to teach you some words in sign. Why don't you ask Esther? I'm sure she'd do it."

"I wanted to surprise her."

Jonah folded his arms and cupped his chin with one hand. "You're sweet on my sister, aren't you?"

"We are friends, but would you have a problem with it if I was?"

"Only that it would make Waneta think she is right about her gift for matchmaking."

"Esther doesn't get along with Waneta. Why is that?"

"They just don't see eye to eye about a lot of things. I'm not sure they ever will. Esther and Waneta can both be stubborn."

Gabe's mother came into the kitchen. "What are you two discussing so intently?"

Jonah winked at Gabe. "Bears." The boy went back outside.

"I like that kid," Gabe said.

"Are you enjoying our visitors? I want our two families to be close friends."

Gabe wagged a finger at her. "You want your sons to fall head over heels for Waneta's girls."

She grinned. "Maybe I do. They are wonderful women. I wouldn't mind having one or more of them as daughters-in-law. What's wrong with that?"

"Nothing, I reckon." They were nice women, but they sometimes neglected Esther. He wasn't sure how to broach the subject but decided he needed to say something. "I did notice that they deserted Esther yesterday at the picnic."

His mother nodded. "I saw that, too."

"Tomorrow is our church service. There will be a lot of visiting afterward. Could you suggest to them that they include Esther rather than leaving her on her own?

Without someone to sign for her, she is uncomfortable in a crowd of people."

"I'm not sure it's my place, but I will speak to Waneta. Sometimes we take our family members for granted without realizing that they may need our attention as much as others do."

"I appreciate that, *Mamm*."

"Where are you off to?"

"Esther and I are going over to the Arnett farm to do some bird-watching."

"The two of you have been spending a lot of time together. Is it because you feel responsible for her after saving her life, or do you feel sorry for her?"

"Neither. The fact that she is deaf makes things more difficult, but I don't pity her. I enjoy her company. She has a very lively mind."

"Her type of deafness is inherited. Any children she might have may also be deaf."

He frowned. "Any of us can have a child born with a disability. *Gott* decides."

"He does, but I thought you should be aware of the fact."

"I'm not planning to marry her, *Mamm*. We've only known each other a few days."

"I knew I was going to marry your father the day I first laid eyes on him. Love comes slowly to some and quickly to others."

Gabe gazed at her intently. "How did you know?"

She clasped her hands over her chest. "My heart lifted when he smiled at me. It may sound silly, but that's how I knew. I couldn't imagine going through life without seeing his smile every day."

"I reckon the Lord didn't want it any other way. For which I am grateful. We'll be back before supper."

"All right. I will speak to Waneta about making sure the girls don't abandon Esther at church."

"Danki."

He headed outside and saw Esther waiting for him beside the shop. She came over to join him. As they rounded the barn, Gabe saw Pamela and Seth walking toward them holding hands. They were intent on each other and didn't notice they weren't alone until they were only a few feet away. Seth stopped abruptly and let go of her hand. "Were you looking for me?"

"Nee, we are going to do some bird-watching."

"Okay. Have a good time," Seth said as he stepped aside. Gabe walked on, but he heard Pamela giggle behind him. He glanced back. She pressed a hand to her lips and turned away.

"I may not have given Waneta enough credit as a matchmaker," Esther said. She looked over her shoulder. "They seem to have hit it off."

"As have we," Gabe said. She wasn't looking at him, so he knew she couldn't hear him. It was just as well. He had no idea how she felt about him other than a shared friendship. He didn't want to risk losing that by making her uncomfortable.

They traveled through the woods without talking. Twice Esther paused to pluck a few flowers and place them in her pocket. When they reached the pond, Gabe stopped and turned to her. He pointed to the violets she had sketched on their first walk. "Do you want to take some of these?"

She shook her head. "Lilly said they are a rare flower, so I will leave them be. I have my drawings and that is enough."

"What are you going to do with the ones in your pocket?"

"I'll press them and add them to my albums."

"Do you have a lot?"

"Several albums with about thirty flowers in each."

"That's a lot of petals."

She smiled. "The Lord has made a lot of flowers. I'll never gather them all. Just like He has made many types of birds."

He held out his identification book. "I mark off each one that I've seen. Someday I'd like to travel down south to view the egrets and storks of the Everglades."

A small frown appeared on her face. "I'm sorry, I didn't understand that."

He wasn't sure how to say it so she could. How many times had she simply smiled instead of comprehending his words? He tried to phrase it more simply. "I want to visit Florida."

"The Amish community in Pinecrest?"

It was close enough. "That's right. We should get going."

He kept a wary watch for wildlife, but their trip through the bog was uneventful. She retrieved her sketch pad and brushed off the dirt before sitting down as far away from the tree as she could get without stepping into the bog. He tried not to smile. She saw him struggling.

"Laugh if you want, but I am not going to sit where a snake could fall on me."

"You know there are more of them in the water than in the trees."

She quickly moved back. "Now you tell me. Will we be here long?"

He shook his head then lifted his binoculars to scan the sky and trees. After several minutes he noticed an olive-sided flycatcher perched in a dead tree a few dozen yards away. He glanced at Esther. She was drawing the red-stemmed feather moss.

He touched her shoulder. "Do you want to see a rare bird?"

"Is it the one you had hoped to see?"

"No, but this one is almost as interesting. An olive-sided flycatcher." He pointed to the tree. "He's perched at the very top on that dead limb. He's a gray fellow with a white strip down his chest."

Gabe handed her the glasses. He moved closer to help her focus them. They were sitting shoulder to shoulder. He could easily put his arm around her. Would she object?

"I don't see him. Oh, wait. Now I do. He looks like he's wearing a gray vest over a white shirt. How cute."

She lowered the glasses and turned to Gabe. Her smile faded as she gazed at him. She reached out and touched his lips with one finger. "You have a beautiful mouth."

He sucked in a quick breath. More than anything he wanted to kiss her, but he held himself in check.

She blushed and looked away. "I shouldn't have said that."

He cupped her chin to turn her face toward his. "I don't mind that you like my mouth. I like a lot of things about you."

"Such as?"

"You have amazing expressive eyes. They look like amber honey in the sunlight. I've never seen anyone with that color."

"I have my mother's eyes."

"I imagine she was a special person."

Esther turned to look out over the water. Memories of her mother were bittersweet. Her childhood had been wonderful, but all that changed. "When I lost my hearing, she couldn't accept it. She took me to doctor after doctor hoping to find a cure. There wasn't one, but she never gave up hope. It consumed her. She neglected my father and my sisters, and they resented it. Eventually our bishop came to speak with her. I don't think she realized the harm she was doing our family until then.

"After that she saw to it that my sisters and I learned sign language, but she didn't stop searching for something that would help me hear again."

She looked at Gabe. He was watching her intently, his eyes full of compassion. "It was *Gott's* will."

"I knew this is the life He has chosen for me. I was content. My mother couldn't understand that. When I was fifteen, she finally found the 'cure' she had been seeking." Esther knew her bitterness was seeping out in her words.

Gabe tipped his head slightly. "Waneta suggested that you refused to be healed. What did she mean?"

Esther picked up a small stick and threw it in the murky water. "She would say that. My father believes the same thing. My parents insisted I have a cochlear implant. A CI is a device that is placed under the skin behind the ear. It bypasses the ear and sends signals to the nerves that carry sounds to the brain. The doctor said the success rate of the operation was nearly one hundred percent."

She hadn't wanted them to spend their life savings on the surgery or to have the entire church pay for her hospital stay, but no one listened to her.

"Is it the same device Nurse Heather talked about?"

"*Nee*, it isn't." She sat staring at the swamp grasses blowing in the breeze for a long time. Finally she looked at Gabe. He was waiting patiently for her to continue.

She sighed. "I had the surgery, but when they turned the device on, it didn't work the way they said it would. I could hear again, but everything was distorted. There was an awful ringing that wouldn't stop unless I turned the implant off. No one believed me when I said it didn't work right. *Mamm* insisted I just needed to get used to it. My parents had sacrificed so much to get the treatment for me that I kept trying. It was awful. Then my mother got sick and died quite suddenly. After that I put my CI away and didn't use it again until I met Barnabas King. After he and I parted ways, I left it off for good. I'm Deaf. I accept it."

"Waneta believes you could hear if you wanted to."

"She thinks I like the attention of being the only deaf person in the family."

"I heard it was an inherited disease. No one else in the family is affected?"

"Both my father and my mother have cousins that are deaf. There is a higher-than-average number of deaf children in our community. That's why a special school was started. I'm a teacher's assistant there, and I love it. I have Deaf friends. We have great times together. Everyone at the school uses ASL. I never have to guess what someone is saying." It was the one place she felt safe and valued for who she was.

"Thank you for telling me this."

She shook her head, amazed and a bit embarrassed by how much she had revealed about herself. "I don't know why I did."

"Maybe because I'm your friend, too."

"I reckon you're right." What would he think if she said she wanted to be more than a friend?

Did she?

Gabe wasn't deaf. He couldn't know what it was like, but he was kind and understanding. Could she overlook the fact that he was a hearing person and grow to care for him? She already liked him more than she thought possible, but would he want to court a deaf woman? How could she risk her heart only to hear she wasn't seen as a whole person by the man who wanted to marry her?

Chapter Ten

Unlike the previous two days, Esther went down to breakfast devoid of any eagerness to greet the day. It was Sunday. The families would be going to the prayer meeting that was held every other week. She was expected to join them.

In her Amish community, there was a bishop and two ministers who shared the preaching during the three- or four-hour service. It was unlikely that she would understand much of what was said today. Preachers normally moved about as they spoke to the congregation or read from the Bible. There would be singing that she couldn't join. Afterward families would visit with each other while the children played together. Her one new friend, Lilly, would not be there this time. While she had met many of the women in the community already, she never felt comfortable in large groups. Today was likely to be a repeat of the picnic, where she watched others enjoying themselves from afar.

The Fisher men were still out doing the morning

chores when Esther entered the kitchen. Waneta, Julia, Pamela and Nancy were standing in a semicircle around Talitha. The discussion looked serious, but as soon as Talitha caught sight of her, she smiled and said, "Good morning, Esther. I hope you slept well. How is your headache?"

"Gone. *Danki.*"

Waneta looked right at Esther. "I'm pleased to hear it," she said slowly. She then turned and began cracking eggs into a skillet on the stove.

Esther's sisters all signed, "Good morning." Then they began to pack several coolers with food that would be served for the noon meal.

It was a strange start to the morning but a welcome change. Esther couldn't help wondering what they had been discussing. "What can I do?" she asked.

Talitha gestured toward several boxes sitting at the end of the counter. "If you would take the pies out to the buggy, that would be a help. We're almost ready to go as soon as everyone has had their breakfast."

Esther stacked the two boxes together and went out the door. She met Zeke coming in. He stepped back to let her pass. Gabe was behind him. He took the boxes from her. "Where do you want these?"

"Your mother said in the back of the buggy."

"Can you get the buggy door for me?"

"Of course." She hurried to open it.

After he had the boxes stowed, he leaned against the door frame. "I hope you enjoy the preaching today. Bishop Schultz can be a little long-winded, but he does a fine job."

"You will have to tell me what he preached about afterward. I doubt I'll be able to grasp much of it."

Gabe frowned. "Why?"

"I have yet to meet a preacher who stands still and looks straight at one person for the entire sermon."

"You have a point. He does like to use the room."

"I hope you won't desert me after the meal. That way I know I'll have at least one person to visit with."

"You can count on me, but you will find you are welcome in New Covenant. Others will seek you out to get to know you better. We should go in to breakfast."

She nodded and walked into the house. Everyone was seated at the places. She took her chair across from Gabe and bowed her head for the silent blessing that Zeke would lead. She glanced occasionally at him, waiting for him to signal the end of the prayers. When he did, his sons began passing the plates of food around.

She buttered some toast and sipped her coffee. She wasn't hungry. She was dreading the morning. At least she might be able to spend time with Gabe in the afternoon.

Everyone finished eating quickly, and the table was cleared. Gabe's brothers carried out the coolers while the women put on clean, crisp white aprons, black shawls and their black traveling bonnets before heading out to the buggy.

She was seated beside the door in the back seat as they got underway. At the end of the lane, they turned out onto the highway. As they passed the large pond where Gabe had saved her life, she saw a moose step out of the forest and into the water. It was a female with twin calves by her side. Esther reached over and tapped Jonah. "There is your moose."

He launched himself across her lap to look out the window. He stared at the animals until the buggy rounded a curve in the road. He looked at her with a huge grin on his face. "A cow with two babies. That was so amazing."

"Better than playing a game of baseball with your friends?" she asked.

"Almost as good as winning against the Mount Hope team."

As his team had only beaten their rival school once, she was glad she'd seen the animals and pointed them out to him.

The church service was being held at the home of members who lived five miles away, on the other side of New Covenant. It took almost an hour to reach the farm. A cluster of buggies was lined up on the side of the hill below the house. Zeke turned into the last row. A boy in his teens came to take the horse. He led Topper away, still in his harness, and tied him up at the corral fence beside the barn, where another dozen or so buggy horses were munching on the hay that had been spread on the ground for them.

An enclosed gray wagon was parked beside the house. A group of men was unloading and carrying in the backless benches that would be used to seat the congregation. Zeke and his sons headed toward the barn where a large group of men stood talking. She recognized Tully, Danny and the bishop among them.

Crops and the weather were no doubt the main topics

being discussed. It was that way in every Amish farming community. Zeke took the bishop by the elbow and led him a few feet away from the group, where Gabe joined them. They were soon deep in conversation.

Nancy touched Esther's arm. "How are you and Gabe getting along?" she signed.

"We have a good working relationship. I think we're becoming friends. How are you and Moses doing?"

"He's a very sweet boy. Much more mature than the fellows back home. He plans on being baptized in the fall."

"That sounds promising. Do you like him?"

"I do, but don't tell Waneta. We'll never hear the end of her bragging about her matchmaking skills if she were to suspect Moses and I will be courting."

"He has asked you to walk out with him?" Esther was surprised.

"He knows I am going home at the end of the month. He has asked if he may write to me, and he has invited me to visit again next summer."

"I'm happy for you. The Fishers are a warm and caring family." She would miss Nancy if she moved to Maine, but she wanted her little sister to be happy. It was easy to imagine being content in the Fishers' home.

"I see they are finished unloading the bench wagon. We can go in."

Esther followed her sister inside. Julia and Pamela were already seated. The benches had been set out in rows in the living room with an aisle down the middle. Men would sit on one side of the aisle. The women would sit on the other. Married men and women occu-

pied the front rows, while the single women and men
sat behind them. Esther soon realized she and her sisters
were almost the only single women in the congregation.
There were several young girls but none old enough to
be courting. It was no wonder Talitha had hatched a
plan with Waneta to bring her stepdaughters for a visit.

Across the way Esther saw the Fisher brothers file in
and take their seats. Jonah sat with them. Gabe smiled
and nodded to her. Behind him, Danny and Jedidiah
were also smiling in her direction. Esther quickly realized their eyes were on Julia and Pamela. Did the Fisher
brothers know they were in for some competition?

A few minutes later, the bishop and the ministers came
into the room. Nancy turned to Esther. As soon as the
bishop began to speak, Nancy began to sign his words.
Esther normally sat through a service trying to grasp frag-
ments of what was being said by reading the speaker's lips.

According to Nancy the bishop was informing the
congregation that Waneta and her stepdaughters were
visiting in the area and that one of the daughters was
deaf. Because of that her family members would use
sign language to convey the preaching to her.

To Esther's surprise, he held his hand out flat with
his palm up and then brought it toward his chest. "This
is the sign for 'welcome.' I ask that we all use it to make
our deaf visitor feel we are pleased she is among us."

Nearly everyone turned and looked in Esther's direction and repeated the sign. She felt heat rising in her
face as she made the sign for "thank you."

Around her people reached for their hymnal, the *Aus-
bund*, and opened it. She could see the first song had

started. Nancy signed the page number, and Esther flipped to the song so that she could read the lyrics even though she chose not to sing. She remembered many hymns from her childhood, but she couldn't be certain she was in tune or in time with others. For the rest of the service, Nancy and Pamela traded off signing for Esther so that she was able to understand all that the bishop and the ministers had to say. The sisters received many curious glances. A toddler in the row ahead of them mimicked the signs as she grinned at Esther.

When the prayer meeting was over, they filed outside so that the benches could be rearranged into tables and seating for the meal. Her sisters stayed close beside her and continued to sign for her as she was introduced again to the members of the community. She became reacquainted with the bishop's wife and the wives of the ministers and their families. Some of the younger women held babies or had toddlers clinging to their skirts. The little girl who had been trying to sign toddled over to Esther and reached up to be held.

Esther picked her up and was struck with a sharp pang of longing to have a family of her own. But that would require a husband. There wasn't one in her immediate future. The child quickly wanted down and went to play with a little boy near her age.

When Esther had a free moment, she caught Nancy's arm. "I can't tell you how much I appreciate you doing this."

Nancy blushed. "I confess it was Talitha's suggestion."

"You're always so quick to want to do things on your own," Julia signed.

Pamela nodded. "You can be abrupt and self-absorbed. Sometimes we forget that you do need us."

"Of course I need you. You're my sisters." Esther hugged each of them in turn. "I will try not to be abrupt in the future."

"And we'll remind you when you are doing exactly that again." **Julia grinned.**

Esther gave her another quick hug. "And I'll point out when you're ignoring me."

"I fear we may have some sisterly squabbles in the future," **Nancy signed.**

"We may, but we'll always make up, because we love each other." Esther wiped a tear from her eye. "Which one of you taught the bishop how to sign 'welcome'?"

Nancy shook her head. "It wasn't us."

Then it must have been Jonah. "I need to thank Talitha for her thoughtful suggestion."

She found Waneta and Gabe's mother in the kitchen setting out the food with some of the other women. "Talitha, my sisters tell me I have you to thank for encouraging them to assist me today."

"It wasn't my idea. I merely pointed out to some members of your family that they were being unkind, although I know that was never their intention." She looked at Waneta.

"Of course it wasn't the girls' intention," Waneta said.

"Did Jonah tell you I dislike crowds?"

"Actually, it was Gabe who mentioned it. He taught the bishop the sign for 'welcome.' That was his idea, too," Talitha said with a knowing smile.

"Gabe did?" For her.

"He thinks a great deal of you," Waneta said.

Esther kept her face carefully blank. "I value him as a friend, too. Excuse me. I need to thank him."

Outside she caught a glimpse of Gabe watching from across the way. He was leaning against an empty hay wagon. She crossed the distance between them with her heart pounding in her chest. How could she adequately thank him for everything he had done?

She stopped in front of him and placed her hands on her hips. "I understand you taught the bishop the sign for 'welcome.' Who taught you?"

He spelled out "Jonah" in sign.

Her jaw dropped. "Why did you do this?"

"Because I didn't like the way your sisters ignored you."

"We used to be close. Now I hope we can be that way again. We simply got used to going our separate ways."

"I'm glad if I helped."

She found herself swamped with emotions. Gratitude and something else. A sincere warmth for this man filled her heart. If she wasn't careful, she would blurt out how special he made her feel. "I have a sign name. Deaf people often choose one so they don't have to spell it out each time. Would you like to know it?"

"Sure."

"It's the sign for 'flower.'" She made the motion of holding a flower by the stem and bringing it to her nose to sniff.

"Flower. It suits you." He repeated the sign.

"I should get back to my sisters."

"That's fine. Enjoy the day. We have plenty of work waiting for us tomorrow."

She took a step back. "It's the kind of work I don't mind if you're there to help." She clamped her lips shut and spun on her heels. She managed to walk, not run, away from him and her growing feelings for this generous and thoughtful man.

Gabe smiled as she walked off. He was glad he had managed to improve her relationship with her sisters and allow her to understand the preaching today. Hearing the words God moved their ministers and bishop to speak brought them all closer to God and to each other. No one should be alone in this life.

Seth stopped beside Gabe. "You like her a lot, don't you?"

He couldn't fool his brother, so he didn't try. "I do."

"I think she likes you, too."

"As a friend."

"Maybe a little more than that?" Seth suggested.

"She doesn't want a hearing fellow. She has made that plain."

"Maybe that is what her head says. Sometimes the heart leads one down an unexpected path."

"Is that what happened to you? Pamela and you seem fond of each other in spite of the fact that you claimed you had no interest in finding a wife yet."

"I'm not ready to marry her, but I do like her a lot. Should I ask her to be your go-between and find out if Esther is interested in dating you?"

Gabe considered it. The question would be better coming from someone who knew how to talk to Esther. But was the time right?

He decided against the idea. "*Danki*, but not yet."

He needed Esther to help him finish his work before the festival. If she found out he was interested in courting her and she didn't return those feelings, she might be uncomfortable working with him. It was more than her sewing skills he wanted to keep. Seeing her every day all day long made him happy. He couldn't risk losing that.

What he wanted to say could wait until after the festival. By then perhaps his lessons with Jonah would give him a good enough grasp of sign language to make himself understood without worrying that she didn't get what he was trying to say.

Later in the afternoon, when the families had returned from the church service, Gabe was reading a book in the living room when Esther and Jonah came in. Jonah sat on the sofa beside Gabe while Esther sank to the floor in front of him. He closed his book, keeping his finger between the pages to hold his place. "Did you want something?"

Eagerness filled her amber-colored eyes and made them sparkle. "Bethany Shetler mentioned there is a farmers market in Fort Craig every Wednesday afternoon during the summer."

"That's true. Do you have produce you wish to sell? Have you been growing radishes on the side?" He could see that Jonah was signing everything he said.

Esther rolled her eyes. "Be serious a moment. Bethany told me her husband takes some of his clocks to sell, so it doesn't have to be just vegetables. Apparently a lot of *Englisch* people come to it."

"I've seen a fair number of them there. What is your point?"

"That the farmers market might be a good place to see how well your items sell, particularly the purses we have made."

He rubbed his chin as he considered the idea. "There is some merit in your suggestion. But none of the purses are lined yet. How many could we have finished by Wednesday? We still have a lot of pieces to make before the festival."

"I've talked to my sisters, and they are all willing to sew linings for us. We could have a dozen done to take, plus a few of your other items to show people samples of what you make. I said you couldn't depend on a single festival for your income. Selling at this market could give you income all summer long after the festival is finished. What do you think?"

"I think it is something we should try to see if it is indeed worth our while."

She clapped her hands together. "I knew you would see the benefits. Perhaps your mother has some leftover fabric from her quilting we can use without adding the expense of buying new material. I'll go ask her."

Gabe leaned forward and put his hand on her head to stop her from rising. "It is Sunday. A day of rest. We do only essential work on the Lord's day."

"Asking about supplies and looking to see what's available isn't working."

He tipped his head. "Isn't it?"

She nodded. "Okay. Maybe I am getting carried away."

He removed his hand and sat back. She sighed deeply. "What are you reading?"

"A book about birds."

"Is there something you don't already know in it?"

"The author talks about how the migration patterns of birds are changing due to the changes in our climate."

"Must be fascinating." Her expression said just the opposite.

He held back a smile. "Shall I read some since Jonah is here to interpret?"

Jonah shook his head and stood up. "I'm going to play a game or two of horseshoes with Moses."

The boy left the room, leaving Esther still sitting at Gabe's feet. He closed his book and put it aside. "What do you like to read?"

She crossed her arms and raised her nose in the air. "What makes you think I enjoy reading?"

"You have a sharp mind. I can't imagine you would ignore all books have to offer."

She chuckled. "I do like to read. I enjoy mystery stories and some romances."

"Love stories? You seem so practical. I wouldn't have pegged you as a romantic."

"Well, I am. I think there is someone out there for everyone. Despite the obstacles that life places in our way, the Lord will see that faith and love win the day."

He leaned forward to gaze into her eyes. "Do you truly believe that?"

Chapter Eleven

Esther gazed up at Gabe. His bright blue eyes were fixed on her intently. What was he thinking? She knew in her heart that this was about more than his question. She did believe there was someone for everyone. Gabe would certainly make some woman a wonderful husband. Esther cared for him dearly, but they weren't meant for each other. Had she given him the impression that she thought they might be? Was that what he wanted to know?

She wouldn't hurt him for the world. She had to convince him that his friendship was all that mattered. Because it did, more than she could say.

"I fervently pray the Lord has someone in mind for me to love. A man I can respect and who respects me in return. One who understands what it is to be deaf in a hearing world. I pray *Gott* has a kind and generous woman in mind for you to love, too."

Gabe sat back. His gaze became shuttered. "We have

both been disappointed in the past. I admire that you still believe in love."

"Don't you?"

"I hope to marry someday. I want a family. But trusting that a woman has my best interest at heart is hard."

"I know what you mean. It is difficult, but at least we know what we want."

Hearing Barnabas tell her that she needed to be "fixed" before he could marry her had crushed her. It had taken a long time and the wise counsel of her Deaf friends for her to recover her self-esteem. She never wanted to feel that despondent again.

She rose. "I will let you get back to your reading."

"What will you do this evening?"

"I may take my sketch pad outside. Your mother has a lovely flower garden."

"Would you like to take a walk? We can choose a different path through the woods. Perhaps you can discover some new wildflowers."

"I would like that."

He got to his feet and nodded toward the window. "Our challenge may be avoiding other couples strolling in the woods."

She looked out and saw Danny talking to her sister Julia in the garden. They headed toward the gate that led to a grove of fruit trees behind the house.

"I'm glad I straightened the ribbons on her *kapp*."

Gabe gave her an odd look. "What does that mean?"

"She was insistent that I finish a new head covering for her before church today. This explains whom she was hoping to impress. Let me get my sketch pad."

She hurried upstairs, eager to spend more time with Gabe. He wasn't the man for her. She accepted that, but she still cherished their time together. What little of it they had left.

When she returned, he was waiting with his binoculars and his birding book. Together they went out the back door and across the garden. At the gate he took a path that led away from the orchard. They crossed a small meadow with a lone gnarled tree at its center. The remnants of an old rock wall extended a few feet out from its trunk. He took a seat and raised his binoculars to his eyes. Esther settled herself on the ground. A cluster of small yellow flowers were poking their heads out from between the blades of grass. She opened her sketchbook and was soon trying to capture their beauty silhouetted against the moss-covered rocks behind them.

When she finally looked up, she saw Gabe had set his binoculars aside and was watching her. "No birds?" she asked.

"Ordinary ones. Nothing special in the skies or the trees this evening. What did you find?"

She handed him her pad. "I don't know the name, but they are very pretty and delicate."

"They're called Quaker ladies."

"Are there flowers called Amish ladies anywhere?"

"I see a lovely one right in front of me."

She felt a blush rising to her face. "I'm sure I don't compare favorably to these beauties."

"I'm forced to disagree." He looked through the pages at the drawings she had made. He paused at one page and then closed the pad.

"Are you ready to go back?" she asked.

"*Nee*, I'm content right here." He handed her sketchbook back to her. "Don't let me interrupt you."

She tried to concentrate on drawing a small blue violet she spied a few feet away, but she couldn't keep her mind on what she was doing with Gabe staring at her.

She looked at him. "It's disconcerting."

"What is?"

"You. Gawking at me."

"I was studying your mouth."

She raised her fingers to her lips. "Why?"

"You once told me I had a pretty mouth."

"I shouldn't have said that."

"You captured a good likeness of someone's lips." He nodded toward her drawing pad.

She had forgotten this one contained the sketches she had made of him at the bog that day. "I spend a lot of time looking at people's mouths."

"I was trying to imagine what that must be like."

"Would you kindly stop staring at mine?"

"It's pleasing. I like the way you smile. It sneaks out like you aren't quite ready for it, but then you give in and it's lovely."

She stared at her hands. "Now you're making fun of me."

He reached out to lift her chin until she was looking at him. "Not in the least."

She noticed something beyond him in the sky. "You are missing what you came here for."

"I came here to spend an hour with you."

"I thought you came out here hoping to see the swallow-tailed kite. He's flying over your left shoulder."

"Is he?"

She cocked one eyebrow. "Aren't you going to look?"

"I've discovered observing flowers is more interesting than watching birds."

Esther wasn't sure she understood him, but there was no mistaking the tenderness in his eyes. He was making it almost impossible to pretend that friendship was all she wanted.

Gabe realized his mistake almost as soon as the words were out of his mouth. His intention had been to keep their relationship friendly. It wasn't to reveal his growing attraction to her. But gazing at her lovely face so close to his own was almost his undoing. He had to put some distance between them.

"It's getting late. We should head back." He got to his feet and clenched his hands into fists so he wouldn't reach out to help her up. He didn't trust himself to hold her hand and not pull her into his embrace. He moved a few steps away.

"Okay." She scrambled to her feet and dusted off her skirt. She gathered her drawing materials and put them in her bag.

He started walking. After a few steps, he glanced back to make sure that she was following. She kept her eyes downcast. Maybe she didn't want to know if he spoke again. He told himself it was for the best. She was praying that God would bring a deaf man for her to love. Someone who understood her silent world.

Gabe gave a heavy sigh. She would never believe that he could be such a man.

"Are you in a hurry?"

He stopped and looked back. He had outpaced her by several yards. "I'm sorry. I was lost in thought."

"Then I'm sorry I interrupted."

He waited for her to catch up. "Don't be. I was being rude."

"Were you thinking about the farmers market?"

Not until she mentioned it, but it was a safe subject. "I may purchase some dyed leather from my supplier. The dog collars and purses might do better if they were more colorful. What do you think?"

"I like the idea. Will you be able to get it soon enough? We absolutely need pink."

"Maybe not a large assortment of colors. It wouldn't be wise to invest heavily in something until we know if it will be popular. I'm supposed to have my stitches out tomorrow. I'll stop at Ed Carson's when I'm done at the clinic and see what he has available. He tans hides. I know he has some leather already dyed. I can order more if your plan works."

"If? Do I detect some doubt?" A spark of defiance appeared in her eyes. "May I remind you that you doubted my ability to sew leather goods."

He decided to goad her a little. "I may have been wrong once, but developing a marketing plan isn't like planning a meal for the family."

She crossed her arms over her chest. "How many meals have you planned?"

"Well, none."

"Then you don't know if it's more difficult or not."

He grinned. "Do you feel better now that you have put me in my place?"

She cracked a smile. "A little."

"If this doesn't work and I have stacks of pink leather left over, it will be your fault."

"It won't come to that. I'm sure of it."

He leaned toward her. "And how many times have you successfully sold leather goods at a farmers market?"

She turned her head slightly to the side. "Never," she mumbled.

He tapped her shoulder to make her look at him. When she did, he cupped his hand around his ear. "I'm sorry, I didn't hear that."

"Going deaf, are you?" He heard the amusement in her voice.

"*Nee*, and I'm not going broke over this project, either. We'll take a small selection and see how it goes."

"Agreed."

"*Goot*, now can we go home? It's getting dark, and soon you won't be able to hear me."

She chuckled. "I'm glad to see you can finally joke about my condition and not worry that you are insulting me."

"Friends do that, right? They tease each other."

"They do. Go ahead, but don't walk so fast. Your legs are longer than mine."

He started toward the house again but stayed by her side. They were back on friendly terms, and he was glad of it. He hadn't ruined their relationship, but he would have to be careful not to be alone with her outside of their work lest he slip up again. It wouldn't take much to prod him into kissing her adorable mouth.

The next morning Gabe's conversation with Esther remained lighthearted and focused on their work together and nothing personal. He wasn't going to make the same mistake twice. After seeing that she had everything she needed to work on, he took the small wagon into Fort Craig. The clinic was busy. He had to wait almost an hour to be seen. Nurse Heather was the one who called him back to the exam room. "How is that arm?" she asked.

"Much better. I did tear a stitch out the day after the doctor put them in."

She scowled at him. "And you didn't come back to see us?"

"It didn't seem worth the trouble of a trip into town. Someone taped it for me."

"I forget that you have to come by horse and buggy. Let me get your vital signs and then we'll have a look."

When she finished her assessment, he rolled up his sleeve. She unwound the bandage. After pressing in several places, she nodded with satisfaction. "It seems to have healed well despite popping a stitch. Once the doctor has a look, I'll remove them and send you on your way. How is Esther? Is she still staying with your family?"

"She is, and she's doing fine. She had a pretty bad headache for a couple of days, but she hasn't complained of anything since."

"I'm glad to hear that. She seemed like a very nice woman."

"You mentioned something about a special kind of hearing aid that your daughters were getting. Is it like a cochlear implant?"

She shook her head. "They are very different, but both do require surgery. Why?"

"Esther had a cochlear implant that didn't work."

She looked surprised. "Really? That's very unusual, but it does happen. How disappointing for her."

"Could she have this other type of hearing aid even if the kind she has failed?"

"As long as she only had a single cochlear implant, yes. If she had two then the bone-anchored hearing aid isn't an option for her."

"Why?"

"In most instances the patient's own cochlea, an internal part of the ear, is permanently impaired by the implant. Some people have residual hearing after the surgery, but most don't. The bone-anchored device needs an intact cochlea in order to work."

Maybe that was why Esther hadn't been interested in learning about this different type of hearing aid. Because she already knew it wouldn't work for her. But it didn't explain why Nancy had taken a brochure.

The door to the room opened, and the doctor came in. Heather handed him Gabe's chart. "He popped one of the stitches the first day, but the rest look fine," she said.

"How did you manage to do that?" the doctor asked with a sour look.

"Our neighbor's feed wagon broke down. It took several of us to raise it and replace the wheel."

The doctor looked at the nurse with an amused grin. "Remind me to add wheel changing to the list of restricted activities for our next Amish patient."

She nodded solemnly. "Yes, Doctor."

"Go ahead and remove those sutures. Mr. Fisher, it was a pleasure meeting you." He walked out of the room still smiling.

It only took Heather a few minutes to snip the stitches in Gabe's arm. She disposed of the instruments and pulled off her gloves. "You are free to go. Please tell Esther I said hello."

"I'll be sure and do that."

As he paid his bill at the desk, he noticed the stack of information about hearing screens and hearing aids on the counter. He took one about the bone-anchored hearing device to read later. If it wasn't something that would help Esther, he didn't want to bring it up. But if there was a chance that she could be helped, he wanted to learn more about it.

Gabe left the doctor's office and drove to his leather supplier at the edge of town. Ed Carson was a small, bald man with a sour disposition. Gabe didn't hold out much hope that he would have an assortment of colored leather. It turned out that he was wrong. Ed had everything from ivory to deep purple in small quantities. Gabe selected a few and went to pay the man.

"Making pink horse harnesses now?" Ed asked.

"If I could sell them, I'd make them."

"You mentioned last month that you might be wanting a goodly pile of harness leather. I went ahead and tanned some in case you were ready to buy more."

Harness leather wasn't like shoe leather or any other type of leather. It had to be tanned with a lot of oil and waxes to stand up to the elements. "I'm sorry you went to the trouble. My customer decided not to buy from me after all."

"Hank Jefferson, right?"

"That is his name."

"He was in the other day asking who else made harnesses in the area. I gave him a few names. I also told him no one makes them as well as you do."

"I appreciate that."

"Ours are trades that few people value anymore. They want quick and cheap. Pleather instead of real leather. If I can throw any business your way, I will. I admire how the Amish live and work." He bundled up Gabe's purchase and handed it over.

On the trip home, Gabe couldn't help thinking about Esther and how much he wanted to help her. Her last attempt to regain her hearing had failed miserably. There was no guarantee the bone-anchored device would work better for her. He didn't want her to be disappointed again. Nor did he want to suggest she investigate something she already knew wouldn't work. Maybe Waneta was the person he needed to talk with. She would know if Esther had had one or two implants.

When he reached home, he found Esther was bent over her sewing in his workshop. She hadn't noticed him come in. He took care to walk softly across the floor so as not to alert her to his presence by the vibration. He carefully slid the pink leather into her view.

She stopped sewing and looked up with a bright smile. "You found some. This is the exact color I was hoping for. It will make a beautiful purse."

"With a matching dog collar and leash."

"What a good idea."

"I have them sometimes." She wasn't looking at him. He knew he was wasting his breath, but he wanted to say what was on his mind. "I wonder if kissing you would be a good idea or a very bad one," he said softly.

She smoothed the leather with one hand. "This is quite supple. It will be easy to sew." She looked up at him. "Can you cut a few for me now? I'd love to get started on them. Let me finish these ax head covers while you do that."

"I'll get right on it." He took the leather from her and went to his desk. He put the information on the bone-anchored hearing aid in the top drawer. One day soon, when this rush of work was over, he would talk to Esther about it. It might not be something her family could afford or that her church would consider paying for, but he would help if it meant she could hear again. He closed the drawer and stepped to his cutting table. It wasn't long before he deposited the new purse pieces in front of her.

"*Danki.* It will just take me another minute to finish this," she said, looking up at him.

"All right. I'm going to the house."

"Okay. Send Pamela out. I need to speak to her about the patterns for the lining I want."

"I'll do that."

Gabe found all the women in his mother's quilting room. He gave Pamela Esther's message and then looked at Waneta. "May I speak to you for a few moments?"

"Of course." She got up from her chair beside the quilting frame and followed him into the kitchen. "Has Esther become a problem?"

He frowned. "*Nee*, nothing like that."

"Then how may I help you?"

"Esther told me that her cochlear implant failed."

"So she claims."

"You don't believe that?"

"Her father doesn't. He thinks she refuses to use it so she can continue her work with deaf children at the special-needs school. Some of the deaf teachers there are not Amish. They are proud of being deaf. They don't believe deafness is something that needs to be corrected."

"It is decided by *Gott* that they should be as they are."

"It is His will, to be sure, but we are not prevented by our faith from seeking medical cures for our children when they have an illness. Esther's parents sought a cure for her disability that she felt she didn't need. They sacrificed a great deal to get her surgery. In her father's eyes, she is being selfish by refusing to use it. I agree with him. She could have been happily married with children of her own by now. Something her father and I dearly want to see. I went to great lengths to encourage a match for her. We would have made her husband a half owner in our bakery. All she had to do was learn to live with the sounds the device allowed her to hear. Perhaps it isn't perfect, but it has to be better than nothing."

There were always two sides to a story. This was Waneta's view. Esther's refusal to marry Waneta's choice was at the heart of the hard feelings between them. Should he tell Waneta he agreed with Esther? A man who would court a deaf woman in order to gain ownership in a business wasn't much of a catch.

Gabe drew a deep breath. He was being unfair to the man. He could have had deep feelings for Esther. She was an easy woman to love.

"I'm sorry the two of you have remained at odds over her decision, but it is her life. Because she is deaf doesn't mean she had to settle for a man she believed didn't love her."

Waneta looked affronted, but she simply folded her arms over her chest. "What is it you wanted to ask me?"

"Did Esther have two cochlear implants or only one?"

"One was deemed enough by her doctor."

"*Danki.* I want you to know she isn't a problem for me. She works very hard and she has some *goot* ideas about growing my business. With her help I'm sure I can produce enough items to make having a booth at the festival worthwhile."

"It's a shame she won't be there to see your success or the lack of it."

"Why wouldn't she attend the festival? Are you leaving sooner than planned?"

"We aren't. She is."

Chapter Twelve

Esther looked up from her sewing machine when Gabe came in. She knew at once that he was upset by the expression on his face. "What's wrong?"

He walked over to lean against the cutting table and crossed his arms over his chest as he faced her. "You're leaving."

"You knew that."

"I didn't know you were leaving in five days."

She pushed her chair back and clasped her hands together in her lap. "Who told you?"

"Does it matter?"

"Waneta?"

"Is it true?"

"I didn't want to come on this trip. My father insisted. The woman he hired to drive us out here went on to stay with some family in Bar Harbor for several weeks. She agreed that when she was ready to drive back to Ohio, she would take any of us who wanted to go along with her. I was delighted to learn of her offer.

I thought two weeks would be more than enough time to satisfy my father. However, that was before I became involved with you and your work."

"Then I don't understand."

"Waneta called Bessie and then wrote to my father to tell him I was coming home. I never said I wanted to leave so soon. I didn't agree to go. I like to finish what I start, Gabe."

Some of the tenseness left his body. "So you aren't leaving before the Potato Blossom Festival."

"I want to see you succeed. I think *Gott* has given you a wonderful talent and more people should know about the things you create. I'm sorry if Waneta upset you. I will make it clear to her that I am not going home until she and my sisters are ready to go."

A half smile pulled up the corner of his mouth. "I can't tell you how relieved that makes me. I've gotten used to having you around."

She grinned. "The feeling is mutual."

"I guess we can get back to work now. What did Pamela say about the linings?"

"She can have three of them ready for us by tomorrow morning. It won't take me long to stitch them in."

"Then I had better get busy cutting more leather. How do you say that in ASL?"

"Say what?"

"Get busy."

She giggled and showed him. He repeated the motion. She nodded and turned back to her machine.

He tapped her shoulder. "Thank you," he signed, surprising her.

"Has Jonah been teaching you more sign language?"

"A little. Not good yet."

Her heart swelled with gratitude for Gabe's kindness and willingness to learn to communicate with her. Every day she discovered something about him that made him dearer to her. When she did finally leave Maine, she was going to miss him dreadfully.

Esther and Gabe worked long into the evening that night and started again early the next morning. After they finished, she had a conversation with Waneta to let her know she wasn't going to leave with Bessie. She had been surprised when Waneta didn't object.

Now, late in the afternoon, Esther's eyes were scratchy from staring at the sewing needle for hours on end. Her back ached from leaning over the machine, but she was finished. It was time to pack up their items for the trip into town in the morning. She looked around the workshop with a sense of great satisfaction. They had accomplished a lot together.

Gabe stood in front of her. "Tired?"

"A little," she said and signed the same.

His signing was improving. Jonah had told her that Gabe sent away for a book on ASL so he could continue to study it even after they went back to Ohio. It was one thing to memorize the signs. It was another thing to be able to communicate effortlessly. Unless Gabe had someone he could practice with, he wouldn't become fluent. She didn't tell him that. He was so pleased with what he had learned.

Daily he demonstrated a new phrase or two that he had mastered. She adored helping him. It was cute watching him try, fail sometimes and then try harder. He had an aptitude for it that surprised her. She had started signing whenever she spoke to him to help him learn.

Suddenly he winced. "We don't need that."

"What?"

"Thunder. The forecast said there was a chance of storms tonight and for tomorrow."

"*Nee.* It can't rain tomorrow." They had worked so hard to get ready. If it rained, few if any people would come to the market.

He looked at the ceiling. "I don't know about tomorrow, but it's raining now. I hear it on the roof."

She looked up, too. "I remember what that sounded like. Soothing. It meant we wouldn't be working in the fields the next day."

"The crops need rain. We shouldn't wish it away."

"Can we pray for a pause from ten o'clock to four o'clock tomorrow?"

"I think that will be acceptable. Are you ready to make a dash to the house?"

"I won't melt."

"You won't? Aren't you sugar and spice and everything nice?" His words were teasing, but his expression became oddly serious.

"You are confusing me with my sisters." She grew warm beneath his intense scrutiny.

He tugged gently on her *kapp* ribbon. "I think not. They may be sweet, but I haven't seen a sign of spice among them."

"Sweet is usually enough for most young men."

He didn't take his eyes off her face. "Not me. I like spicy."

She knew she was blushing. "We should go to the house before the storm gets worse."

He took a step back. "You're right."

She quickly headed for the door. When she opened it, the rain was coming down in sheets. Gabe caught her by the shoulder. She turned to see him holding a large piece of hide.

"I don't have an umbrella, but this should work. Stay close to me."

She nodded. He held the hide over his head and stepped out. She pressed against his side to keep from getting wet as they rushed toward the front porch of the house, but she stumbled and fell to her knees. Gabe lifted her up and kept one arm around her. He couldn't control the hide with one hand. The wind carried the rain into her face in spite of his efforts to keep her dry. Her *kapp* and her hem were soaked by the time they reached cover.

She laughed as she ran up the steps and shook out her dress. Gabe dropped the hide on the porch floor. He pulled a handkerchief from his pocket and began to mop her face. "I didn't help much."

They stood close together. His hand stilled. She saw his eyes darken. She couldn't look away from him. She didn't want to.

Why hadn't she realized it before now? She was half-way to falling in love with this wonderful man.

He leaned toward her. She knew he was going to kiss her. She raised her face and closed her eyes.

His lips touched hers. Gently. As softly as a rose petal, and then they were gone. Her heart began racing as her breath caught in her throat. His hands settled on her shoulders. Nothing mattered except being closer to him. She pressed her hands to his chest and leaned against him as his arms circled her and drew her near. She wanted to keep kissing him.

Part of Gabe's mind said he was making a mistake. There would be no going back from this, but he was past caring. She was in his arms. He wanted to hold her forever. Her lips were as sweet as honeysuckle nectar. One kiss would never be enough. She was everything he'd ever wanted and never knew he needed.

The sound of the door opening behind him brought reality crashing back into view. He glanced over his shoulder. His father stood in the doorway. "I saw you running through the rain, but then you didn't come in. Is everything all right?"

"It's fine. We'll be a minute."

"Okay." His father appeared puzzled, but he went back inside and closed the door.

Gabe looked down at Esther. Her eyes were filled with confusion as she gazed at him. He nodded toward the door. "My father wanted to know if we were all right."

She pressed a hand to her cheek. "He saw us? You—me?"

"Did he see me kiss you? I don't think so."

"I'm so embarrassed. How will I face him?"

"Like nothing happened except that you got wet and took a moment to dry your face with my kerchief." He pressed the damp cloth into her hand. "Go in. The longer we stand out here, the stranger it will look."

"What? I didn't catch all that you said."

"Dry your face and go in."

She stepped around him and looked back. There was so much he wanted to say to her. He didn't know where to start, and this wasn't the time to sort it out. "Go."

She went inside. He picked up the wet hide and shook it off. A moment later he opened the door and leaned in. "*Mamm*, have you got something I can use to dry this piece of leather? I don't want the water to stain it."

His mother appeared with a dish towel. "Will this work?"

"Great. *Danki.*"

"Is Esther okay? She ran upstairs without a word."

"I'm sure she just wanted to get out of her wet things. She slipped and fell."

"Oh, the poor child. I'll fix some hot tea for her. And for you. You look like you need it."

"Sounds *goot.*"

She made a tsking sound. "The two of you have been working entirely too hard."

"I don't think we'll be putting in any more long hours." He began to dry the leather he'd used as an ineffective umbrella. He couldn't be sure Esther would want to see him again, let alone work beside him. Why hadn't he kept his feelings under wraps?

Because of the way she had looked at him. With such wonder in her eyes. Like she had discovered a new rare flower.

She wasn't indifferent to him. But what did it really

mean? She would be leaving. Not in a few days but in a few weeks with her family. She had made no secret of the fact that she wouldn't marry a hearing man. Where did that leave him? Was it possible he could change her mind?

"What are Seth and Asher doing?"

Gabe followed his mother's gaze. His brothers were standing in the barn door. When they saw they had his attention, they beckoned to him.

His heart sank. Something told him his interlude with Esther hadn't gone unnoticed after all. He managed a half-hearted smile for his mother and handed her the towel. "I'll go see what they want."

"Don't stay out there long. Supper will be ready in half an hour." She smiled, patted his cheek the way she had done since he was a child and went in.

Gabe dashed across to the open barn door. Asher and Seth took a step back to let him inside. He shook the rain from his hat. "What do you fellows want?"

"An explanation would be nice," Seth said.

"About what?"

"Don't play coy," Asher grumbled.

"Okay. I suspect you saw me kiss Esther. What do you want to know?"

Seth planted his hands on his hips. "Your intentions, for one thing? Please tell me you aren't just feeling sorry for her. That would not be fair to her."

"I haven't had time to sort out how I feel. What are your intentions toward Pamela?"

"Don't change the subject," Seth snapped, then he took a deep breath. "Pamela and I are walking out together. I may be courting her in earnest before they leave. We get along amazingly well. Your turn."

"Esther and I have been working long hours, and I think the strain got to us. We finished enough pieces to take to the farmers market tomorrow, and the relief went to my head. Maybe to hers, too. I didn't intend to kiss her—it just happened."

"Now that it has, what next?" Asher asked. "You are the one who warned us that Waneta was intent on getting husbands for the girls while they were here. Are you sure you aren't being manipulated?"

Gabe scoffed at the idea. "*Nee*, Esther doesn't want me for a husband."

Asher gave him a hard look. "What makes you say that?"

"Because I'm not deaf. She believes only a deaf man can understand all that she endures and enjoys in her silent world."

Seth laid a hand on Gabe's shoulder. "I think it's time the two of you revisited that assumption, because she didn't look like she cared if you could hear or not."

"I'd love to have that conversation, but I'm not sure I can make her understand all that I want to tell her."

Esther sat on the edge of her bed in her damp clothing. She had one hand pressed to her mouth as if she could hold on to the feeling of Gabe's lips against hers. Why had he kissed her? Why had she let him? They were so wrong for each other. How, then, could a kiss feel so right? It had been perfect in every way. Her heart soared at the memory and then plunged to the pit of her stomach when she realized she had no idea what to do next.

She was startled when Julia sat down on the cot across from hers. "What's the matter?" she signed.

Esther took one look at her sister's concerned face and burst into tears. Julia moved to Esther's side and gathered her close, patting her back until Esther's sobs abated. Esther scrubbed away her tears with both hands. "I'm sorry I'm being so silly."

"Gabe?" Julia signed.

Esther didn't question how Julia had guessed the cause of her distress. She simply nodded.

Julia took both of Esther's hands in her own and leaned forward to make sure Esther could see her. "Tell me."

"He kissed me."

"Was it awful?"

"It was wonderful."

Julia sat back with a puzzled expression on her face. "Then why the tears?" she signed.

"He's not the man I want to be in love with," she said.

"Who is?" Julia signed.

"I don't know, but Gabe shouldn't be the one who makes my heart beat faster."

Julia shook her head. "Esther, you are not the one who decides that."

"What do you mean?"

"*Gott* decides our partners for life. He chooses. We can say yes or no to that decision. We have free will, but surely we must put our faith in His plan for us if we are to live as He desires."

"I'm so confused. I don't know what to do or what to say to Gabe now."

"Foolish little sister. One kiss does not mean you must marry him. It means the two of you are drawn to each other. Give yourself a chance to see if he is the right one or not. Open your heart to *Gott's* plan. Don't turn your back on it because it isn't the path you think you want."

"How do I face him?"

"I would suggest you start by changing into dry clothes and then come down for supper the way you always have."

"You mean pretend the kiss didn't happen?"

"I mean act like it isn't the end of the world or the end of your friendship with Gabe. See what he has to say with an open mind. I know you like him."

"I think I'm falling in love with him."

"Then give him a chance. The two of you have worked very hard to make a success of his business. Don't let him down now."

Esther nodded and then threw her arms around her sister. "You're so wise. How did you get that way?" She drew back to look at Julia's face.

"Trial and error."

"I saw you with Danny Coblentz Sunday evening. Do you like him?"

Julia's eyes suddenly snapped with anger. "Not in the least."

Shocked, Esther laid a hand on Julia's arm. "What happened?"

"I discovered that we aren't suited. Nancy and Pamela

seem to have found happiness here. Waneta will have to be content with that." She stood and left the room.

Esther chided herself for being wrapped up in her own feelings and not paying more attention to her sister. She had often accused her siblings of the same thing. It wasn't gratifying to discover she had the same flaw.

After changing, she went downstairs in time to see everyone heading into the kitchen. She took a deep breath and squared her shoulders. She would act like it wasn't the end of the world or of her friendship with Gabe. She could do that.

Maybe.

She went into the kitchen and took her place at the table opposite Gabe. She forced herself to smile. Everyone bowed their heads to pray except for him.

"Are you okay?" he signed.

She kept her smile in place. "I am. Thank you." She folded her hands and closed her eyes.

After a minute, Nancy nudged her to signal the prayer had ended. Esther kept her eyes on her plate for the rest of the meal, ignoring any conversation that might have gone on.

After the meal ended, the men filed out of the kitchen and into the living room. The women made quick work of the dishes and the cleanup and soon followed the men. Nancy went to sit beside Moses. Pamela and Seth joined the couple, where they began playing a board game pitting the boys against the girls. Asher was reading. Zeke had a book beside him but was dozing in his favorite chair. Julia was stitching another purse lining. Waneta and Talitha were both knitting and conversing at a small table in the corner. Gabe sat by the window with Jonah perched beside him on the arm of his chair. There was nowhere left for her to sit except across from Gabe.

Act like it's not the end of the world or the end of our friendship, she repeated to herself and sat in the chair. There was a book on birds beside it. She opened it and began reading about the birds of Florida. After a few minutes, she glanced up to find Gabe staring at her.

"Jonah, teach me some new words. What is the sign for 'I apologize' or 'I'm sorry'?"

"That's an easy one. Close your fist with your thumb outside. It's also the letter *A*. Bring your hand to your chest and make several circles." Jonah demonstrated. Gabe took his time making the gesture slowly.

Gabe repeated it several times while keeping his gaze fixed on Esther. "What about 'please forgive me'?"

Jonah glanced between Gabe and Esther as if he wasn't sure what was going on. "Hold one hand palm up and stroke it away from yourself with the tips of the fingers on your other hand. Like this."

"How do I say, 'you're forgiven'?" Gabe asked, looking at Esther.

"You're forgiven," Esther signed before Jonah could show him.

Jonah frowned at her. "Gabe asked me to teach him," he signed quickly.

"Then I am sorry, too," she said softly and signed it.

A faint smile curved Gabe's lips as he nodded slightly in her direction. "Jonah, show me how to say, 'we should talk about it tomorrow.'"

She focused on the book she held, refusing to think about the way his lips had touched hers only a little while ago. "Gabe, did you know that flamingos are gray but they turn pink because of a natural pink dye called can-thax-an-thin? I think that's how you say it. They get it from the brine shrimp and blue-green algae they eat."

She glanced at him. His grin widened. "I did."

She went back to her book. "Birds are interesting creatures." She slanted a glance his way.

"Almost as unique as flowers." He held her sketch pad toward her. "You forgot this in the garden. I brought it in last night."

"Thank you for rescuing it before the rain."

"Do you have any new sketches for leather decorations in here?"

"Actually, I do."

"May I see them?"

She scooted her chair closer to him, took the sketch pad and opened it. She skipped past the drawings of his mouth, but she was sure she was blushing, anyway. When she reached the drawings she'd made of the roses, she held the book for him to see a couple of the items that she had envisioned. "I thought a single rose on a leather key chain might be something that would sell."

He considered it for a few seconds and then nodded. "I like the idea." Then he signed, "We should talk about it tomorrow."

Esther was sure he didn't mean her sketches.

Chapter Thirteen

Esther didn't sleep much that night. She woke early and went downstairs to the kitchen. Gabe was the only other person up. He had the coffee can and the percolator in front of him by the sink.

"Let me do that," she said.

He stepped aside. She couldn't bring herself to look at his face. She was too nervous about what he would say. She couldn't bear it if he said he regretted kissing her. She would treasure the memory of those few moments for the rest of her life.

After spooning in the grounds and setting the percolator on the stove, she finally faced him. He was sitting at the table in his usual place turning an empty coffee mug around and around in his hands. He looked more nervous than she felt. In that moment she took pity on him. She hadn't considered that this might be difficult for him, too.

Pulling out her chair, she sat down, propped her elbows on the table and rested her chin on her hands. "I believe it is tomorrow. Did you have something you wanted to say?"

"I had it all rehearsed in my head, but sitting across from you now, I realize that is not what I really wanted to tell you."

"Gabe, it was a nice kiss. Plain and simple."

His eyebrows shot up. "I thought you would be angry with me."

"Surprised, but not angry. As someone recently reminded me, a kiss does not mean we are going to get married. If you are worried that I am expecting a proposal this morning, I can assure you that I'm not."

"I honestly didn't know what I thought you were expecting from me today. I care for you a lot, Esther."

"And I feel the same. You have become a very dear friend. If we let it, a simple kiss could make things awkward between us. I don't want that."

"I wouldn't call it a simple kiss."

She crossed her arms on the tabletop. Didn't he realize he was making it harder for her? "It was short but sweet."

"You're being very mature about this."

She was glad he thought so, because she wasn't feeling that way. She was shaking on the inside. "I could wring my hands and wail if you want." Oh, so easily.

Gabe relaxed for the first time since he'd left the barn with his brothers the night before. "*Nee.* I'm pleased with your attitude. I got carried away yesterday. I'm not going to say that I regret it, because I don't. I won't lie to you. I've thought about it more than once. You are a very attractive woman. But you are also my friend, and the last thing I want is for my lack of self-control to jeopardize that friendship."

She remained silent, and he wasn't sure why. "Did you understand what I said?"

"You start talking too fast when you have a lot to say. I got most of it."

"I could write it down for you if you'd like."

"I think the important part was that you don't want what happened to affect our friendship. Am I right?"

He thought the main point was that he'd considered kissing her before. Either she hadn't understood that part or she was choosing to ignore it. Whichever it was, he'd probably do best to follow her lead. "Absolutely."

She nodded and stood up. "Then we won't let it affect us. We still have some work to do to get ready for the farmers market today. We need to price the items and then pack them. We need to take enough money to make change and something for lunch, unless you want to eat at the market. Is there anything else?"

He held up his empty cup. "Can I get some coffee first?"

She grinned. "I reckon you may."

She took his cup and moved to the stove.

Gabe let out a sigh of relief. The morning was turning out so much better than he'd expected. Esther wasn't angry with him. She still intended to help him with his business, and he was going to have the pleasure of her company until she and her family left Maine after the Potato Blossom Festival. It was more than he deserved.

The one thing that nagged at him was how easily she

dismissed the moment they'd shared as a simple kiss. For him it had been anything but simple. Perhaps she didn't care for him the way he'd hoped she would. As a friend, yes, but he wanted to be more to her.

It didn't take them long to price and load his merchandise. Because it was his first time at the market, he had no idea how much he could reasonably expect to sell. Taking a lot might mean coming home with a lot, and he didn't want that. He still had his hopes pinned on the festival to generate the most income, but Esther was right. He couldn't depend on a single event to maintain his business. If Jefferson had purchased the harnesses he had talked about, it would've made all the difference. Instead Gabe was left trying to nickel and dime his way through his family's financial difficulties.

After loading the boxes in the back of the small wagon, Gabe climbed up and held his hand out to assist Esther. She hesitated, and his spirits sank. While she might claim their kiss hadn't affected their friendship, he could see that it had.

She took a step back. "I almost forgot my sketchbook."

She hurried to the house and returned a few minutes later with her quilted satchel over her shoulder. She smiled up at him and held out her hand.

"I doubt you will find any wildflowers to draw," he said.

"Perhaps not, but I can show customers other items we can make for them and even how we might personalize them."

He happily took her hand and helped her up. If his

venture was a success, it would be due to her business savvy and determination.

The trip into Fort Craig took nearly an hour. He had decided to drive one of the draft horses. Olive was a dappled gray Percheron. She wasn't as fleet of foot as Topper, but she was impressive wearing the parade harness he had made for Jefferson. The more people who saw Gabe's work, the more likely he was to find a customer for the piece.

The area set aside for the market was in the parking lot of a restaurant that had closed several years before. When they reached it, Gabe saw there were already dozens of folding tables covered in red checkered tablecloths arranged around the perimeter along with tents and wagons. There were signs for everything—straw bales, seasonal vegetables, local pork products, honey, eggs, herbs, flowers, baked goods, handmade jewelry and even fresh-brewed coffee.

He stopped Olive beside Michael Shetler's tent. Olive pawed the pavement with her huge steel-shod hooves, making a loud clatter. When she tossed her head, the bright diamond-shaped chrome dots on her bridle flashed in the sunlight. It wasn't long before she began drawing admirers.

Michael and Bethany stepped out of their tent. "I confess I'm a little jealous, Gabe. I wish I had a clock the size of your horse to advertise my merchandise."

Gabe chuckled. "She is more fidgety than our other horses. I thought her color would show off the harness nicely."

"It does."

Bethany helped Esther down from the wagon seat. "Welcome to our farmers market."

Gabe was pleased to note that his friend's wife was speaking slowly and looking directly at Esther. He wanted Esther to feel comfortable in an unfamiliar place. He needn't have worried. She and Bethany went straight to the flower stand.

Michael helped Gabe get his makeshift table of hay bales and wide boards set up beside the wagon. Esther returned with several small pots of flowers. "I thought your mother might like these for her garden."

"That's very thoughtful. I'm sure she will. Do you feel uneasy working beside me?"

"Gabe, I already told you that what happened isn't going to make a difference in our friendship."

He shoved his hands in his pockets. "That's not what I meant. Are you going to be comfortable dealing with customers?"

"Oh." Her cheeks blossomed bright red. "Of course. I will just make sure people know that I'm deaf and that I have to read their lips. I must warn you that many of them will shout at me when they learn that. You may have to learn to ignore it."

"Thanks for the warning."

Olive did her job of attracting people to Gabe's area. He spent more time letting children and adults pet her and answering their questions than selling his leather pieces. Esther did the bulk of the work behind the table. A few times he had to step in when she couldn't understand what the customer was asking. The men with bushy beards she couldn't read at all, but for the most part she did well without Gabe's assistance.

They had been at the market for almost two hours when he heard a familiar voice. "Mr. Fisher. How nice to see you."

Heather, the nurse from the clinic, came up to the table with a group of kids and adults. She smiled at Esther. "This is my husband, Randy, and our children, Frank, Carmen and Sophie. These women are Polly and Frances Minor. Friends from the School for the Deaf in Portland. They're visiting our hobby farm this week," she said as she signed.

The little boy tugged on her skirt and signed something. Heather nodded.

Esther came around from behind the table, knelt in front of the children and began signing. Her smile was bright, her motions larger and more energetic than Gabe had seen before. It was as if she had suddenly been let out of a small box. The women with Heather were equally animated and fluid in their signing. In that moment he realized ASL was a true language, not simply a string of hand motions. Even with her sisters she wasn't this expressive. Her family was always reserved when signing.

Esther rose to her feet and looked at him. Her expression was joyful. She was in her element. He was the one on the outside looking in.

"Frank would like to meet Olive, if that's okay."

"Tell him that's fine. Come along and I'll introduce you."

Esther quickly signed his reply, and the little boy

beamed with delight. Randy took the boy's hand and followed Gabe to where the mare was dozing. Gabe picked up the boy and spoke softly to Olive. She reached out to nuzzle Frank's arm. He drew back in fright. "*Nee*, it's okay. That's how she gets to know you," Gabe said.

The boy turned to his father, who signed Gabe's reassurance. The child nodded and held out his hand. His grin widened as the horse touched him with her lips. He pulled his hand away, but he was still smiling.

Gabe glanced at Randy. "Would it be okay if I put him on Olive's back?"

"Sure." The man signed for the boy, who clapped eagerly.

Gabe settled the child and showed him how to hold on to Olive's harness. The boy made a quick motion with his hands. Gabe turned to his father.

Randy chuckled. "He wants to go for a ride."

"Would your daughters like to join him?" Gabe glanced at the girls, who were standing with downcast faces.

"I'll ask." Frank signed to them, and they dashed toward Gabe.

He held up his hand to stop them. "Don't run near a horse. It can frighten them."

"Okay." The one with a pink headband signed to her sister. She turned and held up her arms to Gabe. "I'm Sophie. This is Carmen. She's deaf."

Gabe lifted Sophie to Olive's back behind Frank and noticed the girl's headband had one of the hearing aids attached to it. The second little girl wasn't wearing one.

With Randy walking beside the children, Gabe led

them on a circuit around the parking lot. Olive had given up her fidgeting and walked patiently and carefully. She knew she had children on her back.

When the ride was over, Gabe and Randy lowered the kids to the ground. They hurried away to their mother, where they vied with each other to tell the story in sign for her.

"Thanks, that was kind of you," Randy said.

"You are blessed. Children are *Gott's* most marvelous gift to us."

"I am, although some people wouldn't see three hearing-impaired children as a blessing."

Gabe nodded solemnly. "Those are the people in most need of our prayers, for they are blind in the spiritual sense no matter how good their eyesight is. Can I ask you a question about Sophie?"

"You are wondering why she wears a hearing aid and Carmen doesn't. Heather mentioned you had questions about the same kind of device for Esther."

"Ja."

"Carmen couldn't get used to being bombarded with sounds after being deaf for four years. She found it distressing. It may be a reaction to the neglect she suffered. To her, silence may be better than the screaming, shouting and fighting she witnessed when she was with her mother. We can't be sure. She is happier not hearing. Heather and I are comfortable with her choice. Frank will never hear. He was born without the nerve that connects his inner ear to his brain. No hearing aid can help him. We are a blended family in more ways than one."

"Danki—thank you."

"Sure. I do have to say you may have ruined my son's upcoming birthday."

Gabe frowned. "How so?"

"My wife and I are getting a pony for the kids. He may not measure up to Olive in their eyes."

Gabe laughed. "A horse of their own is a fine gift that they will soon love. They are welcome to come see Olive anytime they want a ride on a giant again."

"I'll tell them."

Sophie dashed toward them but slowed a few feet away and walked slowly to Gabe. "Mommy says you and Esther are invited to Frank's birthday party on Friday. Can you come?"

"Tell your mother I thank her for the invitation."

"Can you bring Olive?" Sophie asked hopefully.

Gabe glanced at Randy, smothered a smile and shook his head. "Olive will be busy working that day. My brothers are cutting wood for the winter, and she must pull the big logs with her sister Honey."

"Oh. Well, you can still come. You really have two giant horses?"

"My family owns six draft horses, plus two ordinary ones that pull our buggy."

"It must be nice to be Amish. We don't even have one horse. But we do have a dog." She turned and went back to her siblings.

Randy patted Olive's shoulder. "That's a fine harness Olive is wearing. Did you make it?"

"I did. That's my main business."

"I've been thinking about having our pony trained

to pull a cart for the children. Can you recommend a trainer?"

"My brother Asher. Olive is an example of his success. We bought her as an untrained two-year-old. She's four now. You can see how well she turned out. I'm sure Asher would be interested in training your pony."

"Great. How do I get ahold of him if I decide to go that route?"

"We have an answering machine in the phone booth we share with our Amish neighbors. You can leave a message there." Gabe gave him the number, and Randy typed it into his cell phone.

"Esther appears to be in a spirited conversation with the teachers from the School for the Deaf," Gabe said. "I've seen her using ASL with her family, but it isn't like that."

"Are her other family members deaf?"

"They aren't."

"I've read that the Amish speak their own language called Pennsylvania Dutch. Is that true?"

"It is. We call it Pennsylvania *Deitsh* or just *Deitsh*. I learned *Englisch* when I started school, as do most Amish children."

"Do you speak more freely in *Deitsh*?"

"I do. I have to think about my *Englisch* words."

"It's the same with ASL. If you use it every day, all day long, it becomes second nature. If you only use it when the deaf family member is in the room, you need to think about what you are signing. It doesn't come naturally." Randy walked back to join his wife.

As Gabe watched Esther, he wondered if his attempts

to sign amused her. He was little more than a toddler uttering his first words compared to the people she was talking to now. She was like one of the wild birds he liked to watch. She was freely fluttering her wings in the sunshine. Her song was one that only another deaf person could hear.

No matter how hard he studied sign language, it would take him years to become so accomplished. How much of what he wanted to tell her would remain unsaid or missed? He tried to imagine being married to her. How would he speak to her in the night?

Now he saw why she wanted a deaf spouse. She deserved a man she could understand and converse with easily. A man she didn't have to try to guess at what he was saying.

He cared deeply for her, but was that enough? Unless there was a hearing device that worked for her, Gabe wasn't sure he could sway her to consider him or that he should try. He wanted more than the half life she had with him now.

By the time the market closed at four o'clock, Esther had helped sell almost all of the merchandise she and Gabe had brought with them. She was delighted that her pink purses with their flowered borders had sold out, and she had orders for six more in different colors. When they finished packing up and headed for home, Esther realized that Gabe had been very quiet for the past few hours.

"We did well today," she said, looking for his reaction. He merely nodded.

"I have orders for a half dozen more purses."

He glanced her way. "That's good."

"This trip to the farmers market was a success. And yet you don't seem happy."

That drew his attention. "Of course I'm happy."

"So what is on your mind?"

He shrugged. "Nothing in particular."

"There must be, because you don't usually snub me."

He looked startled. "I'm not snubbing you. I had a nice day. I saw you had a wonderful time with your new friends."

"Is that why you are upset? Because I made new friends?"

"Of course not." He didn't say anything else.

She studied his profile as he kept his eyes straight ahead, but she couldn't drop the issue.

"Yesterday you kissed me, and this afternoon you can barely look at me. Are the two related?"

He turned Olive off the highway onto a patch of grass and stopped. He twisted in his seat to look at Esther.

"Maybe they are related. Today I saw you as you truly are."

"I don't know what you mean."

"I saw you excited to be with people like yourself."

"Deaf people." She crossed her arms against the chill that suddenly struck her. "You didn't like what you saw."

"*Nee*, that's just it. I loved what I saw. I've never seen you so comfortable and happy. Watching you I realized you are always focused on trying to understand what is being said by me and others. I thought your intense concentration was just part of who you are. I didn't realize it was part of your struggle. Jonah told me speech-reading is hard, but I didn't realize how much effort you put into it until today. With those people, you didn't have to work at understanding them. It was amazing to see."

She had no idea what to say. After a few moments, he got the horse moving again. She traveled beside him in silence wondering how his revelation would change things between them, because she sensed that it had. When they reached his home, he carried the leftover merchandise back in the shop and set the box on his desk.

"Are we going to work this evening?" she asked.

He shook his head and then turned around. "I must help my father and brothers cut wood. They are working down along the river. I'll join them shortly. I'd like you to make a few dozen more purses and key chains. Those were popular."

She didn't want him to leave with this strain between them. "It was nice of you to give Heather's children a ride on Olive."

A smile tugged at the corner of his mouth. "I liked Heather's *kinder* and her husband."

"Are you going to Frank's birthday party?"

"Maybe. Will you go?"

"I'd love to, if you wouldn't mind taking me. I don't like to drive."

"I did not know that. Of course I'll take you."

"*Danki.* Gabe, are we okay?"

"Sure."

"I'm not any different than I was two days ago."

He pressed his lips into a tight line and nodded. "Maybe I am. I want you to be happy. You know that, don't you?"

She gestured around the room. "Well, this makes me happy."

He pushed away from the desk. "That's good, because we have a lot more work to do."

After he left, Esther set about cutting out several more patterns. She had been working for about half an hour when the outside door opened. Mr. Jefferson walked in. He scanned the room. "Where's Gabe?"

"Down at the river, cutting wood. If you would like to leave a message, I think I have a pen and paper here somewhere."

She opened her satchel, searched for a suitable piece of paper and then pulled it out along with a pencil. When she looked up, Jefferson was walking out.

"So no message?" she signed in annoyance.

She walked to the door to look out and saw him driving away. Shrugging off his brusque manner, she went back to work.

That evening after supper, she sat on the sofa putting the finishing touches on a new dress. Jonah walked by with the book of sign language that had come in the mail for Gabe that day and carried it to him. She couldn't see what Jonah was saying, but she imagined he was asking Gabe if he wanted to learn some new signs.

Gabe shook his head, took the book from Jonah and laid it aside. "Let's play a game of checkers instead."

"Mr. Jefferson stopped by," she said. "Did he find you?"

Jonah turned to her. "Gabe wants to know what he wanted."

"He didn't say. He just left."

Gabe never even glanced at her.

Esther focused on her needlework again. Something had changed today. In her heart she knew they weren't okay.

Chapter Fourteen

Esther was glad when Gabe left to cut wood again after lunch. Their morning work had kept them both busy. They found little time to speak to each other. Or rather, they had avoided speaking to one another. She didn't understand it. Had his amazing kiss meant nothing?

If he wasn't upset that she had made new friends, what was the issue? Had she somehow offended him? It wasn't like Gabe to be so withdrawn. They had been able to talk about almost anything. Why couldn't he tell her what was wrong? Should she press him when he returned? She wasn't sure what she should do.

She was cleaning up the leather scraps from around his cutting table when Julia came in.

"I came to let you know that I'm leaving with Bessie on Saturday," she signed.

Esther set her broom aside. "Why?"

"I'm ready to go home."

"Is it because of Danny?"

Julia nodded. "He came to see me yesterday. I told

him not to come back. I think the best thing is to leave before he does."

"Sister, you must tell me what's going on."

"You know I rejected Ogden Martin's proposal last fall, but you don't know everything. I tried to let him down gently, but he was persistent. He followed me wherever I went, to town, to visit friends. The worst of it was when his parents came to chastise me for treating their son so poorly."

"I knew they came to see you. I didn't realize that was why."

"Ogden cornered me in the grocery store a few days later to tell me I had broken his mother's heart. It was the last straw. I told him to stay away from me or the bishop would hear about his behavior. I honestly never thought I would have to do that, but when Ogden stopped me on the road a few days later, I felt I had no choice. The bishop was sympathetic to me. I had feared he would take Ogden's side, but he went to Ogden's home to speak to him. Ogden's parents were mortified, but at least he finally stopped bothering me."

"What does that have to do with Danny? Is he behaving poorly?"

"Danny and Ogden are cousins who were very close when they were young. Ogden wrote Danny to tell him I would be visiting the Fishers. Danny sought me out here to find out if I was as heartless as Ogden said and to ask why I treated him so badly. I foolishly thought it was because he liked me."

"He didn't say that, did he?" Esther was shocked.

Danny had seemed like such a nice man, though she had only met him briefly.

"Danny has his mind made up about me. I am not going to try to change it. So I'm leaving."

"Julia, I'm so sorry."

"Don't be. I believe the Lord is leading me toward a single life. I will be the doting *aenti* for Nancy and Pamela's children. And for yours."

"You will be a wonderful *aenti*. Clearly, Danny is a fool if he can't see what a sweet person you are."

"What about you? Are you ready to go home? You looked so glum at breakfast this morning."

Maybe that was what she was supposed to do—go home. Gabe would have to manage his business alone, but she had done a lot to improve his chances of success. "I'm not sure what I should do. Part of me wants to stay here until after the festival. Another part of me says there isn't much point." Not unless something changed.

"I would dearly love to have your company on the trip home."

"I'll consider it." She gave her sister a hug. "I will miss you, even if it's only for a short time."

Julia drew back and signed, "I will miss you, too."

After Julia left, Esther sat down at the sewing machine. It didn't seem fair that her oldest sister's hopes for marriage and motherhood had been dashed by two men in the same family. Danny was a friend of Gabe's. Would Gabe intervene if Esther told him what Julia said?

After five hours spent with a chain saw, Gabe was happy to finally get the wood chips and sawdust out of his hair. As he stepped out of the bathroom after washing up, he almost ran into Nancy as she came bouncing down the hall.

"Have you seen Moses?" she asked cheerfully.

"He's bringing up the last sled load of logs. He should be here any time."

"Okay, *danki*." She turned to go back the way she had come, but Gabe stopped her. "Nancy, can I ask you something?"

"Sure."

He took a few steps closer to her. "The day Esther and I went to the clinic, you picked up a brochure on a new kind of hearing aid."

"I did. What about it?"

"Esther said she wasn't interested, but you took one, anyway. Why? Was it for Esther? Do you think it can help her?"

Nancy grew serious. "I took it for myself."

He frowned. "Are you losing your hearing? Jonah said he believed it skipped you and your sisters."

"My hearing is fine. It's just that I know that any children I have may go deaf. I want to be prepared. I want to learn as much about treatments as I can."

"I see."

She smiled. "I have told Moses about my concern. He said *Gott* decides."

"He is absolutely right and a man of strong faith. If you are discussing children, the two of you must be getting serious."

"We are. I didn't think I would like anyone that Waneta picked out for me. I was wrong. Moses is adorable."

"I never thought of him like that."

"What about you and Esther? The two of you are spending a lot of time together."

"I can't deny that I care for her, but she doesn't want me." It was painful to think the two women he had come to love in his life didn't desire him as a husband. The truth was he did love Esther, even if he couldn't admit it to anyone.

"Julia got the impression that Esther was getting very serious about you. Maybe the two of you should talk. If you need someone to sign for you to make sure she understands what you're saying, any one of us would be glad to help."

She walked off with a happy bounce in her step. She and Moses would be well suited.

Gabe raided the kitchen for a couple of cookies and then walked into the living room. Through the window he saw Esther in the garden with her sketchbook in hand. His heart filled with love at the mere sight of her. There were things he couldn't imagine. Not having her in his life was the hardest.

Maybe he was the wrong man for her, but that must be her decision. She deserved to know that he loved her, but first he needed to apologize and rebuild her trust.

Gabe went out the door into the garden. Esther didn't notice him until his shadow fell across her. She squinted at him silhouetted against the sun. "You're back."

He moved to stand in front of her and held out his hand. "Cookie?"

She gave him a funny look but took it. *"Danki."*

He squatted on his heels and pointed to her sketch pad. "What are you working on?"

"A few more rose sketches and some of the iris." She turned the paper so he could see.

He tapped the last rose she had drawn. "I like this one."

"So do I. What about putting it on a few of your tool belts? Women like Lilly also own tools."

He gazed into her troubled eyes. "Some men appreciate the beauty of flowers, too." He held his fist against his chest and made two circles. "I'm sorry."

"For what?"

"Acting like a cranky toddler."

A grin twitched at the corner of her mouth. "Which time?"

He smiled and nodded. "I deserved that."

"What did I do?"

That shocked him. "You didn't do anything. Yesterday I watched you signing with such eagerness. You and those other people were so fluid in your movements. I felt awkward and left out. That must be how you feel sometimes."

"That's true."

"I've gotten used to having you all to myself. I don't begrudge you making friends. You should have more. I wanted to join the conversation, but I didn't know how. I've never felt so inadequate."

"Signing easily takes time. You are learning, Gabe."

"Not fast enough to suit me. I guess I'm impatient. Anyway, that's what caused my sour mood. And don't say 'which time.'"

"Thank you for telling me."

"I hope we can always share what's on our minds. Both *goot* and not so *goot*."

Her forgiving smile warmed his heart, but she looked away, leading him to suspect she had something else she wanted to say. He didn't have to wonder long.

"Gabe, how well do you know Danny Coblentz?"

"Pretty well, I think."

"He has upset Julia. She's leaving Saturday because of it."

"Upset her how?"

"He accused her of smearing his cousin's good name back home."

That didn't sound like his friend. "Are you sure?"

"Danny's cousin proposed to Julia last fall. She refused him. He wouldn't take no for an answer. He was constantly nagging her to change her mind. He even had his parents try to persuade her. She finally had the bishop confront him and his family. There were a lot of hard feelings. He wrote to Danny that we were coming here."

"What would you like me to do?"

"Just speak to him. Tell him Julia isn't the callous woman he believes her to be."

"I'll talk to him. Hear his side."

"That's fair enough. I don't want Julia to leave under these circumstances. I don't want her to leave at all."

"So. Are we okay now?"

"I believe we are."

"Until the next time I behave foolishly."

She tipped her head slightly. "Will there be a next time?"

"I'm pretty sure there will be. It's a hard habit to break. I wanted to ask you about a gift for Frank."

"I've thought about that, too. Any ideas?"

"How difficult would it be to make him a cowboy vest? He's getting a pony."

"Not hard at all if I have the right kind of leather."

"I may have some thin scraps you can use. We can look later."

"We may as well go look now." She held out her hand.

He rose and helped her to her feet. He didn't release her hand. Instead he twined her fingers with his. The look of longing in her eyes almost broke his control, but he didn't kiss her. Instead he began walking with her at his side. Which was exactly where he wanted her for the rest of his life.

He glanced at her face. She was looking down, but a gentle smile curved her lips. He resisted the urge to kiss her and looked straight ahead. Their fragile relationship wasn't meant to be rushed. He squeezed her fingers. It was meant to be cherished.

Esther allowed Gabe to hold her hand as they crossed the farmyard. He wasn't a perfect man, but he was a good one. It had taken some courage to tell her he felt inadequate compared to the new Deaf friends she had made. Not every fellow could do that.

She sensed more than saw his restraint when he had helped her to her feet. She almost wished that he had kissed her. She wanted to see if it would be as breath-taking as it had been the first time. He held open the door of the workshop, and she slipped past him. If she were bold enough, she might entice him to repeat the gesture. Only she wasn't sure she had that much spice in her makeup.

The next morning Gabe brought around the buggy. His mother came out as Esther was getting in to press a box into her hands. "Just a few cinnamon rolls for them to enjoy. They are Gabe's favorite treat."

"Which explains why you are making me give them away. That's cruel, *Mamm*," he said.

"There are more for you to have later."

Gabe pointed his finger at her. "Keep Moses away from them or all I'll get are crumbs."

It was nearly fifteen miles to Heather and Randy's hobby farm. Topper's gait was unflagging as his trot ate up the miles, but it still took over an hour and a half to reach their destination.

As they pulled up in front of the house, the children came rushing out to see the horse first, and then Sophie went to Esther's door. She opened it and the child climbed up the step. Today she was wearing a yellow headband with white polka dots. "You'll never guess what Frank got for his birthday present. Never in a million years. Go ahead, guess," she said as she signed for Esther's benefit.

Esther looked at Gabe. He cupped his fingers over his chin and winked at her. "I am going to guess that he got a pony."

Sophie's eyes widened, then she smacked her forehead with her hand. "How did you know?"

"I'm sure a little birdie told him," Esther said.

Sophie's eyes narrowed. "I think it was my dad."

Randy came to take the box of cinnamon rolls from Esther and help her out of the buggy. He sniffed the packet. "This smells good."

"A gift from Gabe's mother," Esther told him.

"I believe she's someone I want to know better. Please come inside."

With Gabe beside her, Esther followed Randy into the house. The kitchen table held a cake with blue and white frosting with five candles off to the side. It had already been cut. There were smears of blue frosting on the table and glasses.

Balloons had been tied to the backs of each chair. Polly and Frances Minor were seated at the table. Polly held a toddler on her lap. There were five other children playing a game in the living room.

Heather, looking slightly frazzled, came to greet Esther. "I'm so glad you could come," she said as she signed. Esther knew she spoke aloud for Gabe's sake, and she was grateful.

"She brought these," Randy signed and handed the box to his wife.

She lifted the lid, looked inside and set the box down. "Oh, good. More sugar. Just what the little monsters need."

The toddler on Polly's lap signed that she wanted one. Heather relented and cut her a small piece. The child's eyes lit up with delight at her first bite. She signed her thanks.

Gabe stepped close to Esther. She almost laughed at the hangdog expression on his face. "Talk about feeling inadequate. That baby signs better than I do."

She patted his arm reassuringly. "Babies can learn to sign before they learn to speak."

"Really?"

"It's true."

"I'm going to go see the new horse. At least I am something of an expert in the barn."

Esther enjoyed visiting with Polly and Frances again. She learned a lot about their programs at the school where they taught. She shared some of her concerns about the special-needs school where she worked. After discussing it, they assured her the Amish community was supplying their students with the latest curriculum and teaching tools. One by one the parents of the other children came to take them home until only Heather's children remained. Frank went outside to find his father.

Heather sat down. "I wish we had a School for the Deaf closer to us. The local school board assures us their public school can accommodate our needs, but I have some doubts. Especially for Carmen. She is easily frightened. We don't want her to regress because we've pushed her too hard. We bought this place because we wanted our children to grow up in the country and because Randy is from this area. I think we're going to homeschool the children this year or until we can find a private tutor."

Sophie and Carmen rushed to Esther's side. "We are having a tea party. Won't you join us?"

Esther saw Carmen wore a headband identical to Sophie's. Esther glanced at Heather and signed, "Is Carmen wearing her hearing aid in her headband?"

"She is, but it's turned off. She wanted to match her sister today."

Esther turned to the girls. "I would love to join your tea party." She signed as she spoke so both could understand.

Carmen took Esther's hand and tugged on it. Laughing, Esther allowed the child to lead her to their room, where they had a teapot and cups arranged on a small table with chairs. Carmen promptly took her headband off and laid it aside, messing up her fine blond hair in the process.

Sophie gave everyone a cup and began to pour the imaginary tea. Carmen passed around a plate of plastic cookies that Esther pretended to eat. The scene reminded her of how she and her sisters used to play on the kitchen floor while their mother looked on and cooked. There was always the smell of fresh-baked bread in the house.

Sophie picked up Carmen's headband. "This is for you, Esther. Carmen doesn't want it."

"Thank you, Sophie." Esther held out her hand for the gift.

"I'll put it on. I know how it goes." She slipped the headband over Esther's *kapp* and adjusted it. Esther didn't hear anything.

"Oh, I need to turn it on." Sophie touched the hearing

aid. A loud squeal filled Esther's head. She flinched at the painful shock of the sound. "Turn it off."

Before Sophie touched it again, the squealing stopped and a jumble of sounds rushed in to fill the void. Esther held her breath. She concentrated to try to identify them. Carmen was clacking two cups together. The wind whistled softly beneath the partially opened window. She heard birds outside. The sound was piercing. She hadn't heard a bird's song in years. Then she heard laughter coming from the kitchen.

Sophie looked over Esther's shoulder. "Would you like a cup of tea, sir?" Was that right? Had she heard correctly. It was so disorienting.

A deep, rumbling laugh sent chills down Esther's spine. "No, thank you. I would take a cup of coffee if you have one to go with my cinnamon roll?"

The sounds faded in and out. Esther struggled to stay upright as she grew faint.

"Sure. Here you are." Sophie carried a cup behind Esther.

"*Danki*, lovely lady."

Esther's vision blurred. She knew whose voice it was. One she had heard in her dreams but never expected to hear in her lifetime. She slowly turned around. Gabe stood sipping from his tiny cup and smiling at his hostess.

He handed the cup back to Sophie. "I've come to take my Esther home with me. Is she ready?"

Carmen patted Esther's arm. "You're crying. I don't like that thing, either."

Esther pulled off the headband and rubbed her face

with both hands. "I'm ready to go. Thank you for the tea."

She kept her face down so Gabe wouldn't notice her tearstained face. In the kitchen Heather spied her and quickly came to her side. "What's wrong?"

"Nothing. I'll be fine. Thank you for the invitation. I hope Frank likes his vest. Goodbye."

She wanted to run out the door, but she walked slowly to the buggy and got in. She closed her eyes and turned her face to the window. "I'm sorry. I have a headache."

Gabe touched her arm. She couldn't look at him. He set Topper in motion and headed home.

As the fields of potato blossoms rolled past, Esther came to grips with what had happened. She had heard Gabe's voice. The voice of the man she was falling in love with. Fresh tears threatened, but she blinked them back.

She had once met a deaf man who sometimes wore his cochlear hearing aid and sometimes didn't. When she asked him why he didn't choose one or the other, he said it didn't matter. He was a Deaf person who could sometimes hear sounds, but he was still a Deaf man.

It was the same with her. She didn't need to hear to be happy. Today had been a traumatic, painful and thankfully brief visit into the hearing world, but it had given her a gift she would cherish forever. The sound of Gabe's voice. But she was part of the Deaf community, and she wouldn't change that. They were people with a vibrant language, their own heroes, history and folk stories. God allowed her to be deaf, but He had given her much more than He had taken away.

By the time Gabe stopped the buggy, she had her emotions well in check. She turned to face him and smiled. "I'm sorry I was poor company."

"Are you better?"

"I am."

He took her hand. "I'm glad. I was worried about you."

"You needn't be."

"Maybe not, but I'd like to be the one who has the right to be concerned for you. What happened in the girls' bedroom? I saw your tears. Was it because of the hearing aid the children let you wear?"

He saw way too much. She had once told him he was observant. Now she had more proof. "I can't talk about it yet, Gabe."

"But someday?"

"Someday. I promise. Gabe, can you accept me as I am?"

"Of course. I adore you the way you are." He leaned in and kissed her forehead. "I'm the flawed one. Can you accept me?"

"Without question."

He cupped her cheek with his hand. "You're a brave woman. We have a lot more to discuss, but not right now."

She looked outside and saw they were at the school. "What are we doing here?"

"I told you I would talk to Danny. He lives beside the school. I won't be long."

"Okay. I'll be fine."

He got out and crossed to a small house on the south side of the school building. He opened the door and went inside.

He had said he would speak to Danny. She was glad he was keeping his word.

His words. *I've come to take my Esther home with me.* She recalled the exact timbre of his voice. *My Esther.*

She was—or she wanted to be—his Esther. It didn't matter that he could hear any more than it mattered that she couldn't. His heart spoke to hers.

There were going to be challenges for them, she knew that. He could be impatient. She was stubborn. They might clash on any number of subjects, but he accepted her.

She pressed both hands over her chest as joy flooded her heart. He accepted her.

Chapter Fifteen

Gabe stepped into Danny's kitchen. His friend was washing the dishes. Danny dried his hands on a towel. "I'm ashamed to say I let them pile up until I run out of clean plates. Shall I guess why you're here?"

"Sounds like you already have an idea."

"I was rude to one of your guests. I'm not proud of the fact. I intend to apologize and beg forgiveness."

"You may not get that opportunity. I told Esther that I would speak to you and hear your side, but Julia currently plans to leave tomorrow."

Danny hung his head. "I'm sorry to hear that."

"I have come to know Julia as a sweet, modest woman. I understand you have cause to think otherwise."

"I may have been misinformed. I was shocked when I received my cousin's letters detailing his humiliation and asking me to plead his case to Julia while she was here. If she wouldn't reconsider his offer, he wanted me to make sure folks here knew she wasn't to be trusted.

I believed every word he wrote, but I wasn't going to ruin her reputation. After talking to Julia, I belatedly came to realize that my cousin may have misled me. This morning I put a call through to the bishop of his district. He corroborated Julia's story. In all honesty, I never thought my cousin was capable of such behavior. I must forgive him. So must Julia. I'll come to your home this evening and beg her forgiveness."

"I don't think she'll see you."

"In that case, please assure her that I won't bother her again. Tell her I'm sorry and I hope she can forgive me."

"I will give her your message. The family plans to stay until after the Potato Blossom Festival. Hopefully Julia will stay, too." He turned on his heels and left his friend's house, disappointed in his behavior toward Esther's sister.

Esther was waiting impatiently in the buggy. "What did he say?"

"He sends his apologies and promises not to see her again. And he asks her forgiveness. Will that be enough to keep Julia here?"

"I don't know. She was very upset. I don't want her to leave. We are finally becoming friends again."

Because it meant so much to Esther, Gabe would do his best to convince Julia to stay. "I'll speak to her."

"Thank you," she signed. "I think I'll take over Jonah's teaching duties."

He tweaked her nose. "I'd like that. A lot."

Her laughter was music to his ears. He drove home in a happy mood. Things were looking up between them.

At the house, he stopped Topper by the front gate

and turned to Esther. "Why don't you ask Julia to come see me in my workshop?"

"All right. I'll be down later to start working on the rose patterns."

"While I was in the barn with Randy today, he suggested we make some laptop carrying cases. I think the idea has merit. I'll have to find a pattern that's simple but sturdy."

"Perhaps Lilly has a laptop we can use to get dimensions."

"*Goot* idea. We can go see her tomorrow."

Gabe gave Topper a rubdown, watered him and stabled him with fresh hay. When he opened his workshop door, he found Julia waiting for him. She was sitting in Esther's chair in front of the leather stitcher.

"You wanted to speak to me?"

He leaned against his cutting table. "I went to see Danny today."

Julia pressed her lips into a tight line and tipped her head back. "I can't believe Esther involved you in this."

"She cares about you. So do I. She doesn't want you to leave. She feels she has grown closer to you and your sisters since your arrival here."

"We have. I love Esther, but I'm not going to endure the same treatment I suffered at home."

"Danny has realized he made a mistake taking his cousin's word about your behavior."

"Well, good. Better late than never," she snapped.

"He called your bishop and heard the whole story. He's ashamed and embarrassed. He has promised not to see you again. He begs your forgiveness."

"You think he means it? He won't bother me again?"

"I believe he is sincere. I've known Danny for two years. He's never done anything like this. He knows he made a mistake, and he regrets it. I hope this eases your mind enough to feel you can stay with us awhile longer."

"Ogden can be very persuasive. I should know. All right, I'll stay."

"Esther will be delighted."

She tipped her head slightly. "That's important to you, isn't it?"

"More than you know. I've made several missteps in my relationship with Esther. I don't want that to happen again. She is very dear to me."

"As long as you accept Esther for who she is without reservations, you'll do fine. If I can help in any way, please let me know."

"I may hold you to that."

The outside door opened, and Esther came in. "Are you staying, sister?"

Julia nodded. "Your young man has convinced me to remain."

"I'm so glad." She hugged her sister and then reached for his hand. She squeezed his fingers. *"Danki."*

The happiness in her eyes was all the reward Gabe could have asked for.

Over the next two days, Esther wasn't sure she had ever been so happy. She and Gabe worked side by side in the shop all day Saturday. In the evening they walked to Lilly's farm through the woods. Lilly used her computer to show Gabe what kind of carrying cases were on the market for laptops.

The off Sunday, the one without a church service, was spent in quiet reflection and Bible reading during the morning. The afternoon was devoted to visiting friends. Three local families stopped in to enjoy Talitha's cinnamon rolls and coffee. Esther's sisters and Jonah took turns signing so she was able to enjoy the company, too.

On Monday Gabe and Esther were back at work in the shop. Gabe took inventory of the leather they had available and discovered he didn't have enough to make more than one laptop case. "I reckon I'll have to take another trip into Fort Craig. I hope Ed has enough of the weight I need."

"We are low on the dyed leather for purses, too."

"I think it's best we don't go to the farmers market this Wednesday. That way will have more merchandise to take with us to the festival next week."

"Have we made enough pieces?"

"To fill our booth, yes. Will we earn enough money to make the venture worthwhile? I'm not sure."

She wanted to ease his concern. "What more can we do?"

"Keep working. I'll go to Fort Craig tomorrow. That will give us a few days yet to produce more."

"I wish we knew what would sell the best. We could concentrate on making more of those."

"Unfortunately, this first year will be mostly trial and error."

That evening Esther began teaching Gabe the sign

language alphabet. Talitha joined them for her first lesson. To Esther's surprise, Waneta asked to sit in, too. Nancy and Pamela decided to instruct Moses and Seth in signing. Both couples managed to find quiet corners in the garden to practice. Esther wasn't sure how much teaching was actually accomplished.

On Tuesday morning Gabe left early for the trip into Fort Craig. Esther was stitching the last two belts when her stepmother came in. Waneta made a circuit of the room examining the machinery and boxes of items Esther had finished embellishing. She finally stopped in front of Esther's machine.

"How can you abide working in this smelly place?"

"I like the scent of leather."

"That's fortunate."

"Did you want something?"

Waneta clasped her hands together. "I believe I owe you an apology."

"For?"

"My impatience with you. Julia pointed out that I have—" She turned to the side, and Esther wasn't able to read what she was saying.

"I'm afraid you must face me, Waneta. I can't see what you're saying otherwise."

Waneta flushed bright red and stammered, "Of— of course. I was saying that I may have treated you poorly. For that I'm sorry. You may not believe it, but I love your father. He has struggled with your decision not to use your cochlear implant, and I felt I had to support him."

"I'm aware of my father's feelings."

"That being said, Talitha and I have noticed how much Gabe depends on you and how happy he seems lately. I have always liked the boy, and it's gratifying to know my decision to bring you along has met with his approval. That's really all I wanted to say. We should—" She turned away and walked out, leaving Esther wondering what it was they should do.

She shrugged and went back to sewing.

When Gabe returned in the early afternoon, bright joy filled Esther at the sight of him. She cared for him so much. She couldn't deny her feelings any longer. She loved him. He cared for her, too. She knew by the way his eyes lit up when he caught sight of her.

"Ed Carson's place was closed," he said and hung his hat on the peg by the door. He held a small package in one hand.

"You had a wasted trip. That's too bad. Will you go again tomorrow?"

"There isn't any point. He's closed until after the festival. The shopkeeper next door said he's gone to visit his daughter in New York. She just had a baby."

Gabe walked across the shop floor and sat down at his desk. He laid the package on top of it then he slumped forward with his elbows on his knees. "There isn't another tanner in the region."

"We can't get more leather?"

"I'm afraid not. This is a setback I didn't foresee."

"There's no way you could have."

"Okay. Well, my trip wasn't a complete waste of time." He picked up the package and held it out to her.

She took it gingerly. "What's this?"

"A small gift for you."

She opened it and pulled out a book. Colorful flowers adorned the cover. *"Wildflowers of Maine, Quebec and New Brunswick."* She smiled as her heart grew light at the thought of his kindness. "For me?"

"The shop next to Ed's place is a bookstore. Do you like it?"

"I love it. Now I can discover the names of the flowers I see."

"Weeds. There's an index. Look under *W.*"

She hugged it to her chest. *"Danki.* It was very thoughtful of you."

"You've worked hard without pay this past two weeks. It's only a small token of my appreciation."

"I'll treasure it always."

She was smiling now, and that was all Gabe wanted. To make her happy. "You've done enough work in here today. Let's go find out how good your book is. Maybe you can find a flower that isn't in it."

"All right. Where to?"

"The woods and then the bog. Unless you have somewhere else you'd like to explore."

"That sounds lovely. I'll get my sketch pad."

"I'll raid the kitchen for some snacks. I missed lunch."

Fifteen minutes later, they entered the cool woods behind the barn. Instead of taking the path to the Arnett farm, Gabe chose one that led toward a small clearing where an old cabin stood. He and his brothers had discovered it when they first came to Maine. It had been deserted for years, but he remembered the place being surround by flowers when he first saw it.

The path led upward into the wooded hills above New Covenant. There were several places with fine views of the mountains and the winding river below. He took Esther's hand to help her over fallen logs or boulders that jutted out of the ground. When the path widened out and they could walk side by side, he took her hand again and held it. She smiled shyly but didn't pull away.

They stopped at an opening in the trees. The valley lay spread out below in a checkered patchwork of fields and farms. She grinned. "This is beautiful."

He gazed at her face. "Yes, you are," he said softly, knowing that she wasn't looking at him.

She opened her book. "Let me see what these little white flowers are."

He took the book from her. "The better flower show is a little farther down the trail."

"If you say so, but I would like to know the name of this one."

"It's a weed."

"You have no appreciation for the simple things."

"Not when spectacular looms just around the corner."

"Lead on to this amazing scene, if you must."

He took her hand and led the way. A group of cedar trees had overgrown part of the path. He stopped there. "Cover your eyes."

"What?"

"Cover your eyes. I won't let you stumble."

She did. "What are you up to?"

He didn't answer. She couldn't see his mouth, anyway. He led her around the trees and stopped. Then he gently pulled her hands away from her face. "Not weeds."

He stepped aside. The clearing was filled with a carpet of pink, lavender, purple and white spires of lupine. She gasped and stepped out into the masses. "They're beautiful."

He moved close to her and caught her by the shoulders. "You're beautiful. I think I love you, Esther. I'm going to kiss you."

"It's about time." She smiled and circled his neck with her arms.

He pulled her close. She fit so perfectly next to him. She lifted her face to his. He couldn't resist a moment longer. He gently kissed her lips. When she didn't pull away, he cupped her head in his hands and deepened the kiss as tenderness flooded his soul. She hadn't said that she loved him, but he knew in his heart that she did. He could wait until she was ready to say the words.

Joy filled every fiber of Esther's being. She tightened her arms around Gabe's neck, drawing closer to him. His lips left hers. Before she could protest, his mouth moved across her cheek to her temple. Then he kissed her eyes and nuzzled her ear. She sighed with contentment. When he drew away, she opened her eyes. "That was better than the first time."

He chuckled. She could feel the vibrations in his chest beneath her hands. He slipped a finger under her chin and lifted her face. "Practice makes perfect."

"Then we should practice some more." She planted a peck on his lips.

He held her away. "It's a long walk back, and we still have work to do."

"Did I mention that my arm and shoulder ache from working the lever on the stitcher so much?"

"I can take over now that my arm is better. Any other excuses? A headache, perhaps?"

"My head is fine. Thank you for bringing me here. This is lovely."

"I knew you'd like it."

Together they started back to the house. Halfway there she saw Pamela and Seth strolling toward them.

Esther smiled at her sister. "The view is lovely up ahead, but go all the way to the little cabin."

"I know." Pamela slanted a glance at Seth. "We've been there already."

"Is Gabe a good kisser?" **Pamela signed.** "Your lips are a little puffy."

Esther touched them with one finger. The feel of Gabe's kiss lingered there still. She cast a covert glance his way. "He's good, but he needs more practice."

Pamela burst out laughing while Gabe and Seth looked on with confused expressions. She linked her arm with Seth and drew him along the path.

Gabe arched one eyebrow as he stared at Esther. "What did you say?"

"It was just a little sisterly gossip."

He took her hand and walked on. When they came around the barn, Esther saw a car parked in front of the house. She recognized it as the one Mr. Jefferson had driven away in. He appeared to be in a heated discussion with Zeke as Asher and Moses stood behind their father.

She looked up at Gabe. "What's going on?"

"I don't know."

As they drew closer, Mr. Jefferson caught sight of her. He pointed. "She's the one. She took my order. I needed those harnesses today."

Zeke turned to Esther. "Did you take an order from this man for six parade harnesses?"

"No. He came into the workshop. I told him Gabe was out cutting wood. I asked if he wanted to leave a message. I searched for a pen and paper. When I found them and looked up, he was leaving."

"So you didn't hear me say I needed eight parade harnesses like the one you folks showed me by today? If you people can't get the work done, then I'll take my business elsewhere."

Esther's heart was about to pound out of her chest. "I didn't hear you because I'm Deaf, sir. I can lip-read, but only if you are looking at me."

His anger deflated. "Oh. Well, how was I to know? Why didn't you say something?"

"You didn't give me the chance."

"I'm sorry about that, but you shouldn't be working where folks expect verbal orders to be taken. I could sue you people for breach of contract."

Zeke scowled. "A handshake is how we seal a contract, Mr. Jefferson. That's the way we do business. If there was no handshake, there was no deal."

"You Amish." Hank Jefferson stomped off to his car and drove away.

Esther pressed a hand to her cheek as she looked at Gabe. "I've cost you thousands of dollars in lost business. I'm so sorry."

Zeke laid a hand on her shoulder. "*Gott* allowed it. Who are we to question His will?" He walked into the barn. Asher and Moses followed him.

Gabe seemed to sag under the weight of what had happened. "It would have made all the difference, but—"

She didn't catch what else he said, for he had started walking away. She followed him to the workshop. He went to the desk and sat down with his head in his hands.

"I'm sorry."

He shrugged and looked up. "It was my fault as much as yours. I have invoice order forms. I should have told you about them and put them out for you to use."

He pulled open the desk drawer. His hand froze in midair. He slowly lifted out a piece of paper and looked at her. "This is something else I've been meaning to speak to you about."

She saw it was a brochure like the ones in the doctor's office about hearing aids. Esther took a step back. Pain shot through her chest. She couldn't breathe. *Not again. Don't let it happen again, God.* "No! No. Put it away. Better yet, throw it in the trash."

His eyes were full of confusion and disappointment. "Tell me why you won't at least consider this option? It's not the same as a cochlear implant. Don't you want to hear?"

"I am as *Gott* made me. I'm Deaf. I'm not broken. I

don't need to be fixed. Do you understand me? I'm not broken! I thought you loved me." Tears began streaming down her cheeks.

He took a step toward her with his hand out. "Esther, I do love you, but I don't understand."

She moved back out of his reach. "Then it's not the kind of love I want."

She spun around and ran out of the building.

Chapter Sixteen

Gabe paced at the foot of the stairs until Julia appeared at the top of them. It was Esther he wanted to see. Needed to see. She had retreated to her bedroom yesterday, and she hadn't come down since. It was almost noon.

"How is she?" he asked.

"Surprisingly calm." Julia came down the stairs.

"Will she see me?"

Julia sadly shook her head. "She won't."

"I have to see her. I have to make her understand. I was disappointed by what happened, but I don't blame her."

"She blames herself for the loss of Mr. Jefferson's business. She knows how important it was to you."

"I don't care about his business. I care about Esther." He turned around and paced across the hall and back. "She has to talk to me eventually."

"*Nee*, she doesn't. She sent Jonah to Lilly Arnett."

"For what reason?"

"She needs a ride to the bus station in Fort Craig this afternoon. She's leaving."

Gabe sank onto the bottom step and cupped his hands over the back of his neck. "She can't do that."

Julia patted his shoulder. "You don't know my sister as well as you think you do. She can and she will travel by bus all the way home to Millersburg, Ohio, by herself unless I go with her."

He looked up at Julia. "Tell me what I can do to change her mind," he pleaded.

"I honestly don't know. She has been deeply hurt, but it is frightening how calm she is."

"I don't believe this is happening. How could it have all gone so wrong?"

"That's something only you can answer."

He looked up the stairwell. He wanted to shout Esther's name, make her see him, but no matter how loudly he called for her, she would never hear it. And that was part of his fear. She could shut him out completely whenever she wanted.

He heard a car drive up outside. If it was Lilly, maybe he could talk her out of taking Esther to the bus station. He went to the window and saw it was Heather and Randy. Asher came in. "There's a couple here who want to purchase a harness for their pony. Do you know anything about it?"

"They are friends of Esther's. Would you be interested in training a pony to pull a cart?"

"Sure. Little horses don't hurt as much when they step on your foot."

His brother was trying to be funny, but Gabe didn't

see the humor in anything. "I'll speak to them." He wasn't doing himself or the family any good keeping vigil at the foot of the stairs.

Heather smiled brightly at him. "We have decided there will be less squabbling over the pony if the children can all ride in a cart together."

"It's a *goot* plan."

"Do you need to take measurements for the harness?" Randy asked.

"*Nee*, I've seen your fellow. My pony-size harness will fit him fine. There is plenty of room to make adjustments in the straps."

Heather glanced toward the house. "Where is Esther?"

"Avoiding me."

"Oh. That doesn't sound good."

"She's leaving Maine today."

Zeke walked up. "What is this?"

Gabe nodded. "Esther is leaving."

"I'm sorry, *sohn*." Zeke laid a hand on Gabe's shoulder. Gabe had to fight back tears.

"I'm sorry, too," Heather said. "What happened, if it is any of my business?"

Maybe Heather could shine some light on Esther's behavior. She was familiar with a few Deaf people. He repeated what had happened as best he could. "I still don't understand why she refused to consider a hearing aid. Surely it would make life so much easier for her."

Heather sighed heavily. "I've done a lot of reading about the Amish since I met you and Esther. I just don't get you people."

Gabe and Zeke frowned.

"What harm is there in using electricity? You short-change your children by denying them advanced education. Why not allow them to go to high school and college? You are setting them up to fail in our society.

"You cling to things that have no purpose. Your language is a case in point. Why use a means of communication that only other Amish can understand? You live in America with millions of Americans. Yes, you learn English in school, but that isn't the language you prefer to speak. *Deitsh* is how you define yourself. It's what you teach your children when they are growing up. You revere the stories of the men and women who were martyred for your faith, but is that important in this day and age? I don't see that it is. You could easily become part of this world."

"An outsider cannot understand our ways," Zeke said.

"But things would be so much easier for you if you gave up your antique way of life. Have I made my point, Gabe?"

His mind was churning. "It isn't easy for me to accept that Esther can turn her back on something that would allow her to hear. That she would prefer to remain deaf."

"I may not understand the Amish, but I respect you. The way you live is your choice. It doesn't make sense to me. I couldn't go a single day without using my cell phone or computer. You have the right to live as you choose without anyone making you feel guilty or inferior. You are different, but I don't truly see that you need to be fixed. The Deaf culture has their own language—they have their own heroes and history, their own way of caring for others like themselves. Many of them accept God's will in everything. Sound familiar?"

"A little," he admitted. "How do I convince Esther that I finally understand when she won't even look at me?"

"You are going to need some help," Julia said as she came up behind him.

Esther decided to wait for Lilly in the garden. She had grown tired of crying into her pillow. Flowers had always been her comfort. She needed comfort today. She struggled to hold back her tears as she sat on a wooden bench. She loved Gabe, but he didn't see her as a whole person. There was no way to describe the pain and humiliation she felt. All she could hope was that distance would bring some relief.

She stood and wrapped her arms tightly across her middle as if she could hold back her disappointment. She paced across the garden. Why wasn't Lilly here yet? How much longer would she have to wait?

Esther turned back toward the house and saw him standing beside his mother's rose-covered trellis. "Please go away." She couldn't bear this. Not now. Not when she was so close to making her escape.

He held up one hand. "Please hear what I have to say."

She closed her eyes. She couldn't give him another chance to hurt her. She thought he would go away, but instead she found herself enveloped in his arms. She pressed her hands against his chest, but she couldn't bring herself to push him away. In spite of everything, she still loved him. She still needed him.

His lips moved softly against her temple. He was saying something. She turned her face away. "You need to let me go. The car will be here soon."

When he didn't release her, she opened her eyes. Tears glistened on his eyelashes and left a trail down his cheeks. "Don't go."

She could hear the echo of his voice in her mind. He stepped away from her. "Don't go," he signed.

"I'm not broken. I am the way God made me. Why couldn't you accept that?"

"You aren't broken. I am. I'm incomplete without you at my side, Esther. You are the better part of me. If you go, you will leave a wreck of a man behind. I'm sorry I hurt you. Heather was here, and she helped me to understand. I didn't know."

Esther turned away from the pain in his eyes. She wanted to believe him. She wasn't sure she could. "It's too late, Gabe."

He took her gently by the shoulders and turned her around. "Is it too late for forgiveness?"

"Of course not. I forgive you." She meant it. In her heart she knew he hadn't intended to hurt her. He had only been trying to help, but it was help she didn't need and didn't want.

"Forgiveness is a first—first step—" He shook his head. "I—I can't do this." He looked over Esther's shoulder. "Julia, please help me."

Esther saw her sister walk up beside him. A wry smile curved Julia's mouth. "He's a little overcome with emotion. He's afraid you won't hear everything he needs to say," she signed.

Esther raised her chin and looked at him. "I'm listening."

"Okay. I knew from the day we met that you were the most amazing woman. I fell in love with you the morning you went back to the pond to see the moose. I tried to deny it, but the harder I fought the more embedded you became in my heart."

He looked down. Esther watched Julia to see what he was saying.

"I was scared, Esther. I tried to imagine a life with you. I knew I could learn to sign, but how long would it take me to be able to speak as freely as Heather and her friends? A year? Two? How many times would you miss what I was saying because I spoke too fast or wasn't looking at you?"

He raised his face to her. "How can I whisper that I love you in the dark when I'm holding you in my arms? How can I warn you of danger? All these things went through my head. In spite of my fears, I still wanted you in my life. When I learned about the bone-anchored hearing aid, I thought it was the answer for me. For the things I feared. I never asked if it was the answer for you. And for that I'm truly sorry."

Julia wiped a tear from her eye. "He deserves another chance, sister," she signed.

"I'm thinking about it," Esther signed back.

Julia smiled sadly. "One of us should be happy."

"Am I missing something?" Gabe asked.

Esther didn't need her sister to tell her what he said. "Thank you, Julia. You are a wonderful sister, but I can take it from here."

Julia gripped Esther's hand, then patted Gabe's shoulder and walked into the house.

Esther took both Gabe's hands in hers. "I did not consider your fears any more than you thought about mine. We really are going to have to work on our communication skills."

"I'm willing to do anything you ask."

She put her hand in his and began to spell. "This is how you say 'I love you' in the dark. Or this way." She pressed her lips softly at the corner of his mouth and whispered the words she wanted so badly to say. "I love you, Gabriel Fisher."

He took a step back and began to sign, "Flower, will you marry me?"

Esther drew a sharp breath, unable to speak for the tightness in her throat.

Disappointment filled his eyes. "Is that a no?"

She swallowed hard. "You used my sign name. That's the first time."

"But not the last. Will you marry me, Flower? I love you," he signed.

"Our children may be deaf."

"They will have an amazing mother to inspire and teach them."

"I won't hear you shout if I'm in danger."

"I'll keep throwing myself in front of trucks to protect you."

She folded her arms. "We will disagree."

"We'll make up."

"My deafness cost you thousands of dollars in lost work."

"I'll take it out of your wages. You'll have to sew for me for the next sixty or seventy years."

"Gabe, I'm serious. I know how badly you want to keep your family together."

"My brothers and I are grown men. We will do what needs to be done. Even if that means leaving for a while."

"I reckon I'm all out of objections."

His eyes lit up. "Really? You'll marry me? You will love, honor and obey me until death do us part?"

"About the obey part."

He stepped close and took her hands. "Will you love, honor and cherish me?"

"I can agree to that."

"*Goot.* I will be the head of the house. You be the heart. My heart."

"I'm going to marry you, but only because I can't live without you."

"I'll take what I can get." He drew her into his arms. Where she belonged and never wanted to leave. His lips touched the corner of her mouth. She knew exactly what he was saying when he whispered, "I love you."

"*Gott* is great," she whispered back. "He has brought me my one true love. I love you, Gabe Fisher."

He drew back to look at her. "I have waited and longed to hear those words. Say them again."

She cupped his cheek. "I love you, Gabe."

He blew out a deep breath. "Finally. It was worth the wait. I pray you never grow tired of saying it."

She pulled him close. "Oh, I won't. I can promise you that," she said as she kissed his pretty mouth again.

Epilogue

The first day of the Potato Blossom Festival was a whirlwind of excitement. There was a parade, a carnival, games, livestock shows and children everywhere. Esther took a moment between customers in Gabe's booth to gaze at him and wonder what their children would look like. Hopefully like him. He had the most beautiful mouth.

He waved his hand in front of her face. "Where are you?"

"Admiring the man I love."

"Talk like that and I'll start kissing you."

"I'm okay with that."

She was a little disappointed he didn't make good on his promise. Instead he pointed to a nearby booth. "I see Seth and Pamela."

Esther sighed. "They look so happy. I'm glad she said yes when he proposed."

"That's two engagements this summer. I reckon *Mamm* and Waneta's plan worked out pretty well after all."

Esther grinned at him. "In spite of our resistance to their matchmaking."

He smiled. "Thankfully we both had a change of heart. Are we out of purses?"

"We have one left in the box in back. I'll get it." Gabe had been taking care of the customers while Esther kept the display case and shelves stocked.

She stepped out to the counter with the last pink rose-embossed purse when she saw who the customer was.

"Heather. How are you?"

"In need of your help," she signed.

"What can I do?"

"I need a nanny-slash-tutor for my children. Please tell me you are available."

Esther couldn't believe what she was hearing. Her only regret about her upcoming marriage to Gabe was that she would have to give up her position in the special-needs school back home. "Let me ask Gabe."

Since Amish women rarely worked outside the home after marrying, she wanted to be sure he was okay with it. Not that she wouldn't take the job. She wasn't married yet.

Heather grinned. "I already spoke to him. He agreed it would be a fine idea. I don't know why I didn't think of it sooner. Randy and I will pick you up and take you home so you don't have to worry about driving a buggy so far. The kids love the idea."

So did Esther. "Where is Gabe?"

Heather pointed toward the side of the booth. "He stepped out to talk to a man I don't know."

Esther leaned over the counter and saw Gabe with Mr. Jefferson. The two men shook hands. Jefferson walked away, and Gabe came into the booth with a huge grin on his face.

"What did he want?" she asked, not sure she wanted to hear anything about the man.

"It seems none of the other harness makers in the area can beat my prices. He had to eat crow, but it wasn't as painful for him as having to part with an extra thousand dollars. I've got an order for an eight-horse full parade hitch."

She clasped her hands together. "Gabe, that's wonderful. I take back all my bad thoughts about the man."

"Me, too. At least until his check clears the bank." He gave her a sheepish look. "I shouldn't have said that. I have forgiven him. Are you going to work for Heather?"

"I am. Are you sure you don't mind?"

"You are free to do as you please within the rules of our church. That obey thing with me won't kick in until November."

She grabbed his hand and squeezed. "I can hardly wait."

"You haven't seen northern Maine in winter. We can get up to five feet of snow. You may regret your choice."

She winked at him. "Snowbound with my new husband. However will I manage?"

"Very well, I think," he said as he pulled her into the back of the booth where they wouldn't be seen and proceeded to kiss her breathless.

* * * * *

HER FORBIDDEN
AMISH LOVE

Jocelyn McClay

First and always, thanks to God for this opportunity.

This book is dedicated to my mom, Barbara.
Thanks for exposing me to the joy of exploring
quilt shops. I'm so glad I have projects that we found
in them together. You don't own a quilt shop
in real life, so here is one for you in this story.

Thanks to my uncle Gale, who lives within
an Amish community, for his insight.

Thanks to Misti and Joe, who began as
terrific resources of paramedic work
and quickly became wonderful friends.

Thank you to Saundra for answering my quilt shop
questions and having lovely inventory
to tempt me for future undertakings.

Thanks to Amy of the local animal shelter,
who took the time to advise on puppy care.

Any mistakes made on the above topics
are entirely my own.

Ask, and it shall be given you; seek, and ye shall find; knock, and it shall be opened unto you.
—*Matthew* 7:7

Chapter One

It was Socks's soft yip that alerted her. Hannah Lapp looked up from snipping across the dark green material to see her expectant friend, Ruth Schrock, sway as she rose from her seat. Dropping the scissors, Hannah shot out a helpless hand as Ruth grabbed at the shelf behind her, bolts of fabric slowing her descent as she slid to the floor. Now the brightly hued material lay about Ruth's unmoving figure in a kaleidoscope of color.

"Is she having the baby?" Barbara Fastle, the *Englisch* owner of The Stitch quilt shop, asked as she and Rachel, an Amish customer, hurried from the back of the shop. "She seemed fine when she was sitting there a moment ago."

Hannah darted around the counter to kneel at Ruth's side. Tentatively touching her friend's face, she took in her closed eyes and pale color. "I don't think so. But I'm not sure." She carefully moved a nearly empty bolt that lay over Ruth's torso and placed a gentle hand on the woman's protruding stomach. When she felt an abrupt kick against her palm, but no tightening of flesh, Hannah exhaled in relief.

Looking up, her gaze connected with two hovering faces that shared her concern. It was obvious that Louisa Weaver's death a short month ago, along with her unborn child's, was foremost in their collective minds. Hannah's stomach clenched at the possibility of her friend meeting the same fate. "Rachel, run down to the furniture shop and get Malachi. He needs to be here." An instant later, the bell over the door jangled frantically as the young Amish woman dashed out.

"That EMT guy—" hastening toward the counter and the portable phone, Barb waggled her hand urgently as if it would assist her in what she was trying to say "—the one they had the grant for. He rented the apartment upstairs. Moved in this weekend. He'd be the fastest help. Run up and see if he's there. If not, I'll call 911 and get something rolling from out of town, but it'll be a while before they can get here."

Jumping to her feet, Hannah rushed toward the rear of the store where an exit opened into a short hallway, her dog Socks at her heels. Bursting through the brightly painted door, Hannah pivoted from the alley entrance and toward the interior stairway that led up to the small apartment the elderly shop owner occasionally rented out. Hannah's heart was racing faster than her black-soled shoes as she pounded up the steps' worn linoleum.

Hammering rapidly on the paneled wooden door, Hannah shot a worried look back down the narrow stairway as if she could still see her friend lying among the fallen bolts of fabric. Spying a concerned Socks on the steps, Hannah pointed for the Border collie to retreat to the bottom. When the door clicked open, she whipped her head back.

At the sight of the man in the open doorway, Hannah gasped and her eyes widened. Mind whirling, she stepped back into the empty space of the stairwell. Only the hand that shot out to close around her wrist kept Hannah from tumbling down to land in a heap at the base of the stairs. She found herself pulled against a broad chest as strong arms wrapped about her back. The sensation was as riotous as the fall down the stairs would've been. Socks's anxious bark barely penetrated the buzzing in her ears.

Her nose was tucked under a smooth-shaven jaw. If anything, her heart rate accelerated at the sensation. She knew that jawline. If her sister hadn't left that day, it would've been the one Hannah gazed at across the breakfast table for the past five years.

But Gail had walked away.

And Hannah had made the difficult decision to cut Gabriel Bartel out of her life.

Her fingers throbbing against the sturdy chest that cushioned her, Hannah inhaled the scent of male and fresh soap before gingerly pushing away, careful this time to stay on the small landing. Gabriel's hands slid from her back and down the sleeves of her dress to lightly encircle her wrists. Tapping with her toe into the area behind her until she felt the first step, Hannah hastily stepped onto it. Their arms stretched out between them before he opened his hands and released her. From the base of the stairs, Socks's barks receded to a few concerned woofs.

"I need…" Hannah swallowed, firmly pushed her shock aside and started again. "*We* need your help downstairs. Ruth has—a woman has fainted, a woman who's with child…" The blood drained from Hannah's face when Gabe stepped back into the apartment, leaving her standing on the step. Surely he wouldn't refuse to help because of their past? She puffed out a breath in relief when he reappeared a moment later, carrying a small pack.

"My jump bag. Contains a few necessary pieces of equipment. Let's go." He gestured for Hannah to lead them down the narrow steps.

She fled down them as if the turbulent waters of a broken dam were lashing at her heels. What followed her down was even more frightening. Memories of her past, suppressed these past years, now unleashed churning emotions—shock, excitement, longing, regret. If it wasn't for her fear for Ruth, Hannah might've taken the exit to the alley, hastily hitched up her buggy horse, Daisy, and headed home to lick wounds—long-thought healed—that now throbbed anew.

Instead, she burst through the back door into the quilt shop, Socks at her heels, to find Ruth still slumped on the floor with Barbara, her brow creased in deep lines, crouched beside her. The shop owner stood and backed away, relief apparent on her face as Gabe hastened forward.

"She hasn't moved."

Gabe nodded as he took her place beside the unconscious woman. Sliding Ruth's black cloak aside, he picked up her limp wrist, resting his fingers on the blue-veined skin. "Her pulse is slow, but steady. Did she hit her head in the fall?" When Barb and Hannah promptly shook their heads, he untied and gently loosened the black bonnet.

Ruth's arms and legs shifted. Conscious of keeping out of the way, Hannah crouched down close enough to see her friend's eyes flutter. Hannah opened her mouth to talk to Ruth, before glancing at Gabe to see if she should do so. Apparently interpreting her look, he nodded as he continued his examination.

"Ruth! Are you all right?"

"Just got a little dizzy when I stood up." Eyes fully open now, Ruth looked confused at finding herself on the floor amid the bolts of fabric. She leaned forward, attempting to stand.

"Let's not be in any hurry to get up." Gabe moved into her line of sight, a reassuring smile on his face. Hannah swallowed, trying not to remember when his smiles had been directed at her. When his comforting baritone could make her believe that everything would be all right for them, too. "You've had a fall. Let's make sure you and your little passenger are ready before we stand. Just think of it as a moment to examine some of this lovely material more closely, okay?"

Ruth's eyes rounded and her arms swept protectively around her stomach. "My *boppeli*!"

"Seems like he's doing okay and not interested in making his first appearance in a quilt shop," Gabe responded immediately, his voice soothing. "Does your head, neck or back hurt? No? Then let's get you on to your side and give you two another moment before we go further." He assisted Ruth in shifting her position, cushioning her protruding stomach with a bolt of dark blue fabric. "Do you get dizzy often?"

"*Nee.* Only when I…" Ruth stopped and frowned.

"Only when you…?" Gabe slipped a blood pressure cuff on her arm.

"Only when I forget to eat." The admission seemed dragged from the prone woman.

"Ah, that does make a difference." With a glance at the reading, he slipped the cuff off. "What is it that they say? You're eating for two? Me, I'm starved by this time of day just eating for one." He sat back on his heels. "You want to try sitting up?"

Hannah, still rooted where she knelt by Ruth, couldn't tear her eyes from Gabe's confident, fluid movements. The light brown curly hair and deep green eyes were the same, but this wasn't the youth she'd met and quickly fallen for at a party almost five years earlier. That'd been a charming boy. This was a capable man. And she was sure she'd memorized every detail about him then, down to the crease in his lean cheeks when he smiled, but she couldn't recall him ever mentioning an interest in medical care.

"*Ja.*" Ruth's mutter, her voice tinged with self-disgust drew Hannah's attention.

Gabe smiled gently. "Your vitals are fine. Probably low blood sugar. I can't recommend missing meals in your state." Following a pointed look from him that scattered her breathing until she understood his intent, Hannah helped Gabe settle Ruth into the chair her friend had been sitting on ten minutes earlier. Once settled, Ruth wrapped her hands around her stomach again and looked fully into Gabe's attentive face.

Her brows furrowed. "I remember you."

Hannah opened her mouth to say something—offer to run for cookies or juice, or promise to make another quilt for the baby—anything to change the imminent subject. She didn't want Ruth's sharp mind to place where she'd previously seen the man now tending her.

Ruth had been with her at the first party, but any further meetings Hannah had had with Gabe—and there'd been several—had been private. Treasured. Innocent. And too precious to share even with her closest friend.

To her relief, before Hannah could say a word, bells jangled wildly as the shop's front door burst open and Ruth's husband, pale-faced and coatless, rushed in. Rachel Mast, a few steps behind, shut the door against the January cold. Dodging through the rows of multihued fabric, Malachi Schrock was kneeling at his wife's side a moment later.

Along with the blast of winter air, a tension pervaded the shop. Now that Ruth was alert and seemingly recovered, Hannah felt the weight of Gabe's gaze. Knotting her fingers together, she tried to ignore its compelling lure. Her heart raced as if she was still running up the stairs. She expelled her breath in a rush when Barbara spoke. "Good thing you're here, Malachi. Ruth is remembering strange men."

Hannah's eyes finally met Gabe's. He wasn't a stranger. He was the man she'd loved. The man she'd

been going to build a life with. Until she'd been reminded her community was more important. A community whose leaders were now mentioning more and
more often that it was past time Hannah Lapp be baptized and marry one of its men. Dropping her gaze, she
knelt to slide her fingers into Socks's soft, comforting fur. Hannah knew she should, and would, do as
they willed, even though it would be without love for
the man. Because she'd only ever loved once. And the
Mennonite man standing before her was definitely not
an acceptable option for her to marry.

She wasn't going to acknowledge him. Dropping his
gaze, Gabe watched the man entwine his work-rough-
ened fingers with his wife's. Gabe returned his attention
to Hannah, longing to do the same. Her slender hands
were tangled in the dog's black fur. Just like years ago,
she'd withdrawn.

But this time, unlike years ago, he wasn't going to
let her avoid him and disappear.

The married couple held a brief, private discussion,
while Gabe ran an assessing eye over his temporary
patient. He didn't ask when the baby was due. Amish
women weren't fixated on their due dates like *Englisch*
women were, figuring babies would arrive when they
were ready. After checking with Gabe that it was all
right to move her, Malachi Schrock gathered his auburn-
haired wife protectively under his arm and they exited
the shop. Their voices trailed behind them as he shoul-
dered the door open to let in a stream of cold air along
with a few whirling snowflakes. The wood-and-glass

door shut with a rattle. When the accompanying clatter of the bell faded away, the remaining four in the shop glanced at each other in the silence.

Correction, Hannah glanced at Gabe before her gaze skittered away again. She immediately straightened and busied herself, picking up the fallen bolts of fabric. The Border collie at her side evaluated Gabe through intelligent brown eyes before trotting to a dog bed tucked along the wall. He watched her rest her muzzle on her white legs as she continued to study him.

Well, at least he had the attention of one of them. *You're here now, Bartel. Begin as you mean to go on.* This time, he wasn't going to let Hannah avoid him. Picking up a bolt of dark blue material, he handed it to her. Eyes he knew were almost a matching shade remained carefully averted as Hannah hesitated before accepting the fabric. Gabe picked up another bolt, this time shifting it in his hands to ensure his fingers touched Hannah's when she tentatively reached for it. Flinching at the contact, she darted a look at him as the heavy bolt sagged between them. Gabe met Hannah's wary look with a bland smile. *You're not going to ignore me.* She must've gotten the hint, as she hefted the fabric onto the shelf, turning her back to him as she did so.

The gray-haired shop owner had stepped behind a wide counter and picked up the orange-handled scissors lying on dark green material spread out upon it. "Well, that was exciting. I thought we might have to pull down the baby quilts and put them to use. I hope Ruth is all right. Rachel, was there anything else you needed?"

Gabe didn't recognize the young woman who'd entered with Ruth's husband. She looked younger than Hannah, so she might not have been in her *rumspringa* at the same time as the slender woman whose blue eyes continued to avoid his as she smoothed out the bolts, which were now lining the shelf again.

He'd recognized Ruth, though. She'd been there when he'd first met Hannah. And had looked on doubtfully as he'd introduced himself and clumsily tried to charm her beautiful, reserved friend.

Fortunately for him, something he'd said that night had worked. Either that, or Hannah had taken pity on him, because she'd agreed to meet with him again. And again. And many times over during the wonderful beginning of that summer. Until the night Gabe had paced the ground of their prearranged location, anxiously rehearsing a marriage proposal. And she'd never shown.

He hadn't seen her since.

But he hadn't forgotten her. And he'd always kept his ear to the ground in regard to Miller's Creek.

When this job opportunity arose at the same time he'd heard rumors that Hannah would be taking baptism classes so she could marry, it was like God was giving him a nudge. Gabe knew that once Hannah became a baptized member of the church, she'd never marry a Mennonite like himself and be shunned from her family and community. He'd been given a second chance.

He was going to make the most of it.

Frowning, Gabe repacked his jump bag as he regarded the precisely pleated back of the *kapp* covering Hannah's neatly pinned golden blond hair. As he retraced his steps to the back of the shop at a much slower pace than when he'd entered, his new landlady looked up from cutting fabric and called out to thank him. His glance at Hannah was rewarded only with a brief, cool nod before she studiously continued her task.

Her composed profile was the last thing Gabe saw before he ducked through the cheerful rear door. Climbing the steps to his apartment, he snorted wryly. What had he been expecting? That she'd just fall into his arms once she saw him again? Gabe's lips twisted as he recalled she'd done just that, for a moment. But whatever had prevented her from meeting him that night still had her shutting him out. Well, he faced challenges every day in his job. He wasn't one to shy away from a tough situation. Gabe knew convincing Hannah to marry him would be that and more.

Chapter Two

Hannah was glad to be out of The Stitch for even the few minutes it took to walk to the post office and retrieve the shop's mail. At least these were moments when her ears weren't tuned to the bang of the shop's back door. After two days, she could finally resist whipping her head toward the door at any sound generated behind it, as it might announce Gabriel Bartel's appearance. It was surely understandable to be jumpy regarding Gabe's actions. The man had just popped unexpectedly back into her life. It certainly wasn't eagerness to see him that had her looking in that direction at the sound of his feet on the stairs. Or so she told herself.

Ruth, thankfully, seemed to have recovered from the incident. Hannah didn't know if she ever would. The night she'd forced herself to stay home from meeting with Gabe had been one of the hardest things she'd ever done. Second only to watching her pregnant sister, Gail, walk away from home and the Amish community earlier that day.

If Gail hadn't left, Hannah might've made a different choice. But seeing what her departure had done to her family had made Hannah ill. The heartache of her parents. The whispering of those that gossiped. The pitying looks of those that didn't. The suspicious eyes on her and her younger brothers, wondering if they too might abandon the Amish lifestyle. Hannah, who'd always abided by *gelassenheit*, obeying the will of those in authority, had felt the heavy weight of their stares and disapproval.

She'd vowed, in the lonely bedroom she'd shared with her sister, to never disappoint her parents. And so her dreams for a life with the Mennonite man she loved had disappeared down the road with Gail.

Hannah jumped at the harsh scrape of metal on concrete behind her. Spinning around, she and Socks, who'd been trotting on a leash at her side, watched as a man hastily exited the car that'd just slid its rusted nose onto the high sidewalk. Hannah backed away as the man lunged up the steep step and stood swaying before her. She flinched again at Socks's unexpected soft growl.

The man's stringy hair blew over his face. He made an attempt to straighten his jacket, a futile action, as the coat was buttoned crooked. Something had congealed into dark patches on his worn blue jeans. A sliver of unease rippled up Hannah's spine. She slid another step back as Socks brushed against her leg.

"Nice dog." The man's voice was low and rough, like scraping a shovel over a bed of rocks. There was something in it that made the comment sound not like a compliment, but a threat. Giving a faint nod, Hannah slipped her hand through the end of Socks's leash and tightened her grip on the leather.

"Border collie, right? They're good working dogs. Does she bite?"

Hannah huffed out a tight breath when another car pulled up to the sidewalk, briefly drawing the man's attention. "I...I need to get back to work." Pivoting, she doubled her speed, willing to take her chances of sliding over the snow-frosted surface. Several steps farther, she risked a glance back. The man was watching them. Hannah was used to *Englisch* visitors to town staring at times, curious about Amish dress and lifestyle. But this one wasn't looking at her. His attention was on Socks.

Hannah was breathless when she and Socks swept into the shop and closed the heavy door behind them. A condition that wasn't helped when she looked over the tops of the myriad bolts of fabric to see the curly-haired man talking with her employer. Striving to collect herself, she leaned down and unsnapped Socks's leash.

Upon straightening, she almost headed out the door again at Barb's words. "We were just talking about you."

"Oh, really?" Chagrined to hear her voice an octave higher than normal, Hannah cleared her throat and tried again as she hung up her cloak on the wall peg by the door. "How so?"

"Gabe was asking if we made the quilts." The older woman gestured to the collection of intricately designed blankets that lined the walls of the shop. "I was telling him I make some, but you're the more talented one." Barb turned back to Gabe who, one muscular shoulder leaning against the wall, was watching Hannah as she threaded her way through the maze of fabric.

After facing the unsettling man on the sidewalk, Hannah blinked her eyes at the surge of temptation to tuck against Gabe's side. Feel his arm slide over her shoulder. Relax in the remembered comfort of being close to his solid form. Stumbling, she reached out to put a hand on the smooth cotton of a bolt beside her, steadying herself. She could not fall again for this man. He was not for her. She should've forgotten him years ago. Pressing her lips together, Hannah stiffened her resolve and her knees along with it.

His eyes never leaving her face, Gabe tilted one corner of his mouth into a crooked smile and straightened from his slouch against the wall when she reached them.

"Who made the rest of them?"

To Hannah's relief, Barb fielded his question. "Some of the Amish ladies in the community bring their projects in, and we sell them on commission. I'd love to carry more, but they're busy women."

"I can imagine." He winced, frowning in consideration. "That might make my request unfeasible."

"Much is lost for want of asking." Barb repinned some loose fabric back onto a bolt on the counter and returned it to the shelf.

"I was wondering if it would be possible to get some curtains for the windows upstairs that face the street. I never know when I might be called out and I don't want to disturb neighbors when my lights come on in the middle of the night." He shrugged. "I suppose I could stop at the big box store in Portage my next time through and

buy some premade ones, but I noticed some of your...
art." He glanced around him at the displays. "There's really no other word for it. I thought something like that
might be cheery, as well as functional upstairs."

"It is pretty dreary up there, isn't it? I should've
thought of that. I haven't rented it out since the young
Hershberger couple lived there for some months after
they were married, waiting for their house to be built."
The gray-haired woman grinned. "With Ophelia the
oldest of thirteen children, there wasn't room for them
to stay with her folks other than the traditional night
after their wedding."

Hannah frowned. Freeman and Ophelia Hershberger
already had a two-year-old son and another one on the
way. Why hadn't Barb rented out the apartment since
then? Why now? It would've been considerably easier on Hannah's peace of mind to have another young
Amish couple banging their way through the back door
to the alley instead of the current tenant.

The shop owner leaned an elbow on a row of various shades of blue fabric. "Which reminds me of something else. Besides curtains, do you have everything you
need? The apartment has electricity, but it hasn't been
used by an *Englisch* person for some time."

Hannah sucked in a quiet breath at Gabe's grin. The
sight of it still made her stomach jump like a summer
night full of fireflies.

"I did find that I'm well supplied with oil lamps in
case the power goes out. And the additional heat source
is nice. And I'm Mennonite. As were the Amish originally. There was a falling out sometime in the 17th cen-

tury and we're a bit more comfortable with technology, but there are still similarities to the Amish. Some of us even speak the same language. At least we used to. *Ja?*"

Hannah's cheeks heated when Gabe turned to her with a raised eyebrow. She knew he was referring to their earlier time together, not Pennsylvania Dutch, the dialect Amish and some Mennonite spoke. She and Gabe used to want the same thing—to live their lives together. Hannah wasn't sure what he wanted now, dropping back into her life. But what she wanted had changed. It had to have. She wanted to stay in her community. To not cause ripples. To submit to the will of the *Diener*—the district's elected officials—and not distress her parents. Still, her mouth grew dry and the flush crept down her neck under Gabe's intent regard.

"Well, we're glad the grant went through to establish an EMS program in town. But there are probably better places in the area to rent." Barb wagged a finger toward the ceiling and the living space above it. "Whatever prompted you to want my little apartment upstairs?"

"Oh, the price was right. And I liked the location." Gabe smiled at her employer, but his tone and the glance he returned to Hannah were deceptively neutral. Still, Hannah figured her cheeks were now the hue of the brightest red fabric in the shop. Peering at the door, she willed a customer to walk in. To her dismay, their side of the snow-covered street was empty. She focused her attention on Barb, only to find her employer looking between her and Gabe speculatively.

The older woman straightened away from the bolts of fabric. "So you need curtains. You're right. You're living above a quilt shop. We can't let you put store-bought curtains up there. Hannah can make them for you."

Hannah's jaw dropped. She barely managed to squeak, "Me? Amish don't generally have curtains."

"*Englisch* customers love to see you working on the treadle sewing machine when they come in. Helps make the shop seem quaint. Besides, you're a better seamstress than I am. If you can figure pattern calculations for quilting, you can figure out curtains. I can handle other things while you work on them."

"But…"

Ignoring her, Barb turned to Gabe and waved her hand at the surrounding shop. "What color did you have in mind?"

His attention on Hannah's rounded eyes, Gabe offered, "I'm partial to blue."

The shop owner patted the fabric beside her. "We can certainly do that. Anything here you like?"

Gabe's eyes remained locked with Hannah's. "Yes," he drawled.

She looked away. He was flustering her, charming her, all over again. She couldn't let it happen.

Striding over to the row of blue fabrics, she smacked the bolted material. "Pick one." Forcing a smile, Hannah released a breath. Her smile faded as she recalled how close she'd come to disrupting her world for this man. Crossing her arms over her chest, Hannah reminded herself Gabe was as out of place in her life as his muscular and masculine form was in the bright-colored quilt shop that surrounded him.

Although she stood her ground, her heart rate escalated as Gabe strolled closer to survey the vast collection of fabrics, some plain in keeping with Amish needs, some with printed design to accommodate *Englisch* shoppers. All in shades of blue from the lightest pastel to the deepest navy. "Hmm. That's a tough one." He glanced over at Hannah, standing stiffly at the end of the row.

"Well, it'd be nice to wake up to something beautiful. Although beauty isn't everything. It's more how it makes you feel." Reaching out a hand, he traced a finger down the length of a nearby bolt. Hannah forced her attention away from it. "I'd like something that seems cool at the outset." Gabe paused as his eyes slid to the fabric before returning to her rigid form. "But vibrant upon closer scrutiny."

Pressing her lips together, Hannah glanced over to see Barb watching with raised eyebrows. She wanted to put her hand over Gabe's mouth to keep him from continuing. But the thought of touching him reminded her of the warm skin of his cheek, and the soft bristle that grew there when they would meet late in the day. Hannah curled her hands into fists to dismiss the sensation. Her short nails dug into her palms as he continued.

"I want something that makes me feel alive as I start the day, but is restful at the end of it." Gabe squinted thoughtfully as he deliberated. "Something that's more complicated than it actually seems. Something that has a bit of glow to it."

At each description, Gabe's gaze shifted from the fabric to her face. Hannah fixed her gaze away from him and blew out another breath, determined not to let him fluster her further. She remembered how he'd always made her laugh. She'd never laughed so much as when they'd been together. Hannah frowned. She'd missed that. It was almost as if the colors of her life were somehow muted now that Gabe was no longer in it.

She narrowed her eyes at the row of material she faced. Beige. A neutral color, normally a background in the concept of the quilt. That was her. She wasn't a vibrant blue. Gabe was describing someone Hannah didn't recognize. One who didn't exist anymore. Or maybe only had with him. Hannah swallowed. And she wasn't just beige. She was beige without a pattern in the fabric, like the *Englisch* preferred. Bland. Muted.

Only Gabe had made her feel like the primary focus of a design.

Hannah's eyes burned. She blinked until the fabric went from a blur back to individual shades of pale, sandy, yellowish-brown.

Biting the inside of her cheek, Hannah reminded herself that background colors were always needed. She'd heard murmurings from the district's *Diener*. According to those ministers, she'd soon be bound into some arrangement with another for life. Just not one of her choosing. With a slight turn of her head, Hannah met Gabe's green eyes. No, she'd given up her chance for creating her own design.

And it was past time Gabe finished this and choose his. Whirling to face the blue fabrics, Hannah jerked a bolt out of the row.

"No, not that one. The one next to it," Gabe directed.

Hannah stuffed the one she had back and pulled the

one he'd indicated. Striding over to the counter, she dropped it with a thud next to Barb.

"Nice shade," Barb commented as she eyed the bolt before sliding it over to the side. "It matches Hannah's eyes. But before I cut it, I need to know the required length. Hannah, you'll have to go up and measure the windows for him." The shop owner returned her attention to Gabe. "I'm assuming you know what style you want?"

"Plain," he responded immediately, his eyes dancing. "I like a plain style."

Hannah stifled a snort, her face flaming again. He'd keep this up until the silly curtains were made and hung. Her best recourse was to avoid him and be coolly pleasant when he was around. No one needed to know they had a history. And she couldn't allow them to have a future. Snagging the tape measure from the counter, Hannah strove for a composed stroll toward the back door. The sooner the measurements were taken, the sooner she could finish the project. These would be the fastest curtains ever made. And then she could go back to being beige. Where she'd been content these past few years.

Hadn't she?

Watching Hannah march to the store's rear exit, Gabe couldn't suppress the grin that spread across his face. He pulled out his billfold.

Barb waved it away. "Don't know what the cost is until we know how much material you're getting. Besides, I'll provide these with the apartment."

He repocketed the billfold. "When we know, I'll pay.

I have a feeling I might take them with me no matter where I go." They both looked over when the back door slammed behind Hannah.

Barb narrowed her eyes at Gabe. "Where did you say you two had met?"

Gabe headed for the rear exit when he heard Hannah's determined tread on the stairs. "I didn't," he tossed back over his shoulder.

Since the door to the apartment wasn't locked, Hannah was already inside and at the window with her tape measure by the time Gabe stepped through the door. He wasn't surprised she had went straight to the task. From her behavior since he'd arrived, he figured it was so she could leave immediately, continuing to avoid him as much as possible.

She wasn't fooling him. Hannah was as aware of him as he was of her. Although she didn't turn when the door clicked closed, under the dark green fabric of her dress he saw her shoulder give a barely discernible flinch at the sound.

Gabe sighed. He paused, then reached back to open the door again. Maybe that'd been part of the problem before. The wonderful times they'd had together, the joy they'd felt with each other, the relationship they'd built—innocent except for their growing feelings—it hadn't been in the open.

If he was going to convince her to marry him, he'd have to drag it there.

Hannah rose on tiptoe, a lovely slender silhouette in front of the window, the weak winter light shining in around her. She stretched out her arm toward the top of the frame. Her reach was about four inches short of the wooden trim on the tall window.

"Here, let me help." Gabe's feet echoed on the bare wood floor as he hustled over to where she stood.

"I think you've helped enough," Hannah responded as she let the end of the tape measure dangle, leaving ample room for him to grab it without touching her fingers.

Gabe took the metal end tab and held it up above their heads. The stiff organza of her *kapp* was right under his chin. Her golden-blond hair was within kissing distance. Gabe was sorely tempted to drop a tender caress upon it as he'd done years before. Appreciated then, that action now would probably send Hannah skittering down the stairs. Frowning, he considered the scarred wooden trim of the window. "Where do you want it measured from?"

When Hannah looked up to assess, their eyes met and held for a moment before she slid hers away to peer at small holes in the wall just outside the trim. "Are those nail holes? They're probably from brackets for previous shades or curtain rods. Measure from there."

He moved the tape as she requested, trying to focus on the street below him instead of the citrus-shampoo scent of her hair. Only when she bent to measure the bottom of the window was he able to draw a full breath. "Funny how holes are left when something is no longer there that used to be."

She'd certainly left holes in him. Some he'd managed to plaster over through the years. Some that might never be filled again. Especially if he couldn't breach whatever barrier she'd put between them.

Hannah spoke to the sill below him. "Maybe it never should've been there in the first place."

Dropping his arm, he released the tape. "You don't believe that." He watched as she straightened, rolling the white length into a tight coil. "I've missed you, Hannah."

Her eyes were wide, liquid with tears. "I…"

Gabe held his breath, waiting to hear why she'd abruptly abandoned him years before. Pressing her lips together, Hannah glanced away to stare out the window. Instantly, she stiffened.

"What is it?" Gabe looked out the window when Hannah backed to the center of the room. Nothing seemed out of the ordinary on the street below. Shallow piles of snow edged the street. A scattering of cars were passing by. A handful of people were on the sidewalk, including a man directly below them.

"Barb mentioned you were all moved in." Arms crossed tightly over her chest, Hannah was scanning the rest of the small, sparsely furnished apartment. "There's not much here."

At least her comment admitted that she had talked with her employer about him. It wasn't much, but he'd take it. His breath escaped in a slow hiss at her obvious avoidance of their history as Gabe followed her gaze. "Well, I haven't collected much. There are some boxes yet to unpack in the kitchen. Some more still in my vehicle. Otherwise, that's about it. Did you think

I was kidding when I said I needed curtains to cheer the place up?"

Her gaze was fixed on his well-worn brown couch. "I thought you had other motives."

It was the closest she'd come to mentioning their past. "I did." Gabe studied her face. There were signs of strain under the polite composure. He longed to press her, but recognized the need to pursue a light present instead of bringing up their fractured past. "But it still was pretty dreary up here. I don't suppose you could make me a pillow for the couch, as well?"

"You'll be lucky to get the curtains," she retorted, but her lips curved in the first genuine smile he'd encountered since he'd seen her again. Ah, this was the Hannah he remembered.

"Well. What was it Barb had said? 'Much is lost for want of asking.'" He trailed after her to the apartment door. "Don't forget the window in the bedroom. It's the same size. Basically." He wobbled a hand in a so-so movement. "As far as old buildings go, anyway. I truly don't want to be a sideshow for anyone when I'm home. Or bother anyone else who happens to live downtown when I respond to a call at odd hours."

Hannah paused in the open doorway. "The community was thrilled when the grant went through to start the EMS service. How did you end up being the one...?"

"I saw the job opening and I was looking." *For a way to get into the area* remained unsaid. As did any mention of the solid-paying job he'd left to come here in exchange for the baseline salary the grant provided and a collection of part-time work that barely scraped up enough for the apartment and other living expenses. But if he could convince Hannah they belonged together, that and the difference he knew he could make in emergency care for the rural area would be enough reward.

"Will you be driving an ambulance and such?"

"I'll be going out on local calls, but there's a bit of groundwork to set up at first, like working with the newly identified medical director. The grant budget won't stretch to an ambulance." It barely paid for him to do local EMS work while he helped establish the program. "A share of the schedule will still be covered with volunteers. Part of the work I'll be doing is local fire department and EMS training, so folks like the Amish volunteers don't have to travel so far for it. Also, I'll be teaching CPR classes at the Portage hospital, as well as businesses and the junior college."

Hannah's brows furrowed. Gabe figured it was the mention of the college. He'd been studying something else years ago when, on a whim, he'd joined some friends at a weekend party that'd involved a mixture of local youth, including the woman before him.

The muffled jangle of the shop door drifted up the stairs. With a slight frown, Hannah turned her head in that direction. "I have to go. Barb might need some help downstairs."

Gabe winked at her. "Remember the measurements?"

Hannah's face went blank, and her blue eyes blinked a few rapid times before she recited the width and length of the window with a grin. "You were trying to distract me."

Gabe's own smile ebbed. "It's the other way around,

Hannah. I've been distracted since I met you. You know why I really came to Miller's Creek."

The flawless skin of Hannah's cheeks bloomed in color. She fled down the worn linoleum steps of the narrow stairway. Gabe watched her descent. Had he made progress? It was hard to tell. But at least, for this moment, he knew why she was running away. And where he could find her again.

Hannah's heart was pounding as she raced down the stairs. She'd forgotten the joy of just being with Gabe. Maybe they could figure out some way of spending time together? Surely no harm could come of a few casual meetings? The possibility brought a smile to her face as she hustled along the short hallway. Her breathless grin abruptly faded as she stepped into the shop and pulled the back door closed. Facing the occupants in the shop who looked over at her entrance, she shuttered her mind to the thrill and temptation of being with Gabe.

Here was her life. Here was where her mind and obedience needed to be focused. Clasping her hands at her waist, she nodded to Barb to indicate she'd take care of these particular customers and propped up a composed smile to replace the earlier genuine one. Stepping away from the door, she greeted the two who'd arrived while she'd been upstairs. Enjoying herself. Hannah pushed the errant thought away.

"Ruby Weaver, Bishop Weaver, what a pleasure to see you both today. Is there anything I can help you with?" The statement was a stretch. The pleasure would be if they were truly here for material. And not to see her for some reason.

Any hope of that quickly died at the bishop's next words.

"Hannah Lapp. I need to talk with you." Bishop Weaver motioned Hannah over to the corner of racks displaying different quilting tools and patterns, away from where the *Englisch* store owner was working.

Hannah tried not to drag her feet. But she remembered all too well that Bishop Weaver and his wife were the reasons her *schweschder*, Gail, almost didn't return to Miller's Creek with her young daughter Lily. It was only thanks to *Gott* and the persistence of Samuel Schrock, now Gail's husband, that they'd rejoined the Amish community some months ago.

Shortly after Gail and Samuel's wedding, the bishop's only daughter-in-law and her unborn child had unexpectedly died. Bishop Weaver had pulled Hannah aside at Louisa's funeral and admonished her that it was time for her to take baptism classes and thereby become a member of the church.

As a member, she was eligible to marry.

Dread pooled in her stomach like water running into a dry creek bed following a hard rain. She knew what he was going to say. She knew what she was going to have to say in return as an Amish woman for whom *gelassenheit* was a way of life. Hannah swallowed hard to keep the hint of tears from glistening.

"Hannah Lapp. It is selfish of you to remain single at your age when our unmarried men need wives."

At twenty-three, Hannah was older than many single

Amish women. It wasn't what she'd planned when she'd started her *rumspringa*. But then she'd met Gabriel. Even though she'd intentionally dropped out of his life, she hadn't been able to erase him from her mind. She'd since had many admirers, but no other young man in the Amish community had been tempting enough for Hannah to want to share their lives. Not in the way she'd wanted to share Gabe's. So she'd delayed. And delayed.

"You will marry one of our men shortly after your baptism. You might as well see who will suit." The bishop droned on, expecting her full attention and co-operation. Hannah bowed her head. *And why shouldn't he be? You've always done what was expected of you.*

Hannah braced herself. She knew who he was going to mention. It wasn't that she had anything against the man. He was hardworking and honorable. It was just that, in the times she'd been around him at different functions and church events, there was no spark. Nothing like she'd shared with…Gabe.

But that was years ago, when the man had been single. Hannah admonished herself to be open-minded. Perhaps things had changed since then. There were other Amish marriages that'd started out with not much more than friendship and respect and had grown into solid relationships. She could live with that. She'd just hoped for…something more.

"There is a man, recently widowed, in the community. I will tell him that you expect him to come calling. Plan for Jethro to be here tomorrow to take you to lunch."

And there it was. Bishop Weaver might state that she

should start seeing the single men to see with whom she might suit, but what he'd meant was she was to marry his widowed son. His only son. Hannah felt the burn of distress in the back of her throat at the same time she stifled an inappropriate snort at the possibility that Jethro might have plans for the morrow, and his life, that his father wasn't aware of. Or more likely, didn't care about.

"*Denki*, Bishop Weaver. I will expect to see Jethro tomorrow. I appreciate your consideration and concern for my welfare." Hannah didn't know how she got the words out. They must have risen from the deep reservoir of practiced obedience she'd lived all her life, except for the brief, stolen time with Gabe years ago.

She'd always done the right thing. Been the well-behaved daughter to her sister Gail's more rebellious actions. Always thought of others first and herself later, if at all. Years of that behavior enabled her to respond appropriately to the bishop. But inside, her heart was breaking. *Oh, Gabe!* Hannah gently set her teeth together to keep her chin from trembling.

Bishop Weaver nodded jerkily before flinching. He raised a hand to rub it along his jaw and down his neck. Furrowing her brow at his actions, Hannah pushed aside her distress when she noted, even in the shop's temperate environment, beads of sweat were dotting his forehead under the brim of his hat.

"Are you all right?"

"*Ja*," he mumbled, but his response was more distracted than his usual brusqueness. "Ruby," he called across the shop in a strained voice. "It's time to go."

Ruby's narrow face reflected her surprise at the abrupt directive. Hannah supposed it didn't happen very often. Probably, much more frequently, the other way around. But, with a glance at Hannah and Barb, she turned toward the front exit, her mouth pressed in a lipless line. Hand against his stomach, Bishop Weaver struggled to open the front door of the shop, the bell jangling with his repeated attempts. Finally he succeeded and shuffled out with hunched shoulders, his wife at his heels.

Hannah and Barb watched them climb into a nearby buggy, the bishop pausing on the step before he pulled himself in. "He didn't look like he felt well," Barb observed, frowning as her fingers automatically resumed the task of stocking a recent delivery of fat quarters—precut pieces of fabric popular among quilters.

Neither did Hannah after their conversation. The bishop's health was forgotten as she went to the counter, found a pad of paper and jotted down the measurements of the window upstairs. She was surprised she remembered them after her talk with the bishop. But then, she'd always remembered every moment of her interactions with Gabriel Bartel. Much as she'd once hoped differently, she knew now it was all she'd ever have of him.

Chapter Three

Hannah had always liked the cheery jingle of The Stitch's doorbell, knowing it announced a customer or someone just dropping by to visit. Today, she flinched at the jarring sound, growing increasingly tense as the wall clock ticked toward noon.

It wasn't that she disliked Jethro Weaver. He was a *gut* man. While measuring Gabriel's fabric to the length needed for his curtains, Hannah mentally listed the bishop's son's qualities. He was hardworking. He was quiet. He was… Smoothing the fabric, her lips quirked as she recalled Gabe's foolish description of what he was looking for. In fabric, or so he had said. In other things as well, she knew he had meant. It wasn't her. Not anymore. The scissors felt abnormally heavy when Hannah picked them up. She winced at the first snip.

It's what you have to do with him in your life. Cut him out. You've done it before, you can do it again. It didn't help that she hadn't heard the other sound her ear had been tuned for—the muted bang of the back door leading into the street—all morning. Was Gabe still upstairs in his apartment? Or had he already left for the day? Where was he?

She couldn't let it matter. She would do what was expected of her. That was the essence of *gelassenheit*. Yielding oneself to the will of a higher authority, be it *Gott*, the bishop or others, with contentment and a calm spirit was a core value of who they were as an Amish community. Hannah resolutely cut across the fabric. She needed to remember that she was beige. Not this vibrant blue.

What mattered now was Jethro. Who was hard-working. And reserved. And—she jumped, slashing the material jaggedly at the jarring bell announcing an arrival—here. Setting the scissors down, Hannah wiped her hands down the side of her skirt and stepped around the counter with a weak smile.

Jethro Weaver responded with a stiff nod as he shut the door. Hannah couldn't see his eyes below the flat brim of his black hat, but from the set of his jaw, evident even under his short beard, it looked as if he was as uncomfortable being there as she was having him there. Hannah wasn't sure if the realization made her feel better or worse. Allowing herself a last glance at the fabric on the counter and memory of the man who'd chosen it, she corrected herself. She couldn't feel much worse.

Injecting pleasant interest in her voice, she started for the door and the man standing rigidly beside it. "Mrs. Fastle should be back from lunch momentarily. When she arrives, we can go. Where did you have in mind?"

"The D-Dew D-Drop."

She'd forgotten Jethro had a stutter. When she got closer, Hannah could see the faint line of a scar perpendicular to his unsmiling upper lip. Standing just inside the door, they faced each other awkwardly. Jethro shuffled his feet. Hannah shifted hers. She was about to suggest he remove his coat while they waited when she heard the muffled bang of the door to the alley. Her heart jolted at the possibility that it was Gabe. Much more likely, it was announcing Barb's return. Stifling a sigh, as it meant she was now free to join the man before her for what would surely be an uncomfortable meal, Hannah reached for her black cloak and bonnet that hung on the nearby peg rack.

Hannah hissed in a breath when a smiling Gabe followed Barb through the shop's back door. Although he was chatting with her employer, his eyes scanned the shop until they locked with her own. Gabe's gaze shifted from her to the tall, lean man beside her and back again. Hannah found herself holding her breath until Gabe returned his attention to Barb. Fumbling the cloak off the peg, Hannah tossed it over her shoulders.

Nodding to Jethro to open the door, she called over her shoulder to her boss, "Now that you're back, I'll be going."

A cheery "Have a nice lunch!" followed them as they exited. Careful to keep a space between her and Jethro as they walked down the snow-dusted sidewalk, Hannah figured the best outcome she could hope for regarding the pending meal was for it to be tolerable.

Even that seemed unlikely when all heads turned in their direction as she and Jethro came through the door of Miller's Creek's main eating establishment. Hannah could almost tell from the ensuing expressions who was going to gossip about the two of them and who wasn't. By the time they sat down next to the window, she'd lost her appetite. Ordering a cup of soup, Hannah figured she might've agreed to the outing, but she didn't have to make it last long. She made a few feeble attempts at conversation, only to have Jethro nod or shake his head in response. When her soup arrived and he hadn't said a word other than to place his order, thoughts of three silent meals a day filled her heart with dread and her stomach with lead, prompting her to stir the soup more than eat it.

In the silence at her table, it was easy to listen to the conversation at the one behind her. Hannah stopped stirring at the words *stolen dog*. Straightening in her chair, she tipped her head back in order to hear what else was being said by the two *Englisch* diners.

"Found him down by Milwaukee. Wouldn't have if the new owners in the city hadn't taken him to the vet to be checked out and they discovered his microchip."

The other man grunted. "I'd heard some folks had dogs missing. Some mixed breeds, but mainly purebreds. Mine raised a ruckus the other night. Since then, I make sure if she's outside, I am, too. So glad you got Ace returned. Scary to think of how many might not be. Do they have any idea who—"

Hannah jumped when the waitress stopped by to refill their coffee cups. Reluctantly tuning out the men behind her, she glanced over to Jethro. Fortunately for future silent meals, he seemed to be a fast eater. Hannah frowned down at her soup. *Easy to do, when you're not saying a word.* But, she reminded herself, conversation worked both ways. Hannah had a feeling this courtship wasn't his idea, either. She needed to make more of an attempt herself. Pasting on a smile, Hannah looked up, just in time to see Gabe walk into the restaurant.

"What's he doing here?" was not what she'd intended to ask the man across the table.

Jethro glanced over his shoulder to see Gabe closing the door. Raising his eyebrows, Jethro lifted his freshly filled coffee cup. "Eating?"

Hannah stirred her soup faster as heat flamed her ears, until she was tempted to tug her *kapp* down over what she knew would be their fiery red edges. It shouldn't have been a surprise that Gabe was there. Miller's Creek had few restaurants and The Dew Drop was the only one downtown. And she'd seen Gabe's kitchen, what there was of it. If he hadn't unpacked the boxes since yesterday, it would've been difficult for him to make even a sandwich in the apartment. No wonder he was eating all his meals here.

Still, Hannah almost groaned when Gabe sat in her line of sight. The restaurant was busy, but not so busy that he couldn't have sat somewhere else. She made a face when the young Amish waitress hurried over to him. Rebecca hadn't served their table that quickly.

"Your soup isn't *g-gut*?"

"*Nee.* The soup's fine." Hannah struggled not to stutter herself, caught as she was with her eyes and attention on another man and an alien twinge of jealousy racing through her. "Everything's fine." Keeping her gaze on Jethro, she strangled her spoon as Gabe laughed at something the pretty waitress said. At Jethro's furrowed brow, Hannah forced herself to take a bite of the baked potato soup in front of her. "Can't beat hot soup on a cold day."

Raising his sandy-blond eyebrows again at the congealing mixture in her cup, Jethro swiveled in his chair to take another look at the man seated behind him. Now heat infused Hannah's cheeks until she was sure they were hotter than the soup had ever been as the two men nodded stiffly to each other. Jethro swung back to regard her quizzically. Under the intense regard of both men, the heat crept down her neck. Determinedly, she took another bite. As she chewed the lumpy mass, Hannah struggled to push up the corners of her mouth into what she hoped was a friendly smile. They felt heavier than the bales of hay that she helped her *brieder* load on wagons in the summer.

Scooping up another bite, she winced at the sound of the spoon scraping the crockery. She had no interest in food. But if eating while watching the flirtation across the room curbed her misplaced hunger for a life with the man sitting there, it was worth forcing it down.

The approaching waitress was a needed distraction as Gabe tried not to stare at Hannah.

"What can I get you today?" she asked cheerfully, the smile on her lips matching the one in her eyes.

You can get the man sitting by Hannah to move to another table. Gabe's own smile was a trial to keep in place. "The daily special sounds good." He'd eaten at the restaurant several times already. Usually he enjoyed his interactions with the pretty waitress. Not today.

Rebecca laughed. "I haven't told you what it is yet."

"Doesn't matter. Anything The Dew Drop makes is good." It was true. But Gabe knew anything he'd eat today would be tasteless with Hannah sitting across the room with another man. An Amish man and an unmarried Amish woman didn't normally sit together unless something was going on. The only thing that gave Gabe a smidgen of peace was that the man had a beard. In the Plain world, that meant he was already married.

"Pretty good crowd today," he observed, making a point to look around the room as Rebecca topped his water glass off for the second time. "I'm getting to know by face a number of folks in town, but have a ways to go yet. For example, the couple next to the window? I've seen the woman at the quilt shop below my apartment, but I'm not familiar with the man."

The waitress swiveled to see where he was looking. "Oh, that's Hannah Lapp. She's worked for the shop's *Englisch* owner for a number of years." Her gaze sharpened at the sight of the man. "She's sitting with Jethro Weaver, the bishop's son. Poor man just lost his wife and unborn child about a month ago."

Gabe nodded stiffly when the man turned to look at him. He remembered the case. Tragic indeed. The gossip was the woman had suffered a stroke, probably from eclampsia. So heartbreaking, as the condition was preventable. But sometimes Amish women didn't always seek prenatal care, at least until later months of their pregnancy.

From what he'd understood, the awful incident had helped push the grant responsible for his job through. "Time is tissue" was a mantra in the EMS world. Prompt help increased positive outcomes. A factor that Gabe was all too familiar with.

A cold burst of air swept over the table. Needing to distract himself from the pair at the window, Gabe glanced toward the door to see the bishop and his wife, whom he'd already had pointed out to him, come through it. The older couple scanned the room before pausing in their apparent search, a smug look settling over both their thin faces. Gabe followed their gazes to where Hannah and the bishop's son sat. From the Weavers' faces, the sight of the two together was met with a great deal of satisfaction. The younger couple's relationship was obviously an arranged match.

Gabe's mouth went dry. Leaning back in the booth, he pushed the plate Rebecca had set in from of him off to the side, his appetite suddenly gone.

Rebecca stopped by his booth again, water pitcher in hand. Her smile drooped a little when she saw the rejected plate. "Is everything all right?"

"Everything's just fine," he murmured, looking at the couple across the restaurant. Gabe knew, in order to convince Hannah to marry him, he already needed to overcome whatever had spooked her from their deepening relationship years earlier. Now he'd be confronting the will of the community's leader. The community he knew was important to the woman he loved.

Persuading Hannah that they belonged together seemed impossible.

Chapter Four

The truck rocked to a stop in front of a team of draft horses. The Belgians jerked up their heads when Gabe flung open the door. A quick glance behind the team revealed a wagon of cut lumber. One end of the load was unsecured, with boards sliding from the wagon to rest on the ground. Snagging his jump bag from the passenger seat, Gabe was a step away from the cab before the last rumble of the truck's engine faded on the crisp winter morning.

Bounding through the foot-deep snow in the ditch, he climbed over the barbed wire fence. His eyes stayed focused on the figures gathered at the edge of a small pond in the cow pasture beyond.

"Is he out?" he called as he ran, crunching across the snow-crusted grass loosely braided with cattle paths.

"Ben's got him!"

Dodging through the handful of youngsters clustered anxiously along the pond's bank, he saw an Amish man, garbed in a dark coat and watch cap, holding on to a rope. Gabe's sharp gaze followed the line across the frozen pond, its surface splintered with cracks like a broken windshield, to another man sprawled on the ice. This man's dark hair was plastered to his head, his arm hooked over a boy's chest. The youth sagged against the man's blue coat. His head bounced gently with each jerk of the rope as the Amish man pulled it in. An ominous crackle and pop drew gasps from the boys as another long splinter appeared on the pond's surface next to the prone pair. Gabe grabbed the icy rope and heaved in sync with the man.

"Did he go under?"

"Ja."

"How long?"

"About five minutes before Ben pulled him out."

"You know the kid?"

"Nee. He's *Englisch."*

The pair was sliding closer to the ragged brown weeds that fringed the pond. "Hey, kids!" Gabe called to the hovering crowd of boys. "What's your friend's name?"

"Alex," one of the older boys responded shakily. "Is he going to be okay?"

"We'll do everything we can," Gabe assured him, although his stomach clenched at the sight of the boy's limp figure. *Keep calm, Bartel. Maybe you can save this one.* His muscles strained with another coordinated pull on the line. "What happened?"

"It looked like a good place to play hockey. Then we heard a crash, and Alex went down. We tried to get to him, but the ice was popping and we thought we all might go under, so we got off. Derek called 911 and when we saw these guys coming… We should have gone out there to help him." The boy's voice started to crack.

"Nah. You did good. Otherwise we'd be pulling more of you out." Gabe's attention was on the pair, close enough now to reach from the frozen ground of the bank. Both man and boy were white-faced, the boy's lips growing bluer as Gabe watched. Reaching out a hand, the Amish rescuer assisted his friend off the ice. Rivulets of water ran from the other man's dark hair, streaming down over his face as he tried to lift the boy toward Gabe.

"That's okay. I got him." Snagging his jump bag, Gabe swept the limp boy into his arms, the sopping blond head lolling over his elbow. Working his way over the jagged terrain to the first flat ground he could find, Gabe gently laid the boy on his back. The kid wasn't breathing. He pressed fingers to the cold skin of the boy's neck. Nothing. No chest movement. No faint throbbing under his fingertips to indicate the kid was still alive. Gabe's own heart was pounding like he'd been thrashing in icy waters. Quickly snagging a CPR mask, he adjusted it over the boy's face.

"Stay with me, Alex," he muttered as he positioned himself over the motionless form. Without conscious thought, he began chest compressions to the rhythmic beat of an old disco tune. Thirty compressions, two quick breaths, back to the compressions, the process was automatic. Two minutes into the sequence, Gabe checked again for a pulse. Still nothing. "Come on, Alex," he begged, resuming compressions.

For a moment, the scenery surrounding Gabe shifted

from frozen water and snow-skiffed earth to one lush and green. The slack face below him was not an unknown boy, but his well-loved little brother. Only muscle memory kept Gabe's rhythm from breaking. But he had to draw in a shuddering gasp before he could breathe for himself, much less for the boy.

One of the two men hovering tensely nearby shifted. Gabe welcomed the distraction. "How'd you get here so fast?"

The dry one, blond hair curling up from under his dark blue watch cap, responded. "We were taking a load of lumber to the furniture shop in town. Heard the boys calling. Ben cut the rope on the load and we used it as a line in case he went down with the boy. Which he did. I think intentionally."

Gabe glanced up while he continued pressing the heels of his hands against the boy's chest. The Amish man's words might've been flippant, but his face was strained. Gabe followed the man's concerned gaze when it shifted to his companion.

The dark-haired man was shaking under his wet coat. "He went under." The words were barely audible due to his chattering teeth. Gabe's brow lowered at the sight of the man's pinched, white face.

"Ben, right?" After Gabe gave the boy two more breaths and resumed compressions, he shot another look at the man crouched beside him.

"Ja."

Gabe couldn't tell if the man responded with a nod or was just shaking. "I can't take care of both of you. Get in my truck. Can you turn it on? Good. Start it up and get the heater going. Behind the seat I have an extra jacket. Take off your wet clothes and put it on. Hopefully by then the ambulance will have arrived and you can fill them in when you bring them over here. Got it? Good."

"Nothing yet?" the blond man asked, watching his friend stumble across the field toward the truck.

"Nobody is dead until they're warm and dead," Gabe panted in time with the compressions. "You know CPR?" He grunted in relief at the man's hesitant nod. After giving the boy two more quick breaths, he checked again for a pulse. Nothing. Resuming compressions, Gabe hoped the sound in his ears was the faint wail of the ambulance and not encroaching fatigue. Or the memory of a brother he couldn't save. *Please, God, no. Don't let me lose another one.*

Hannah hesitantly tapped on the apartment's door. Holding her breath, she listened for the sound of someone crossing the floor to respond to her knock. At the continued silence, she rapped again, slightly louder. With no ensuing footfalls as the seconds passed, her shoulders sagged. Hannah told herself it was with relief, not disappointment. Gabe was still out.

She'd thought she'd heard him leave earlier in the day. *Who are you trying to fool, Hannah Lapp? You're aware of every single sound that comes from this apartment. I'm surprised you don't hear the dust settling. You know he left thirty minutes after you arrived this morning and hasn't come back yet.*

Hannah winced at the guilt that bounced through her head like popcorn on a hot stove. She hadn't seen

Gabe since her uncomfortable meal at The Dew Drop earlier that week. She'd finished his curtains at home last night. Her *mamm* had regarded her curiously when Hannah awkwardly explained what she was making, but hadn't said anything further. Hannah had wanted to get the curtains done quickly and to not have a reason to think about him...*them* anymore.

Which didn't explain the extra care she'd taken to ensure they were some of her best work. Or the fact that when she'd heard his tread on the stairs and the thud of the back door this morning, she'd battled briefly with dismay that he'd left before she could get upstairs to hang them. She was glad he'd be gone when she went upstairs with the curtains and the rods Barb had provided. Wasn't she? It was only because she'd been busy with customers and other duties that she hadn't been able to get upstairs to take care of it while he was out. Not because she'd been hoping he'd return before she went up.

Which he hadn't. With a sigh, Hannah tentatively twisted the door knob and entered the apartment.

Gabe had been right. He hadn't collected much in the way of household goods. The apartment was Spartan beyond a tired couch, bordered by a scuffed wooden coffee table and worn end tables. The simple mismatched collection faced an oil-burning stove. Hannah glanced at the blue material in her hands and smiled wryly. He'd also been right that the apartment needed some cheering up.

Closing the door behind her, Hannah headed for the window, making note of every detail of the room. It wasn't because it was his. She was just curious. That was all. She wrinkled her nose as her feet echoed on the wooden floor. A rug would warm up the room both in appearance and functionality. Pursing her lips, Hannah recalled some old wool her *mamm* had been keeping for years. Perhaps she'd let Hannah have it to braid a rug, just a little one, to lie between the couch and coffee table. Just something warm he could put his feet on over the winter—

Shrieking, Hannah clutched the curtains to her chest at the sight of the body lying on the floor beyond the couch. Staring at the motionless figure, she froze. It took a few frantic heartbeats for her to realize it wasn't a body…exactly. Although the yellow hair was almost lifelike, the rigid face beneath it obviously was not. The blue sweatshirt on the—Man? Woman? Doll?—was zipped up to just under a plastic chin.

Still, she backed away from the lifeless form. When she reached the window, following one last look to ensure the figure didn't move, she pivoted. Setting the rods and curtains at the base, Hannah looked up at the tall window. Realizing she didn't have any nails to attach the rod's brackets to the wall or a hammer to secure them, Hannah wrinkled her nose in dismay. *It's no wonder, you* dummkopf. *You were more concerned with the missing man than the job at hand.*

Keeping a wary eye on the body at the end of the couch, Hannah headed for the door. And shrieked again when it swung open toward her. The heavy beat of her heart thrummed under her fingertips as she clutched her chest. Gabe swept through the door and jerked it closed, his alarmed green eyes touching on her before they scrutinized the rest of the small apartment. Ascertaining no threat, he frowned and set down the black backpack in his hand. Closing the distance between them, he gently curled his hands around her upper arms. "Are you all right?"

"*Ja*. I just wasn't expecting you to come through the door."

As Gabe searched her face, his gaze gradually softened its intensity. His fingers twitched on her arms and, for a moment, it seemed he would draw her to him. Hannah held her breath. When Gabe relaxed his hold and stepped away, she let it out in a quiet sigh. *Surely not of disappointment?*

With a furrowed brow, Gabe glanced around the apartment again before returning his attention to Hannah, his cheek creasing at the slight lift in the corner of his mouth. "What are you doing up here?"

Her own cheeks heating, Hannah closed her eyes in frustration. *I was going to be calm when I saw him again. In control. Distantly pleasant, as should a woman be who is going to marry another man. Not screeching throughout his apartment like a startled owl. Or trembling like a leaf in a breeze when he touches me.* Opening her eyes, she gestured uncomfortably toward the window before crossing her arms in front of her. "I finished your curtains. I was going to hang them, but I didn't have all the tools I needed."

Shrugging off his coat, Gabe hung it on a peg on the wall before he looked toward the stack of blue fabric lying under the window. "Oh," he said distractedly. He smiled at her. But it wasn't the teasing, personal smile that'd originally drawn her to him at the party years ago. It didn't involve his eyes that Hannah knew could dance like a flame in a fireplace. If her behavior was different than she'd envisioned, his was dramatically so. *What was going on?*

Crossing to the window with a heavy tread, Gabe picked up the curtains. Staring down at the blue fabric, he absently stroked his hand over the top of the stack. "They're beautiful. They'll really brighten up the place. Thank you." His normally rich baritone barely deviated from a monotone.

Something was definitely wrong. Hannah frowned. Arms still folded, she trailed after him to the window. "I almost decorated your apartment by tossing them in the air to land willy-nilly. And stabbing myself in with the rods in the process."

"What?" Gabe turned to her, with sharper attention in his gaze.

"I was afraid you'd committed a murder up here and I'd discovered the body."

He lowered the hand holding the curtains, the material tumbling down his side to look like he was dangling a rich blue cape. "What?" he repeated.

At least she'd broken through his stupor. Whatever'd been bothering him, she'd succeeded in cracking through its disturbing hold on the man. Unfolding her arms, Hannah pointed to the end of the couch. "That thing over there."

His gaze followed the direction of her finger. "Oh—" a little bit of Gabe's normally endearing smile twitched on his lips "—Annie."

"It has a name?"

"Oh, yeah. Rescue Annie, CPR Annie, Resuscitation Annie, or simply Resusci Annie. She and I are old buddies." His smile expanded. "Currently, she's my only partner."

Now it was Hannah's turn to be a little startled. "What?"

Gathering up the material, Gabe refolded it before setting it against the wall. He strode over, more enthusiasm in his step now, toward the form at the end of the couch. He picked up the doll, its legs dangling below the stiff chest. "I teach CPR. Cardiopulmonary resuscitation. If you can keep the heart going, you have a chance to keep someone alive. If a person's heart stops, or they stop breathing, CPR manually pumps blood to the vital organs of the body until it can get started again. Or until it's determined…" Gabe's legs seemed to give out from under him. Clasping the mannequin, he sank down onto the couch.

"There was a boy today. A drowning. He was gone. I didn't know if we could get him back. He was the same age as…" Gabe pressed his lips together for a moment. "As I was doing CPR, all I could see was Will. Will's face. Will's blue lips. Will's slack body that I couldn't bring back." Gabe's voice was barely audible with his last words. One tear, followed shortly by another, tracked down the edge of his nose to drip onto on the doll's blue shirt.

Shaken, and gripped with the need to comfort him, Hannah found herself seated beside him. The worn cushion sagged, tipping her toward Gabe. She reached out a hand to his upper arm, both to console him and to brace herself from drifting in farther. "Will?" she whispered.

Gabe's hands clenched on the mannequin, his knuckles showing white for a moment before they relaxed their grip. "Will was my little brother." He exhaled deeply, his shoulders sagging with the action. "He drowned. I was preoccupied with…things. By the time I noticed he was…" He stared at the scarred wooden floor at his feet. "It was too late. I hadn't paid much attention in high school health class the day we did CPR. I mean, who really expects to use that?" His throat worked in a hard swallow. "If I had, maybe…" He bowed his head.

Hannah's own eyes prickled with tears. She rubbed her hand lightly over the blue sleeve covering his bicep, wanting to soothe. "When did this happen? You'd mentioned a little *bruder* when we were together, but you never said…"

When Gabe didn't respond, Hannah figured he wasn't going to answer her question. When he did, she wished he hadn't.

"It was shortly after you didn't show up that night. I didn't know how to find you. It wasn't like we'd been seen together, so I could go asking around the Amish folks. I did a bit." He snorted softly. "You can imagine what kind of reception I got. After a while, I figured if you'd wanted to see me, you would have. So I went home to Madison that weekend, trying to forget you. Or at least trying to understand what might've happened to make you disappear. I thought we…" His voice died off.

Squeezing her eyes shut to keep her tears at bay, Hannah recalled her own grief when she'd known she had to break off their relationship. She hadn't thought of him. *How selfish of me.* Her fingers tightened on his arm. Gabe's eyes remained focused on the scarred wooden floor in front of the couch.

"To distract myself, I decided to go swimming at a local lake my family frequented. My little brother wanted to come along. As we'd been there before, I figured, sure, why not." His lips twisted. "I went out into the deeper water. I was swimming hard, trying to forget… Will tried to follow me. When I finally looked around, he was gone. I—I found him, but I couldn't bring him back." Gabe tipped his head to the back of the worn couch and closed his eyes.

"I dropped out of school up here. Went back home for the rest of the semester to be with my folks. That fall, I changed my major. If I couldn't save Will, at least I could learn to save others." He exhaled in a shuddering sigh. "Today it helped me save the boy, Alex."

Wrung out just listening to his excruciating tale, Hannah remained rooted in her position on the couch. Knowing she played a part in it filled her with sorrow that couldn't be extinguished by tears. She swallowed against the swelling in her throat.

In their time together, she'd known Gabe as a fun and interesting companion. A caring, considerate man who'd made her laugh. She'd known joy with him, unlike anything she'd felt with anyone else. Enough that she'd almost left everything she'd known to be with him. In their interactions, she hadn't seen this depth of compassion. Her heart ached for him. It felt odd, yet right to be the one to comfort him. But how?

"Praise God for the two guys that beat me there today. They were Amish. Maybe you know them?" Opening his eyes, Gabe lifted his head to look at her. "Apparently they work for the furniture company in town. Gideon Schrock spelled me for a bit on CPR before the ambulance got there. A guy named Ben Raber went into the pond after the kid. They were amazing. It was their quick thinking more than my actions that saved the day. Good men. Said they're on the volunteer fire department. I look forward to working with them."

Hannah knew she needed to respond, but wasn't sure how. He needed her. How could she assuage and distract him from his grief? She latched on to the last things he'd said.

"I've known Ben most of my life. Gideon moved in a year or so ago." Clearing her throat, she forced emotions she didn't feel into her voice. "Are you telling me Ben can do something I can't? And if Gideon knows, then in all likelihood, my new brother-in-law Samuel Schrock knows how to do it, as well. And he'd never let me live that down. I don't suppose you could show me how to do this CPR thing on…Annie, was it?"

Gabe regarded her doubtfully. "You really want to learn?"

"Of course! Assuming you're a *gut* teacher."

His eyes began to dance in the way Hannah realized she treasured. His lips hooked in a half smile. "I haven't lost a mannequin yet."

"Let's see if you can keep it that way." Gabe's gaze traveled from her smiling face to where her hand still lightly rested on his upper arm. Jerking it away, Hannah clasped it in her lap.

Annie under one arm, Gabe agilely pushed up from the couch and turned to offer his hand to assist Hannah. "These old cushions have made it a possessive couch. Once you're in it, it doesn't want to let you go."

Her fingers still humming from their contact with his muscular bicep and her sensibilities from his unexpected vulnerability, Hannah smiled, but avoided touching him. She could relate to the couch's sentiments in regard to the man in front of her. It'd been difficult to let him go. Wedging an elbow against the arm of the worn sofa, she levered herself out.

"While doing CPR, you want the person on their back on a firm surface." Gabe laid the mannequin in the middle of the wooden floor and knelt beside it. "You're going to regret not making me pillows," he commented, with a rueful look at the scarred floor. The look he shot Hannah acknowledged there were other things in their relationship that he was regretting, as well.

So was Hannah. She was regretting that she couldn't wrap her arms around his neck to comfort him. To stroke a gentle finger over a furrowed brow. To brush a kiss on his wind-tousled hair. To ask more about a little *bruder* whom he'd obviously loved very much. But they didn't have that kind of relationship. They couldn't. But that didn't mean Hannah's heart didn't ache for Gabe's loss. That she didn't love... Hannah stepped back from the thought, bumping into the couch and almost sinking into it again.

Gabe wanting to help people was very noble. It was

admiration she felt. That was all. Hannah thought of her own young *brieder.* She couldn't imagine them being in danger because of her and failing to help them. If teaching her CPR diminished the pain from Gabe's eyes…

Briskly, Hannah circled the mannequin and knelt on its other side. "At home, our floor is covered with linoleum. It's not much softer. What should I do?"

"Hmm," Gabe regarded her across the blue-shirted figure. "There's a bit to it, but it's not difficult. If you're really interested, I can see about having you attend the volunteer firefighters' training meeting tomorrow evening. I'm re-certifying them on CPR. So for now, I'm just going to give you the basics, which can still help you save a life. Lack of oxygenated blood can cause brain damage within a few minutes. A person can die within eight to ten. CPR keeps that blood moving."

Hannah was afraid to ask, but she wanted to know. "What about the boy today?"

Gabe smiled slightly. "Time will tell, but praise God, it was looking good when I left the hospital."

Hannah couldn't prevent her corresponding grin. "*Gut.* I'm glad."

Her breath caught when Gabe didn't look away. Shifting, he leaned fractionally closer. Pulled by a seemingly invisible thread Hannah edged forward. Lowering a hand to brace him, Gabe flinched when the heel of it pressed into Annie's chest. Abruptly straightening, he sank back.

"Okay, the first thing you want to be aware of when you come upon someone needing aid is BSI, body substance isolation, and scene safety. Kind of a problem doing chest compressions on a person if you're surrounded by fire or in the middle of a road and could get hit by a car."

Hannah's eyes rounded.

"So check to see if the surroundings are safe. Then determine if the person is conscious." Gabe glanced at Hannah to see if she followed. At her nod, he continued, "If they're unconscious, tap them or shake their shoulder and ask, 'Are you okay?'" Annie wiggled under his hand as Gabe's loud voice echoed around the small apartment.

"You try now."

Feeling a little silly, Hannah did as he instructed.

"If you don't get any response, you need to take immediate action. If you're with someone, have them call 911." Gabe sat back on his heels as he regarded her. "Which might be difficult in your community. Although, come to think of it, a number of your youth carry cell phones during their *rumspringa*. Well, if you're with someone, have them get to a phone and dial 911 to get help. If you're alone and you have a phone close, make the call before you start compressions. If you don't have a phone close and you're alone, go straight into chest compressions. Got it?"

Knowing he expected some response from her, Hannah nodded weakly. It was a lot to think about.

"Okay, the normal acronym is C-A-B. The C stands for compressions, which is keeping the blood circulating. The A is airway. Open the airway. The B is for breathing. You have to breathe for the person."

Her concern must have shown, as Gabe paused.

"Hmm. Yeah, well, for you, we're just going to teach chest compressions. Keep doing them until there's movement or someone else can take over. Compressions may still keep someone alive until help arrives. If you want to learn more, come tomorrow night."

"Ah, I think this will be enough. I, um, wouldn't want to show them up with my new skills."

"I understand." From the way Gabe looked at her, she knew he also understood why she was doing this. Understood and was grateful. Hannah's pulse accelerated. She couldn't look away. *What happens when you're breathless and your heart is pounding too hard? Is there something that's the opposite of CPR to assist with that before you make a fool of yourself?*

Blinking dazedly, Gabe glanced down at Annie. "Um, let's see." He pointed to where the material of Hannah's skirt almost brushed the mannequin's shoulder. "You're kneeling in the right position." He unzipped the doll's blue jacket to expose the plastic chest. "Now, place the heel of one hand over the center of the person's chest right here." He placed his hand in the center of the mannequin's chest, right above the V indicating the end of the rib cage. "Then put your other hand on top of the first hand. Like so." He demonstrated. "Make sure your shoulders are directly above your hands and keep your elbows straight. Now you try."

Gabe retreated. Hannah leaned forward to hesitantly put the heel of her palm against Annie's cool, hard plastic. She placed her other hand on top of it.

"Just a little farther over here." Gabe reached out to gently shift her position and adjust her fingers. Hannah froze at the warm touch of his hands enveloping hers. Breathlessly, she glanced up to meet Gabe's eyes. They were equally shaken. His fingers flexed on hers a moment before he drew in a ragged breath and shifted away. "That's…it. Right there."

And it was. The unexplained, unanticipated, incomparable feeling that'd happened the first time their hands had touched.

Gabe cleared his throat. He reached out as if he was going to touch her shoulders to reposition her before thinking better of it. "Okay, elbows straight, and shoulders directly over your hands. That's good."

Flushing under his praise, Hannah composed a bland, interested expression as she sat back.

Gabe repositioned himself over the mannequin. "You can't use just your arms, you have to use your upper body weight. Push straight down on the chest about two inches."

Wincing, Hannah bit her lip. It seemed so much.

"Remember, you are beating their heart for them. You're saving their life. Believe me, if their heart isn't beating, they'd rather you do it than not." He demonstrated. "You want to do compressions at a rate of 100 to 120 per minute." He hooked a smile at her. "I don't suppose you listen to a lot of music?"

Frowning, Hannah shook her head.

"Well, there was a song that came out during the disco craze that has the perfect beat. It's called, ironically, 'Stayin' Alive.'"

"Was the song written for CPR?"

"No," he laughed softly, "but it fits." He sat back again. "You try now."

Hannah positioned herself over Annie, careful to put her hands in the correct position. She tentatively pressed down, surprised at the give of the mannequin. Rebounding, she pressed again.

"You got it. Now a little faster."

Hannah picked up the speed of her compressions.

"That's it. Now take it from the top. You find a person unresponsive."

Hannah went through the steps, pleased she remembered them all, ending with a minute of compressions. Strong as she knew herself to be from helping with farm work, she was surprised at how fatiguing CPR could be. She was slightly winded when she looked over to see Gabe nodding in satisfaction.

"I know. An untrained person can usually last about ten to fifteen minutes doing CPR. You did great. Do you want more?"

Hannah knew he only meant further training. She needed to get back downstairs. Away from him, away from the truth that she wanted so much more from him. She wanted to be able to give so much more. Her hand, her heart, her life to share with him. But that would mean giving up her community and opening her parents to more pain. Which she couldn't do. The most she could get from and give to Gabe was a careful friendship.

Shaking her head, she cleared her throat awkwardly. "*Denki* for the lesson. Now I can hold my head up around Ben, Gideon and Samuel. But I pray I never have to use it."

"My pleasure. And you won't be the first one leaving a CPR class with that thought."

As Hannah rose to her feet, she noticed the splash of blue against the wall. "The curtains! I was going to hang them for you. If you'll give me a moment, I'll run down for a hammer and some nails to hang the rods."

Gabe picked up the mannequin and returned it to the end of the couch. "I've unpacked recently enough that I remember where I put mine. I'll help you."

Within minutes, they had the rods and curtains up. Gabe had been correct. They certainly brightened up the place. As did the smile that Gabe now wore. Trotting downstairs, Hannah couldn't deny the pleasure she felt in knowing she'd put it there. Her descent slowed as she realized that even though she'd never stopped loving Gabriel Bartel, she was still going to marry another man.

Chapter Five

Gabe turned off the highway onto the country road.
It wasn't exactly out of the way. Okay, it was a bit out
of the way, but he was going to take this route on his
return from teaching an early-morning CPR recertifi-
cation class at the Portage hospital. If the route just happened to go past Hannah's farm, which he'd recently
discovered the address of, well, a critical part of his
job involved being able to quickly find locations in the
county. Surely it made sense to explore his new area?

Perhaps knowing where Hannah lived might prevent
her from disappearing from his life again. Although,
Gabe mused that not knowing her address didn't rate
high now among their obstacles. But while Hannah had
learned a bit about CPR yesterday, Gabe had learned
that she wasn't indifferent to him. There might still be
reason to maintain a sliver of hope for their relationship.
What could he say, he was a hopeful guy.

Gabe slowed as he passed her family's pristine farm
yard, raising his eyebrows as he noted clothes on the

line, even on a cold winter morning. But the pants and dresses shifting in the slight breeze were the only movement at the farm. What had he expected? Just because it was her day off didn't mean she'd spend it outside so he could see her as he drove by.

Turning at the next corner, he frowned at the sight of a black-cloaked figure walking on the side of the road some distance ahead. As the truck slowed, his heartbeat increased as he knew, without seeing the Amish woman's face, it was Hannah. He lowered the window as the vehicle rolled along at the quick pace of the woman beside it.

"Do you need a ride?" When she turned to him, Gabe's smile immediately disappeared at the sight of her face. Jabbing the brakes, he slammed the truck into Park. A second later, he was out the door and wrapping his arms about her unresisting form. "What's wrong?"

Red-faced in spite of the cold, Hannah was obviously striving for composure. Gabe rubbed her back in slow circles as he felt her hiccupping breaths. "Socks is missing," she got out in a high, tight voice. Like a dam breaking, her face crumpled and she began to sob. Gabe pulled her more tightly into an embrace, gently rocking her back and forth as he felt hot tears against his neck.

Gabe knew what the Border collie meant to her. "How long?"

He could barely make out the words that were spoken into his shoulder in between sharp inhalations. "She disappeared when I let her out last night. I heard a few sharp barks, but I didn't think anything of it as she and Dash sometimes play. When I went looking for her, I found Dash with my folks in the barn for milking, and Socks was gone. I wanted to search last night, but *Daed* discouraged me from going out in the dark." Gabe's arms tightened about her as Hannah's slender shoulders shook with renewed sobs.

"Shh. It'll be okay. We'll find her." Gabe rested his chin on the wool of her black bonnet. "Have you seen any sign of her along the road?"

"N-No. I've been looking since daylight. What if she was stuck in a fence and couldn't get to me? What if she fell through the ice like that boy? What if someone t-took her?" Hannah tipped her head back. Gabe's heart almost broke at the misery in her blue eyes.

Unwrapping one arm from around her, Gabe wiped a tear from her cheek. "We'll keep looking. But you won't do her any good by freezing before you find her." He shepherded her to the other side of the truck. "Get in. We can cover more ground this way. We'll go slow and keep the windows cracked so you can call and listen."

Upon assisting Hannah into the vehicle, Gabe quickly returned to the driver's side, climbed in and turned up the heat. They continued slowly down the country road with Hannah intermittently calling for Socks in an increasingly quavering voice before straining to listen for any responding bark over the quiet rumble of the engine. When they reached the first lane, Gabe stopped and turned to Hannah, who sat forlornly in the passenger seat.

"You want me to go in and ask? I can check to see if they've heard anything."

Hannah looked up the lane to the large white house

before shifting her gaze to his face. "It's Amish," she murmured.

"I know." He regarded her solemnly. "Still, much is lost for want of asking. If they know something about Socks, it might be worth it." Gabe ached for her, though. Being seen with a young man from outside her community was an issue for Hannah. In hindsight, he'd realized the unintentional covertness of their previous meetings had probably contributed to her disappearance years ago. If they had any chance for a relationship now, it had to be held out in the open. Gabe kept himself from trying to persuade her further. Since the risk was hers, the decision had to be hers, as well.

His heart rate rocketed, and he found it hard to breathe when Hannah reached out a hand to where his rested on the console. "All right."

Rotating his hand, they entwined fingers. Gabe turned into the lane. When they parked in front of the house, he gave her hand a squeeze before reluctantly releasing it. "We'll find her."

But they didn't find her there. The Amish woman who came to the door hadn't seen a Border collie. She made sure they knew she didn't like seeing Hannah traveling with an *Englisch*.

When Gabe returned to the truck, Hannah had tugged her black cloak more closely about her and kept her hands in her lap. Her eyes glistened with tears and her mouth trembled. "She's a neighborhood gossip. Everyone will know."

"Good, that way everyone knows we're looking for your dog, so if they see Socks, they'll contact you."

Hannah's smile was weak, but her eyes were grateful for his support. "Maybe."

They stopped at three more houses, two Amish and one *Englisch*, before turning onto the highway. The woman at one Amish home was neutral, but curious. The man's gaze at the other had shifted repeatedly between Gabe and where Hannah remained in the truck during the brief conversation. No one had seen Socks.

Hannah sat in the passenger seat, head bowed, silently weeping. "I don't think she would have come this far."

Gabe handed her some napkins from his stash in the console. "Well, there's one way to find out." He pulled into the first lane off the highway. They heard a dog barking before they were halfway up it. Jerking up her head, Hannah shot Gabe a wide-eyed look.

"Could be any," he cautioned her.

"I know that bark." Hannah's hand was on the door latch before he braked to a halt. Her door bounced on its hinges as she jumped out to rush for a fenced-in backyard, the source of the barking. Before she could reach it, a black-and-white dog scrambled over the fence and raced toward her. With a sob, Hannah crumpled to the ground, the dog leaping into her arms. Exiting the truck, Gabe watched as Socks licked Hannah's face exuberantly.

As he walked up the concrete steps, a gray-haired *Englisch* woman opened the door, dish towel in her hand. "I'm so glad someone came for her. She's too sweet of a dog not to have come from a loving home. Wondered if she was from the Amish community. Anyway, glad you found her."

Frowning, Gabe turned his head to look at the joyous reunion. "She's usually wearing a collar."

The woman shook her head. "There wasn't a collar on her when we found her early this morning. Only a rope with a short tail. Looked like it might've been gnawed through. I took it off her. You want it?"

"Thanks. I'd like to see it if you don't mind."

The woman disappeared to return a moment later, a rope with a knotted loop on one end and a frayed braid on the other in her hand. Examining it, Gabe agreed with her assessment. Socks had been tied up somewhere and chewed her way free. But where? And by whom?

Returning his attention to the woman, Gabe opened his mouth to thank her, only to be forestalled when she fixed her attention on his name tag and trailed it down over his shirt and the blue pants common to his profession.

"Are you that new paramedic guy that came with the grant? Sure glad that came through. Saw in the local paper that there were some issues with it, though. Hopefully they can get those resolved. Never know what's going to happen when county administrations change."

Gabe just nodded. He'd heard the rumors, as well. Maybe that's why the old guard had been so quick to hire him in. His stomach clenched at the thought of what he'd do if the grant fell through. With another polite nod for the loquacious woman, he looked over to see Hannah's smile as she rested her cheek on Socks's head. Any concern for himself evaporated in relief at having her reunited with her dog.

"So you'd be the one that saved the Winston boy? He lives just down the road. That would've been such a tragedy. Can't imagine the heartache in this neighborhood if you weren't there."

Gabe shook his head, wanting to be sure she knew who deserved the credit. "Some Amish men on the volunteer fire department got him out first. The boy owes his life more to them than me."

The woman nodded. "Some folks around here aren't sure about the Amish. Don't like to see them buying up the land. I imagine the feelings might be mutual. Human nature, I guess. I think the Amish have been good neighbors to us. Polite. Hardworking. Now who's this, so I know who to contact if that lovely dog shows up again?"

"This is Hannah Lapp. She lives around the corner, down the road. The dog is Socks."

"I'm Cindy Borders." She firmly shook Gabe's hand. "You ever need anything, just let me know."

Hannah was coming up the steps, Socks following closely at her heels. *"Denki."*

The woman smiled. "You're welcome."

Gabe turned to Hannah. "You ready to go?"

Waving to Mrs. Borders, they returned to the truck. When Hannah motioned Socks to get into the cab, the collie backed away.

Gabe raised his eyebrows at the dog's behavior. "You ever have that issue with her before?"

Hannah shook her head. *"Nee.* Not that I'm aware of. She doesn't ride in many trucks, but she jumps right into the buggy."

"Hmm." Gabe wondered if it had something to do with the dog's disappearance. "Get in. I'll hand her to you."

Moments later, Gabe settled into his seat to find Hannah with her arms around her dog, regarding him from across the console. "Gabe. I can't thank you enough for helping me find her."

He gripped the steering wheel with both hands to keep himself from reaching for her. Didn't Hannah know how he felt about her? That he was still hoping they could marry and have a lifetime together? If not, should he tell her? Hadn't he acknowledged that if there was a chance for their relationship, they had to bring things out into the open? Hoping he wasn't making a mistake, he drew in a deep breath and turned to meet her appreciative gaze. "It was my pleasure. Truly. You know I'd do anything to make you happy, Hannah. Except leave. I can't do that. Not when I think there's a chance for us."

Hannah's mouth dropped open, and she blinked rapidly. For a moment, as he'd recently witnessed it when they'd found Socks, Gabe recognized pure joy on her face. His breathing stilled. He leaned closer, reaching his hand toward her when the *clip-clop* of hooves on the pavement cut through the crisp weather. Hannah looked toward the highway, her profile blocked by the brim of her black bonnet.

When she looked back, her beautiful face was as frozen as the ice in some of the farmyard's winter puddles. Ignoring his outstretched hand, she shifted in her seat to be as close to the passenger door as possible. The Border collie immediately put her front paws in Hannah's lap and stuck her head out the window as Gabe drove down the lane. A horse and buggy passed when they reached the end of it, the driver and his passenger peering at the truck through the windshield.

As they pulled out and the hoof beats faded away, the ensuing silence in the truck cab was uncomfortable. Striving not to feel dejected, Gabe knew something needed to be said to break it. "Might want to pull her back in, I'm rolling up the window." He nodded toward Socks. "She has the makings of a good truck dog."

Hannah didn't reply, but her tepid smile disagreed.

Gabe packed up the practice mannequins used in the evening's training. Even with his head bent, his attention was on the group of Amish men not far from the table where he was working. One of them was the man who'd been with Hannah at the restaurant. Gabe concentrated on ignoring the impulse to scrutinize the man, or eavesdrop on the conversation. He'd say this for the guy, he didn't say much, he'd been quick to be recertified and he had the obvious respect of the men in the community.

Two of the group broke off and approached the table. One of them Gabe recognized as the blond man who'd been at the pond. The other's similarity in looks suggested he was a relative.

His fellow rescuer greeted him with a nod. "I'd have felt a lot more confident if I'd have had this refresher *before* I had to use CPR the other day."

Gabe grinned at the young Amish man. "You did great, Gideon. I should've had you teaching the course."

"*Ja*, well, it helped that you were right there beside me at the pond. Helps also that you're able to teach these classes locally. Otherwise we'd have had to hire drivers and travel some distance to take the training."

"All part of my job now. I aim to do whatever I can. Who knows when it might save a life, right?"

"*Ach*, as long as Ben's the one who goes into the freezing water, I'm game. Now, if it was Samuel with me the other day, we'd still be debating about who went out on the ice."

The other blond man shook his head. "No, we wouldn't have. It would've been you. Being the older *bruder* has to count for something."

Gabe grinned at the siblings' interaction. Closing the lid on the mannequin case, he snapped it shut and looked up to see Samuel studying him.

"I'm also now older *bruder*, at least by a few months, to Hannah Lapp. I understand you were seen with her today. Is there anything that an older *bruder* needs to know about that?"

Gabe met his gaze. "The Amish grapevine works very quickly."

The man shrugged good-naturedly. "Almost as fast as the *Englisch*'s information highway."

"You probably already know that she found her dog then. That's all there was to it." *For now.* Call him foolish, but he hadn't given up yet. "I wish Hannah nothing but the best." *Which hopefully includes me in her life.*

Hannah's brother-in-law scrutinized him further before smiling slightly. "It was horses that got me. See you around."

Gabe shook his head as he watched the brothers leave. He didn't have long to ponder the curious remark when another Amish man approached the table.

With a grin, Gabe nodded at the newcomer. "Aaron.

It's good to see you. How've you been?" He'd met Aaron Raber at a party when Gabe was taking classes at the nearby junior college years ago. In his *rumspringa*, the Amish man had been one of the young men in their run-around years that seemed to find anything within horse-and-buggy—or for a few, even car—range that remotely resembled a party. Aaron was the one who'd invited Gabe to the gathering where he'd met Hannah. He nodded to the short cast the man was wearing on his arm. They'd worked around it in order to complete his training. "You doing all right?"

"I'm *gut*. I see you found a way back into the area."

"Well, God opens doors. Although maybe sometimes it's windows."

"This isn't what I remember you doing when you left. You were in some kind of…mechanics, *ja*?"

"Yeah, well. I had a change of heart. Went home to Madison. Finished up there. Still mechanics of some kind, I guess. Human body mechanics. Speaking of which, is your brother the one that went in after the boy?"

"That'd be Ben. Never hesitates to step up when needed. *Gut* man to have in a pinch." The man quickly moved on from his younger brother's heroics. "Were there any classes for mechanics down in Madison?"

Obviously, the man wanted to draw the conversation back to his topic. Gabe didn't have a problem with that. He nodded. "There are some good tech schools in Madison. I hear it has one of the best diesel programs in the country."

The dark-haired Amish man leaned in from the opposite side of the table. "Any way of getting *gut* training without taking the classes?"

Gabe frowned as he considered the question. "In what way?"

"We don't use electricity from the grid, so the community gets its power from motors, both gasoline and diesel. From refrigerators in the home to huge machinery at the sawmill and Schrock Brothers' Furniture. Things are changing. Land's tight. Not as many opportunities to farm. Have to come up with other ways to make a living and support a family. Someone in the Plain community needs to be able to repair and sell all these motors, big and small. Why not me?"

The man had a point. And had found a potential niche into the community business environment. "I met a guy at school," Gabe said. "His dad has a repair shop in Madison where some of the students interned. He'd know more than I do. I can get you his number if you think it'll help."

At the man's enthusiastic nod, Gabe pulled out his phone and shuffled through his contacts. He looked over at Aaron. "You got a phone?"

Aaron pulled out a device and rattled off the number. "For the moment. Until I get baptized." He half smiled. "Followed shortly after by marriage."

Gabe wanted to be happy for the man, but the emotion that initially surfaced was envy instead. Keeping his expression neutral, he bent his head over his phone as he sent the contact information. "Congratulations."

"You might've met her. She was in the fabric shop the day Ruth Schrock became ill."

There might've been another woman in the shop that day. There also might've been a marching band in there. Gabe didn't remember anything about that day except his patient and seeing Hannah again. "Sweet girl. Again, congratulations."

"Denki." Aaron lifted up his phone and tipped it toward Gabe. "And *denki* for this. I appreciate it. I hope things work out for you, as well."

Gabe eyed him sharply, remembering the news that he and Hannah had been together had already raced around the community.

Aaron's eyebrows peaked at his pointed interest. "On your new job." Pocketing his phone, he waved and exited the fire department's meeting room. Although other men nearby, *Englisch* and Amish, nodded as they broke up their conversations and left, no one else approached Gabe as he finished packing up the abbreviated training mannequins and other supplies and loaded them in his truck.

So, Hannah and he were news around the community. As Gabe headed back to his apartment, he wondered what being the new hot topic on the Amish grapevine meant for his chances with the woman he loved.

Chapter Six

Hannah looked up from her needlework at Dash's sharp bark. Socks, curled up beside Hannah's chair, jumped to her feet. Emitting a soft whine, she trotted to the door. Across the room, Hannah's *daed* tipped down the corner of the newspaper he was reading to meet Hannah's frown. Paul, the only one of her four younger brothers currently at home, looked up from where he was whittling at the kitchen table.

A moment later, a series of furious barks had Hannah springing to her feet as well and hurrying to the door. Flinging it open, she stepped out onto the porch with Socks close beside her. Wrapping her arms about her to ward off the cold, Hannah searched the darkness for the male Border collie. Her hand rubbed Socks's silky head as her mind thought back to the dog's disappearance three days earlier and the frayed rope found on her.

Hannah's shoulders sagged in relief when she made out the white markings on the black-and-white dog as he zipped back and forth across the top of the lane.

"Here, Dash. Come here, boy," she called for him. After a moment's hesitation, the dog loped to the house and leaped up onto the porch. With a soft growl, he positioned himself at the top of the steps, looking out.

"Everything all right?" Hannah turned to see her *daed* silhouetted in the doorway, the gas lamps from inside the house a soft glow behind him.

"I think so, *Daed*. I don't see anything."

Zebulun Lapp nodded and disappeared into the house. Calling to Dash, Hannah stepped closer to the door her *daed* had left open.

"Come here, boy. Why don't you come inside?" Although she sighed, Hannah wasn't surprised when the Border collie just turned his head to look at her before facing the darkness beyond the porch again. Dash had never liked it in the house. At most, he might enter and circle the room to ensure everything was as it should be before racing for the door again. Tonight, he remained braced at the edge of the porch. Hannah closed the door and crossed to him, wishing she had his enhanced senses, as she, too, stared into the night.

A dim light glowed where the road was. Then it was gone. Hannah blinked, trying to figure out what it might've been. It wasn't a flashlight beam. She hissed in a breath when it came to her. It'd been a dome light of an *Englisch* car. If that was so, why was it sitting on the dark road beyond the end of their lane? Holding her breath, she focused on listening. In the cold, still night, she made out the quiet rumble of a car engine. But no corresponding headlamps lit up the road. She tried once again to coax Dash inside with the same lack of success; instead, the dog kept looking toward the direction of the vehicle.

Kneeling beside him, Hannah wrapped her arms around his taut shoulders. Socks huddled on her other side. Keeping one arm around Dash, Hannah looped the other around Socks, taking comfort from the contact of their warm, vibrant bodies. All three focused their attention on the road.

Dash stiffened, and Socks lifted her head at the faint sound of barking. Hannah narrowed her eyes on the muted glow in the distance of an *Englisch* neighbor's yard light. From numerous trips past, she knew a large black-and-brown dog roamed their yard. The trio on the porch listened as the barking continued, followed abruptly by the muffled sound of a human yelp. Unbidden, the image of the man who'd approached her and Socks on the sidewalk in town popped into her head. Chilled by the thought of the man, as well as the permeating cold, Hannah hugged her dogs more tightly. A roar of an engine cut through the night, this time with headlamps piercing the darkness. The lights headed in the direction of town.

Conscious now of the cold nipping at her nose and ears and seeping into the parts of her not in contact with the dogs, Hannah stood. With one last look toward disappearing lights, she and Socks returned to the house. Dash stayed planted on the porch.

It took an hour and a hot cup of tea for Hannah to settle down. Still, she poked herself with her needle when Dash barked again. It was a different bark from earlier, but Hannah was up and at the door before the dog's last yips concluded.

There was no questioning the clatter of hooves on the lane's frozen ground as a horse and buggy pulled up in the darkness.

"Malachi?" Hannah watched as an Amish man sprang out, foregoing the buggy's step in his urgency. There was no sign of her friend. Her fingers tightened on the doorknob. "Where's Ruth?"

Malachi was panting as if he'd run the distance between the two farms himself. He braced his hands on both sides of the door. "The *boppeli!*"

There was no need to say more. Hannah jerked her cloak and bonnet from the nearby pegs on the wall. Malachi anxiously looked behind her into the large open room. "Your *mamm?*"

"Not here. Paul!" she called to her younger *bruder*. "Run down to the phone shack and call the midwife. Tell her that Ruth Schrock is having her baby." Hannah was halfway across the yard before Malachi caught up with her. With a hand at her elbow, he assisted her into the buggy, almost tossing her across the seat in his excitement before scrambling in after her.

Hannah braced a hand on the buggy's dash as they swung out of the yard. "How is she?"

Malachi encouraged his gelding to pick up the pace. "She's bossy."

Bringing her hands to her lap, Hannah clasped them so tightly she felt the cut of her short nails on her skin. "That's her normal state. Obviously labor hasn't affected her much."

There was little further conversation as tension filled the buggy on the ride between the two farms. Hannah's heart raced with the cadence of the horse's quick beat on the road. Her friend needed help, but she'd never delivered a *boppeli* before. Her *mamm*, mother of several children, was visiting relatives in another district and wouldn't be home tonight. Rocking with the motion of the buggy, Hannah tried to concentrate on the upcoming event, but her ability to focus vaporized like the condensed air that drifted along the horse's black mane. They needed more help. *Please, Gott, let Paul reach the midwife. Please let her arrive soon.*

It seemed Malachi could hear her thoughts. "You ever done this before?"

The brisk air stung Hannah's nose as she drew in a shaky breath. She considered stretching her experience to comfort both herself and the dad-to-be, but the truth popped out instead. "I've helped *Daed* deliver several of our dairy calves."

Malachi was quiet for a moment before snorting. "Ruth's pragmatic, but I'll leave it to you to tell her you're comparing her delivery to that of a Holstein."

She recognized the humor for what it was, a defense against fear. A quick grab of the buggy's door frame kept her from swaying into Malachi as they swung into the lane before coming to a rocking stop in front of the house.

"You go on in. I need to take care of Kip. I'm… I'm hoping we don't need him the rest of the night."

Although she wanted to dash into the house, Hannah picked her way over the combination of frozen, rutted ground and smooth, icy puddles. When she reached the front door, a guarded woofing emanated from the other side. "It's okay, Rascal," she soothed. "It's me." Twisting the handle, Hannah stepped inside to be greeted by the Border collie Ruth had gotten from her as a puppy a year ago. Shooting a glance toward the door she knew led to a downstairs bedroom, Hannah bent to give the dog's head a brief rub. "I know. It's a pretty exciting night."

Her heart rate jumped at the continued lull from the room as she hastily shed her outer gear to hang it on the nearby pegs. She'd expected some type of greeting. Surely her friend had heard her come in? Hesitantly, Hannah crossed the large open room. "Ruth? Are you there?"

There were a few more beats of heavy silence as she approached the door before an exasperated "Just where did you think I'd be?" floated through the opening.

Hannah exhaled a breath she wasn't aware of holding. Her friend sounded more annoyed than distressed. "With you, it's hard to tell." She stepped into the room, glancing immediately toward the bed. Finding it empty, she blinked in surprise.

"*Ach*, it's a pretty safe guess tonight. Did you leave Malachi at your place?"

At her friend's comment, Hannah whirled to find Ruth across the lantern-lit room, pulling miniature clothing from a wooden chest. Shaking her head, she crossed to join her. "He'll be here in a moment. He's taking care of Kip. What are you doing up? From the way Malachi came racing to our house, I expected to find you…well, not up and around."

"There always seemed to be something to do, other than get these out." Ruth ran a finger down the dark blue material. "I made them months ago. But, after Louisa, I put them away. Just…just in case." She turned toward Hannah, a little gown and cap in her hands. Although she sounded nonchalant, her appearance told a different story. Auburn hair stuck in sweaty tendrils around her flushed face. Her green eyes were clear, but filled with relief at the sight of company. They shifted to the door, obviously searching to see if anyone else would be entering the room.

Hannah bit her lip. "I'm sorry. My *mamm* isn't home tonight. It's only me. Paul's calling for the midwife. I don't know when she'll be able to get here." She forced the reassuring smile she knew her friend needed to see onto her face. "I'm sure we'll be fine until then." Taking Ruth's arm, she steered her toward the bed. They were halfway across the room when Ruth gasped and hunched forward, crossing her arms over her belly. Hannah could only pray as tension gripped the elbow under her fingertips. *Please,* Gott, *let us be fine.*

They stayed rooted in the center of the room until Ruth visibly relaxed. Lifting her head, she squinted at Hannah. "*Gut* thing I always thought you had more sense and composure than any natural woman should have."

Even though she hadn't moved, Hannah felt like she'd run to the neighbors' farm and back in empathy with the physical struggle of the woman beside her. She couldn't take Ruth's pain for her, but she'd help her in any other way she could, even if it was just mild distraction. "Well, one of us needed it," Ruth snorted as they crept the rest of the way to the bed. Flipping back the sheets, Hannah helped the pregnant woman into a sitting position.

Sighing, Ruth leaned her head against the headboard. "If you would do one thing for me?"

"Anything," Hannah immediately agreed. She pulled the sheets up to tuck around Ruth's rounded lap.

"Make sure my *kapp* stays on, as I think I'll be doing a considerable amount of praying tonight."

"I've got it." Hannah straightened Ruth's prayer covering and secured the pins. She understood Ruth's concern. The *Biewel* stated a woman's head should be covered when praying. As it also said they should pray without ceasing, Amish women wore head coverings continuously. Knowing she'd be doing a considerable amount of praying over the next hours as well, Hannah confirmed her own *kapp* was well anchored after the jolting ride.

"And Hannah?" Ruth reached out and clasped her hand. Hannah tried not to wince at the strong grip squeezing her fingers. "If I scream, don't tell anyone. I have a reputation to keep."

"That's *hochmut*." Hannah surreptitiously wiggled her tingling fingers when Ruth released her hand.

"Believe me," Ruth groaned softly as she shifted. "Of the many things I'm feeling right now, pride is not one of them." She eyed Hannah with a frown. "We can't all be models of *demut* and *gelassenheit* like you."

Hannah's lips twitched as she adjusted pillows behind Ruth's back. "I won't tell," she promised. "Besides, no one would believe me if I did. They all figure if you make any sound at all, it'll be to give orders."

"*Ach*, they're right." Ruth settled back in obvious relief at the new position. For a few moments, the room was quiet as she gently massaged her belly. When she spoke, it was so soft that Hannah had to lean forward to hear her whispered words.

"So here's the first one. If anything happens to me, take care of my husband."

Hannah froze. Ruth looked up, and the two women shared a glance. Only clamping her tongue between her teeth kept Hannah from bursting into tears at her friend's obvious concern. They were both thinking of the loss of Louisa Weaver and her unborn baby. Careful not to jostle the other woman, Hannah sat on the side of the bed and took both of Ruth's unresisting hands in hers.

"Whatever happens will be according to *Gott*'s will. So we shouldn't worry about that. I'm thinking your worry should be more about the sleep you'll be missing when a beautiful *boppeli* keeps you up at nights. And you and Malachi will be *wunderbar* parents who'll give this child many siblings to play with in the future. Everything will be fine." Hannah pressed her lips together in a trembling smile. *Please,* Gott, *let me be right about that.*

With a final squeeze of her friend's hands, Hannah stood and made her way to the open door. Facing the living room, she spoke over her shoulder. She didn't want Ruth to see her face, as she was struggling to mask her own fears. "Now I have some things to get ready. I'll be back in a moment." Striding quickly into the kitchen, Hannah ensured she wasn't in the line of sight of the open bedroom door when she hugged herself and bowed her head. *Please,* Gott, *let me know what to do to help her. And please, please have the midwife hurry.* With a deep breath, she raised her head. Moving about Ruth's home, she gathered clean sheets, towels and rubbing alcohol while racking her brain for anything else that might be needed for the pending birth.

Chapter Seven

Gabe forked up another bite of meat loaf. He'd made a few lunches at his apartment—meaning he'd opened up a few cans of soup—but had been eating all his suppers at The Dew Drop. It wasn't that he was at a loss in a kitchen, but that the Dew was such a winner. And its warm, cheery atmosphere was much better than spending an evening at home. Alone. Thinking about a woman who wasn't likely to be sharing any home with him.

Among the clatter of silverware and quiet buzz of conversations, he heard the ringtone and vibration of a phone on a nearby table. Idly looking over, Gabe saw Martha Edigers, fellow Mennonite and the local midwife, frown as she put down her fork and picked up the device. The older woman must struggle with her hearing, as the volume was turned up loud enough for Gabe to hear from his own booth. He straightened abruptly at one of the names mentioned as Mrs. Edigers listened to the excited male voice on the phone. Gabe had his wallet out and was tossing a bill on the table by the time the woman disconnected the call. He slid out of the booth and was in front of Mrs. Ediger's table in time to see her gather up her coat and fill in her husband on the call.

"That was Paul Lapp. Ruth Schrock is having her baby. Hannah Lapp is with her, but I need to go now."

"Anything I can do to help?" Gabe nodded at the woman's husband before shifting his gaze back to the midwife. The gray-haired woman studied him with narrowed eyes for a moment.

"You know, I might need you. I usually have an assistant, but she's laid up following a foot surgery. I've heard you know what you're about. Does that include birthing babies?"

"Once. I was more anxious than the new parents. But I can bring along some equipment in case it's needed and add a hand if necessary." As Mr. Edigers made a move to rise, Gabe continued, "And I'd be happy to drive."

Mrs. Edigers covered her husband's hand with her own. "You finish your dinner. I'll see you at home. It's hard to tell on these first ones. I don't know when I'll be back." They shared a smile. It apparently was a common farewell for them. Reaching out a hand, Gabe assisted the midwife out of her chair and on with her coat.

"I need to grab some supplies before we head out."

"My truck's out front. Just tell me where we're going first."

After swinging by the midwife's house to pick up necessities, they were headed out of town minutes later. They'd reached the highway before Gabe felt a sting of chagrin for inviting himself along. Granted, it was always helpful to have medical assistance available for a home delivery. From what he'd heard, though, the older woman seated beside him had been successfully delivering babies in Miller's Creek for as long as anyone could remember. But once he'd heard Hannah's name, Gabe acknowledged it would've been difficult to dissuade him from offering assistance, just for the chance to see her and ensure she was all right.

Squirming with embarrassment, he glanced over at his passenger. "I appreciate you letting me come along."

Mrs. Edigers smiled benignly. "Glad to have your help. You never know in these situations." Her smile ebbed. "The community's somewhat tense after a recent loss."

"I'd heard about that."

"The Amish don't carry health insurance. When someone has bills to cover, they rally around with fundraisers. But they try to keep costs down. For them, childbirth is natural and quite common. That's why many of the women don't seek medical help until later in the pregnancy. Sometimes things that could be caught and prevented, aren't." She shook her head. "Things like eclampsia."

Gabe had heard something to that effect. The complication could be fatal to mother and child.

Mrs. Edigers sighed. "Some women go to chiropractors, asking for help on pregnancies. I don't know why they're more comfortable going there than other medical facilities. I help where I can. Over the years, I've gained a level of trust. It would be wonderful, though, if someone from their community would become a midwife."

"How is that possible? They stop school after eighth grade."

"There are certifications that can be earned through apprenticeships. Wisconsin currently recognizes them." She directed his turn onto a country road. "You know the Schrocks?"

"Met them." Gabe couldn't recall if introductions had been done that day in the fabric shop. Beyond his patient's needs, all he'd seen and known that day was Hannah. But he'd remembered Ruth from before. "Briefly. I…um…am more acquainted with Hannah Lapp."

From the weight of the gaze he felt across the truck's cab, Gabe figured the Amish information highway must have tracks through the midwife's office. Mrs. Edigers didn't comment, but a quick glance in her direction revealed an enigmatic smile. "I'm sure everything will work out fine."

With Mrs. Edigers's directions and Gabe's heavy foot on the pedal, they were soon pulling in front of a large white farmhouse. In the moment before he shut off the truck, the headlights revealed a man stepping out onto the porch, a black-and-white dog at his side. Gabe gathered equipment from his side of the cab and hurried around to help the midwife over the rough, frozen yard. Woofing once to let them know he knew they were there, the Border collie stayed beside the man, his white-tipped tail waving gently over his back.

Geared to respond to any medical or emergency situation, Gabe blew out a few breaths to remind himself it wasn't him who'd been called out to the farm. He was self-invited backup. Keeping a hand under the older woman's elbow, he assisted her up the stairs.

"Hello, Malachi. How's she doing?"

The blond man looked like he wasn't sure how to answer the question. *"Gut?"*

Mrs. Edigers patted his arm. "Don't get too comfortable out here. Even if Ruth isn't looking for you again soon, I will be to have you help catch the baby."

The man's broad shoulders rose and fell in a shaky sigh. With a smile, the midwife patted his arm again and disappeared into the house.

Turning to Gabe, Malachi reached out a hand. *"Denki* for bringing her out." Raising an eyebrow at the unusual action for an Amish man, Gabe shifted the bag of equipment to his other hand and shook it. It was surely an unusual evening for the pending father.

"You Samuel and Gideon's brother?" It was a logical assumption. There was a family resemblance to the two men who'd been at the fire department training session. Gideon had said the day of the cold water rescue that he worked at the furniture business in town. The only one Gabe had seen so far was called Schrock Brothers. But in Amish communities, where certain surnames were very common, there could be ten different Schrock families.

"Depends on if they were behaving."

Gabe grinned and reached down to acquaint himself with the dog before running his hand over its smooth head. "Very much so. I saw them at a CPR training session last night and met Gideon when he and Ben Raber rescued the boy at the pond."

"Then I guess I'll claim them." Malachi looked over his shoulder through the door into the house. "I…ah… need to go back inside." The man twisted his work-hardened hands together. Gabe read both apprehension and eagerness in the gesture.

"Absolutely." Gabe quickly crossed the porch. Malachi followed, looking immediately to a closed door across the large, simply furnished room once they stepped inside the house.

He closed the outer door with a quiet click. "Actually, it was *gut* to step away for a moment. It's hard to see her in… She isn't saying much of anything." Malachi's smile was wry, but his eyes remained solemn. "Which is abnormal for Ruth." He exhaled in a long stream through pursed lips. "I feel…helpless. I'm so glad Hannah came earlier. She's been a comfort to Ruth."

Gabe gripped the man's shoulder and squeezed it gently. Even though she wasn't and may never be his, the thought of Hannah someday bringing his child into the world swept him with empathy for this obviously strong man who felt powerless in the face of his wife's pain. "I'm sure you are a great comfort to Ruth, as well."

Malachi swallowed and nodded. "I'm going to go back in. Help yourself to anything you want in the kitchen." He glanced toward the dog. "All I can offer is Rascal for company while you wait."

"We'll be fine." Releasing his grip, Gabe glanced down at the dog. Relieving Gabe of the supplies with a final nod, Malachi crossed to the closed door, his tread slow on the linoleum floor. Pausing in front of it, he took a deep breath, turned the handle, stepped decisively into the quiet room and closed the door behind him.

The Border collie looked toward the door and whined softly. Gabe knelt to give him a few reassuring pats. "They'll be fine, as well." Rising to his feet, he wandered briefly around the room before stopping in front of an oak rocker. Marveling at the workmanship, he decided it was too small for him and settled into the upholstered mission-style chair nearby. Shifting through a stack of *Budgets*, he began flipping through the Amish newspaper by the illumination of a nearby gas light. The dog lay down between the two chairs, chin on paws, to face the bedroom door. The room was quiet except for the ticking of the nearby wall clock and the soft rustle of turning pages.

Fifteen minutes later, both man and dog started when a strident tone intruded in the silence. It took Gabe a moment to process that his pager was going off in the room otherwise void of electronics. Hushing the device, he quickly contacted dispatch. A moment later, he rapped softly on the closed bedroom door.

When Hannah cracked the door open, he smiled in relief at the composure on her face. "How are things going?"

"*Gut.* We're still waiting. The *boppeli* is being a little shy."

"I need to go on a call. I don't know how long I'll be gone. Will that be an issue for Mrs. Edigers?"

Hannah turned back toward the unseen room. Following a short, murmured discussion, she shook her head. "*Nee*. She's expecting to be here a *gut* while yet."

Gabe nodded. "Okay. I'll see you later." Although he wished for a more lingering farewell, he needed to get going. Giving another abrupt nod, he headed for the door. That Hannah was still watching him when he'd looked back while closing it prompted an extra zip in his step as Gabe hustled across the frozen ground to his truck.

The flashing blue light on his vehicle reflected over the snowy landscape as he retraced his way toward Miller's Creek. Gabe recognized the address. On the distant outskirts of town, he swung into a driveway, the truck shuddering as it slid into the frozen ruts in the unplowed surface. Abandoned vehicles lined the lane to a dilapidated house and machine shed. The sign above the wide shed door was shattered on the left side, leaving only the word REPAIR visible, like it was making a plea instead of advertising a business.

A dim glow, generating from a bare bulb in a simple white socket, lit the porch. Gear in hand, Gabe headed for the ragged door beyond. He'd heard of this guy. Clay Weathers had been a respected local mechanic until a snowmobile accident a few years ago. He'd eventually recovered from his back injury. He hadn't recovered from the pain medications he'd become addicted to during the process. His business, health, friends and family had been left behind in the wake of the hold opioids now had on him.

Gabe brushed his pocket to confirm he had naloxone as he trod across the weathered porch. The call had been for a deep laceration but, given the story on the man, other issues were possible. Rapping firmly on the warped screen door, he loudly announced himself. Gabe was about to try the handle when a muffled "Come in" filtered through the door.

Pushing it open, Gabe stepped into a small, shabby living room to find who he presumed to be his patient, sitting in a worn recliner with the footrest extended. A bloody towel was wrapped around the man's hand. The man's left calf was bare except for the blood-stained towel pressed to it with his free hand. A few more similarly soiled towels lay beside the chair.

"Looks like you tangled with something." Upon setting down his gear, Gabe donned his personal protective equipment and leaned over the man. He nodded to the man's leg. "May I?"

Wearily nodding, the man pulled his hand back. Gabe examined the leg. Through the smeared blood, he could see some gashes and a seeping puncture wound. "Dog bite?" he confirmed.

"Yup, but he didn't mean it. Was my fault. I startled him."

Placing clean gauze on the puncture wound, Gabe directed the man to place pressure against it. "Let's get that bleeding stopped before we clean you up." Turning his attention to the man's hand, Gabe unwrapped the soiled towel to find similar wounds, although these were no longer bleeding. "Do you know the dog? Is this normal behavior for it? Do you know if it's up-to-date on its rabies shots?"

"No, no. He's a good dog. He's in good shape."

Gabe frowned. He didn't know if he was talking

more to Clay Weathers or to what the man was under the influence of. Gathering what he needed, Gabe began cleaning and treating the man's hand.

"When was the last time you had a tetanus shot?"

Now the man frowned. His eyes, even with their constricted pupils, looked melancholy. "I used to keep up with that. Because of the shop. I... I've had one."

"Do you want to go to the hospital? I don't think these will require stitches, but I recommend having them checked out, as dog bites are prone to infection." He couldn't make the man go to the hospital. And the choice not to go affected what Gabe could do for him. But if he went, perhaps Clay Weathers would allow the hospital to assist him with other issues.

"Nah. I'll be all right." The man's head dropped to the worn headrest of the recliner, and he closed his eyes.

Gabe sighed as he wrapped gauze around the man's hand. "You'll need to continue to clean the wounds and put antibiotic ointment on them." Finishing with the hand, Gabe turned his attention to the leg to find the bleeding had stopped. "I highly recommend seeking out your personal physician for future care, especially if it gets infected."

Attending to the man's calf, Gabe felt rather than saw the man's shrug. He wasn't surprised with the reaction. It was what he'd expected. The man had his reasons not to want to see a health official. Still, the situation saddened Gabe.

After doing all he could to ensure Clay Weathers had the best possible chance he could give him for healthy recovery, Gabe packed up his gear to go. Stopping at the door, he turned back toward the man. "I can't emphasize enough that you follow up with your doctor."

"I'll be fine. I sure do thank you for your help. I got a little concerned when the bleeding wouldn't stop."

Gabe nodded in acknowledgment. He met the man's listless gaze across the small room. "I hope you seek out help, sir."

Clay lifted his unbandaged hand and waved. Lips pressed in a firm line, Gabe stepped out the door and closed it behind him. His spirits only lifted when he got to the truck and remembered he was returning to Hannah.

Hannah stepped through the bedroom door and closed it softly behind her. Heading across the large open living area, she froze, wide-eyed, at the sight of Gabe, reading in the dim light of the gaslight, Rascal lying beside him on a braided rug.

"You're back."

Gabe rose from the chair. "How are things going?"

Emotions still high from recent events, Hannah had trouble finding her tongue. "*Gut*. Really *gut*. Everyone is doing fine." Her heart swelled. If things had been different, it might have been her in the adjoining room, with Gabe supporting and encouraging her through the delivery of their child. If she had met him that night, this might've been their second child.

Without thinking, she found herself moving across the room toward Gabe, unable to contain the wide smile that spread over her face. "The *boppeli* just arrived. A beautiful baby girl. New *mamm* and *daed* are getting acquainted with her." As if on cue, the sound of a newborn's cry penetrated the room.

"From the sound of it, she takes after her mother?" Gabe wore a teasing grin as he glanced at the closed bedroom door.

"*Ach*, that's unfair. Ruth was as quiet as a mouse all through delivery."

"I've heard that about Amish women." He shook his head. "I don't know how they do it."

"Neither do I." Hannah shared his smile. The volume of the cries increased. Although reluctant to break eye contact, Hannah turned toward the bathroom. "I have to gather some things and return." Gabe followed her across the room, the dog at his heels. Rummaging in a cupboard, she slid him a shy glance. "I'm glad you're back." Hannah blushed when she realized she'd verbalized her thought, hoping the murmur was low enough that Gabe hadn't heard it.

She caught her breath when he gently touched her elbow. "So am I." His hand slid down her arm to tangle with her fingers. "Do you ever think...?"

Yes. She did. Way too frequently recently. Hannah studied the floor. "I shouldn't."

Goosebumps rose on her forearms at the realization they'd both been thinking the same thing. She turned to look at this man who might have been her husband. Beyond his dear face, she saw the room behind him.

The contrast was blatant. Gabe's light brown hair wasn't in a bowl style, but curled closely to his head. There was no beard on his chin, a length determined by their years of marriage. If she'd been married to Gabe, the house where they lived wouldn't have a room lit with gas and lantern light. It probably wouldn't have a gas-powered refrigerator. There wouldn't be a few buggy and draft horses in the barn. But most critical of all, it wouldn't be with the support of the Amish community that would gather around, visiting the new *boppeli*. To support her, the new mother.

Because of the new father.

Which one did she want more? Which could she more easily live without? Right now, flush with the miracle of new life, and after witnessing the wonder of two awe-struck parents holding their newborn, with her hand clasped in Gabe's warm, strong grip, and his green eyes soft on hers, Hannah knew if he would ask what she thought he'd wanted to ask years ago, she'd say yes.

Her eyes must have mirrored her confusion, as Gabe leaned closer, his other hand lifting to gently cup the back of her neck under her *kapp*. Eyelids fluttering down, Hannah swayed toward him.

Only to jerk back when the dog at their side yipped excitedly and trotted toward the bedroom door. Hastily dropping Gabe's hand, Hannah stepped away from him. Turning back to the cupboard, she stared into its depth a moment before she could recall what she was supposed to gather. When the bedroom door swung open a short while later, she was halfway across the room with her arms full of towels and other items.

Malachi stuck his head out the door. "Did you find everything you needed?"

"Ja." Hannah nodded, slipping past him into the room.

"I'm a *daed*," she heard Malachi announce to Gabe with some amazement.

Gabe's soft "Congratulations" followed them into the room before Malachi closed the door behind them.

Ruth was sitting up in bed, holding the baby, a captivated smile on her weary face as she looked down at her newborn daughter. Malachi crossed to the pair. Carefully setting a hip on the bed, he slid his arm about Ruth's shoulders.

"I'm glad it's a *dochder*," he murmured.

"Really?" Ruth's smile widened as she leaned against her husband.

"Really," he echoed. "I hope she's just like you."

Ruth turned her head toward Malachi. This time her tone was heavy with skepticism. "Really?"

"*Ja*. The world needs people like you." Dipping his head, he kissed her nose. "Just not too many of them."

Hannah busied herself on the other side of the room, her emotions warring between yearning and mild embarrassment at having witnessed the tender exchange.

She was so, so happy for her friend. Sliding another glance at the trio on the bed, Hannah bit her tongue when a sliver of envy slipped in to dilute her joy. Quickly, she quashed the errant feeling as she assisted Mrs. Edigers in tidying up the room. Still, she conceded, as she sniffed back a few tears, a family would be *wunderbar*. She yearned to be a mother. Gabe would be a tender father. If only...

When Mrs. Edigers instructed Gabe to take Hannah home some time later, despite her exhaustion, Hannah was reluctant to go. What had begun with anxiety had ended with awe.

Before they left, Gabe accepted Malachi's offer to

hold his daughter, Deborah. Hannah's breath had caught at seeing the tiny infant in his strong arms. She'd turned away, but not before Ruth noticed Hannah's expression and raised her eyebrows almost to her hairline.

If the ride over had seemed endless, the return trip was too short. They didn't talk, but by tacit agreement, held hands over the front seat's console. Gabe helped her out of the truck and walked her to the door, fingers again entwined. Although it was still a few hours until sunrise, Hannah was conscious that any minute her parents might be rising to prepare for chores. Still, she tightened her grip and didn't resist when Gabe used their grasp to swing her around and take her other hand.

"That could've been us, you know." His breath in the cold morning air wafted away an inch from her face.

"Ja," she whispered.

"It still could."

Hannah didn't say anything. She couldn't. She was breathless. Maybe it was the wonder of the night, but anything seemed possible at the moment. Even marrying the man she'd fallen in love with years ago.

Gabe tugged gently on her fingers, and she eased forward. The warm air of his breath caressed her cheek as he leaned closer.

A light flicked on in her parent's bedroom. She immediately took a step back. In the light of the now-shadowed porch, she saw Gabe's eyes as he sighed ruefully.

With a subdued smile on her face, Hannah dropped his hands. "Good night."

"Good night," he echoed, mirroring her expression.

Walking back to the truck, Gabe gave her a last look before getting in.

In his eyes, she'd seen hope. And a promise.

Hope for them? A promise for their future? Hannah knew what she hoped for and the future she was beginning to acknowledge she wanted, but it needed to be *Gott*'s will, not hers. Knowing she wouldn't sleep the rest of the night, Hannah quietly made her way into the house.

Chapter Eight

"Yes, I understand." Although he didn't. Gabe's hand tightened around the phone. "No, I appreciate you calling. I'd much rather hear it direct than from another source. Okay. I'll… I'll work with that. Sure. Thanks. I appreciate it. Bye." Gabe slowly lowered the phone. There was no need for him to disconnect the call. The caller, obviously relieved to have finished the conversation, had hung up almost before Gabe's distracted farewell. Gabe couldn't blame her. Most people didn't like being the bearer of bad news.

The grant for his position had fallen through. No grant, no funding. No funding, no job. No job, no reason for him to be here. No reason for him to be here, no chance to build a future with Hannah.

Tucking the phone back into his pocket, Gabe chided himself for thinking of the situation only from his perspective. He'd been brought in as a paid employee to assist the local volunteer fire department with EMS needs. The local department was very good, but with more residents working outside of the district, along with other factors, the number of volunteers had decreased. As over fifty percent of service calls were for EMS, Gabe's involvement greatly reduced the stress on the diminished squad. Due to his training, he could also provide more advanced emergency care. Miller's Creek would be affected by the loss of Gabe's contributions to the community. The emergency needs of the area were more important than his personal issues.

Gabe wanted to be completely altruistic, but the progress he'd been making with a local EMS service wasn't running through his mind as he stared across the apartment he'd finally finished moving into. *We've come so far. Last night at the Schrocks', I know she felt what I felt. That we could have something precious and rare.*

Now the only things precious and rare were the few days he had left in Miller's Creek. He was going to be paid through the end of the month. The administrator had assured him they'd apply for another grant, but it might take months before it went through. And although he was a careful money manager, he wasn't in a position to go without a job. Gabe shoved himself up from the couch. He shouldn't be surprised. Halfway through the interview process, the administration that'd hired him had become evasive with some of his questions. But he'd been so thrilled to find a job in Miller's Creek he hadn't noticed their ambiguity. When he'd been advised to report to someone else before he'd even moved into the area, he'd shrugged it off, more focused on the challenge of setting up the program than caring who his supervisor was.

Gabe stalked to the window, seeing not the view outside it, but the blue curtains that surrounded the wooden frame. Well, he had a few weeks left. A few weeks to complete the training he'd already started. Reaching out, he slid a finger down the fabric. A few short weeks to convince the woman he'd never stopped loving that he was worth all she'd have to give up to be with him.

The bolt of fabric dropped with a thud to the floor. Cindy Borders and the other *Englisch* customer who'd been talking at the counter looked over to Hannah at the sound.

"Are you all right?"

"Ja," Hannah mumbled, hastening to pick up the dark green material and set it on the counter. "It slipped through my fingers."

As Gabe was going to, if what the women were discussing was true.

"The grant fell through? We're losing our new EMS service?" She swallowed as she unrolled material from the bolt to stretch it across the ruler embedded in the counter's surface. Would there be any reason for Gabe to stay in the area if the grant was lost?

"Yes. A shame, isn't it? We were so excited for the town to have a program established. Even if they leave right away from a neighboring area, it still takes extra time to arrive. And when the weather gets bad out, it takes even longer." The *Englisch* woman who'd found Hannah's dog shook her head.

The other woman nodded. "Hate to think of what would've happened to the Winston boy without the young man that's been working in the area." She smiled at Hannah. "And of course, the Amish men that pulled him from the pond."

"A yard and a half of this fabric?" Hannah gave her a small smile in return. She picked up the scissors, her thoughts not on the green material, but on the young man just mentioned.

"Yes, please." Mrs. Borders sighed. "Too bad the whole community won't do something like the Amish do." Cocking her head, she regarded Hannah. "Don't you do different types of fundraisers to help cover medical costs and other things for your members? If I recall correctly, there was a whole slew of events before the Amish school was built some years back. And what is it I read about in some Amish communities?" Her forehead furrowed like a freshly plowed field. "Mud sales?"

It was true. Hannah recalled the numerous bake sales, pancake breakfasts and BBQ dinners held to raise money for the local teacher's salary and other school expenses. A mud sale, an auction usually held in the spring when the footing was soggy, hence the name, was a traditional way some Amish districts raised money for their volunteer fire departments.

"Ja." Folding the now-cut material and setting the rewrapped bolt on the table behind her, she reached for the next color in the stack. "How much of this one?"

"Half a yard. Hopefully it will look like it's supposed to when I'm done. I don't have near the talent displayed in your shop." Mrs. Borders's attention rested on the quilt hung on the wall behind where Hannah worked, before straying to the others that decorated the borders of the room. "These are so beautiful. If something like a quilt auction were held, I'd be sitting in the front row, spending much more than my husband would like." She gently elbowed the woman beside her. "Or knows about."

"I tell mine it's worth it as they serve a dual purpose. It's a feast for the eyes and warmth for the toes. And I don't complain about the money he spends on fishing gear."

Mrs. Borders smiled conspiratorially. "Just think of the money an auction selling both could raise. With something like that, we might not even need a grant in order to keep the EMS service."

The women's conversation drifted to other topics as they paid for their purchases and left the store, but Hannah's thoughts lingered on what they'd said. While restocking the fabric bolts, her eyes drifted around the shop as the woman's had earlier, touching on each quilt. She had a good idea of what the *Englisch* would pay for a quilt. Amish, too, if the occasion was right. Would they see saving the EMS service for the community at large as a worthwhile cause? Her gaze lifted from the walls to the ceiling overhead. If they determined it was, could it happen in time to keep Gabe from leaving?

Winding her way through the rows back to the counter, Hannah pondered who she knew had recently completed quilts or nearly finished works-in-progress. And wondered if they could be convinced to part with them.

It might not be possible. But, as her employer had said, much is lost for want of asking. Hannah knew just the place to start. If she had the courage.

* * *

Although her eyes were on the scrolling stitch in front of her, Hannah's ears were tuned to the chatter about the room. A considerable portion of the female Amish community, among them her *mamm* and younger *schweschder*, bordered the quilt frame stretched across the large room. Little girls in *kapps* and dresses played beneath its surface, including her niece, Lily. Hannah could hear the girl's infectious giggle drift up from under the center of the friendship star design.

Outwardly calm in appearance, Hannah's heart was beating so fast her hand trembled, making it a struggle to keep her normally precise stitches even. Since she'd heard the news yesterday about the grant, she'd known something needed to be done about the situation. Someone needed to step up. If not, the community would lose a resource that had already proven valuable. And she'd lose… Hannah glanced at the faces of the women lined along the borders of the quilt. Faces of women her age and older. Women she'd been raised to respect. A lifestyle she'd been raised to respect. A lifestyle in which she'd never caused a ripple.

Bowing her head to the fabric in front of her again, Hannah pressed her lips together. *This isn't about me. It's about what's best for the community. Who knows who might need emergency care at some critical time? Someone should do something.*

Her thread broke with a quiet pop. Leaning back from the framed material, Hannah wondered if maybe that was a *gut* thing, as her stitches today were lopsided and inconsistent. She flinched imperceptibly when a young girl instantly appeared beside her and handed her another threaded needle. Too old to play under the quilt and too young to take her place along its edge, the girl was one of a handful who contributed to quilting by threading needles for the older women while they sewed. Taking the needle, Hannah smiled at the earnest young face. It was a good thing the girl had threaded it because her own hands were shaking so much she couldn't have found the eye were it the size of a hay-mow door. *Someone needs to do something. I need to do something.*

But doing so meant making waves when she never had before.

Drawing in a shaky breath, she also drew a puzzled look from the young girl beside her. Hannah dropped her gaze to the thin pointed metal pinched between their fingers. The most elaborate quilt couldn't come together without the simple act of threading a needle. Not a big step, but one that had to happen in order for bigger things to come together. To save the extended emergency service program, and keep Gabe in the area, a first step needed to be taken. Could she thread that needle?

Much is lost for want of asking.

Her throat felt like it was coated with church spread. Hannah cleared it. When the voices around the room dropped one by one, she looked up to find herself the center of attention. Her thimbled finger clattered against the quilt frame. She took strength from Socks's warm weight, where the collie lay against her ankles.

Reaching forward with the newly threaded needle, Hannah pushed it into the fabric. "I was talking with

Ben Raber the other day. Asked him if he'd warmed up yet from going into the pond after the *Englisch* boy. He said he'd only recently stopped shivering." Hannah knew she'd have to rip out any stitches she was inflicting on the quilt in front of her, but she continued poking her needle through the fabric. "He said he'd heard the boy had made a complete recovery, thanks be to *Gott*. It amazed him, because when he pulled the boy out, there was no sign of life. *Gut* thing we had emergency service close."

"The *Englisch* need to take care of their own." The mutter came from the far end of the quilt. Although her attention remained unseeing on the quilt before her, Hannah took a deep breath and pitched her voice a little higher. "It could've easily been an Amish boy that went in. I know my *brieder* have skated on that pond before. It seems the ice wasn't the only thing that broke through. I heard the grant supporting local EMS did, as well. It would be a shame to lose the service now when we know it can save lives."

Murmurs rose from around the room. Due to the general buzz, Hannah couldn't tell if the comments were pro or con. She closed her eyes. An ally would be *wunderbar* about now. If only Ruth had been here, she wouldn't have hesitated to speak up. But her friend was still at home, getting acquainted with her new *dochder*. Hannah stabbed her finger with the needle when a voice cut through the murmurs.

"Samuel said it's a real benefit having someone local teach the required training needed for volunteer firefighters. It saves the men time when taking the classes.

Before, they had to hire drivers to take them out of the county. Classes are more economical, too, with a local trainer."

Hannah glanced up to see her sister's impish smile. Gail's comment had been both sly and convincing. Amish women loved nothing more than a bargain.

Comments flowed around the room like creeks after a spring thaw.

"Well, there's no money for it now."

"Since when has the current lack of funds stopped a Plain community from doing what was needed? Didn't we raise money to expand the school?"

"We all know how dangerous farmwork can be. Faster arrival from local care could save a life, or a limb." The voice was elderly and tinged with experience.

For a moment, the only sounds in the room were the giggles and murmurs from the children under the quilt. All the women at its edges knew a friend or relative who'd been affected by some type of farming accident.

"What type of fundraiser are you thinking?"

As Hannah opened her mouth to respond, another voice forestalled her.

"You just want to keep this particular man here." Even the chatter under the quilt faded as Ruby Weaver's voice cut through the room. All faces turned toward the bishop's wife. Some with agreeing nods and sharp looks back toward Hannah. Concentrating on keeping a flush from rising in her cheeks, Hannah glanced around the quilt's border, searching for friendly faces before she faced the pale blue eyes on the far end of the patterned material. She was surprised at the number of frowning expressions she saw. Frowning at whom? Her or the bishop's wife? When Gail's was one of them, Hannah grasped a sliver of hope that they weren't all directed at her.

"I don't care who provides the service, I just think there will be times we wished we had it, and in those times it'll be too late for whoever is affected." Hannah knew she spoke the truth. But would she be willing to push past her reluctance to cause ripples in the community if Gabe wasn't involved?

"I'll ask again," prompted a voice across the room. "What type of fundraiser do you propose?"

Hannah could feel her pulse beating at the sides of her throat. She swallowed. "Well, many communities do mud sales to support their volunteer fire departments. This is something of an extension of that. So I was thinking we could arrange one for Miller's Creek."

"Does that mean you're going to organize it?" From Ruby, it sounded like an accusation.

Hannah's stomach hollowed at the question. It wasn't reluctance to tackle the amount of work in the project that flashed through her. But she'd already stepped out of her comfort zone. The tight-lipped woman across the quilt's friendship star design was probably going to be her future mother-in-law. One who was already unhappy with her. Should Hannah cause even more discord? She recalled how Ruby Weaver had been instrumental in driving Gail from the community. Not just once, but nearly again.

Should she continue on this path? This project idea was more Hannah's will than the will of the community. Hannah had always obeyed what was best for the district. She darted a glance toward her *mamm*, working beside Gail on the opposite end of the quilt. Willa Lapp met her gaze with a small smile. Hannah relaxed. She glanced down at her hands, poised above the fabric. Fabric that wasn't useful if it remained on a bolt. Unless someone began working with it, it couldn't fulfill its purpose. What if it was *Gott*'s will that she do this? Just because it was what she wanted, did that mean it wasn't His wish, as well? Had He put the two *Englisch* women in the shop to talk about the topic?

The attention in the room was all on her. Hannah quickly searched for any nudging of self-will and found a snippet of peace instead.

She nodded. "*Ja*. I am. I propose we hold an auction. Any objections if we start with this quilt? I'm sure that Barbara at the shop would donate to the cause, as well. What else can we provide to raise money for this project?" She made eye contact with each woman around the room, although it was difficult to hold Ruby Weaver's stony gaze. "And I'm counting on you to bring other items, as well."

Hannah released Daisy from where the mare had been tied to the post. She'd done it. And she'd survived. After some initial reluctance, and with furtive glances toward the bishop's wife after every positive comment, an excited buzz had generated regarding the project.

"We'll show the *Englisch* how a fundraiser is done." Hannah had overheard the comments of a gray-haired stitcher a few seats down the quilt's border.

"Hush now, Waneta. That's *hochmut*," her neighbor had chided, but it'd been said with a conspirator's smile.

The project was launched. Now she had much work ahead to manage a successful execution.

Hannah's mouth was tired from the effort of keeping a smile on it for the past few hours. An initial grin had risen from the ladies growing enthusiasm, but she'd had to prop it up several times to encourage and persuade participants. And wear it as armor against Ruby Weaver's undisguised disapproval. When it was finally time to wrap up for the day, after polite goodbyes, Hannah had been one of the first out the door.

She felt guilty for wanting to escape. Although they'd come together, her *mamm* was catching a ride home with a neighbor while Hannah went into town to grab some groceries from the Bent 'N Dent. Hannah was looking forward to a few moments alone, except for Daisy and the *clip-clop* of her hooves on the road, to gather her thoughts.

Sighing, she stroked a hand down the mare's wintercoated neck. Had she done the right thing? She'd always striven to abandon her will for *Gott*'s. Was this His? Or hers? While some of the women had smiled benevolently as she'd left, assuming her motives were altruistic for the community, Hannah knew better. Trailing a hand along Daisy's side as she walked back to the buggy, she winced. Ruby Weaver had been right. Hannah wouldn't have even thought to raise funds if Gabe hadn't been involved.

"Well, sister. It's not like you to make waves. I always thought that was my role." At the sound of Gail's voice, Hannah turned to see her sister approaching, hand in hand with a skipping Lily. "You were more of a 'one who rows the boat seldom has time to rock it' type."

Hannah smiled at the old Amish saying. "Maybe I learned from you."

"*Ach*, forgive me for that. But if that's the case, you handle it with much more grace than I ever did."

Hannah knelt to smooth her niece's *kapp* over the little girl's blond hair. "What's the saying about honey versus vinegar?"

"I don't think it's flies you want to catch. I think it's a handsome Mennonite man I've seen around town."

Straightening so quickly that Daisy jerked her head at the abrupt motion, Hannah shot her sister a quelling look. "Where did you get that idea?"

Gail snorted as she attended to her own horse, tied along the fence beside Daisy. "Your current romances, and the fact that you are finally having them, are the talk of the district." She paused, slanting a glance toward Lily, who'd bent to pet the patiently waiting Socks. "At least you didn't have an ill-advised one like my first romance."

Conscious of the heat rising to her cheeks, Hannah turned to straighten a harness strap that'd twisted over Daisy's flank. "Yours was no more ill-advised than mine at the time."

"I disagree. The players were completely different. Even if Atlee had married me instead of Louisa five years ago, we'd most likely be miserable by now. I think what you're most unhappy about is that you're not with the man, this Gabriel Bartel." Gail turned to lift Lily into the buggy. "Come on, sweetie. We need to get home to fix supper for *daed*." She stepped back from the rig to pin Hannah with a gaze. "Which makes me wonder why you aren't."

"*You* should know the answer to that." Hannah nodded subtly toward the little girl visible behind the windshield.

"Are you saying you broke it off with him because of me?" Gail sounded as horrified as she looked.

Hannah shrugged a defensive shoulder at the accusation. "We couldn't both leave." Seeing the instant dismay on her sister's face, Hannah reached for her hand. "I know you didn't want to go. You didn't expect the way things went with Atlee. But you didn't see what leaving did to *Mamm* and *Daed*. The reaction and whispers of some in the community. How could I leave right behind you to marry someone from outside our community? And you know as well as I do, if more than one child from a Plain family leaves to the outside, the others in the family are more likely to follow. I couldn't do that to our younger *brieder* or our folks."

Gail's smile was cynical. "The same community you just mentioned as distressing our parents by hurtful actions and gossip?"

"The same community that welcomed you back."

At the bang of a door, they turned to watch Ruby Weaver cross the porch and stride to her buggy, parked in a position of honor close to the house. "For the most part," Gail quipped.

Releasing her hand after a light squeeze, Hannah shared a smile with her sister. "You take the good with the bad."

"Well, I think you should take what would be good for you and go after your Mennonite man."

Hannah's smile instantly ebbed. "I shouldn't. I can't." She shook her head. "I'm not you."

"*Ach*, you'd have made so many more foolish mistakes if you were. It's okay to allow yourself one or two." Gail sighed. "It's just that, after so many years of being afraid and essentially alone, I'm so happy now. I just want you to be happy, as well."

"I am happy having you and Lily back in the community and with family. Maybe that's why I feel I shouldn't leave. It'd be a mistake I'm not willing to make."

"*Ja*. It's *wunderbar* to be back. Though I think it's more because of the man. It wouldn't be the same without Samuel. But I wouldn't have gone against my fears and mild—" she rolled her eyes at the understatement "—resistance at returning if I hadn't been pushed. And look what I would've missed. I was doing what I thought was best for me and Lily. But *Gott* had a plan for me. I just had to face my biggest fear."

A tapping on the windshield behind them drew their attention. They looked up to see Lily waving from inside the buggy. Wrapped in a blanket, she shivered exaggeratedly, a big grin on her face. Hannah laughed.

"I get the hint." Gail shook her head at her daughter's antics.

As she turned to go, Hannah touched her arm. "Don't worry about me. I'll be all right. Like the old saying goes, if you can't have the best of everything, make the best of everything you have. That's what I intend to do."

"*Ja*, well, don't be alarmed if *Gott* has some surprises for you along the way. And unexpected methods of bringing them about." With a wave, Gail climbed into the buggy. Hannah watched as Lily immediately scooted over and snuggled under her mother's arm.

Sniffing against an unexpected surge of melancholy as she watched the two, Hannah slowly returned the wave as Gail backed the rig out and they clattered down the lane. Upon directing Socks into her own buggy, Hannah climbed in and sat a moment, absently fiddling with the reins.

Dear Gott, *Your will is right and good. And I will trust in it.* Hannah stared through the windshield, splattered here and there with residue from its travels. Through the streaks and splotches, she considered her future. Happy in community and family, and content in her… She sighed deeply. *I will be content in my marriage.* If not to Jethro Weaver, then to some other Amish man. As she tried to envision other single men from the community, Gabe's face filled her mind, his teasing smile, his caring eyes. Hannah squeezed her eyes shut, hoping to block out his image. But what filled her head instead was a quick, unbidden plea. *Oh,* Gott, *You work in mysterious ways. If only one of those ways would lead to Gabe…*

Blinking her eyes open at the rebellious thought, Hannah backed Daisy away from the fence. It might've worked out for Gail to have the best of everything. She was thrilled for her sister.

And Hannah knew that for her, what *Gott* provided would be good, even if not necessarily everything. Besides, there was so much more to life than love. Wasn't there?

Chapter Nine

The winter sun was winking at the horizon as Gabe drove into town. These days, when the sun seemed to set in the middle of frigid afternoons as the calendar climbed away from the shortest day of the year, usually made him melancholy. But today, Gabe couldn't keep the smile from his face as he watched the purple-and-pink-streaked sky spread over the snowy landscape.

It'd been difficult, given yesterday morning's dismal news, to get enthused about today's appointments, but Gabe compelled himself to do more than just go through the motions. It wasn't his nature to be lackadaisical in his work. Besides, surely someday the town would be able to support a more robust emergency medical service. As long as he was here, he was going to lay as solid a foundation as possible for whatever might follow.

He'd been stunned when he stopped by the administration office late in the day. He'd expected to be advised on how they wanted things wrapped up. Instead, he was told another possible source of funding for the project had been proposed. By the Amish community.

When he recovered from his shock, Gabe had asked the administrator if she was kidding. The woman had primly advised him that she didn't joke. And as the Amish were usually quite successful in their fundraising—although she wasn't familiar with this particular Amish woman—the administration was willing to leave the situation open-ended for the moment to see how things played out. Further determination would be made based on how much money was raised. If Gabe had any questions, he needed to contact—the woman had checked her notes—a Hannah Lapp, who could be reached at The Stitch quilt shop in town.

After returning to the truck, Gabe had sat for a moment, staring through the windshield. He had questions all right. This was out of character for the demure Amish woman he knew. Why was Hannah doing this? His hands clenched on the steering wheel. Was it because of him? Was she trying to save his job? His heart rate picked up, as did his hopes. Was it more than just trying to extend the EMS service for the township? Could it be a sign she wanted to extend their relationship, as well?

Just the possibility filled Gabe with a warmth that surely exceeded even the glow of a sunny mid-June afternoon. It stayed with him through his last appointment of the day.

His smile expanded when, slowing for the upcoming intersection, he glanced toward the Bent 'N Dent store on the corner. Gabe touched the brakes when he recognized one of the few Amish rigs in the parking lot. The district's *Ordnung* dictated the design and color of the buggies in the community. Given they all looked the same, who'd have thought Gabe would learn to pick out Daisy from all the brown Standardbreds in the area? But seeing her numerous times behind the shop always generated a little thrill through him, as it meant her driver was nearby. He'd unconsciously memorized every minute detail of the mare and the buggy she generally pulled. The sight of Daisy at the hitching post made his pulse spike.

Daisy's owner was just the person he'd love…well, he'd love to see today.

Gabe pulled into the Bent 'N Dent's lot. When he stepped inside, he was surprised at the dimness. The store's interior, lit as it was by skylights and some lanterns, was even darker without the aid of the now-set sun. No wonder the place closed at 5:00 p.m. in the wintertime. At the checkout counter just inside the door, an older Amish woman looked him over before giving a slow nod.

"Folks come in to search for bargains. With the day drawing to an early close, you might need something to aid you in your hunt today." She handed him a flashlight, her eyes crinkling at the corners as she smiled.

Hooking a nearby basket on his elbow, Gabe took the flashlight with a matching grin. It would be a big help in scrutinizing things on the shelves. In Bent 'N Dent stores, some of the cans and cartons were just that, bent and dented. Many items were past their prime, with dates inked on the package—whether they be best by or expiration—having passed days, weeks or even months earlier. It made for a buyer-beware shopping experience. The shelves might be dark, but it was still light enough, as Gabe passed the ends of the aisles, to identify the few folks shopping this late in the day.

Besides, he wasn't looking for canned goods, he was looking for...

Gabe stopped at the end of an aisle. Hannah, her own flashlight in hand, was on the opposite end, minutely examining the can in her hand. Keeping his beam off, Gabe took a moment to just absorb the sight of her.

What was it about this woman that'd caused him to instantaneously fall for her years ago and never forget her? Certainly she was beautiful, with her golden-blond hair, deep blue eyes and exquisite features. That might've been what drew him to her in the first place. Had that weighed on him more than it should? Most men were intrigued by a pretty face. Because of his job, he'd seen enough to know that beauty was only skin deep. Besides, he'd met other beautiful women over the years and had easily forgotten them. No. That wasn't what had kept him wanting to be with Hannah again and again.

It wasn't her beauty that captivated him. At least not her outward beauty. Over the long five years without her, it wasn't her pretty face Gabe had missed, or her slender figure. It was their mutually giddy smiles. The laughs they'd shared. Her calm, quiet presence in the occasional moments when they weren't talking. Her peaceful silence, almost as precious as a solid conversation—and they'd had plenty of those. Her thoughtful perspective. Her generous encouragement. The way she filled a part of him as nothing other than saving lives did.

The Amish spoke of finding God's chosen one for them. Gabe could understand that. It would certainly be a lot easier for him if God had chosen for him someone other than Hannah, but Gabe didn't think He had.

So he'd jumped, maybe foolishly so given the current precarious job situation, at the chance to get back into her orbit so he could persuade her that they could have something together. Something wonderful. Was she finally starting to feel that, too?

Taking a deep breath, Gabe started down the aisle toward her. "Are you finding any bargains?"

Hannah's unguarded expression when she saw him told him everything he could've hoped for. They had a chance. Whatever the obstacles, they had a chance. That was all he needed to know. Enough to prevent a sigh when she quickly masked her elation with composed features and a shy smile.

"Right now, it's a bit of a challenge to find anything."

Gabe glanced in the blue plastic basket hanging from her elbow. "Looks like you found a few."

"*Ja.* Enough to make it worth the drive into town."

"I heard you've already had quite a busy one today."

Even in the darkening light through the skylights, her bewilderment was apparent.

"The fundraiser," he prompted.

Her bemusement transitioned to astonishment. "How did you find out about that so quickly?"

Gabe shook his head. "It's amazing what your community accomplishes without a phone on everyone's hip. I don't know how, but they knew in the administration office when I stopped in." He hesitated, because his next question made all the difference. "It's true? That it was your idea?"

For the span of a few heartbeats, he wondered if she'd answer. She fastidiously placed the can she held into her basket and seemed to find it fascinating before meeting his eyes again. "I'm sure if I hadn't come up with it, someone else would have. It is a *gut* thing for the community."

Raising an eyebrow, Gabe held her gaze. "Just the community?"

"Well, the *Englisch* one, as well."

"*Gut* thing." Gabe echoed her Amish dialect. "Because of it, they're delaying the ending date of the program to see how it progresses. Looks like I might not be leaving so soon after all."

Hannah's eyes rounded. "Really?" Her voice rose on the word. She immediately glanced down toward her basket again. He wasn't sure, in the dim light of the aisle, whether it was a blush or shadows that darkened her cheek.

"Really." Gabe reached out to touch her porcelain skin with a gentle finger. Hannah looked up at his touch. Gabe lost himself for a moment in what he saw there. He would have stayed frozen forever if the beam of a flashlight hadn't shot across the now-dark skylights overhead. This wasn't the place. They had observers, most likely Amish ones, an aisle over.

This wasn't the moment. But after years of wishing

and wondering, Gabe now knew they'd have one. Hopefully a lifetime of them. But he still had to be patient.

Lowering his hand, he stepped back. "So, what's for supper?"

Hannah's shoulders lifted and sank in a deep sigh. "Maybe not for supper, but I did find some prizes. The breakfast bars are only a month past their 'best buy' date. My four younger *brieder* will surely have them gone in a few days. *Mamm* can hardly keep enough food around to satisfy them. I also found these cookies." She pointed to a crushed package in her basket. "They're likely smashed, but the boys won't care when they put them into a bowl and pour milk over them for dessert. What are you here to find?"

Gabe didn't say "you," but he knew his eyes did. And Hannah obviously understood, as another flush rose up her cheeks. "Actually, supper for me. I figured I'd skip The Dew Drop a few nights and give my wallet a break from eating out. Although it's pretty relieved at potentially having a few more weeks of a job. Can you help me find something to put on my limited menu?"

"What do you like?"

"Depends more on what I can find." Turning on his flashlight, Gabe directed it to scan the aisle they were in. The surrounding shelves were well-stocked. There was obviously order to the system, but Gabe couldn't identify what it was. "Unfortunately, in this, I sometimes can't see the trees for the forest. How do you find what you're looking for?"

Hannah opened her mouth, abruptly closing it when a beam of a flashlight, followed by an Amish woman, turned into the aisle. Although she kept the beam lowered, the middle-aged woman paused at the sight of them before she nodded and proceeded down the aisle, quickly evaluating and picking up a few items as she went.

Gabe braced for Hannah to step away from him in the woman's presence, to act like they weren't together. When she didn't move from his side, his shoulders relaxed and he briefly closed his eyes. Was it because Hannah was getting less concerned about what the community thought when he was with her, or was it simply because she figured it was dark enough they weren't easily recognized? Either way, it was progress.

The woman was still in the aisle when Hannah continued. "I've been navigating this and other stores like it since I was a *meedel*." Hannah moved a few steps down the aisle. "How does soup sound?" She gestured to several stacks of cans, all of them with some type of dent in their sides. "Always make sure it's dented in, not bulged out. They try to catch those, but you need to be aware."

"Got it. In, not out." Shining his light on a few nearby cans, Gabe raised his eyebrows at the prices. "Wow. These are bargains."

"*Ja.* If you're a bargain hunter, you'll have to be careful about not leaving with more than you intended."

Selecting two cans, Gabe put them in his basket. "Well, I'll just have to hope a certain someone can manage it so I can stay long enough to eat what I take."

She smiled. "Do you like spaghetti? Usually some

good options on sauces here. And pasta that's not too far from the buy-by date."

"Lead on." Gabe gestured with his basket. On the other side of the aisle, he followed the beam of her flashlight when she directed it to an array of taller cans. "Oh my. You're right," Gabe murmured as he looked them over. "So what's the best bet? Big dents or little dents?"

"*Ach*, that's a serious question. It's one each person will have to make up their own mind on. I'm not sure I know you well enough to answer."

"It's okay. I trust you." After all, he was trusting her with his heart. Gabe just hoped it didn't end up the most dented of all.

A few more items, including breakfast bars for himself, went into his basket as they worked their way down the aisles. Although many cans had only a few tears on the labels, Gabe found one that had no label at all. Tipping the top toward his light, he saw, whatever the contents were, they had yet to expire.

He held the can up to Hannah. "What do you think is in here?"

She shook her head. "Hmm. I don't know. The rest of the things here are fruits. So peaches maybe? Pears?"

"My luck I'll open it, hungry for some peach halves, only to find more olives than I can eat in a year. But… then again, it could be the best thing I've ever eaten out of a can." Gabe frowned at the silver container in his hand. "What's life without some risks? We don't always know how things will turn out." He shifted his gaze to Hannah. "Sometimes you have to be brave. Sometimes things might not end like you want, but on the other hand, sometimes they might be even better. Could be missing some of the best deals if you're afraid to take a chance on the unknown." His flashlight was lowered, leaving her face in shadow. But her solemn expression revealed she understood Gabe wasn't talking about the can he tucked into his basket.

They rounded the end of that aisle and looked down the final one. "How are you set for shampoo, soap and such?"

"Pretty good. My patients haven't complained at least." He winked at her.

By tacit agreement, they headed toward the checkout. Both carried their baskets on the outside, their inside hands only a short span apart. Gabe flexed his fingers, aware that just a slight extension of them would brush Hannah's delicate ones.

"Let me know if there's anything I can do to help with the fundraiser." Gabe glanced dubiously at the items in his basket. "I wouldn't be much good at baking, but I'd be more than happy to help with other things. Community awareness, publicity among the *Englisch*, helping set up a location. You name it. Let me know." He indicated for her to go ahead of him at the cashier. "I can't thank you enough for doing this, Hannah."

She set her basket down on the counter in front of the gray-haired Amish woman manning the old-fashioned cash register. "It's *gut* for the community."

When it was his turn, Gabe pulled some bills from his wallet, glad he had cash on him as the store didn't take credit. Even seeing some of the prices, he was surprised at how low his bill was.

When he got outside, Hannah was climbing into her buggy. Gabe smiled when, inside the rig, he barely made out Socks peeking out from under a blanket.

"Gabe." Hannah paused on the buggy step and turned toward him. "It wasn't only because it was *gut* for the community." Before he could answer, the door was closed behind her. But he could see her soft smile through the windshield as she backed Daisy out.

Gabe headed for his truck, his grin big enough to light up the dreary twilight of the abbreviated winter day all by himself.

In the dim glow of her battery-powered headlamps, Hannah could see Daisy's ears flick back, alerting her that someone was behind them on the dark road. Glancing in the side-view mirrors, she saw the distant glow of headlights. Directing Daisy closer to the side of the paved country road, she waited for the whoosh of someone rushing by now they had the room. It remained silent except for the quick cadence of the mare's hooves as no vehicle passed.

For a moment, Hannah's heart leaped, thinking maybe Gabe was following her home. She craned around to look out the back. The vehicle was closer. Instead of truck lights, these were lower, nearer to the ground. It was a car. Following slowly. Her pounding heart accelerated as she shifted from excitement to trepidation. In hope of prompting the driver to pass, Hannah slowed Daisy to a walk and pulled more to the road's edge. She slid in her seat as the buggy tipped slightly toward the ditch. The car behind slowed even further.

Socks huddled next to her. Even lazy Daisy was jerking her head, impacted by the tension running down the reins. Hands clenched tightly on the leather, Hannah guided the mare back onto the pavement and urged her to road-speed again.

When they made the final turn to their road, Hannah swung wide, hoping to get a glimpse of the vehicle. When she did, her breath hitched and she slapped the reins on Daisy's hindquarters, startling the Standardbred into a speed the mare hadn't used in some time. Hannah recognized the car that was turning onto the road behind them. It was the one that'd scraped onto the sidewalk. The one the man had sprung from. The man who'd focused his eerie attention on Socks. Had he been the one who'd taken her? Was he going to make sure she didn't get away this time?

Oh, Gabe, I wish you were here.

Dear Gott, *please protect Your servant.*

Her family's home and barn, silhouetted by the rising moon, were visible ahead. Their large, dark shapes had never looked so good.

As they charged toward that haven, Hannah began to shake, not with fear, but with anger. She was angry that someone would threaten her dog. She was angry that dogs belonging to others were lost, some only returned to their loving owners because of something called a microchip. What about the dogs that hadn't been recovered? Whose owners didn't know where they were?

Hannah gritted her teeth as Daisy pounded down the road. Someone had to do something.

Upon swinging into the lane, she pulled Daisy to

a stop and set the brake. With a trembling hand, she rooted in one of the buggy's many compartments for a flashlight. Finding one, she pushed open the rig's door. Her knees were so wobbly, she almost fell down the step. Socks jumped down behind her. Hannah urged the dog to go to the house, but the collie stayed by her side. Socks whined, but didn't bark. Dash was at the top of the lane, barking enough for both of them. Barking enough to rouse the whole neighborhood. Hannah drew strength from his indignant clamor.

She heard the bang of one of the barn doors. Hannah risked a glance in that direction to see a lantern light framed in a doorway in the area where at least some of her family would be milking. It gave her further courage.

Striding a few steps away from the buggy, she looked down the lane to see the car idling on the road at the end of it. Hannah knew it was the man from town, although she couldn't see him in the dim light. She knew, in her black cloak and bonnet, she stood out in dark relief against the snow of the lane and surrounding farmyard. Socks's warm weight snugged up against her leg.

"What do you want?" Hannah curled her fingers into the palm of her hand, wanting to force the tremor from her voice. "You're frightening me. Are you the one who took my dog? The *Biewel* says Do Not Steal. I don't know why you are doing these things, but it's not right." Something compelled her to continue, "I'm sure you don't mean to scare people. You need to stop. It's not right."

There was no response from the car. No sound except the quiet rumble of the engine. Even to Hannah's untrained ear, the sound was much smoother than the car's appearance. After a long moment, through which Hannah could count her heartbeats from the way they throbbed in her ears, the car rolled forward. It began picking up speed as it went down the road. Seconds later, all that was visible were the red taillights in the distance.

Shaking, Hannah sank to her knees and pulled Socks to her. Her legs wouldn't hold her and she tipped to sit in the middle of the lane. Socks crawled into her lap and licked her face. An instant later, Hannah started at the nudge against the back of her bonnet. Dash joined Socks in nosing at the tears on her face. Tears Hannah hadn't been aware of shedding.

"Are you all right?" The call wafted down from the direction of the barn. Twisting on her cold seat, Hannah saw the silhouette of a figure come out of one of the doors.

Stiffly, she rose to her feet and dusted off the back of her cloak. "*Ja. Ja.* I'm *gut.*" And, oddly enough, she was. She'd faced a fear. She'd protected her dog. Something else had shifted inside of her, but she wasn't sure yet what it was.

Shuffling over, she patted Daisy's sweaty hip. She needed to get the mare to the barn. As she climbed back into the buggy, Hannah realized she'd proposed the idea of a fundraiser auction to the community and confronted a threat to her pet today.

If she could do that, what else could she face?

Chapter Ten

At the jangle from the bell above the door, Hannah looked up from where she was cutting material for project packets. Her ready smile evaporated from her face quickly when she saw who entered. Knowing she should greet the new arrival, Hannah couldn't make her feet step away from the counter. Since quilting yesterday—and her launch of the fundraising project—she'd known this encounter was possible. Make that probable. She'd been dreading it.

"Bishop Weaver." Setting down the scissors, Hannah folded her arms across her chest. It was a struggle to form her mouth into a smile. "What can I do for you today?"

The bishop slowly wove his way through the rows of fabric to reach the far side of the wide counter. Hannah furrowed her brow as he approached. Under his flat-brimmed black hat, the bishop's face was pale and dotted with sweat. Perhaps his obvious agitation was due to an ailment, but it still didn't bode well for her.

"I understand that you are getting mixed up in *Englisch* things, Hannah Lapp. You would do better to devote your time to convincing my son that you'd welcome an offer from him."

Hannah clenched her hands into fists. Her contrived smile slipped into more of a grimace. "I...I do." Wincing, Hannah recognized the similarity of her words to wedding vows. She would marry Jethro. Even though she cared for another man. Surely *Gott* knew she would do what she should in action, even if her spirit was reluctant?

"You should make sure he's aware of that. He says he doesn't want to marry right now."

Although relieved to not immediately discuss the auction, Hannah's heart went out to Jethro. The man was caught in the strong currents of his parents' demanding wills as much as she was. Lowering her arms, she clasped her hands at her waist. "Perhaps it is a little soon," she began tentatively. "After such a recent loss of his wife and child."

"He will marry as his parents wish. As he did before. As *you* should do."

Hannah flinched as the bishop slapped his hand down, rattling the nearby scissors on the counter.

"Your duty is to do what is best for the community as I—as *Gott* wills it." Now inexplicably panting, the man leaned an elbow against the workbench when he finished his decree. At the spasm that contorted his features, Hannah circled the counter to approach him.

"Bishop Weaver, are you all right?" She gasped when the man grabbed his left shoulder. As he teetered backward, Hannah reached out a hand to guide him toward the chair kept nearby for waiting customers.

The bishop slumped hard into the seat. When he looked up at her, bewilderment and fear were evident in his face. "I don't think I'm going to make it," he whispered.

Wide-eyed, Hannah opened her mouth to assure the bishop he would be fine, only to be left gaping when he fell forward from the chair to the floor, her hand curling into his jacket to slow the tumble.

Hannah followed him down until she was on her knees beside the inert man. "Bishop Weaver! Can you hear me?" The bishop's mouth sagged open, and his eyes were rolled back in his head. He was obviously unconscious.

Unlike when Ruth collapsed, there wasn't anyone to run for assistance. Barbara had left that morning to visit her adult children living out of state. Hannah knew, as she'd been listening, that Gabe had left earlier in the day and hadn't returned. She was alone. Springing up like a jack-in-the-box, she frantically looked out the window, hoping someone was passing by on the sidewalk and could be flagged down.

The street outside the shop was empty.

The phone! Heart pounding like a runaway horse, Hannah grabbed for the landline on the counter. She fumbled with the receiver, almost dropping it as she knelt again beside the motionless man. The strident drone of the dial tone was abnormally loud in the silent room. Fingers trembling, she stabbed out 911 on the keypad.

As she waited breathlessly, the three numbers reminded her faintly of another series of three. An alphabet one. What was it? Oh yes! CPR. CAB. The C was for...? Contractions? No! What had Gabe taught her upstairs...? Compressions! That was it! And they needed to start immediately. But before that, she needed to...

Propping the handset against the base of the counter, Hannah jumped when a composed voice came over the line.

"911. Where is your emergency?"

Hannah pressed the speaker button and shifted to ease the limp bishop onto his back. "Ah, The Stitch," she responded breathlessly. "It's a shop in Miller's Creek."

"Do you have a street number?"

"Ja." Hannah searched her memory until she was able to recite it for the dispatcher.

"And what is your phone number?"

Hannah froze in her actions of unfastening the bishop's coat and tugging it back toward his shoulders. She rarely called the shop. Staring at the handset, she noticed the number taped to the inside and rattled it off.

"What is your emergency?"

"The bishop is unwell. He grabbed his shoulder and fell out of the chair."

"Is he conscious?"

"Nee, I mean no."

"Is he breathing?"

There was no discernable movement in the chest underneath her fingers. "I don't think so," she whispered.

"Stay on the line," directed the calm voice. "I'm going to get an ambulance on the way."

While the phone line was quiet—it seemed forever to Hannah but was probably only a few seconds—she tentatively started compressions. She froze after two. It was so different than working on the mannequin upstairs. Drawing in a steadying breath, she began again. After a few motions, Hannah recalled the rhythm of it. But how she missed Gabe's presence beside her and calm tutelage.

The voice came back on the line. "Does the patient have a cardiac history?"

"I don't know," Hannah responded, huffing lightly with the surprising exertion required in giving compressions. The dispatcher asked other questions that Hannah had no answer to. She wanted to weep at her ignorance, but had no time for it.

"You're doing fine," the woman advised her. "I can hear you. Do I understand you're doing compressions?"

"*Ja.* But I'm not sure I'm doing them right."

"That's okay. You're doing a great job. We'll talk you through it." As the dispatcher talked her through the process, Hannah made adjustments where needed. The woman counted with her, helping her keep her in rhythm. It wasn't long before Hannah was panting in time with the compressions. Her heavier breathing must've been audible over the phone.

"You're doing great. Help will be there very soon. Is there anyone else nearby who knows how to do CPR?"

"*Nee*, there's no one here but me." Hearing the growing whimper in her voice, Hannah cleared her throat and struggled to regain composure.

"He's fortunate you're there to help him. Any change in his condition?"

Hannah studied the slack face below hers. Were his lips slightly blue? Or had they already been that way before she started compressions and were now better? Was a little color returning to his face? Her arms were growing tired. Biting her lip, Hannah prayed for reserves of strength. Reserves she drew upon as a young woman who'd done physical labor throughout her life. *Please,* Gott, *help him. Please help me help him.*

Over her ragged breathing and the encouragement of the dispatcher, Hannah thought she heard the bang of the shop's alley door. Had she just imagined it? Or wished it? She had no time to wonder when Gabe burst through the door into the store. "Hannah!"

Never faltering in her rhythm, Hannah erupted into tears.

"Ma'am," the dispatcher's voice was sharp and insistent. "Are you all right?"

"Ja! Ja!" Weeping with relief, Hannah hastened to assure the dispatcher. "Help has arrived!"

Dropping to his knees, Gabe slid into place on the other side of the bishop. "This is Gabe Bartel, Miller's Creek EMS. I'm taking over CPR." Jerking a device from his key chain, he quickly used it to cover the bishop's mouth. With a motion to Hannah to pause, he gave the man two breaths.

"Copy. ETA for ambulance is 8 minutes. Dispatch is disconnecting."

"Copy."

Hannah sagged back against the base of the counter, and Gabe shifted over the bishop, taking over compressions. Hugging her weary arms, Hannah tried to ward off the trembling that instantly besieged her. She watched through tear-blurred eyes as Gabe kept up a decisive rotation of compressions and breaths.

"How long was he out before you started compressions?"

"A minute or two? It all happened so fast. It took a moment to remember what you told me. I'm sorry. It happened so fast…" Hannah knew she was babbling. In a moment, she'd be crying again, as well. She was just so glad to see him. So glad to have help. She'd been so scared.

"You did great." Gabe met her eyes. There was no mistaking the intent sincerity in their green depths. "I'm so proud of you. If he makes it, and we're going to do everything we can to make that happen, it's because of you."

Sniffing back tears in response to his encouraging smile, Hannah straightened from where she'd slumped against the counter. "What can I do to help?"

Gabe winked at her. "Atta girl. The ambulance should be here soon. Could you go outside and flag them down? Every moment helps."

"Of course." Pushing to her feet, Hannah wobbled, wincing at the tingling in her lower limbs, the result of long tense minutes in a cramped position.

Concern instantly covered Gabe's features. "You okay?"

She couldn't stop herself from reaching out to touch him as she hustled past to the door. "*Ja.* I am so much more than okay now that you're here." Jerking open the shop door, she dashed onto the sidewalk, sliding a bit on the slick, snow-swept surface. When the winter breeze ruffled the damp hair in front of her *kapp*, Hannah realized she'd been sweating. Lifting her hand to her prayer covering, she found it askew. Releasing a few deep breaths through pursed lips, the everyday task of repinning her *kapp* helped steady her.

She was just starting to feel the cold when the wind carried the beautiful sound of an approaching ambulance siren.

When she led the EMS personnel inside, it was to the welcomed sight of Bishop Weaver stirring and blinking his eyes. Ensuring she stayed out of the way, Hannah sagged bonelessly against a row of fabric, uncaring that she knocked the bolts crooked from their normally pristine arrangement.

When Gabe followed the gurney to the ambulance a short time later, she stayed inside the store, numbly watching the small crowd that'd gathered outside. A few of the onlookers were Amish, their faces mirroring shock and dismay as their bishop was loaded into the ambulance.

By the time Gabe reentered the shop, Hannah had straightened the fabric bolts, hung up the phone and shakily lowered herself into the chair by the counter. At the sound of the bell and the tread of his shoes, she surged to her feet and into his arms. She almost wept anew with relief and comfort as they closed securely about her. Her eyes fluttered closed at his light kiss on her forehead.

"You probably saved his life," he murmured into her hair.

Hannah sniffed once before succumbing to tears. They leaked onto his shirt.

Gabe rocked her gently. "Shh. It's okay. You did fantastic. His vitals were good when they left. They'll take good care of him. You did everything you could and did it well."

Hannah inhaled raggedly. "How can you do what you do? I was so frightened."

"How can I not?" Another soft kiss, this time on her hair. "If I can save one life, or help one person on what might be their worst day, I feel like I'm fulfilling a major part of the purpose God has for my life."

Her knees still shaky, Hannah snuggled closer into his embrace. She'd felt that, too. Once the fear had subsided, when the outlook had become hopeful, among the myriad of emotions that'd bombarded her had been a sliver of satisfaction in making a difference.

Gabe rocked her a moment more, before he eased back to look down into her face. Lifting a hand, he gently thumbed away the remaining tears from her cheeks. "God has a purpose for all of us. When I found mine, it was like something falling so obviously into place, I'm surprised there wasn't an audible click. I don't always save everyone." Gabe paused, his face solemn as his thoughts went somewhere far away from the brightly colored store. When he spoke again, his voice was initially hoarse. "But I do all I can to make a difference, to create a positive outcome."

He took another small step back, his arm drifting

away from her shoulder. Hannah felt its absence, the loss of its warmth and support, immediately. Reaching out a hand, she grasped the back of the chair she'd been sitting on earlier. Gabe's gaze followed the movement with lowered eyebrows.

After a moment, his attention remaining on the seat, he half smiled. "I'd be careful sitting in that."

Hannah cautiously pulled her hand away, as if the chair suddenly presented a danger.

"There must be something about it. People keep passing out whenever they sit there. Of course—" his crooked smile expanded into a teasing grin "—the other common denominator is you. And that I can understand. You take my breath away whenever I'm around you."

Hannah slapped her hands to her face to cover her flaming cheeks. The action also served to hide her smile. Ducking her head, she hurried to the other side of the counter in order to get some barrier between her and Gabe. Just in case she did something foolish, like jump back into his arms.

When he gave her a wink and a wave and headed for the back door, she waved farewell. Gabe felt certain of his purpose in life. Hannah hoped she could learn to be as certain in hers. But with her hands still reveling in the feel of Gabe's gentle fingers touching her skin, it was hard to imagine that her purpose was to marry the bishop's son.

Chapter Eleven

Pausing at the back door to the quilt shop, Gabe took a deep breath. He was going to ask Hannah to join him for lunch at The Dew Drop. The question was weightier than a simple meal together. He was asking her to make a public acknowledgment of a relationship—a *possible* relationship, he reminded himself.

Although they hadn't seen each other for the past few days, she was never far from his mind. He knew Hannah felt the same as he did—that they could have something precious and rare. Gabe ran a hand through his hair. He'd also thought the same thing years earlier. And been left alone, never to see her again until earlier this month. But if she said yes to being with him today…in full view of her Amish community…

Taking another deep breath, he pushed the door open.

Hannah poked her head out of one of the many colorful aisles as he closed it behind him. Gabe's shoulders relaxed. His lips curved to share the immediate shy smile that lit her face. He couldn't stop himself from grinning. To his joy, she seemed to be content with the same. It was more than wonderful, but the action wasn't going to get him a public date.

He cleared his throat. "I was wondering how the bishop was doing." Their efforts with Bishop Weaver had been the talk of the community the past few days.

"*Gut.* He should be out of the hospital soon."

"Glad to hear it." Gabe shifted his feet and wiped his sweaty palms against the side of his pants. *Much is lost for want of asking.* "I was also wondering if you'd be interested in joining me for lunch? I'd love to hear how the auction plans are going. Besides, an endless cup of coffee at The Dew Drop would help me get through the rest of the day."

Gabe held his breath as the smile wavered on Hannah's face. His stomach dropped. She was going to say no.

Hannah's gaze darted around the shop before returning to meet his. "I could handle getting something to eat." She put a hand over her stomach. "I think."

Gabe blew out his breath in a slow, quiet stream. Knowing it would be too much, he resisted the urge to reach out and take her hand. "Are you ready?" Hannah would understand the question to mean more than if she was prepared to walk out the door.

Her slender throat worked in a swallow, but she nodded. Unable to keep the elated smile from his face, Gabe waited while Hannah put a sign on the door and donned her cape and bonnet. Then they were out on the street. Together. In public. By her choice, and not because she was worried about her missing dog.

Gabe was abnormally aware of every horse and buggy that *clip-clopped* past them during the short walk to the restaurant. Knowing the speed of the Amish grapevine, Gabe wondered if half the community knew he was taking Hannah to lunch before they pushed open the door into The Dew Drop. If not, from the heads that swiveled in their direction when they entered, he figured they would by the time he and Hannah placed their orders. He understood enough of the Pennsylvania Dutch dialect to know they were the topic of conversation at every table they passed.

By the studied composure of her face, so did Hannah.

Hannah sighed in relief when they settled into a booth at the back of the restaurant, just outside the swinging door to the kitchen. Her face flushed as she recalled a recent lunch here with another man. She bit the inside of her cheek. There had been nothing official about her relationship with Jethro. It'd only been... strongly suggested.

The community had been receptive to the fundraiser, even though rumors were circulating that she was spearheading the event due to her interest in the man rather than the program. Surely the community could become receptive to the man? Outsiders had been accepted before—not into the church, but into the Plain community at large. Why not Gabe? He was a good man. Surely everyone could see that? And a Mennonite. There'd been a pleased rumble throughout the district about him, initiated by the Amish volunteer firefighters who'd gotten to know him.

But what kind of relationship could they have? Knowing his passion for his work, Hannah knew Gabe wouldn't become Plain. That left…her leaving. Could she? She'd pondered it once. The answer had been a tentative yes before it became an adamant no. But with Gail now back, some of that sting was gone.

Slipping off her cloak and bonnet, Hannah tucked them into the corner of the booth's seat before turning to face the man across the table. If they could keep his job here, was there a way they could stay together in the community? She couldn't become a baptized member of the church, but if she could still see and be involved with family and friends…could she live with that?

Studying his dear face, Hannah thought perhaps she could. It felt good to be here together. In the open. Hannah's smile pushed up like daffodils in spring. It felt really good in fact.

Gabe seemed to feel the same way. His green eyes regarded her warmly. "So, how's the auction coming? Have a location? A date?" He raised an eyebrow. "Any participants?"

"*Ja*, to all three. Since it'll help the volunteer fire department, they've offered the use of the building and surrounding area for the auction. As for participants, there's been a lot of discussion. I need to confirm items so I can have posters made to hang around town."

Gabe nodded thoughtfully. "Sounds good. Sounds great, in fact. Anything I can do to help?"

"Do you know how to sew?" Hannah jested.

"Not at all. Guess you'll have to find something else for me to do."

Right now, what Hannah would like for Gabe to do would be reach across the table and hold her hand. Was the community ready for that? Was she? Hannah flattened her hands on the wooden surface to keep from reaching for him herself.

The bang of the kitchen doors beside them made her jump. Rebecca came over, her expression as grim as Hannah had ever seen as she set water glasses on their table.

"You ready to order?"

Gabe raised his eyebrows at the normally cheerful waitress's unusual demeanor. He reached for the menus nestled behind the napkin dispenser. "Sorry, could we have another minute?" With an abrupt nod and a pasted smile, Rebecca turned toward the kitchen.

Concerned, Hannah watched as the young woman pushed through the swinging doors. Now, over the top of them, she noticed the blotchy, tear-streaked face of Rachel Mast. As she watched, Rebecca gave a comforting hug to her older sister.

Hannah frowned. "I wonder what's going on. I hope everyone is all right. You haven't been contacted about anything, have you?"

Gabe pulled his phone out and glanced at the screen. "No missed calls." Putting the phone back, he checked the device at his hip. "Doesn't look like it."

Hannah relaxed, but she was still worried. Traveling on busy roads could be risky for the slower moving buggies. Farming was a dangerous business. Accidents might be more prevalent in the busy summer season, but silos filled with grain could be treacherous. Animals could kick or injure people. The Mast girls had recently lost their *daed* to a lingering illness. It would be awful if something had happened to their *mamm* or younger *bruder*, as well.

A low rumble of male voices heralded the arrival of a group of Amish men into the restaurant. Hannah knew them all. They worked at a local business that made portable buildings. She was surprised when a few frowned at her and Gabe. While she'd expected a few raised eyebrows, their expressions leaned to unfriendliness. Visiting with the customers they passed, the group made their way to a table. Within moments, a ripple of whispers circled the room.

By the time a more-composed Rebecca took their order and delivered it, Hannah discovered she and Gabe had drawn more attention. She straightened against the back of the booth when one of the men who'd come in with the group approached them.

"Why did you tell Aaron Raber to leave for the *Englisch* world?"

Setting down his water glass, Gabe furrowed his brow, trying to recall where he'd seen the man before. "Excuse me?"

"You told Aaron Raber to go to an *Englisch* school. He's gone. He left the community."

Frowning, Gabe shook his head. "I didn't tell Aaron to go."

The man's lips flattened. Gabe couldn't recall the man's name, but he finally placed him as a volunteer fireman who'd attended one of his trainings.

"I think there must be some kind of misunderstanding," Gabe told him. The man's grave expression didn't change. "I've only seen Aaron at the department's training the other night. We spoke briefly…" *about his interest in training on gas and diesel engines, when I gave him a number to contact about it.*

His stomach churning, Gabe strangled his fork. Now he remembered the man as one who'd been in the small cluster near where he and Aaron had spoken. Surely Aaron hadn't taken Gabe's simple action as encouragement to leave?

It took another swallow to force down the previous bite of food that suddenly stuck in his throat. The goodwill of the Amish community was helpful to his job. In fact, if they were going to be the ones financially supporting it, it was vital. His gaze shifted to Hannah. It would be vital for that relationship to work, as well.

Gabe cleared his throat. "We chatted about a business interest he had. I gave him some information. That was all. I certainly didn't encourage him to leave."

The man's expression indicated he believed Gabe was directly responsible for Aaron's departure. He strode back to his companions, who were watching from their table with chilly expressions.

Gabe felt several gazes burn into his back. His meal could've been shredded paper for all he tasted. From Hannah's rounded eyes, she felt the weight of the attention, as well. When an unusually somber Rebecca passed by and gestured with the coffeepot, they shook their heads. Gabe had his wallet out before she brought over the check. Talking in the restaurant ceased as he and Hannah walked to the door. The frosty winter day outside seemed warm in contrast.

"Did you know anything about this?" Hannah whispered as they hurried down the sidewalk toward the shop.

"No more than I said at the booth. Aaron was interested in motors. Something about determining there was a need for that type of work. I gave him a contact number. Did his leaving have anything to do with Rebecca and the other young woman's distress? And why are we whispering?"

Hannah faced forward, although she spoke in a louder voice. "I've never had other Plain folks treat me like that. Not since…not for a while. It brought back memories. Unpleasant ones."

Gabe slowed his stride at her admission, but when Hannah didn't, he hurried to catch up. Before he could address her concerning comment, she spoke again.

"Everyone knows Rebecca Mast's sister Rachel and Aaron Raber are walking out together. They've been together for years. They took the baptism classes so they could be married. Aaron was supposed to be baptized with Rachel, my sister Abigail, Samuel Schrock and others this fall. Although Aaron came the day before to confirm his decision to be baptized, that Sunday morning a horse kicked him. It was obvious his arm was broken."

Gabe lifted his eyebrows. That explained the short cast on Aaron's arm the night of the training.

"They took him to Portage to have it taken care of. Benjamin came and was baptized. I don't know when they were going to complete it for Aaron. I know Rachel has been anxious, because she's waited all this time to marry him. And now he's gone."

Gabe blew out a breath. "No wonder she was upset," he murmured. "How often do young folks leave from your district?"

Hannah stumbled. Gabe automatically shot out a hand to catch her. To his surprise, she shook it off. "Not…often. Rarely. Not since…not since my sister years ago."

"Your sister left? When was this?"

"That day we were supposed to meet." Jerking open the door to the quilt shop, Hannah swept inside, leaving Gabe rooted to the sidewalk.

By the time he followed, she'd hung up her cloak and positioned herself behind the counter, almost as if she wanted a barrier between them. *Why not?* Gabe stopped on the other side. There always had been. Maybe, even beside the differences in religious doctrines, they were getting to the root of it. It certainly wasn't about their compatibility and the way he felt about her. And the way he thought she'd felt about him.

"Was that why you didn't show up that night?"

Hannah picked at the embedded ruler in the countertop. "I walked with her down the lane, trying to convince her to stay. She was determined to go. The man she'd been—" Hannah shot a glance at him from beneath lowered lashes "—secretly walking out with was marrying another, and Gail was going to have a *boppeli*."

Her voice had dropped so much that Gabe leaned over the counter to hear the last bit.

"I…I had to tell *Mamm* and *Daed*. I had never seen them so heartbroken." Hannah shifted from fiddling with the ruler to spinning the orange-handled scissors that lay nearby with her finger. "I couldn't leave them that night. Not when I was secretly meeting someone, as well."

"Why didn't you let me know?"

"How? We didn't exactly plan beyond a meeting at a time," she countered softly. "Besides, after seeing what Gail's leaving did to my family… Their sadness, the shame they felt when those who are prone to judge in the community slighted or gossiped about us. How could I do the same thing to them? How could I have left, as well? Break their hearts again? Provide more fodder for the gossips? What example would that set for my *brieder*?" Her voice grew stronger as she spoke. Hannah looked up now, eyes glistening with tears but the set of her jaw almost daring Gabe to refute her statements.

"Theirs weren't the only hearts involved," he murmured.

Hannah sniffed, her face softening. "I thought you could handle it."

Gabe's lips twitched. "I appreciate your confidence in me. I guess." Twisting to look behind him, he located the chair. "Glad you didn't remove it. I feel like I need it. I'll try not to pitch onto the floor." Stepping back, he dropped into the seat.

Hannah smiled faintly, her eyes telling him she appreciated his attempt at humor. Glad someone did. Gabe heaved a sigh, recalling his own heartache when she never showed, when his attempts to find her failed, when, despondent, he went home, and his little brother died soon after.

"So where does that leave us?" Needing something to do when he wanted to jump up and plead his case, Gabe reached down to wipe moisture, residue of some snow on the sidewalk, from his shoes. Ears tuned to her, he could hear Hannah quietly breathing. *Say something. I love you. But I can't make this relationship work on my own.* He closed his eyes. *And I don't know if I can handle having my heart broken again.*

He snorted ruefully. Maybe there *was* something about this chair's effect on people. Opening his eyes, Gabe pushed up from it to find Hannah standing silently on the other side of the counter. Eyes wet with tears, her hands were pressed to her mouth.

"Your sister's back now, isn't she? So am I. For the moment. Do you think maybe there's a reason that God has given us this second chance?" Shaking his head, Gabe started for the back door, the silence ringing behind him.

Chapter Twelve

Hannah stopped the sewing machine's wheel and her feet paused on the treadle at the angry rattle against the windows. She glanced out at the snow gusting down the street. All afternoon the wind had been battering the windows as if it was trying to blow through the glass.

Frowning, she clipped off her thread. Her *daed* had warned her about the weather. Even cautioned that maybe she shouldn't go to work today. But since Barb had left the store in her care while she was out of town, Hannah didn't want to close it in her employer's absence.

She was thankful she'd left Daisy back at the farm. The trip home over unplowed country roads would've worn the old mare out. The topic of conversation of the few customers she'd had since noon had been the deteriorating weather and the concern they hadn't seen the worst of it yet. Hannah frowned at the snow, blowing so hard the bank's sign across the street was barely visible. A glance at the wall clock revealed it to be an hour to closing. Even Barb would agree it was reasonable to shut the shop for the day.

The window rattled again. As she pushed her chair back from the sewing machine, Hannah bit her lower lip. She needed to call the Thompsons and arrange for a ride home. Hopefully the *Englisch* drivers were willing to go out in these conditions.

She glanced up at the ceiling. She'd heard Gabe come in a short while ago. They hadn't spoken in the past two days she'd been at work, although she'd thought about what he'd said…and that she hadn't responded. Even though he'd frequently stated that much was lost for want of asking, given the current circumstances, asking him for anything was something Hannah couldn't do.

She stared unseeing at the fabric lined up under the sewing machine's presser foot. Due to some rumblings in the community about an *Englischer*'s—Gabe's— alleged involvement in Aaron Raber's absence, the auction was at a standstill. The naysayers had been quick to speak out, which had suppressed the support of others. It was no surprise who the naysayers' leader was. Even though Gabe's work had saved Bishop Weaver's life, the man's wife surreptitiously campaigned to quash the fundraising event.

Hannah didn't know how or whether to proceed. What if it was *Gott*'s will that it be ended?

No auction meant no job for Gabe.

His leaving would remove temptation, so she could focus on what she should be doing. Who she should be intending to marry. Still, the knowledge that in less than two weeks she might never see him again gnawed at Hannah's stomach and made her eyes sting.

There was a brief lull in the wind. Hannah lifted her head at the creak of the building's stairs. A moment later, the back door opened and Gabe poked his head into the shop.

"I didn't see Daisy out back." At another big gust, he looked beyond Hannah to the window. "It's getting pretty rough out there. How are you getting home?"

Hannah couldn't prevent the catch in her breath at the sight of him. She barely managed to keep her face composed. "Ah, I was going to call the Thompsons to hire them for a ride."

"Their car might have a rough time in these conditions. I'll give you a ride home."

Stepping the rest of the way into the shop, Gabe kept his attention on the windblown street. Was he intentionally avoiding her? He had reason to, after the way they'd last parted. Although she nodded solemnly, Hannah's pulse accelerated.

"It's supposed to get worse." Gabe finally looked in Hannah's direction. "How long do you need to stay?"

Hannah sprang up from her chair. "I can be ready to go in a few minutes."

"I'll go grab my gear, then head out to warm up the truck. Meet you in back?"

"Ja." Hannah dashed for the front of the store to grab her cloak and bonnet from their peg and lock the door. Quickly addressing other tasks to close the store for the night, she locked up the shop's back door and headed out.

The alley door was like a live thing, trying to jerk out of her hands. Once outside, Hannah gasped to reclaim some air before the wind whisked it all away. She hopped down the path Gabe had made through the knee-deep snow to reach the truck's passenger door and climb in.

Directing some heat vents toward her with one hand, Gabe hooked a thumb toward the back seat with the other. "There's a blanket and an extra coat in back." He returned his hands to the steering wheel and, moments later, they were heading out of the alley. The wipers barely kept pace with the constant bombardment of white.

Hannah twisted to retrieve the lap-size blanket from the back seat. It could be that Gabe's curtness was due to the dangerous conditions of the trip. Maybe it was just her remorse, but his demeanor seemed almost as chilly as the weather.

"It's worse in the country," he murmured as he leaned forward to peer through the windshield. "I'm glad you didn't drive Daisy today. This weather is nothing to mess around with. How'd you get in?"

"I caught a ride in with a neighbor." Hannah was just relieved they were talking. She didn't care what the subject was.

By the time she'd tucked the blanket around her legs, they'd reached the edge of town. Once the protection of the buildings was gone, the truck shuddered under the onslaught of the buffeting winds.

Hands never leaving the wheel, Gabe darted another glance at her. "Buckle up."

Doing as he directed, Hannah kept her eyes on the white world beyond the windshield. She didn't know how Gabe even knew where the road was, but somehow he kept on it. They crept down the highway leading out of town at a speed her mare Daisy could've outpaced. Even so, Hannah gasped softly every time she felt the truck shift abruptly on the road's treacherous surface. Numerous times she glanced over to Gabe, taking comfort in his focused profile and capable hands on the wheel.

They both jumped when Gabe's pager went off. Finding his way into the nearest driveway, Gabe put the truck in Park and contacted the dispatcher. Following their succinct conversation, he turned to Hannah with a frown.

"I have to respond to a call. I don't have time to take you home beforehand."

"That's...that's all right. You do what you need to do."

With a terse nod, Gabe carefully backed onto the road. Hannah caught her breath and braced a hand against the dashboard when Gabe gently braked and the truck continued to slide backward. She waited until he had their forward motion under control before speaking.

"Accident?"

"Yeah. Fortunately just a little farther up the road." They crept along until Hannah could make out dark shapes against the otherwise uninterrupted white world outside, one car tipped in the ditch on both sides of the road. Putting on his hazard lights in addition to the flashing blue on the dash, Gabe parked at a 45 degree angle on the road to try to block the scene.

Leaving the engine running, Gabe's eyes were riveted on the cars as he grabbed his jump bag. "I might need your help." He glanced at Hannah, his green eyes grave. "For now, stay put."

Easing the driver's door open, he and the wind battled for control of it. Gabe won, but in the short skirmish, frigid air swirled through the cab. Hannah gasped at its vicious bite. She watched anxiously through the window as Gabe fought his way to the car on his side of the road.

When he stepped away from the road's shoulder, he sank to his knees in the snow. With a few lunging strides, he reached the driver's door of the partially buried vehicle. Clearing the snow away, he wedged it open and leaned in.

Fixated on the vehicle, Hannah's eyes widened. Even under these conditions, she recognized the older model car that'd been idling at the end of her lane that night. Heart clenching, she automatically looked around for Socks before remembering she'd left the collie at home today. Hands clasped to her chest, she stared at where Gabe was barely visible in the open driver's door. She caught her breath when he reappeared out of its depths and motioned for her before disappearing again.

Hannah hesitated as she recalled her fear as the car in the ditch had idled at the end of her lane, her anguish when Socks was missing, presumably taken by this man. A moment later, grimacing with trepidation, she pushed open the truck's door. Driving snow stung her face, and the wind whipped her cloak as she worked her way to the ditch. The tracks where Gabe had made his way down were already drifting over. Taking a step, Hannah gasped as wet and cold gripped the thick stockings on her leg.

Gabe ducked back out of the car when she reached him. He scanned her face. "You doing okay?" he shouted above the wind. Hannah didn't know if she was nodding or shaking, but Gabe took it as an affirmative. "I'm so sorry to get you into this, but I need to get his bleeding stopped and check the occupants of the other car. Can you keep pressure on this?"

Ducking with him out of the wind, into the cavity of the car's interior, Hannah saw a man—the man who she'd seen on the street—slumped in the front seat. He was bleeding from the face and head. With a gloved hand, Gabe had a wad of gauze pressed against the man's forehead. Using his free hand, Gabe pulled another medical glove from his pocket and handed it to her.

"Here, put this on. Then I need you to take my place. Ready?" In the cramped situation, they managed to switch positions. "Head wounds bleed a lot. It's not as bad as it looks, but we still have to get it stopped. I'll check the other car and be back as soon as I can. Local police should be here soon and maybe can relieve you." He met her eyes. "You going to be okay with this?"

"Ja." Hannah nodded. As the cold seeped into her feet through her sensible black shoes, she reminded herself that she'd saved a life with Gabe's help a few days ago. She could do this, too.

"You're amazing." Touching her shoulder, Gabe gave her a smile before ducking out of the car's interior.

Even in the frigid surrounding, his parting actions warmed her. Her heart rate steadied with the knowledge of his confidence and support. Turning her focus to the man in front of her, Hannah's brows furrowed as she scrutinized his face. Under the rivulets of blood that tracked down it, the man's skin, instead of being pale with cold, was flushed. Tentatively, she held the backs of her ungloved fingers to an unbloodied space on the man's opposite cheek. Heat radiated into her cold hand. The man was burning up.

When his eyes suddenly fluttered open, Hannah jerked her hand back from his cheek. Only an arm's length apart, she could see some lucidity drifted into their depths.

One corner of the man's lips twitched slightly. "I'm sorry," he murmured. "About your dog."

With the wind buffeting the outside of the car, Hannah wasn't sure she heard correctly. Or if he was even fully coherent. "Hang on. Help is here. We'll get you taken care of."

"I didn't mean to scare you. I…" He sucked in a shuddering breath. "I took care of the dogs when I took them. I tried to find good homes for them. I just needed money to pay for the painkillers…the drugs. Drugs that have…wrecked my life. I'm sorry. So, so sorry." His eyes drifted closed again.

Memories of the sleepless night, the panic and angst of Socks's disappearance flooded Hannah. She never wanted to relive that night. And Socks had only returned because she'd chewed through a rope to escape. Hannah could've lost her forever. "Hello? You probably need to stay awake. Hello?"

The man's eyelids slowly lifted again. He regarded her with dull eyes.

Hannah forgot the wind and the cold as she looked into them. They were filled with obvious pain. Pain that wasn't just physical.

Squeezing her eyes shut, Hannah swallowed as she reflected upon the fear and anguish this man had caused her. She wasn't sure what else she could do for his physical aches, but she knew what she had to do for the other. For both of them.

Opening her eyes to meet his listless ones, Hannah whispered, "I forgive you."

The man's eyes widened. The corners of his mouth lifted slightly, and his shoulders sagged further against the seat as his eyes drifted shut again. While still flushed, he looked…peaceful. Surprisingly, it was a peace she shared.

Hannah's hand was cramped with cold. Glancing through the windshield, she was surprised to see flashing red-and-blue lights against the snow. Her relief knew no bounds when she could make out Gabe, bent almost double against the wind, cross the road toward her. She gasped when he slipped at the edge of the ditch, sliding down its length before regaining his feet. One side of him was caked in white when he ducked beside her to lean into the car.

"How're we doing?" With a glance at Hannah, he took over applying pressure. Gently lifting the gauze, he checked the wound. "The good news is the bleeding stopped." He ran his eyes over the man, lingering on a grubby bandage on the man's ungloved hand. "Mr. Weathers, did you ever see your doctor about your dog bite?"

The man's head weakly wobbled back and forth on the headrest.

"Looks like it's gotten infected. You've got a fever and, I imagine, feel pretty lousy. There's an ambulance en route. I can't make you go to the hospital, but you're very sick, Mr. Weathers."

The man's cracked lips barely moved in his whisper. "I'll go. I was heading for the doctor, but got stuck in the lane. When I gunned it to get out, I shot onto the road and hit something. Are they all right?"

"Yes, sir, they're going to be fine. Getting a ride back into town with the officer."

Hannah could hear the faint sound of a siren. So apparently could the man. His eyes popped open and fixed on her.

"Take care of the puppies."

Chapter Thirteen

Hannah's brow creased. Was he talking about Socks? About dogs he'd taken, in general? Was he simply delirious with fever? Frowning, she caught Gabe's eye. He shook his head, apparently not understanding what the man meant, either.

"There's two. A friend of mine had them. Their momma died and he couldn't handle them. They're in the kitchen. I've been taking care of them. But…" The man was quiet for a moment as Gabe addressed the wound on his head. "I'm going to be away for a while. I…I need help. It's…it's time I got help."

Impulsively, Hannah grasped the man's grubby hand, startled again at the heat of it against her cold fingers. "Don't worry. I'll take care of the puppies. You just get better." She felt the subtle pressure as the man gently squeezed back.

"Thank you," he sighed, his hand dropping open as if the action was too much for him.

Through the windshield, Hannah caught sight of

movement as people in reflective gear descended the ditch. Ducking out of the car's interior to give them room, she stumbled a few feet away through the drifts, blinking against the sting of the snow on her face. She thought she heard Gabe yell something about the truck before the wind whipped his words away. Grasping handfuls of dead grass that barely topped the snow, she pulled herself out of the ditch. Gabe's truck was now among a trio of light-pulsing vehicles. Hannah was glad to see an ambulance was one of them.

Slipping across the slick pavement, she reached the truck and battled the passenger door open to climb inside. She almost wept with relief at the warmth of the cab and break from the incessant wind. When Gabe opened the driver's door to a flurry of flakes and a blast of cold air a few minutes later, Hannah still had her fingers tucked against the blasting heat vent.

"You doing okay?" Gabe stashed his ever-present black bag behind the seat before giving her a quick survey.

Hannah nodded toward where her legs were tucked under the dash. "I can finally feel my feet again."

Gabe frowned. "I'm sorry about that. You aren't dressed for this. I shouldn't have called you out to help."

"*Nee.* I'm glad you did. I—" she ducked her head "—I'm glad you trust me to do so. I'm sorry about the other day…"

Stripping off a glove, Gabe reached for her hand. "Hannah, I don't give up easily."

Lifting his hand, Hannah touched the back of it against her cheek. Though not extremely warm, it was a compelling contact against her chilly skin. Gabe's presence in her life was like that. It added a warmth, a vibrancy, that didn't otherwise exist for her. "I'm glad about that, too."

She returned their clasped hands to her lap. "I need to get the puppies."

"Yes, ma'am." Gabe grinned at her before turning his attention to the two other vehicles maneuvering to turn around on the highway. Their flashing lights dimmed in the growing dusk and blowing snow as they pulled away. His smile faded. "The deputy said to get back into town as soon as possible. They're stretched thin and having trouble getting around themselves." He looked at Hannah, his expression solemn. "They're closing down the highway. I don't know that I'll be able to get you home, especially if the country roads are worse than this."

Hannah hissed in a breath at the dilemma. Staying with Gabe was out of the question. As a single woman, she couldn't stay overnight alone with a single man. And a single man who wasn't Amish? Her folks would be upset. Even the more open-minded ones in the community would be appalled. As for Jethro and the bishop... Well, it wasn't possible.

"The Thompsons said I could stay with them if I ever needed." Hannah liked the *Englisch* couple who frequently drove for the Amish. "But I don't know about taking puppies there."

"You fill me in on what to do. I'll take care of them at my apartment until you can get back to town. I need to call into dispatch and tell them I'm finished here."

With a squeeze of her hand, he freed his to reach for the radio clipped to the driver-side visor. After Gabe advised the situation was wrapped up and they were heading back to town, he reattached it.

"I wish I could let my folks know I was all right. They would've expected me by now."

"Do you have the number of their closest phone hut? We can give them a quick call before we head in." Gabe reached for a side pocket of his pants.

Hannah's gaze sharpened when Gabe shifted abruptly to use both hands in an apparent search. Her heart rate accelerated at his grim expression as he quickly checked other pockets.

"My phone." Gabe's voice was flat as he plucked at an open flap along the edge of his pants. He closed his eyes in obvious frustration. "I'm going to check the car. If I'm lucky, I'll find it in there." Opening his eyes, he puffed out his cheeks. "If I'm not, it probably slipped out when I slid down the ditch." They both looked out the window to where the wind had already filled in the furrow created by his slide down the incline. "And someone will find it in the spring."

With a glance at her face, Gabe hooked a rueful smile. "I won't be long." Once more, wind blasted through the cab when the door opened. Tucking the blanket she'd retrieved more closely about her legs, she watched as a small light bounced around the interior of the stranded car. When Gabe emerged a short time later, she tensed, only to sag against the seat when he waved his arms in obvious failure in his search.

After a brief battle with the wind over the door, Gabe

lunged into the truck. He brushed the snow out of his hair. "It's not there. I'm sorry."

Aware of his obvious distress, Hannah reached out to touch his arm. "Why are you apologizing to me? Having a phone is more of a shock to my life than not having one." Her heart hiccupped when he shared her smile. "When I get to the Thompsons, I'll leave a message for my folks that I'm all right. That way, they'll know when someone goes to check."

"Sounds like a plan." Gabe carefully backed the truck on the highway until his headlights picked up a snow-filled lane. Two perpendicular lines along its length had been blurred to insignificance by the relentless wind. Reaching over to shift something in the console, he sighed deeply. "I hope four-wheel drive can get us out. Otherwise we'll be spending the night here, and I can't guarantee the accommodations. Hang on. It's going to be a bit of a ride."

He wasn't joking. Hannah gripped the handhold next to the ceiling as the truck bucked its way up the lane. They finally made it to the top, where even the driving snow couldn't make the house and nearby building look less dilapidated.

Upon shifting into Park, Gabe kept the engine running. "I'll get them."

Hannah already had her hand on the door handle. "I'm going with you."

She followed in his footsteps along the unshoveled walk. On the porch, they stomped their feet against the worst of the snow and entered the front door. Although not cold, it was definitely cool in the house. Having been there before, Gabe led the way to the dimly lit kitchen. In a large box tucked in the corner of the room, two black-and-white puppies snoozed and cuddled together on an old blanket.

Hannah knelt next to the box. "Oh, you sweeties!"

"Looks like Border collies. How old do you think they are?"

One of the pups lifted its head and yawned. "About four weeks, I'd say." Reaching out a hand, Hannah stroked a finger down the white strip between its little ears.

Gabe was nosing around the shabby kitchen. "I see some supplies here. What do we need to take with us to get them through the night and maybe the next day? I've got blankets, and probably a box, at the apartment."

Hannah was relieved to see that, unlike the kitchen, the pups seemed to be in good shape. Reluctantly, she rose and looked toward where Gabe stood by a counter crowded with many things, among them, fortunately, puppy supplies. "Definitely some of the milk supplement." She spied an open bag of puppy food. "Looks like he's started them on solid food. We'll need that, too. We'll mix it with the supplement. Um…do you have some type of flat pan or bowl they can eat from at your place, or do we need to bring this one?" She toed the empty bowl on the floor by the box.

"I think I'm good. Don't want to take more than we can carry." Gabe met Hannah's gaze across the dimly lit room. "Just in case," he added grimly.

Nodding at the implicit direction to hurry, Hannah turned back to the pups. "If you can grab the supplies,

I've got the pups." Kneeling again, she scooted her hand under each warm little body. Mr. Weathers might not have taken care of himself, but he'd taken care of his young charges. Squirming, the pups squeaked at being rousted from their home. She clutched them to her chest as Gabe secured her cloak to ensure they were covered. When he paused, Hannah glanced up to meet his smiling green gaze. The look in them was as warm as the precious bundles she held. When she smiled hesitantly, Gabe leaned in and gave her a quick kiss on the lips.

Before she could do more than blink, he'd turned to gather the requested supplies from the counter. "Ready?"

He meant to go out the door with him and face the snow storm. Momentarily rooted on the dingy linoleum, Hannah realized she was ready for a lot of things. Including facing whatever storms might come in order to have a life with the man who currently shared a stranger's shoddy kitchen with her.

"Ja," she whispered, exhaling a breath she hadn't been aware of holding.

Supplies gripped in one hand, the other under Hannah's elbow to support her, Gabe led them to the still-running truck. The pups, awakened from the trip over the yard, yipped softly and began nosing their way out of the opening of her cloak as she settled into the seat. Although her lap was warm with the pups there, Hannah frowned when she extended a snow-dusted foot under the dash. The fan was blowing, but the truck's heater was making little headway against the biting cold outside.

Gabe shifted it into gear. "Hang on. Although we have better tracks to follow, the trip out might not be much better than the one in."

They jolted down the lane, windshield wipers battling furiously against the driving snow, then lurched from the end of the lane onto the highway. Hannah's sigh of relief morphed into gasps when the truck kept skidding over the slippery surface.

Gabe wrestled it into control. A moment later, they were creeping back toward town. If Hannah thought the trip out had been slow and treacherous, the return in the gathering darkness was more so. When a collection of weakly glowing lights, as opposed to sporadic ones indicating an *Englisch* farmyard, was visible through the blowing snow, she knew they were approaching Miller's Creek.

Trying to relax tensed muscles, she looked over in question when Gabe made a slow, careful turn into a lane, this one shorter and fortunately plowed sometime during that day.

"The Thompsons. But it's not looking good that they're home."

Gabe's concern was warranted. Hannah stayed in the truck when he went to the door and watched as he knocked once, twice, thrice. No answering light came on throughout the house's dark interior.

Gabe sighed when he got back into the truck. "I doubt they'd mind you staying, but unlike Amish homes, they keep theirs locked. Now what?"

Hannah stroked a hand over the again slumbering puppies. "I don't know when these two have last eaten.

We need to get them someplace warm and feed them. I can stay in the shop." She smiled wryly. "I have access to plenty of blankets. That way I can help you with the puppies. They need to eat every six hours or so."

"If you're sure?"

"*Ja*, I'm sure."

They crept out onto the road again. "Almost there." Gabe glanced over to give her a reassuring smile.

As he negotiated a sweeping curve in the road at the edge of town, a brutal gust of wind hit them, pushing the truck sideways. Immediately, Gabe responded to correct the slide, but the icy surface had them in its grasp. His efforts to counter their careen toward the ditch were futile. Hissing in a breath, Hannah clutched the seat belt that secured her with one hand as she curved her body over the puppies to protect them. She stiffened her legs, as if the action could somehow stop the truck's spin. Wide-eyed, she watched as they skidded toward the ditch and its sharp decline.

Chapter Fourteen

The truck shuddered beneath Hannah as it left the road, skittering over the shoulder and into the ditch. The pickup rocked hard to a halt, ending at a slant toward the passenger's side. Items on the center console tumbled into Hannah as she hovered over the puppies. Something black flew across her vision to crash into the window. She'd slid over the seat, her grip on the seat belt saving her from being plastered against the door. Out her window, the only thing Hannah could see beyond it was the wind-curled top of a snowbank.

"Are you all okay?" Even competing with the moan of the wind and the rumble of the engine, the urgency in Gabe's voice was unmistakable.

Heart rocketing, Hannah took stock of her little passengers. Running a gentle hand over them, she could feel little paws press into her lap as they stretched. One climbed up her cloak to sniff at the ribbon of her *kapp* that dangled on the outside of her cloak.

"*Ja*. I think so." She tried to lean away from the door,

only to find that gravity kept a possessive hold on her. "But I seem to be stuck."

"It's okay. We'll figure this out."

Hannah twisted in her seat to unbuckle the belt now restricting her movements. With feet pressed in the foot wheel and one hand on the steering wheel to brace him, Gabe reached across the console with his other to help. They both froze when the truck creaked and shifted toward the downslope of the steep ditch.

Hannah couldn't seem to find any air. "Is it…going to tip?" she whispered.

With a grunt, Gabe maneuvered in his seat until he was leaning his weight against the driver's door. Mouth flattened into a thin line, he scanned the snow-enshrouded dusk outside the windshield. Hannah gasped as a blast of wind shook the vehicle. As the truck creaked again, Hannah slid a fraction of an inch closer toward her door. With a shared wide-eyed gaze, they both held their breaths.

Gabe's heart squeezed at the fear he saw in Hannah's eyes. He had gotten her into this. If anything happened to her because of him…

He wasn't going to try to drive out. Any rocking motion to get traction in the snow could tip them over. Their tailpipe could be covered already. If it wasn't cleared, the cab could fill with carbon monoxide. If he couldn't keep it cleared, they'd need to shut off the truck. The pickup was shelter from the wind, but not from the cold without the heater. Even with the engine running and the fan full blast, frigid air was seeping in from every corner.

Conventional wisdom was to stay with the vehicle. Biting the inside of his cheek, Gabe narrowed his eyes at the lights that heralded the homes and businesses of town. Downtown and his apartment lay just beyond. A short distance, but was he foolish to even consider trying for it? Would he be risking their lives if they left the shelter of the vehicle?

The truck shuddered under another gust. Hannah's face paled beneath her black bonnet.

Glancing at the gauges, Gabe shut off the truck and withdrew the keys. Without the comforting rumble of the engine, the wail of the wind was unobscured.

"I don't like our options. We have shelter here, but not enough fuel to last the night. If the truck tips…" Gabe pressed his lips together. He wished he was certain he wasn't making a mistake with their lives. He nodded toward the windshield. "Can you see the lights of town?"

Hannah nodded hesitantly.

Gabe rubbed his forehead. "I normally wouldn't recommend this… We can't call out with my phone gone and, if I'm not mistaken, the radio in pieces at your feet. Hard telling how long we'd be here before help can arrive. I haven't seen another vehicle on the trip back into town. If they've closed the roads, we probably wouldn't.

"But if the truck tips, we might then be dealing with injuries." He nodded toward the puppies that were investigating Hannah's lap. "They have needs we can't meet here." Gabe regarded her grimly. "I can walk in and try to find help…"

Hannah drew in a breath as her gaze darted about the cab. "I'd rather not stay here alone. I think… I'd prefer level ground. With you." She gave him a tremulous smile, although Gabe could see it was with effort. "Even when a bad storm would blow up, the cows still need to be milked. We always made it to the barn to take care of the livestock. Of course—" the bow under her chin bobbed as she swallowed "—the barn wasn't quite so far from the house."

"I'll get you to safety." Or he'd die trying, Gabe vowed.

It was agreed. They cautiously maneuvered to gather what they'd need and could carry. Using empty grocery bags Gabe had left in the truck, they condensed the puppy supplies to what they figured would be immediately necessary. Hannah carefully wiggled into Gabe's spare coat, the sleeves long enough to cover her hands to protect them from the cold. A bungee cord used by Gabe while moving his possessions to the apartment was discovered in the console.

Every time the truck rocked under a strong gust, he and Hannah stared at each other with bated breath.

"The wind should be at our backs, which will help. Once we get among buildings, they'll block some of its force." Gabe gazed out the window toward the lights of town. "We're close enough we won't lose direction." He looked back to Hannah. "And you won't lose me. But it will be dangerously cold." Gabe's stomach clenched. He'd seen situations where people had died of exposure within yards of help. Even wearing the extra coat, he eyed Hannah's thick stockings and bonnet doubtfully, and he asked, "Will you be okay in those?"

She nodded with a half smile. "Try riding in an unheated buggy for a couple of hours. I'll be fine."

Across the confines of the tilted cab, Gabe regarded her. Nose red with cold, hair strands straggling from under her bonnet, eyes cautious but calm, delicate hands peeping from outsize sleeves holding two wiggling puppies clutched to her chest. She'd never looked more beautiful.

"You know, I thought you were wonderful when I met you. I've now realized I had no idea how *wunderbar* you really are."

Hannah ducked her head, pressing her cheek against one of the pups. "I…I feel the same."

A blast of wind battered the truck again. Gabe shot a hand to the dash as he felt the vehicle lift off its driver's-side wheels. Hannah squeaked, her mouth open in an unvoiced cry. When the truck bounced back down again, Gabe blew out a breath. Slipping the strap of his jump bag to sling over his chest, he adjusted it so he could unzip his coat and fleece vest. Upon tucking his vest into his belt, he reached a hand toward Hannah.

"Let's go. Give me the babies."

She handed up the puppies one at a time. Gabe carefully tucked them into his vest, resting miniature paws against his chest on both sides before he zipped it up. He then zipped up his coat, ensuring there was room at the neck for air to reach his young passengers.

"Ready?" He winced as she pushed the blanket aside.

"I wish we could take that along, but I think it'd blow around and be more in the way. Okay, I'm going to open the door and ease out. When I'm out, I'll dangle the bungee cord across the seat, and you can use it to lever out, as well." He gave Hannah what he hoped was a reassuring smile and not the grimace of concern he was feeling.

Heart pounding so hard he figured the pups pressed against his chest felt it, Gabe grasped the door handle and clicked it open. Bracing his feet in the driver's footwell, he wedged it open. The wind howled, pushing back. With a grunt, Gabe swung his legs out of the truck, shifting until he found secure footing. The wind slammed the door against him. Gabe winced at the bite of his shins against the truck. Pressing his backside firmly against the quaking door, he reached back into the cab for Hannah.

Down the slant of the truck, Hannah's face revealed the trust that struggled to overcome her fear. Gabe's heart stumbled. When they were out of this, he was going to do everything he could to ensure he was never involved in distressing her again.

Shaking the cord toward Hannah, he raised his voice so she could hear him over the howling wind. "Always knew life with you would be an adventure."

At his words, some of her fear dissipated as she wrapped one hand around the cord and used the other to lever herself along the dash. The bags of supplies were hooked on her elbow. "I could do with a little less adventure right about now."

Braced by Gabe, Hannah climbed up the seat and

over the console and was soon situated beside Gabe in the wedge of the driver's door. At their first step away from the shelter of the truck, they were almost knocked to their knees by the gusts at their back. With one of Gabe's arms supporting his passengers, the other hand gripping Hannah's elbow, they climbed out of the ditch. Finding some traction on the road's shoulder, they stumbled ahead of the wind.

The snow drilled into the back of Gabe's head. Air rushed past so fast that it was hard to get a breath, and when he did gasp one in, the cold bit all the way down his windpipe. After what seemed hours but was probably merely minutes, the wind, though still fierce, was hampered by the intermittent buildings. As they got farther into town, its power decreased. Soon they were walking upright. And faster. The road surface, while covered with snow, wasn't as slick underneath.

Under his gloved fingers, Gabe could feel Hannah shivering. He had to get her to shelter. Heat. Dry clothes. All of which he had in his apartment. Gabe's hand tightened at the thought of wrapping his fingers around a hot cup of coffee. He wanted to cheer when they reached their block of Main Street.

"Just about there," he encouraged Hannah, thrilled that he could speak at a normal decibel instead of shouting against the wind.

Before heading for the alley entrance, they stopped a breathless moment to look down Main Street. It was the first time Gabe had seen it empty of cars. Even in front of The Dew Drop, the parking spaces were deserted. Soft lights glowed from inside the windows, although the restaurant looked empty. The streetlamps shone down on the deepening snow, falling flakes looking like crystals as they drifted into their feeble light.

The fabric shop was illuminated from inside, as well.

"Oh dear, I forgot to turn them off when I left."

Gabe moved his hand from her elbow to wrap it around her shoulders. "That's okay. It looks pretty good to me. It's welcoming us home."

"First thing I want to do is call the phone hut near my folks and let them know I'm okay."

"Sounds like a plan. After you use it, I hope Barb won't mind that I borrow it to check in."

"I'm sure that would be fine…" Hannah's words died off as everything suddenly went dark about them. The street lights, the shop's lights, the lights from The Dew Drop. The street was pitched into darkness, the only light the white of the snow.

Chapter Fifteen

"What happened?" Hannah's voice was shaking as much as her slender shoulders were under his arm.

"Power went out." Gabe tucked her closer to his body.

"Will it come back on? It's not a factor at home, but so many things here depend upon it."

"It will, but I don't know when. Come on, let's get you inside." Gabe urged Hannah around the corner to the alley entrance. Supporting the squirming pups inside his jacket with one arm, Gabe kicked snow away from the door in order to get it open enough for them to stumble through. The hall inside was pitch black and silent. A silence broken by Hannah's surprising giggle.

"I'm just so happy to be here."

"Probably not as happy as I am to have gotten you here. Still, we need to get you dry and warmed up. Thanks to the previous tenants, even without electricity, upstairs we'll have light and heat of various sources. I might run every one of them, just to try to thaw out my feet."

Upon pulling off his gloves with his teeth, Gabe dug into a pocket to find his penlight. A moment later, he and Hannah sighed in relief at the circle of light.

"How about yours?"

Hannah stomped her feet to knock off the snow that covered her shoes. "Cold, but not frozen." Slipping off her shoes, she headed for the store's back door and unlocked it.

"Where are you going? We need to get the pups and you upstairs next to some heat."

"I'm calling the phone hut to let someone know I'm all right."

With a grunt, Gabe quickly slipped off his own boots and followed her into the store. He swept the light ahead of Hannah as she headed for the counter and the cordless phone there.

In the glow of the flashlight, Gabe could see her frown of confusion when she picked up the receiver and lifted it to her ear. "It's dead."

With the beam, Gabe touched on the phone's base and the flat gray cord protruding from it. "The phone may be cordless, but it still uses electricity." As Hannah's face fell into more distress than he'd seen her express all the treacherous evening, Gabe put his arm around her. "The storm is supposed to stop by morning. They might have the power on before that, and we can call then. From what I know of the Amish, once the blowing stops, a little snow on the ground won't prevent them from getting around. In the meantime, let's get you and my wiggling passengers upstairs and warmed up. It's not bad down here right now, but without power and in this cold and wind, the temperature will drop fast. Come on."

He guided her to the back door. "Besides, I need your help in figuring out how to get all this nonelectric stuff upstairs going."

Gabe had never been so thrilled to enter his apartment. With the help of Hannah and the penlight, kerosene lanterns left by the previous tenants were located and lit, along with the gas heater. By this time, the pups were ready to explore. Or something.

"Help," he murmured to Hannah when two cold noses poked under his chin and little tongues began licking his neck.

She came to his rescue, unzipping his coat and vest to collect the puppies. "They're hungry. I dropped the supplies just inside the door downstairs."

"I'll get it." Resurrecting his penlight from his pocket, Gabe slipped off his jump bag, set it next to the door and went on his errand. When he returned to the apartment, Hannah had her outer gear off and was on the floor by the heater with the pups in her lap.

He carried the supplies into the kitchen. "I've got a box in here from when I moved that will help keep them contained." He raised his voice so she could hear him in the other room. "I'm sure I could find a blanket to cushion it to sacrifice for the cause, as well."

"Sounds *gut.* How about a pan or bowl they can use for feeding?"

"I think I can dig something up."

Ten minutes later, he set a bowl of puppy food soaked in milk supplement on the floor. The pups scrambled over from their explorations of the room to eat. He and Hannah chuckled as one climbed into the bowl.

"Hey there, bud. You need to share with your sibling." Picking up the pup, Gabe set him outside the dish. While the puppies ate, their white-tipped tails wagging over their black backs, Hannah rose to her knees and inched her way closer to the heater.

"As the temperature drops, that'll feel even better."

"I don't think it could feel any better than it does right now," Hannah disagreed, holding her hands as close as possible to the emanating heat. She looked over when he knelt beside her. "You know I can't stay up here with you."

Gabe extended his fingers toward the heater. "I didn't risk our life and limb, or at least fingers and toes, to get you safely into town just to let you freeze downstairs. With the power off, there's no heat in the store." He stared at the red glow inside the heater. "If you're going to be stubborn about it, it would be better if you stayed up here and I went downstairs."

Hannah leaned over to poke him with her elbow. "*Ach*, were you always this contrary?"

"Me, contrary?" Gabe snorted. "I doubted my judgment and good sense in getting us out of the blizzard. And you're telling me you can't stay where it's safe and warm? If that's not the definition of contrary, I don't know what is."

They huddled in companionable silence, hands outstretched to the heater. Gabe swallowed audibly. "Another definition might be a woman who knows how much a man loves her, and knows she loves him, but won't agree to marry him."

For a moment, he didn't think she would respond. Was he wrong? Had he pushed too far? Memories of when he'd thought the same thing years before, only to have Hannah disappear, made Gabe feel colder than he had during their snowy walk into town.

"How about a man who pursues a woman when he knows the decision to marry him is...complicated?"

"I'm beginning to think he's just dense," Gabe muttered.

Hannah turned to smile at him. "I've wondered that a time or two myself."

Gabe tipped his little finger to tap against hers. "Should he give up hope?"

She hooked her pinkie around his. "If he can be patient just a little bit longer, there might be a chance."

Gabe shifted until they were touching shoulders. "He's a pretty patient guy."

For several heartbeats, there was only the sound of the flame inside the oil heater beside them and the occasional squeak of the puppies eating. When Hannah spoke again, it was barely above a whisper. "I'll... I'll talk to my parents when I see them again. And...tell Jethro that I can't marry him when I...love someone else."

Gabe's heart pounded enough he didn't need the heater to warm him. Drawing in a breath to respond, he grunted at the needle-sharp teeth that nipped his stockinged foot. Looking over his shoulder, he saw one of the pups had wandered from the bowl to find something else to nibble on. Scooping up the pup, he handed it to Hannah. "Since they're done, I'm going to fix some tea and something hot to eat on my gas stove so—" he looked intently at Hannah "—whoever goes downstairs is further fortified." Rising to his feet, Gabe headed for the kitchen.

"That will be *gut*," Hannah called to his back. "I'll appreciate that when I go downstairs."

Lighting the stove, Gabe snorted.

After the pups were settled and Hannah and Gabe had a meal of soup, tea and whatever else he could scrounge up, it was Hannah who went downstairs for the night. The debate continued as they descended the stairs by way of Gabe's penlight and another flashlight he'd unearthed. He refused to allow an oil or kerosene lamp down among the fabric.

"How do the *Englisch* manage to stay warm in the winter without electricity?" Hannah countered. "Surely they don't all freeze overnight?"

As he feared, the shop was already much cooler, even in the short time they'd been upstairs. "They probably have extra clothes to put on." Gabe considered it a victory that he'd finally persuaded Hannah to put on a pair of his socks. Her stockings were currently hanging on the back of a chair next to the heater to dry overnight. "Or extra blankets for the bed. You don't even have a bed. You'll be on the cold floor. Unless you think you're going to sleep on the countertop." He raised an eyebrow when a smile blossomed on Hannah's face.

"But I have blankets. Probably more than you do upstairs. I just need to get them down. And—" enthusiasm sparked her tone "—bags of batting would make a *wunderbar* mattress. I'll be more comfortable than you will."

When Gabe narrowed his eyes at her logic, Hannah lifted her light to expose all the quilts that lined the upper walls of the shop. He shook his head in reluctant admiration.

"Are you sure?" Gabe called as he fetched the chair by the counter. Sliding it next to the wall, he climbed upon it and started unclipping clothes pins that secured the quilts Hannah pointed out to him.

Hannah took the quilts as he handed them down. "Barb won't care. These are ones I made. In fact, she'd be helping me take them down if she was here."

"What would you have done if you'd worked in a grocery store? Used a bunch of soup cans for a mattress?"

Hannah carried her stack of quilts to the counter. "I'd have figured out something." They quickly made a bed on the floor beside the counter. Gabe had to admit when they were finished that it looked pretty comfy.

"Are you sure you don't want to stay upstairs where it might be warmer? I mean, I could stay here."

"*Nee*, I'll be fine."

"They'll probably have the electricity on by morning," Gabe said. "When you wake up, come upstairs for coffee, if not a little breakfast."

"Little being the key word."

He smiled at her teasing of his near-empty pantry. "I need to get back to the Bent 'N Dent and pick up some more expired breakfast bars." Gabe glanced at her face—this woman who'd endured so much with him tonight—shadowed in the indirect glow of their flashlights. "Well, good night. Call if you need anything. I mean call—" he cupped his hands about his mouth "—not call," he continued, nodding toward the inoperative phone.

"Ja." Hannah held his gaze.

Even in the shadows, Gabe was pulled into the sweet warmth in her eyes. He felt himself lean in—an inch, two, three—before he froze.

With a long exhale, he shifted back. "Well, I probably better go. When did you say those two need to eat again?"

Hannah smiled, but was that disappointment he saw in the shadowy light? "In six hours."

With a brief nod, Gabe reluctantly backed toward the door. He didn't break eye contact until he bumped into the wall. "See you in the morning," he murmured. Her soft "good night" followed him out the door. Jubilant at having her close and at her earlier shy admission, the beam of his flashlight barely kept ahead of him as he took the stairs three at a time.

Hannah tucked the quilts about her. Snuggling more deeply into her nest, she grinned as she listened to the wind whine against the storefront glass and the corresponding creaks of the old building. The room temperature might be dropping, but she was cozy in her pallet. Directing the flashlight's beam to the ceiling overhead, she saw not the shadows it made on the painted surface, but the man in the apartment above it.

They'd been through so much tonight. It was hard to believe it was only a few hours since Gabe had offered to take her home. He'd trusted her to help with his emergency call and, later, she'd trusted him to keep them safe. They made a good team. If they could handle the challenges of the past few hours, surely together they could face any circumstances that would come their way?

She'd admitted she loved him. Hannah hugged the thought to herself. It felt good. The memory of what else she'd said—that she'd talk to her folks and Jethro—not so much. She flexed her fingers in their grip on the blankets. She needed to talk with the bishop, who was still recovering. Hannah's chest tightened with remorse.

She'd always done as she should. Surely just this once she could ignore the bishop's directive? Her parents had married for love, wouldn't they understand? And Jethro, the man had recently lost his wife. Surely any feelings he might have for Hannah were just simple respect at this point? *Gott* had created love and marriage, had he not? Surely he would understand a hope for love in the relationship? Hannah rearranged the batting she was using as a pillow. Her hope was for courage to face the upcoming confrontations.

Shifting to lie on her back, she winced at a poke into her hair. Touching her head, she rolled her eyes when she realized she still wore her prayer *kapp*. Sitting up, she unpinned it and set it on the counter. As she settled back down, her flashlight beam swept across the row of beige fabric that lined part of the aisle.

Redirecting the light onto the light brown material, Hannah recalled the events that'd occurred since Gabe had reentered her life. Saving the bishop, initiating a community project, confronting the man she now knew was Mr. Weathers, helping and forgiving him tonight, rescuing puppies and trudging through a snowstorm to name a few. Maybe she wasn't a drab beige after all. While she might not be the rich blue Gabe saw her as, Hannah mused, drifting off to sleep, perhaps she was at least a green hue.

Blinking open her eyes in the feeble morning light, Hannah found herself in a canyon. It took a moment to recognize its fabric walls. Snuggling into her blanket cocoon, the events of the previous evening came back to her. The accident. The storm. The treacherous walk into town. Gabe. Upstairs. The lack of electricity to call her folks.

Even as Hannah acknowledged her cold nose, compliments of the room's low temperature, a low hum rumbled throughout it. The shop's furnace was kicking on. Ceiling lights she'd forgotten to turn off when she'd abruptly left last night flickered before fully illuminating the area. Hannah smiled. Lights, heat, the phone.

The phone! Scrambling out of her nest, she snatched the receiver off its cradle on the counter. Sighing in relief at the dial tone, she tapped out the number to the phone hut nearest to her farm and left a breathless message for her folks.

Mission accomplished, she pulled a quilt off her makeshift bed to wrap about her. Hannah searched for her shoes before remembering she'd taken them upstairs to dry out next to Gabe's heater. Gabe's heater, which would have kept the apartment reasonably warm. At least warmer than this.

Would Gabe be awake yet? Never having been at the shop this time of day, she didn't know when he got around. Hannah smiled. The pups would probably change his schedule this morning. Tipping her head, Hannah listened for any sounds from the apartment upstairs, but the growl of the furnace drowned out anything else.

He'd mentioned coffee. And she needed her shoes. Surely if she was quiet, it might be possible to obtain both without bothering him? Besides, she wanted to check on the pups. But if Gabe was already up, it would be the first breakfast she'd have with him. That their first of many shared breakfasts might start with expired breakfast bars expanded Hannah's smile.

The need for warmth, coffee and Gabe was superseded by the habit of setting the shop to rights first. Hannah bustled about, gathering and carefully folding the quilts to rehang later. When all looked as it should be, she headed for the back door. Her first steps on the stairs were hesitant, until she heard the tread of someone moving about above her; then she fairly skipped up the stairway.

"Morning." Gabe gestured her into the apartment with the coffee cup he held.

"Good morning." Hannah couldn't stop the flush that bloomed on her cheeks as she entered. Although Gabe was dressed, his light brown hair was tousled. She'd never seen him before with as much stubble on his cheeks.

"Can I get you some?" He lifted his cup again.

"*Ja*. Please." Instead of following him into the kitchen,

she checked on the status of their young charges. The pups were curled up, asleep in the blanketed box.

Gabe reemerged and handed her a cup. "They were fed again just a bit ago. They're…quite effective in making their needs known." He tipped his head toward the lamp emitting a dim glow near the sofa. "Power's on. County should be digging out soon. Did you get your call made?"

"*Ja.* Left a message. Someone should pick it up soon. I just couldn't stand to have them worry."

"I understand. Thankfully I didn't get paged last night, but I need to get another cell phone lined up. And get someone to pull my truck out of the ditch. Hopefully it's still sitting upright. But first, breakfast. Do you want a breakfast bar, or a breakfast bar?"

"Hmm. That's a difficult decision. I think I'll have a breakfast bar."

"Good choice." Gabe disappeared into the kitchen again, brought out two bars and handed one to Hannah. They ate them standing over the heater.

Upon finishing, Hannah gathered up her stockings and shoes from where they'd been set to dry. "I need to go back downstairs. I came to check on the pups and to get my shoes."

Gabe wadded up his wrapper. "Not for my fantastic breakfast?"

Hannah smiled. "Well, that, too. But I…shouldn't be up here alone with you."

Gabe sighed, but his intent gaze reminded Hannah of her agreement last night to talk with the bishop and her family about her relationship with him.

Snagging her outer gear from the pegs near the door, Gabe gestured for Hannah to precede him downstairs. "I'll go down with you to use the phone. I need to leave messages at work and the tow service." Both of them in stocking feet, their treads were quiet on the stairs.

"While I wait, I might wander out to see if the truck's okay. Maybe I'll take a shovel with me, to try to dig it out. And then I might go to where the accident was. Maybe root around in the snow a bit like a St. Bernard and try to find my phone."

Hannah giggled at the image of Gabe pawing in the ditch, snow flying out behind him. "Watching you do that would almost be worth the walk out to the truck."

"Store won't open for a while. You're welcome to join me…"

Gabe held the shop's door open for her. Basking in his smile, Hannah grinned up at him and walked through under his arm. A motion at the shop's wide windows drew her attention. Three men were looking into the shop, a team of draft horses and sleigh behind them. Hannah's breath caught with joy at seeing her father and two oldest brothers. Until she watched the transition from shock to dismay on Zebulun Lapp's face before his expression morphed into somber lines.

Through the glass, Hannah saw his gaze shift from her to Gabe and back again. Glancing at Gabe, unshaven with rumbled hair, his arm at the door practically around her, Hannah then looked down at her wrinkled dress. She instantly knew what her father was thinking.

Zebulun Lapp's attention lingered above her frozen stare. Reaching up with her free hand, Hannah pat-

ted her head, gasping when her fingers touched only
mussed hair. Her glance flew to the counter where her
kapp sat where she'd put it last night. Dropping her
shoes and stockings, Hannah dashed over, snatched
up her prayer covering and pulled it into position, her
fingers fumbling to gather the pins from the counter's
slick surface.

When she looked outside again, her father was turning away from the window. Racing to the door, Hannah
quickly unlocked it and ran outside. *"Daed!"*

Her father turned, his gaze sweeping from the hastily positioned *kapp* to her feet, clad in Gabe's socks, on
the snow covered sidewalk. He sighed. "Your *mamm*
and I worried about you when you didn't come home.
We wanted to make sure you were all right."

Hannah didn't feel the cold of the snow under her
feet or the frigid breeze through the thin material of
her dress. She was too hot with shame. "I'm so sorry.
I helped Gabe with an accident last night. I was going
to call but the power went out and he lost his phone in
the snow." Even to her ears, it sounded far-fetched. "I
left a message this morning at the phone hut. I spent
the night downstairs in the shop. Truly."

Her *daed*'s gaze lifted to above and behind her. Hannah felt a weight settle over her shoulders and discovered Gabe had covered her with her cloak. Zebulun
turned his attention to the draft horses who were stomp-
ing their feet in the snow. "I need to let your *mamm*
know I found you. Do you need anything before I go?"

*I need to know that you're not upset with me. That
you don't think I've let you down. That I haven't brought*

shame upon you. Hannah almost sobbed the words. She'd lived her life striving to always do the right thing. Responding to everything with humble obedience. Except for the times when she first met and secretly went out with Gabe. With a twist in her stomach, she watched her *daed* climb into the sleigh. "Where are you going?"

Zebulun settled onto the bench seat, Hannah's brothers climbed silently into the sleigh beside him. "Your *mamm* wants some groceries since we're in town. And when the feed store opens, I need some minerals for the cows."

"I'll go with you!"

With a look at her feet, Zebulun frowned. "You'll need shoes."

"Just give me a moment, please!" Hannah turned, almost bumping into Gabe as she dashed into the shop. He followed more slowly behind her, standing a few feet away as she jerked off his socks and struggled to put on her air-dried stockings while standing on one foot.

"Hannah."

She set her foot down on the cold floor, stocking bunched at the heel, and clamped her hands to her cheeks. "I can't, Gabe. I'm sorry. I thought I could marry you. But to do so would hurt my family. I can't… I can't bear to shame them like I just did."

"But we didn't do anything…"

"We did. *I* did. I saw his face. I hurt my *daed.* It was something I promised myself I'd never do after seeing the pain and shame they felt when Gail left."

Hannah couldn't see him clearly through her tear-blurred vision. "I need to do as my parents wish. To follow *Gott*'s will as the bishop wishes and…and marry elsewhere." Kneeling, she finished pulling on her stockings and slid her feet into clammy shoes. The laces were too stiff to hurry, so Hannah drew in a few deep breaths as she clumsily tied them. As she straightened to stand, she brushed the tears from her face. She almost sobbed anew at Gabe's expression. Even the man in the wreck last night hadn't looked as defeated.

"I'm sorry," she whispered before turning for the door. As she went through, she locked it. At the heavy click on the old door, Hannah couldn't help but think she was locking up something else, as well.

Her heart.

Chapter Sixteen

Wisconsinites were experts in digging out after winter storms. Within a day, the town was set to rights. Within two days, other than deeper drifts in ditches and across fields, it was as if the storm had never happened.

But Hannah knew better. She pushed peas around her plate with her fork, dodging other uneaten food from The Dew Drop's daily special. In those two days, she hadn't had the courage to talk with her *daed*. It wasn't that they'd been avoiding each other. When Hannah was home, her *daed* had been busy with extra chores due to the storm. At supper, with her folks and her four *brieder* interacting around the table, her subdued silence wasn't noticeable.

Unlike here. Hannah glanced up to find Jethro watching her while he ate. Feeling her cheeks heat, she dropped her gaze again to her plate and set down her fork. Ruby Weaver had stopped by the shop late yesterday, ostensibly to buy fabric to finish binding her quilt. Hannah recognized the visit as judgment to see if she was chastened enough to still be a worthy wife for the bishop's son.

Right now, she didn't feel worthy of anyone. Hannah squeezed her eyes shut at the knowledge of the pain she'd caused Gabe. Of how fickle he must think her. She knew she loved him. But she'd learned from when she was just beyond a *boppeli* how vital *gelassenheit* was to Amish society. Yielding to the will of *Gott* and others was woven into the fabric of their lives. The welfare of the community was more important than individual rights and choices. More important than her choice. Gabe. Who could never be more than just an aching dream or memory to Hannah.

Opening her eyes, she slid her napkin over to wipe away a teardrop from the table's glossy surface. Jethro Weaver was a good man. It was time she focused on reality and not wishes, hopes and dreams. This was her future, if he'd still have her. This man. Whom she needed to get to know.

A concept easier said than done without a conversation. So far, she'd asked how the bishop was doing after his incident. "Fine" had been the reply, with no elaboration. Had Jethro had any problems with the storm? "No." After numerous other one-word answers, she'd left the man to eat his roast beef and potatoes in peace.

Hannah glanced around the restaurant, unintentionally catching Mrs. Edigers's eye. The midwife smiled and waved from where she was eating with her husband. Hannah nodded back, feeling a flash of joy at the memory of working with the woman to bring Ruth's baby into the world. Her expression softened at the reminder of the amazement of *Gott*'s creation, the wonder of birth and the opportunity to help mothers through the anxious time of delivery. Hannah had a great deal of respect and admiration for what the older woman did.

Her attention returned to her dinner companion. Jethro's silence gave her a lot of time to think. That could be a good thing. Or—Hannah's mouth grew dry as she watched someone approach the door through the restaurant's windows—a bad thing.

Appetite now completely gone, Hannah nudged her plate away. She watched Gabe stop outside the restaurant door to stomp snow from his feet. Reaching for the door handle, he glanced inside. And froze when his gaze connected with hers. Hannah sucked in a breath when he pivoted and walked back down the street. She was still watching when he turned the corner.

Mouth quivering, Hannah was concentrating on folding her napkin for the third time when she thought she heard words from across the table.

"How's the f-fundraiser going?"

She'd have been less shocked to hear Daisy ask a question during the drive home. Eyes wide, Hannah stared at her dinner companion.

Jethro raised an eyebrow. "The f-fundraiser?" he prompted.

"Uh, *ja*. I—I don't know if it's going to happen." Hannah pulled the napkin into her lap and proceeded to unfold it.

Jethro raised his other eyebrow.

Hannah interpreted that as asking why. She took a quick sip of water. "Uh, there doesn't seem to be much support for it anymore. Interest was lost when Aaron Raber left. And maybe more after the storm when I... I don't know if I'll continue to pursue it." Setting the glass down, she traced its condensation ring on the wooden table. Surely the man knew his mother was the primary one stifling the project.

When she glanced up, Jethro was watching her as he picked up the last roll from the basket and buttered it. Hannah hunched a shoulder at his continued attention. "Something else will come up to raise the funds." She sighed. "The *Englisch* will probably do something. Someone might write another grant. The community will get local EMS service eventually."

"Eventually," he echoed, breaking the bread into smaller pieces. "T-takes t-time."

"Ja," Hannah murmured. Time that Gabe didn't have. She cleared her throat. "It won't be this particular person. But the community will get the help it needs at some point. Isn't that the important part?" She tried to smile when meeting Jethro's thoughtful gaze, but her lips kept trembling. Retrieving her napkin, she held it against her mouth until her lips were as firm as she knew her resolve needed to be.

Jethro nodded slowly, his eyes solemn. "F-finished?"

Nodding in return, Hannah stood. Yes, with anything to do with Gabe, she needed to be finished.

Gabe trudged up the stairs to his apartment, his legs heavy with the same lead that filled his stomach. If he'd needed proof that it was over between him and Hannah, he'd just had it. Shoving open the door, the first thing he saw when he looked into the room were the blue curtains at the window. He crossed the room to touch the rich fabric.

"It's curtains for me," he murmured as he leaned against the wall. It certainly was. It was the end of any hopes he might have of a future with Hannah. The end of his job here in town. Gabe snorted. He'd learned that bit when he'd called the office as soon as he'd replaced his phone. The administrator had heard the fundraiser was off. With no source of funds in sight, there was no choice but to terminate the position. As the budget was already running in the red, Gabe would be paid for what he'd already worked, but surely he could understand...

Gabe could understand all right. As of this weekend, he had no reason, either personally or professionally, to stay in Miller's Creek. Too bad he'd already unpacked and disposed of the boxes.

Except for one. At the squeaks generating from a large carton, Gabe ambled over to squat down and regard its two occupants. Upon blinking their eyes open, the pups waddled over to greet him. Gabe ran a few fingers over their silky heads. Trying to reach him, they scratched with tiny paws up the side of the box. Scooping a pup in each hand, Gabe returned to the window and settled on the floor next to it with his back against the wall.

"Well, kiddos." He set the pups on his lap. "If I love her, like I say I do, I want her to be happy." He sighed. "Something I thought involved me being in her life. But what makes her happy is being connected with her family and community. And I complicate that. Maybe it's a good thing the job fell through." Gabe smiled ruefully as both pups put their paws on his chest and began licking his chin. "Because I can't stay here and see her married to another man. I...I just can't."

He shifted the pups back to his lap. "But when we go, we're taking these curtains with us. We'll put them up in our next place. That all right with you guys? 'Cause you're going with me. You're part of my family now." Gabe ran a hand down their fuzzy black backs. They felt so warm and vibrant, when he couldn't recall being so cold, even in the midst of the blizzard.

The men were getting up from the tables, which, with much practice, had been hastily arranged after the church service. Hannah was refilling the water pitchers for the next seating while other women were clearing up from the previous one or preparing more food.

With a squeak, Hannah hastily shut off the faucet and drained some excess water from the pitcher. *Gut* thing she wasn't pouring coffee today. Her mind wasn't anywhere near her task. It was where it'd been the past four days since she last saw him. On Gabe. On the ache in her stomach, knowing she'd never see him again. She'd heard he was leaving. And why wouldn't he? She'd chosen family and community over him. Again.

Hannah dodged through the traffic on the way to the tables, her expression grim. Maybe it was understandable that some couples were content to start their marriages with just respect. It was less unsettling than love. Hannah caught her mother's frown of concern as Willa grabbed a cloth to wipe up the water that'd just sloshed over the rim of Hannah's pitcher. Head lowered, Hannah continued to the table and began filling glasses.

Surely she could be happy without Gabe? She'd spent years without him, years when she'd been…beige. Hannah bit the inside of her cheek. Beige wasn't bad. It just wasn't…blue. But maybe blue wasn't for her. At the end of a row, Hannah turned her back to the room, pulled the pitcher to her chest and lowered her head. *Dear* Gott, *I trust in Your will. Help me to respect your chosen one for me and teach me to love him even a small measure of the way I love…someone else.*

Draining what remained in the pitcher into the next glass with tear-bleared eyes, Hannah pivoted to return to the kitchen, before halting abruptly in the middle of the room. Jethro stood before her, eyes on her face. He cleared his throat. His face was so red, the white scar above his lip stood out in sharp relief.

"Hannah L-Lapp." Hannah flinched at the unexpected volume of his voice. It was abnormally pitched to draw attention. Glancing around, she saw if that had been his intent, he'd succeeded immensely. All heads were turned in their direction. Her cheeks heated as her own color began to rise.

"I have s-something I n-need to ask you."

Chapter Seventeen

Pinning a faltering smile on her face, Hannah braced for what Jethro might say next. Even though she knew it was what the bishop willed, inwardly, she cringed. *Please don't let him declare himself here. Please don't let him ask to walk out with me in front of the whole community. I know my duty is to marry him, but please don't let it start out like this.*

This action seemed so out of character for taciturn Jethro, but then again, did she really know him, this man who was to be her husband, at all?

"I have some b-b-birdhouses and a b-b-bushel." He closed his eyes in frustration of getting the words out. This was obviously as painful for him as it was for Hannah. *So why was he doing it?* "Of walnuts. F-for the auction. Where d-do you want them? You're still organizing that, right? Is the d-date for it still the same?"

Hannah's jaw sagged. She'd been braced for a question, but not this one. Should she go on with the auction? This man, who might become her husband, thought she should. And with a quick search of her heart, Hannah knew it was the right decision. Recovering from her shock, she was sorely tempted to throw her arms around the man. Reaching out the hand not holding the pitcher, she grasped his work-calloused fingers. "Oh *denki*, Jethro, *denki*," she whispered for his ears alone.

Dropping his hand as quickly as she'd grabbed it, she cleared her throat and spoke at his previous emphatic volume. "*Ja*. It's still on. The date is the same. *Denki* for the *wunderbar* contributions. If folks aren't able to bring items the day of the auction, I... I'll collect them at our farm."

Jethro nodded stiffly, something closely resembling a smile on his normally solemn face. *"Gut."* Was that almost a twinkle in his eyes?

Hannah swallowed hard as she watched him pivot and rejoin a group of men, who along with all others in the room, were curiously observing the interaction. The expressions on the surrounding faces were intrigued. Positive. Supportive? Just as Jethro had probably anticipated when he'd fairly leaped out of his comfort zone to offer his support. The man who had the most to lose if she succeeded in keeping Gabe in town had just revitalized the project that could keep him there.

Hannah felt... She didn't know what she felt.

She'd just asked *Gott* to help her love the man she would marry. Was this the beginning of His plan? She'd respected Jethro, or what she'd known of him from her minimal acquaintance, but his actions today showed her more of his qualities.

She may never feel for him the way she did about

Gabe, but this solemn man certainly now had her admiration. Surely love could grow from that? Hannah had seen relationships develop into good marriages that had started with less.

Gott was answering her prayer. Showing her how to love another man. The revelation was reason to be elated. But if this was elation, why was she so close to crying?

Hannah was concentrating on blinking back threatening tears when Samuel Schrock kept her the center of attention, calling out, "Hannah, I'll be bringing a horse to the auction. I suppose you'd rather I keep him at home until that day rather than leave him on your porch?" Her brother-in-law's comment drew chuckles from around the room.

"Is that the one that's blind in one eye and has three lame legs?" Someone wasted no time in teasing the local horse trader.

"*Nee*, Freeman Hershberger, I sold that one to you for a hefty profit." The chuckles grew to outright laughs.

Hannah started when someone touched her on the arm. Susannah Mast, Rachel and Rebecca's mother, smiled as she took the pitcher from Hannah's hands. "That reminds me, I have several jars of honey and some goat milk soap I'll be bringing to the auction. Would it be helpful if I just brought them straight in that day? I'll be there. Especially now that I know Jethro is bringing in walnuts. Although—" raising her voice, Susannah turned toward the women still working in the kitchen "—I'll probably have to bid against Naomi for them."

One of the older women drying dishes responded with

a nod of her head. "*Ach*, for certain you will. But at least I know what to do with them once I bring them home."

"You may be right," quipped Susannah over the corresponding giggles. "I've never been known for my baking. Maybe I'll just go for one of the birdhouses." With a hand on Hannah's shoulder, she led her into the kitchen. While some women still hung back, watching dubiously, the pair was stopped by a procession of others, advising Hannah on what they planned to bring to the auction and asking further questions about the project.

By the time everyone had eaten and the dishes were done, Hannah had lost track of all the items being donated and the people who'd assured her they'd be at the auction. Overwhelmed by the abrupt shift of the day and needing a moment to herself during a lull, Hannah grabbed a chore jacket from a peg on the wall and slipped out the back door. Sliding her arms into the oversize sleeves, she was enveloped with the familiar scents of hay and livestock. Knowing the men would be congregating in the barn to visit, she headed instead to a side yard, her objective a picnic table beyond the clothesline that stretched over the snow-tramped ground.

Brushing the snow from the wooden seat, she sank down onto it, tucking the encompassing jacket under her. Although there'd been a few frowns and suspicious gazes, Hannah was humbled by the outpouring of support. Tipping back her head, she considered the winter blue sky overhead. This is why she loved the Plain community. This is why she needed to stay. They took care of each other. Beyond love and obedience to *Gott*, the bands of family, friendship and unity were the foundation of the community.

She squeezed her eyes tight against the prickle of tears. One escaped to slip down her temple into her hairline. If she married Gabe, she'd miss that. Would she eventually resent him for pulling her away? Could she adjust to their new existence? Who would be their community? Her role in the Plain world was so much a part of her identity. Hannah knew her place in it. At least, she knew who she was supposed to be in it. Who would she be without it?

Hannah's lips trembled. She stilled them with chilled fingers.

Oh, but those happy few days with Gabe before Aaron Raber left, when the community had buzzed with gratitude that Bishop Weaver had been saved and it seemed anything was possible.

To the surprise and delight of the congregation, Bishop Weaver was in attendance today. He didn't preach, but had remained seated in the one upholstered chair remaining in the room. She'd caught him watching her speculatively a few times. If he had an opinion on the auction, Hannah hadn't spoken with anyone who'd heard it.

She smiled faintly. She might think one thing in regard to interactions with her future mother-in-law. But whenever she thought of her future father-in-law, she'd be thinking of the man who'd shown her how to save Bishop Weaver's life. Noticeably absent today in expressing any support was Ruby Weaver. If Hannah had caught the bishop's eyes on her, his wife's gaze had seemed to burn a hole through Hannah's *kapp*. She and

Gabe may have saved her husband's heart, but the action certainly hadn't warmed his wife's any.

Hannah tried to shrug off her dismay. She'd find a way of making a marriage with Jethro work. She had to. Still, the prospect of being daughter-in-law to Ruby Weaver filled her mouth with the taste of milk gone sour. But, she drew in a long breath, feeling the cold air as it raced through her nose, it was apparently *Gott*'s plan.

The soft crunching of feet on snow announced someone's presence in the yard. Shifting on the bench, Hannah turned to see her *mamm* crossing the yard. Willa Lapp wore a gentle smile as she approached.

"Is this a private gathering?"

"There's always room for you, *Mamm*." Hannah brushed snow off the seat beside her.

Tucking her black cloak about her, Willa sat. "Sounds like your auction will be a success."

"*Ach*, it's not my auction. But if *Gott* wills it, I certainly hope so. I'll work to make it so." Hannah's voice dropped to a whisper. "It seems it's also His will that I marry Jethro."

Willa nodded. "Jethro is a *gut* man." She put her hand over where Hannah's rested in her lap. "But what is your will?"

Hannah looked at her *mamm* in surprise. "My will doesn't matter. *Gelassenheit* is abandoning my will in favor of following divine will, as Christ has done."

"*Ja*. That is so. You will think me a poor influence today. It's wrong to be *hochmut* as well, but I am so proud of the way you have obeyed throughout your life. I couldn't have asked for a better *dochder*. And now, because I am your *mamm* and love you, I have a question for you. Does the thought of marrying Jethro make you happy?"

She apparently had her answer when Hannah's eyes filled with tears. Willa squeezed her hand. "I rejoice and give thanks to *Gott* that your sister was returned to us. I rejoice more that she is happy. Have you ever wondered if marriage to Jethro is *Gott*'s will, or the bishop's?"

Hannah's eyes widened. "Wouldn't the bishop be implementing *Gott*'s will?"

Her *mamm* smiled. "We would like to think so. And sometimes it is so. But we are all still human and can be selfish in different ways." Her smile ebbed and her eyes softened with compassion. "Large families are a blessing from *Gott*. Bishop Weaver and his wife have suffered many losses. Jethro is their only living child. They want to see him settled with a family of his own. Perhaps the bishop is a bit biased on what he sees as *Gott*'s will, in this case. According to James in the *Biewel*, wisdom from above is many things, including impartial.

"Besides, sometimes *Gott* softly whispers his instructions instead of shouting them from the hayloft. Pray that your heart and mind are open to the subtlety of his direction. His ways are mysterious."

Pausing, Willa sighed. "Jethro recently lost his wife and unborn child. Our faith believes it isn't right to grieve overmuch when a loved one dies, as that is to question *Gott*'s will. I'm sure Jethro wants to be a *gut* son to his parents and do as they wish, but it might be soon for him to be thinking of marrying again. Has he given you any reason to believe he wants this match as much as his parents do?"

Thinking back over the painfully silent meals with Jethro, Hannah realized he'd never given an indication he was interested in a match between them. So why the public support of the auction today? Was it an effort to tilt her toward Gabe and away from himself? Her heart rate accelerated at the possibility.

"If I'd married the man my bishop wanted me to, I'd be in Indiana working in a nursery now. I like animals better than plants. I guess I'd rather help make the fertilizer than sell it."

Hannah's jaw dropped at her *mamm*'s admission.

"The bishop wanted me to marry his nephew. It took me prompting, sometimes subtly, sometimes not so subtly, to get Zebulun Lapp to give me a ride home from a singing before the bishop's choice could ask me. I've never regretted it. The way *Gott* has blessed me since, if following my heart was wrong, He has more than forgiven me, He has blessed me abundantly indeed."

"Mamm!" They shared an amused glance.

"Your *daed* still takes a little bit of prompting now and then. He loves you and is also proud of you, even though he isn't one for saying it. *Ja*, he was surprised the other day. We were desperately worried about you. Your *daed*'s reaction was more his version of relief than of judgment."

"He looked so disheartened. And when Gail left…"

Her *mamm* reached out to wipe tears Hannah wasn't aware of running down her cheek. "The reason we were so upset when Abigail left is that we were worried about her surviving in the *Englisch* world. Not for whatever was happening to us in the community. *Ja*, there was gossip—" Willa raised an eyebrow "—which *Gott* says is a sin, as well. But not from the ones who matter to us, and there were many of those. And Gail is not you. She's a little more…impetuous." Willa lowered her hands to gently encase Hannah's clenched ones. "Sometimes you think too much."

After a light squeeze, her *mamm* released Hannah's hands. "Gabriel Bartel seems like a *gut* man. He must be, or my *dochder* wouldn't care for him so. Your *daed* and I will survive whatever you decide to do. And, as long as you make your choice prior to baptism, you will not truly leave us. Only members baptized into the church risk being shunned.

"Marriage is for life. I milk cows twice a day for three hundred and sixty-five days, because I like who I'm doing it with. You will sit across from your husband for breakfast and supper every day. For many years. If the face across the table isn't dear to you, those years can be very lonely."

They both turned their heads when a voice called her *mamm*'s name. Hannah's *daed* stood at the yard's white fence. "Willa, the cows are waiting on us. The older boys are staying for the singing." Hannah inhaled sharply when he turned his attention to her. It hitched further when his normally reserved expression eased into a gentle smile. "Will you be staying, as well?"

Hannah wanted to leap from the bench and race to her *daed* for a hug. Although her legs tensed for activity, she remained seated, knowing the action would embarrass them both. Just his smile of acceptance was enough to know she was loved. Besides, she had much to think about. For the moment, the quiet yard seemed a good place in which to do so. Sharing her father's smile, she gave a hesitant nod.

Pushing to her feet, Willa brushed the snow from the back of her black cloak. Zebulun Lapp opened the gate and extended a hand to help his wife over an icy patch. Hannah barely heard her *daed*'s words and her *mamm*'s reply.

"Like a singing long ago, I'll be with the prettiest girl in the room."

"I must've aged well then. I've progressed to the prettiest one in the barn. I think *Gott* will forgive me for being *hochmut* that I'm better looking than a herd of Holsteins."

Watching them leave, Hannah's heart warmed at their obvious devotion so many years into marriage. It was the relationship she'd hoped for. One she knew she could have...with Gabe. She mulled over her *mamm*'s words. Over the events of the afternoon. Had not *Gott* renewed the possibility of the fundraiser? And with it, the possibility of Gabe staying? Had not *Gott* had Gabe show Hannah how to do CPR, and because of that knowledge, they'd been able to save the bishop's life? Which in turn had earned latent goodwill for Gabe in the community and displayed the need for the EMS service? And the storm, and the accident? If not for them, nothing would have changed and she'd have remained floundering in her decision, or lack thereof. What else might *Gott* be whispering, if she'd only listen?

Had she herself asked what path *Gott* wanted for

her, or had she just assumed others knew best? Hannah pressed her lips together. Much was lost for want of asking. Her breathing shallow, she bowed her head.

"*Gott*, please help me to do Your will. Help me to be open to know what it is. Direct me to Your path forward." Hannah stared unseeing at the snowy yard beyond her seat. Even motionless, her heart was racing and her breathing shallow. She closed her eyes. "*Gott*, if there is any way that Your will for me could include Gabe, please shout it from the hayloft, as I certainly don't want to risk missing Your gentle whisper on that. Because...because that would be my choice."

Opening her eyes with a deep exhalation, she rose from the wooden seat. Hannah paused when two men, one coming from the house, the other from the direction of the barn, stopped to talk in the middle of the farmyard. From the looks Bishop Weaver and Jethro sent her at interludes, a tight feeling in her stomach told Hannah the discussion involved her.

After a moment, Bishop Weaver turned and headed back to the house, leaving his son in the middle of the farmyard. Jethro hesitated, casting a longing look toward the field where his rig was parked, before heading for the yard gate. Shutting it behind him, he crunched through the snow to where Hannah stood.

He stopped a short distance away, his expression solemn. When he didn't immediately speak, Hannah shifted, feeling the cold seep through her feet for the first time since she'd come out.

Jethro sighed. "Hannah. You are a f-fine woman. I know you will m-make a *g-gut* wife. B-but not for m-me right now." He frowned. "It's t-too soon after..."

Hannah held up her hand, sparing him further words as excitement grew within her. This sounded like more than a whisper. "It's all right. I understand."

Seeming encouraged by her response, he continued. "I understand if you are n-not available after some t-time p-passes." A smile rose, more in his eyes than in the slight curve of his mouth. "I'll l-look around. See if I can f-find more things f-for the auction. I think this auction w-will be successful f-for you. That it will b-bring in everything you hope."

Hannah's eyes widened. Was the cancelation of this relationship *Gott*'s endorsement for another?

Nodding, Jethro left the yard, with a lighter step than when he'd come in, but no more buoyant than Hannah's as she dashed for the house.

She flew in the back door, her heart thumping in her chest. Hanging the borrowed coat on a nearby peg, she felt eyes on her. Turning, Hannah found Bishop Weaver in the mudroom, his frown accented by the ravages of his recent illness on his gaunt face.

"Hannah Lapp. I…"

Hannah stood tensely as the bishop studied her, her heart in her throat. Hadn't *Gott* been displaying His will? And it matched hers, not the bishop's. Hoping she wasn't going to provoke the man into another heart attack, Hannah opened her mouth to tell him so.

Bishop Weaver spoke first. "Martha Edigers came to talk with me in the hospital. She said it's time for her to think about retirement. She knows our community needs a midwife. There's not a large population of Mennonites in the area, but they've always gotten on well with Plain folks. But none of her people are interested."

His gaze pinned Hannah as he frowned. "She said you have the touch. She said if you wanted to apprentice with her, she would work with you to become certified." His brows lowered as if Hannah had challenged him. "You do understand that something else might need to be arranged while you have young children."

Hannah held her breath as she waited for his next words. Surely *Gott* was raising His voice to the barn rafters? If she was allowed, no, instructed to take more training for the community, a rarity for an Amish woman, perhaps she wasn't to stay in the church?

The bishop swallowed, his rawboned throat bobbing. "I have some hens that haven't been laying well. No sense in feeding them if they're not earning their keep. They'd make *gut* fryers for someone. I will have them there for the auction. I…I hope it's a success and…and will get you what you want. It's…it's *gut* to have such fast medical care in the district."

Bishop Weaver's unblinking eyes, huge in his thin face, studied Hannah. "Will you be staying in the community with this Mennonite man?"

Hannah's heart was pounding. "If he'll have me." Her palms sweating, she straightened her shoulders and met his intent gaze.

"All right then. I will inform Mrs. Edigers that you will be contacting her about the apprenticeship."

Grabbing her cloak and bonnet, Hannah nodded hastily to those remaining in the house as she hurried outside. She skidded to a halt at the end of the sidewalk. Her parents had left, and she had no transportation. But she had brothers and a brother-in-law in the barn who did. She started picking her way over the frozen rutted ground of the farmyard.

Jethro was driving his rig out from the field where church attendees had been parked. He pulled alongside her. "D-do you need a r-ride into t-town?"

"Ja. Denki." Hannah scrambled into the buggy beside her previous suitor. "Is your horse fast?"

Jethro gathered the reins. "I hope so. I b-bought him from your b-brother-in-law."

Bursting through the alley door into the hallway, Hannah dashed up the narrow stairs two at a time. Her haste reminded her of her actions a few weeks ago. Then, to revive a friend. Now, to hopefully resuscitate a relationship. When Gabe opened the door to her knock, this time it was his face that displayed shock at who was on the other side.

"Hannah! What are you doing here?" He scanned beyond her. "Are you here alone?"

"Ja and *nee.* There's no one else with me. But, Gabe, I hope I'm no longer alone. I hope there's still a chance to be with you. As your wife. Jethro is donating things for the auction and doesn't want to marry yet, and Samuel has a horse he's offering and many others have things they'll be contributing. Even Bishop Weaver is bringing chickens and he needs me to become Mrs. Edigers for the community. It is so *wunderbar*!"

His gentle hands gripped her upper arms. "Slow down. You lost me at chickens."

"That's what's *wunderbar*! I thought I'd lost you forever but *Gott* showed me His will through chickens and my *mamm* not marrying the bishop's nephew and an apprenticeship that I'm not forgoing His will to marry you. In fact, I'm following it…" Hannah took in Gabe's round-eyed look. Glancing through the apartment's open door, she noticed the boxes. Boxes for him to move away. Her gaze returned to Gabe's green eyes and she took a deep breath. "If you'll have me. Will you?"

Just like before, he tugged her into his arms. Hannah went willingly, holding on to him with all her strength.

"I thought you'd never ask," he murmured before he kissed her.

Epilogue

Hannah turned from paying the auctioneer, her smile as wide as the man's trailer. Even so, it managed to expand even farther when she caught sight of Gabe weaving his way through the thinning crowd.

She gestured with the record book and fat manila envelope in her hand. "Looks like you'll be here a little longer."

His smiling green eyes held hers as he crossed the last few feet. "Good thing, as I'm getting married next Thursday."

Hannah's cheeks flushed. She still was amazed that she'd soon become Gabe's wife. "You must be a risk-taker."

"I had faith. In God, and the person arranging the fundraiser." He winked at her. "And I'd have figured out a backup plan. Much is lost for want of asking, you know."

"So I've heard. Since you haven't asked, I'll tell you that we raised enough to fund the EMS program for the next year. Even maybe expand it so my husband isn't always on call by himself. And perhaps next year, a used service vehicle, if he has the contacts to find one." Gabe's eyes widened and his mouth dropped open. Before he got too excited, Hannah cautioned, "A bargain one."

"Bargains are always good." He smiled wryly. "Particularly with Nip and Tuck growing so much they're eating me out of house and home. When the time comes, I'll certainly explore my resources. And now we know a decent mechanic, as Clay Weathers is working on opening his business again." Taking her free hand, Gabe led her away from the trailer. "In the crowd today, if I heard it once, I heard it ten times—come next year... You've started something amazing. I can't thank you enough for making this possible."

"*Gott* made this possible."

"I can't thank Him enough. Mainly for you."

Hannah felt the same. Her heart was full. The blue dress she'd made for her wedding was hanging in her room. Hannah touched it every night just to remind herself what seemed impossible would soon become real.

Granted, their wedding would be a more subdued event than a normal one in the Plain community. But those who counted would still be there. Because she was marrying outside the faith, she couldn't join the church—which hurt—but she could still interact in the community. As evidenced by support of the auction, she was still accepted by most of the Amish district. And it was early yet. She'd just started apprenticing with Mrs. Edigers. Folks were more relieved they'd continue to have a midwife when the elderly Mennonite woman retired than concerned that a fellow Amish woman was marrying a Mennonite man.

Ja, she had much to thank *Gott* for.

"I don't know how you finished this in time." Gabe's comment drew Hannah's attention to the folded quilt sitting on a nearby table.

Hannah glanced at the intricate design, glad only she would notice the mistakes she'd made working long into the nights. "I couldn't ask everyone else to donate and not provide something myself." She shook her head at him. "You paid too much for it. I would've made you another one after we get married."

"I figured I was just contributing to my own salary. Besides, I recognized something in it." With his free hand, Gabe reached out to trace a repeating triangle of blue fabric in the multicolored quilt.

Hannah also touched the vibrant hue that matched the curtains in Gabe's apartment. Her finger slid over to the beige material right next to it. With a smile that she knew echoed the one in her eyes, she walked her fingers back to the blue.

Clasping Gabe's hand, she looked up at him. "Thank you for seeing me as more than I saw myself."

Gabe raised her hand to his lips and gently kissed the back of it. "Hannah." His voice was hoarse. "There's not enough fabric in the world to represent the color you bring into my life. I found and lost you in my past. And I will want for very little, as long as I have you in my present and future. That's the greatest thing I could ever have asked for."

* * * * *

"Are you okay?" Stone asked, tightening his hold around
her waist and gripping one of her hands.

"I— Yes." She didn't have time to explain to Stone
why this had nothing to do with her sore ankle, nor why
avalanches were her worst nightmare and that was the
real reason why she'd suddenly swayed in his arms.

Not when there was work to be done. There were
people in Holden Springs who needed help, and she knew
she should be there.

Tugger whined and pressed against her leg as he'd
been taught to do as a therapy dog. He could tell her heart
rate had increased and her pulse was pounding in her ears,
even if she didn't show it in her expression, although
there was probably that, too. The dog was responding to
cues most humans couldn't see, and Felicity reached out
and absently ran a hand between Tugger's ears to steady
her insides.

"Have they set up a temporary disaster shelter yet?"
she asked.

"Yes. At Holden High School," her sister said.
"They're using the cafeteria and the gym, I think. I'd go
myself except I have clients in the middle of service dog

training back at the center. Do you mind taking Tugger and heading out there?"

Felicity did mind. More than anyone would ever know, because she never talked about it, not even to her siblings. But now was not the time to give in to those feelings. She could cry into her pillow later when she was alone and the people of Holden Springs were safe.

"I'll take Tugger." She nodded. "And Dandy, too," she said, referring to a young black Labrador retriever who was part of the therapy dog program.

"I can tag along, if there's anything I can do to assist," Stone said. "That way you'll have an extra person for the dogs."

Felicity was going to decline, but Ruby spoke up first. "Thank you, Stone. They need all the help they can get. From what I hear, there are a lot of families who were suddenly evacuated from their homes."

"It's settled, then," Stone said. "I'm going with you."

Felicity didn't feel settled. The last thing she needed was Stone alongside her. It would distract her from her real work.

She sighed deeply.

A bruised ankle.

Stone's unnerving presence.

And now an avalanche.

Could things get any worse?

Don't miss
Their Unbreakable Bond *by Deb Kastner,*
available January 2022 wherever
Love Inspired books and ebooks are sold.

LoveInspired.com

LIEXP1221

IF YOU ENJOYED THIS BOOK, DON'T MISS NEW EXTENDED-LENGTH NOVELS FROM LOVE INSPIRED!

In addition to the Love Inspired books you know and love, we're excited to introduce even more uplifting stories in a longer format, with more inspiring fresh starts and page-turning thrills!

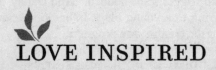

LOVE INSPIRED

Stories to uplift and inspire.

Fall in love with Love Inspired—inspirational and uplifting stories of faith and hope. Find strength and comfort in the bonds of friendship and community. Revel in the warmth of possibility, and the promise of new beginnings.

LOOK FOR THESE LOVE INSPIRED TITLES ONLINE AND IN THE BOOK DEPARTMENT OF YOUR FAVORITE RETAILER!

LOVE INSPIRED

Stories to uplift and inspire

Fall in love with Love Inspired—
inspirational and uplifting stories of faith
and hope. Find strength and comfort in
the bonds of friendship and community.
Revel in the warmth of possibility and the
promise of new beginnings.

Sign up for the Love Inspired newsletter
at **LoveInspired.com** to be the first
to find out about upcoming titles,
special promotions and exclusive content.

CONNECT WITH US AT:

 Facebook.com/LoveInspiredBooks

Twitter.com/LoveInspiredBks